1ˢᵗ Edition

About the Author:

Roman Payne was born in Seattle in 1977. He currently lives in Europe.

For more information about the author, please visit:

www.moderoom.com, or email: info@moderoom.com.

Acknowledgments & Legal Statement:

This book is a work of fiction. Names, characters, places, and incidents either are products of the author's imagination or are used fictitiously. Any resemblance to actual events or locales or persons, living or dead, is entirely coincidental. Special thanks to Aaron Pogue; and my eternal gratitude to Nastya – you know who you are.

© 2004, ModeRoom Press

Cover Design: Roman Payne

CREPUSCULE

by Roman Payne

CHAPTER I

I care not that this moment's lot
was thin and sparsely dealt,
all pleasures sweet can be forgot
the instant they are felt.

"'DIGNITY?' ... 'Dignity!', you cry? ... you sorry fellow ... even the man being hanged is allowed his dignity. If he chooses to soil himself on the gallows, that's his own business. He obviously just doesn't care to have any dignity. But you can't say the executioner isn't allowing him dignity. Quite the contrary! The executioner is a paid servant of the government. And when he hangs a man, he is devoting his time to – that is, he is serving – the man whom he is hanging. Do you understand? Don't be such a sorry fellow. In such a case, the government is paying, out of its own pocket, to have a professionally trained man, who surely doesn't like wasting his time, to go out of his own way, taking precious hours out of his own day, to string this man up on the gallows and watch him sway! ...And if that hanged man doesn't realize the dignity that's wrapped around his neck, he's a sorry fellow. When somebody is paying for another to receive a service – *and a hanging is a service, mind you!* – the one receiving the service is receiving respect and dignity any way you look at it ... he is receiving respect and dignity courtesy of the government treasury. Don't you think it costs money to hang a man? You think these gallows build themselves? You think these executioners are volunteering like Salvation Army workers? No, it costs a pretty penny to hang a man — especially these days, what with the new *Executioners' Union* and all. But why have you gotten me off track? We're not talking about a hanging here! No one's getting hanged. We're just talking about a mere *deportation!* You should feel lucky you're not getting hanged. How would like to be hanged today? And you cry about a lack of dignity ... why it's not like you're being deprived of your life. You are just being deprived of life in America!

"...And remember, you're getting a service here. Our government ... excuse me, *my* government, is paying me to pack you up in this little box and load you in with the rest of the cargo on this steamship so you can get back to Europe where you belong!

"...What? I can't hear you! The wood is too thick! ... No I'm not going to open the lid! I've already sealed you up. I've already hammered in the nails. You're just going to have to yell louder if you want me to understand what you're running your mouth off about in there! But you'd better hurry and say it, your boat is leaving. Just don't cry to me anymore that you're not being treated with dignity by the American government. That's an accusation America doesn't take lightly. Even our non-citizens, *such as yourself,* are treated with dignity in *this* country. Just wait till you get to Europe in a few days. See how those socialists treat you. Boy, you'll be wishing you were American, I tell you! If they treated their citizens with dignity, we wouldn't have this problem of people like you, trying to sneak over here to squat on the land of the free and freeload in the homes of the brave! ... Now off with you!"

Then we hear a loud *thud* as the little pinewood crate, containing the young man being deported from America, is dropped onto the cargo plank of the steamship. Then that gruff man, the government worker at the city port — who had just been giving David a stern lecture about dignity while packing him up in a wooden box — loaded the few straggling pieces of cargo onto the cargo plank, shut the iron door, padlocked it; and, as was his custom when loading a ship bound for a foreign shore, he pulled a silver dime from his pocket, made a wish and threw it in the swells of the saltwater in the sound at the American port. He then walked up the pier, clocked out of his job, and walked on towards Second and Pike to buy a sandwich. By the time he reached the sandwich shop, the cargo ship containing packages, canned fish and, David, the hero of our story, (who was packed up for deportation in a box of pine with three small air-holes on each side just big enough to fit a pinky through) was leaving the harbor. It passed through the Puget Sound and through the great Strait of Juan de Fuca; and by afternoon it reached the cape where the beaches of Washington State lie to the southward eye and the shores of Canada stretch on in the north; and that massive cargo steamship proceeded on into the Pacific Ocean.

That ship saw several storms and many days of calm. It saw the full moon rise over the Panama Canal and the crescent moon drift alongside the black night waters of the Atlantic. The daytimes spent on the great ocean were mostly sunny and calm, though inside the cargo vessel, David saw no light of day, and no sliver of the moon. There were lamps burning near the engine room and a small amount of their kerosene light cast itself across the cargo room, illuminating pallets of canned fish and bottles of corn oil. David, who spent days scrunched up in one position in that small, pine crate kept his lips pressed to the breathing holes; yet, occasionally, when boredom became overwhelming, he took his lips away from the holes and let his eyes peer through them. He saw the beams of light from the kerosene lamps reflect off of the tin fish cans that sat on the pallets in the cargo room and the edges of these tin cans shimmered with this silvery jeweled light reflected from the beams, and this sight pleased David very much.

In his box, beside a scrap of bread, he had a bowl of water from which he could drink. The pine box, in which he was packed, was too small for his arms and hands to have the freedom to hold the bowl up to his mouth, so he had to lap the water up like a cat would do. As he didn't know how long the journey would take, David prudently conserved the water as long as possible – only permitting himself to lap two or three laps per day. Unfortunately, by the fourth day, David's bowl was dry as could be. It appeared as though all the water had evaporated; though as the bowl saw not the sun, and as the ocean air that filled the vessel was wet and humid, it didn't seem at all possible to David that his precious water had evaporated.

"It could not have evaporated," David said to himself on the fourth day of his journey at sea, "an animal must have snuck in through one of my air-holes and sucked the water out!" … "but how could an animal small enough to fit into one of these air-holes be big enough to drink that much water in one day? …as there was quite a bit of water in my bowl yesterday." This puzzled David and the only solution he could think of was that the animal that drank his water had, in fact, been rather big, but had also had a slender snout that could've slipped through the hole and into the water dish. As the sea journey was long and dull, and the hours lagged on and on, David had much time to muse on this question; and so he spent the fourth and the fifth day going over in his head all the world's living animals – great and small, of land and sky and sea – to ascertain exactly what kind of animal it was that drank the last of his water. After giving it a lot of thought, David decided that the animal could be none other than an anteater. "Only an anteater," he concluded, "has a slim enough, and long enough snout to fit through one of these air-holes and drain my water dish."

It may seem to you, dear reader, that David was rather petty and simple-minded to devote so much time and thought to this question of which animal, if any, had stolen his water, but I urge you to realize, for one thing, the importance water had taken at this point in the journey. When David left America, he was already quite ill (that being the cause by which he was being deported to begin with, which I'll explain later); and by the fourth day, the seasickness had fully set in and David was, consequently, very dehydrated. Furthermore, David didn't know exactly how long the journey would take – for he'd never hitherto sailed from the West Coast of America to the shores of France – and he was sincerely afraid that if he didn't conserve his water with the utmost prudence, he would surely die. And, in any way, can one so ill with seasickness, among other ailments – who is trapped in a little box that allows no freedom of movement or circulation of air – really be expected to ruminate on deep and intelligent questions? In those days, David was experiencing traumatic psychological disturbances that would make anyone, you and I included, shudder with fear to the point of incapacity. He had recently been expelled from the hospital and forced to go overseas to live and receive treatment for an illness he didn't really understand – an illness even the doctors didn't understand. And to think of these problems, while seasick and stuffed in a dark cage for days on end, would have surely led to a madness of the most permanent kind. So by musing on petty and simple-minded questions, his brain was actually working in a very intelligent and sensible manner. David's intelligent brain was depriving him of the ability of complex thought in order to save him from madness. ...And so during the voyage, David's only thoughts were of the animal who stole his water.

Yet such musings also created another problem for our poor hero. By the fifth day, he had decided that an anteater was loose in the cargo room, poking it's snout where it pleased; and so the sixth and seventh days at sea were exceptionally bothersome to David for he was, at this time, quite afraid of this strange animal's presence onboard. He had never seen an anteater before and, therefore, didn't know the nature and the capabilities of this beast. Do anteaters attack human beings? Even experienced zoologists have a difficult time answering this question.

The days were dark for David and intermittently, during the journey, he slept. And intermittently during his sleep, he dreamt. And what horrid figures and terrible apparitions haunted these dreams. Had there been any onlookers in that cargo room, they would hear pounding sounds and notice the pine box tremble and shake every few hours with the panicked movements of he who was inside.   The box would tremble at the moments when David woke up from a sleep full of dreams of winged anteaters devouring his liver, or of armies of anteaters marching on a twilit hill, with carbines in their arms, ready to fire on any human who approached; or after other similar nightmares.

I am just touching on the surface of David's internal and external worries. He was unfortunate to the depths, and if we were to explore these depths – especially in these first few pages of our story – we would find ourselves stressing our own brains with imaginings of the darkest and most ugly sort.   So let us now limit our knowledge, for our own sake, to the knowing that David was psychically ill, psychologically irritated, cramped and dehydrated in a wooden box on a journey that would sooner or later bring him – in some state or another, alive or dead – to the shores of France. …And before we arrive in France, let's just mention one other thing, David's body temperature was increasing by a full thermometer degree every day while he was at sea.

Upon our hero's arrival in Bretagne, France

The sun was shining gaily on the port near Concarneau on the coast of Brittany. Down a long grassy hill, fragrant with lavender and honeysuckle flowers, Marc, a jovial man with ruddy cheeks and about fifty years, was running to greet the incoming cargo liner.

It was a spring day in April and the weather was mild but fresh and the sun resounded in the sky. Marc was happy to go to work that day, for it was still just late-morning and he knew he didn't have to spend much time on the docks. He only had to unload a few pieces of cargo, sign a few forms and then he would be off, around noontime, to enjoy the rest of the sunny day in the fashion he chose. There were other men to unload the pallets of canned fish and oil. There were young workmen for that. Marc had worked for the port authority of Brittany for many years and, as he was a really likeable and jovial fellow, he was continually given the more pleasurable and less time- and labor-consuming duties of the trade.

So, Marc reached the bottom of the hill and walked out to the edge of the pier to greet the cargo ship, which had just come from America.

Marc had himself been a sailor before, for many, many years, and had taken several voyages to America. He had seen San Francisco and Seattle, New York and Boston, New Orleans, Philadelphia, Montreal and Vancouver. He could cook American food as spicy as anyone; and he spoke an English that always impressed the tourists – especially due to the large amount of foreign swearwords and vulgar expressions he had learned during his years as a sailor.

The pier near Concarneau was empty on the morning David's ship came in. The workmen who would be unloading the canned fish and oil were still sleeping in their bunks. Marc was up early and had the pleasure of seeing the sun cut through the fog and push away the early morning clouds to reveal a sky of blue azure.

He whistled a French folk tune and clapped his hands together as he walked to the pier. Once on the dock, he helped the enginemen secure the ship and then boarded on the main deck. He then descended to the cargo room to see what it was he would have to unload.

The cargo room was damp and musty, it was dark and smelled from some rotting fish that had burst out of a few cans, which broke in transit. Marc paced the aisles between pallets and parcels a few times until he decided that there wasn't much work for him to do. He was looking forwarded to getting off the ship, climbing that grassy hill and smoking a pipe underneath the laurel tree at its summit. From the summit, he could eat his lunch and see out over the ocean in three directions.

Just when Marc was preparing to leave the ship. He heard the sound of a wooden box sliding a few inches across the ground. He then heard the *thud, thud, thud* of some dull object pounding against wood – and he heard the box slide again. So, Marc took his flashlight and went looking for the box that was making so much noise. He was sure that a dog had gotten onboard and was trying to tear open a wooden box to eat the processed fish inside.

Marc walked the aisles of the cargo room banging his flashlight against wooden crates so as to scare the dog away. Although the smell of rotting fish was thick in the air, the smell of a sick man penetrated Marc's nose when he approached the crate containing our David. Marc could hear struggling from within the crate. He tapped his flashlight against the pine box and gasps could be heard as it rocked from side to side slightly with the movements of the struggling inhabitant.

"They're supposed to kill the damn fish before they pack 'em, the basta'ds!" Marc said aloud in the sailor English he picked up while docked in the Boston harbor years ago. He then tapped his metal flashlight against the crate again, and again the crate jumped a few inches. "Jump fishy!" said Marc.

Then came the muffled voice of the young man inside the crate. Marc couldn't make out exactly what the voice was saying but, as he recognized it not to be the voice of a fish, but the voice of a man, he himself jumped back a few inches, startled. He then left the cargo room in a quick and determined pace.

Back on shore, the late-morning sun was still beaming on the grassy hill and the workmen were still sleeping in their bunks. Marc crossed the pier to the storeroom and took a crowbar off the wall. He poured himself a cup of coffee and walked again down the pier onto the ship where he continued on into the cargo room.

Opening up David might have been a gruesome sight for many, but Marc was a seasoned witness to the cruder things in life; and, after he pried off one facet of the crate and David tumbled out, Marc simply tossed his jolly head back and laughed until his cheeks were ruddier than ever.

"Why it's not a fish, it's a stowaway!"

David lay there on the metal floor of the cargo room gasping for the clean air that now surrounded him. His lips were chaffed and his skin was scaly from dehydration. His forehead was covered in beads of sweat from fever. He lay in the fetal position clenching his abdomen in pain. His eyes were closed but he was conscious. He didn't know where he was and when he tried to open his eyes and look around, hallucinations interfered with his judgment as to what was happening around him. David saw Marc and mistook him for an anteater; and, in fear, tried to crawl as far away and as quickly away as possible. His limbs were too weak to move properly and many portions of his body had been deprived of blood circulation during his transcontinental voyage, so any fanciful notions he had of standing and running or of swatting the giant anteater away were not at all possible, and so they just remained fanciful notions.

Even old Marc, who was accustomed to seeing dying men squirming on the floor of a ship's cargo room after being extracted from pine crates, realized that the young man was in a dreadful condition and could benefit from a glass of water and a cold washcloth. The old sailor went and fetched one of each.

David's forehead enjoyed the washcloth yet his body rejected the glass of water and after a couple sips, he vomited on the cargo room floor. Marc decided that he would leave the mess for the workmen sleeping in the bunks to clean up.

After it was clear to Marc that David would live, he stuffed the sick man back in the crate and tipped it back up so the open-end pointed upwards.

"Why are you putting me back in here?" David managed to say in a most feeble and pained voice.

"It's for your own good, kid. They kill stowaways, you know. I'm going to help you out." And so Marc put the lid back on the crate, took a hammer from his belt and drove a few nails into the lid, locking David inside the odious pinewood crate, once again. David made a few grunts and gasps as Marc loaded the crate onto a dolly, but Marc pounded the crate so hard with his hammer after hearing David make noise that the latter was soon quiet.

"Listen, kid … you don't want anyone to hear you make any noise. Is that clear?"

There was no response. Marc pushed the crate on the dolly out of the cargo room and up onto the pier. As Marc was pushing the dolly up the pier towards the shore, Henry – an English dockworker who had run away from England to become a French dockworker – approached Marc.

"What've you got there?" asked Henry.

"A delivery for the boss!" said Marc.

"Oh. …Any coffee left?" asked Henry.

"Sure. In the storeroom," said Marc.

And Henry continued on his way towards the ship, leaving Marc and the boss's delivery alone.

That crate took a journey on the dolly down a path and through a square and up some steps and up another path and eventually it ended up under the laurel tree at the summit of the same grassy hill where Marc had intended earlier to smoke a pipe and while away the warm spring day.

Once Marc and his crate took a seat on the grass under the laurel tree, Marc lit his pipe, took a few puffs, and once again, extracted the passenger from the crate. This time, when David tumbled out of the crate, he was no longer nearly-dead, but was half-way alive. Marc was relieved. David was given some more water, which his body took well this time, and was permitted to recline against Marc's favorite tree while he nursed himself with clean air, water, and some dry bread that Marc offered him.

"You know," said Marc, after David was in good enough condition to listen to and acknowledge someone, "If I'd had taken you to the boss, he would have chained your legs together and dumped your ass in the Atlantic! …They kill stowaways in this business. …It's up to the ship captain to make sure all the passengers are accounted for and if someone is hiding onboard, and isn't accounted for, and doesn't have the proper documents, it's the ship captain's ass at stake. By law, he has to return the stowaway to the country where he came from. Otherwise, the captain is charged with aiding in illegal immigration and he loses his license, his boat and sometimes is even thrown in the clink for a while! No captain will have that! …It's easier to kill a stowaway than to declare him and sail him back to the other side of the world." Marc talked while eating his bread covered with salted butter and sardines. David slowly sipped his water and listened. Marc continued talking, "Me, I don't like killings, I don't like declarations, I don't even care much for ship captains. So I'm going to save your life here, kid. I'm going to take you into town as soon as I finish my lunch and I'm going to drop you off and not look back. …And if anyone asks, you never saw me, you never heard of me, and you never, never stepped foot on that ship down there – got it?!" Marc pointed to the great cargo liner off in the distance that brought David from America to the coast of France. It looked magnificent in the harbor, from the view on the grassy hill. The steel deck glimmered in the sunlight and one could see all of the workmen, who appeared as little specks in the distance, walking down the pier wheeling dollies filled with pallets of canned fish and oil. "…Don't you even remember the name of that ship – got it?!"

"I never *knew* the name of the ship." David managed to mutter in a feeble voice.

"Good kid," said Marc, "In a few, I'll drop you off in town. A town called Concarneau. It's a beautiful place."

CHAPTER II

Two men and a woman were seated at a table in a sunny backyard around noontime. The woman, wearing a cotton housedress and apron, was helping the two men to large portions of roasted potatoes with melted gruyere, tomatoes with vinegar, and beet salad. The older of the two men was Marc, the fifty year old dockworker. He ate quickly and spoke very little, for he was quite hungry still, even after having eaten with David on the summit of his favorite hill underneath his favorite laurel tree. The woman, an elderly woman, with white hair and a nose full of grey freckles, was Marc's wife. She spoke not at all at first, but instead guessed at the answers to the questions that kept popping in her head about the young man sitting at the table. She didn't speak a word of English, and the young man didn't know French. The young man was David and he was sitting in the sunny backyard in the coastal village of Concarneau, fighting off his illness to seem pleasant to Marc and especially to Marc's wife. He picked at his potatoes and cheese, trying to eat as much as he could. Though his temperature had dropped considerably, he still had an acute pain in his gut and a wretched nausea that made the thought of food unbearable. The elderly woman kept glancing at David, and with each glance, a new question would pop into her head; and, after becoming frustrated trying to answer the questions for herself, she would turn to her husband and ask him about it. Marc answered a few words here and there between bites of lunch, but mostly he kept quiet. It had been his plan to drive David only as far as the entrance to the village of Concarneau, and to drop him off and let him fend for himself; but as Marc's faded blue pickup truck winded the country roads of Brittany, towards Concarneau, the two men talked – Marc, more than David, as the latter was quite ill during the journey – and Marc took a liking to the young man. Consequently, he decided to have him over to his house for lunch.

13

"Make sure, once we get to my house, David, that you don't mention anything about being a stowaway. It will scare my wife, y'hear? Not that she'll understand a word of what you say. She doesn't speak English. But if she finds out you were a stowaway, she'll be scared to death. I'm going to tell her you are an American tourist I picked up hitch-hiking, okay?"

"Okay, no problem." replied David. He had no intention of informing Marc that he was not a stowaway, but that he was rather a deportee. David could not imagine how this bit of information could do him any good – and, although Marc was a decent guy, David didn't plan on knowing him that long. David's goal at that time was not to make friends. His goal was to go to Paris and find a doctor, or a hospital, to cure him of his illness.

"You are as pale as a whale's underbelly, my boy – and you stink like burning whale oil, too! Ha! I'm sorry to say that, but you *do* stink kid! ...And you have a lot of sweat all over your forehead. That sea voyage didn't do you good, did it?"

"No, I have a fever and I'm in terrible pain." replied David.

"Well, I've seen worse than you, that's no doubt. ...Don't worry, kid. You'll be fine. And you don't need a doctor. Just a few good meals. I saw men in worse shape than you survive a whole month at sea without a good meal or any help from doctors. You know, way back, we used to have a doctor on board when we went to sea – back when I was a sailor. But we stopped taking those doctors out with us because they were too expensive; and anyway, *they* were usually the ones who needed the doctoring! ...Never met a doctor built for the sea, that's for sure! After three days they'd be getting sick from the rocking ship and spend the rest of the journey in their cozy private cabins, puking all over themselves. We never knew what to do with them, we weren't doctors. We just let them sleep in their puke. After all, the captain was paying for their voyage, why should *he* clean up their filth? ...No, a doctor is a thinkin' man – and a thinkin' man is not meant for the sea. You have to have strong arms and a strong gut to go to sea. ...I say this because we stopped taking those worthless doctors out with us and everybody did fine. Even stowaways like you, who suffered the most, almost always lived to see the next port – that is, unless they were found out by the captain and thrown overboard. Then the stowaway had no hope for recovery."

While David picked at his beet salad, he felt lucky that it had been a man like Marc who found him stuffed in that crate. Although he wasn't a stowaway, he doubted whether he could have convinced one of the captain's men otherwise. If he'd been found by another dockworker, he thought for sure he'd have been thrown off the pier with shackles around his ankles. Yes, he considered himself very lucky to have met Marc, although he was ill at ease eating with him and his wife in their backyard.

David let his thoughts drift away from Marc and the uncomfortable stares of the old woman; and he let his thoughts drift away from his illness, which was all too unbearable when he thought about it. Instead, he thought of Paris – and all that might await him there. It was a city he knew nothing about but he was sure that it was the nearest place he would find a good doctor – and a doctor was what he needed most.

While David sat in between the two, picking at his lunch, Marc's wife noticed that David smelled pretty bad; and, although she still didn't know whether or not to have a good feeling about this 'American hitchhiker', she decided he'd probably be a fine young man once he put on some clean clothes. David chewed on a little piece of beet soaked in wine vinegar and looked at Marc's wife. She then looked away and said something in French to her husband, and the latter excused himself from the backyard table and disappeared into the house for a moment.

When Marc returned, he had in his hands a man's formal, white summer suit – a jacket and trousers, and a clean white shirt, to boot. He threw the suit into David's lap. "Here, kid. Try this on! It's clean and if it fits, you can have it. I only wore it once – to a wedding – and I'll never wear it again. Never again, that's for sure!"

David felt the fabric of the suit with his fingertips. He loved it. He hoped it would fit, but, being the taller of the two, he was sure the sleeves and the legs would be too short. He asked Marc if he could go change into it. Marc happily pointed to the backdoor of the house and told him to go on inside and try it on. David then stood immediately and walked towards the house. At that moment, the face of Marc's wife took on a distressed, almost panicked, look and she leaned over and muttered something in her husband's ear. Marc nodded his head; then he stood, and followed David into the house.

"You can change in there." Marc said, pointing to the bathroom. David followed his instructions and while he changed in the bathroom, Marc stood by the door, waiting.

The clothes David had worn during his voyage at sea meant nothing to him and he intended to throw them out as soon as he had on this nice, white suit. Once he was naked, he sat on the toilet seat, going through the pockets of his old trousers. He had important things in those pockets and he needed to make sure they stayed with him. He pulled out of his back pocket a French passport issued to him by the consulate in America the day before his deportation. He recalled what a fever he had had while standing in line in that French consulate, under guard and wearing handcuffs. That was an ugly memory, which he wanted to forget.

Still seated on the toilet seat, David pulled out of his front pocket an envelope that was filled with banknotes. Thirteen-thousand dollars in American cash. The most money he had ever seen in his life. He counted and recounted the money in the envelope just for the pleasure of feeling it in his fingers and seeing that it was all there. Then he set the envelope on the back of the toilet, along with his French passport and his other important possession: a small journal with a green leather cover that he had bought months ago in Seattle to write poetry in. He had already filled thirty or forty pages with verse but there were a hundred or so blank pages left to fill.

He tossed his old clothes on the floor, forgetting one last possession that remained in his pockets; then he stood and urinated idly, musing to himself many things – all the while Marc waited outside the door. When he finished urinating, he tried flushing the toilet but failed to figure out how.

"Marc, how do I flush this toilet?" he yelled through the door.

"Pull the chain!" Marc yelled back.

He had never seen a toilet that had a hanging chain to flush it before. It was a strange toilet indeed. David realized then that there were going to be many strange things about this new country that he would discover. He was no longer in America and every event from then on, he realized, would have a new and peculiar essence to it.

David slipped into the white suit, buttoned the white shirt and put on the white jacket. He examined himself in the mirror. He had guessed right. The sleeves were too short and the cuffs of the trousers hovered several inches over the tops of his shoes. But he didn't care … he liked the suit … and the pockets all had buttons to secure their contents. So, after he put his passport in his breast pocket, and buttoned it; and put his money in his other breast pocket, and buttoned it; and his journal in his back pocket, and buttoned it; he felt that his three important belongings were very secure. He forgot about the forth belonging that lay in the pocket of his old clothes on the floor. David looked again into the mirror. The happiness of having that new white suit took some of his illness away. The whiteness of the fabric took some of his paleness away, as well.

Marc, meanwhile, was sitting in his living room waiting for David, and when the latter came out, he said: "Lookin' sharp ... lookin' sharp, kid! Glad I never have to wear that thing again. Let's go back outside, the wife's probably worried."

David carried his old bundle of clothes out to the backyard and asked Marc where he could toss them. Marc said that he would have his wife wash them and then he would give them to one of the new dockworkers who hadn't any suitable working clothes. He said that there were always a few men hired each month to work down on the piers who were coming directly from prison, and the clothes that David had would help them out a lot.

David threw the bundle of clothes on the lawn near the washbasin, and went back to sit down at the table. The new clothes raised his spirits and his appetite. He quickly ate up the last of his potatoes and then asked Marc if he wouldn't mind giving him a ride to the train station.

"There is no train station in Concarneau, kid! There's one up in Quimper, which isn't so far, but why do you want to get on a train? You should stay in Concarneau. It's a beautiful town ... and I could probably get you a job carrying loads off the ships that come in. You could sleep in the bunks with the other dockworkers. ...Just don't tell none of them that you're a stowaway! ...Yeah, you could bunk with the other dockworkers ... sure, some of them are rough, but you'll roughen up soon enough! ... you may need your old clothes back...."

David thought of how what Marc was suggesting was the last thing he wanted to do. What little of Concarneau he saw, didn't appeal to him. Working on the piers didn't appeal to him. And what he needed more than anything was to go into the city and find a good doctor. He had never lived in a village. He had always lived in the city. And he thought that if he was forced to be in France, he might as well begin in Paris. He had thirteen-thousand dollars American in his pocket and certainly that was enough to get a first-class ride on a train, a thorough fix-up at the doctor's, and a decent enough apartment, which he planned on paying off for many months in advance, to keep him secure while he looked for a job.

"Thanks for the offer, Marc; you are really too kind. But the reason I was depor... I mean, the reason I stowawa...." he looked over at Marc's wife, who wasn't even listening; she was busy picking the skins of potatoes from her teeth, "...the reason I was *hitchhiking* was because I need to get to Paris where my mother is. She came to Paris on vacation and, unfortunately, suffered a stroke," he lied, "she's in a hospital there and it looks like she won't live too long, so I really need to get to Paris as soon as possible to see her." David bowed his head in feigned remorse after he finished speaking.

"I'm sorry, kid. That's sad news." said Marc with sincere regret in his voice. "I'll take you Quimper after lunch and you can catch a train to Paris. ...But come back out to Brittany to visit, sometime. Paris is alright but it's no paradise. Here you have the sea, and, the ... well, what else do you need? ...Maybe a woman like her." At that moment, Marc stood up, walked around the table and kissed his white-haired wife on the mouth. She was very surprised and, since she hadn't understood what the two men were talking about, she thought the kiss must have been to make it up to her for making her the butt of some joke or another. She looked at her husband suspiciously and frowned.

The afternoon crickets started chirping and a large cloud of gnats hovered over the lunch table in the backyard belonging to Marc and his wife. The three had finished eating and Marc was checking the oil in his old truck out in the driveway, while David sat in the shade under a nearby tree pressing a cold washcloth to his head to bring his persistent fever down. Meanwhile Marc's wife cleared the dishes from the table in the backyard. She thought about the stranger who came to her house and wasn't able to speak French. She thought about the coming of summer. It was almost May. She loved the month of May. She then mused on how nice the weather would be that day. She could smell the afternoon beginning. She felt quite full from the heavy lunch and wondered how she'd spend the rest of her day. Then the cloud of gnats began to fly into her mouth and eyes; and while spitting and blinking her eyelids rapidly, she ran into the kitchen carrying the last of the dishes.

Concarneau doesn't strike the newcomer to Europe as being very European. There is a small section of town, called the *Closed City* that has narrow, cobbled streets and ancient structures. This *Ville-Close* is fortified by castle walls, which were built to protect the inhabitants from an English attack by sea. But the rest of the village looks as modern and modest as a middle-class coastal town in America. There are no impressive cathedrals, there are no grandiose, stone courtyards with ancient sculptures and fountains. The larger village of Quimper, however, has these ancient squares and gothic cathedrals that are so impressive to the American traveler new to Europe. In Quimper there is a train station. Its tracks run through Rennes – the capital of *Bretagne* – and on into Paris. David and Marc took that pale blue pickup from Concarneau up to Quimper, which took quite a while. Marc made sure David drank out of the truck's canteen every fifteen minutes so as to get healthy. It must not be forgotten that only a few hours before, David was all cramped up in a wooden crate, suffering from a high fever and dehydration – among other ailments, that we'll soon find out about. But all that horrible nonsense seemed like a distant memory to David as he traveled down the country road, with a canteen full of fresh water and the springtime sun pouring its warmth and color on the rolling hills that stretched on into the distance. He was no longer stuffed in a dark box in a dank cargo room. He now had freedom, and clean air and Marc's good company. The lunch out back and the drive through the country was David's first experiences of Europe, and he tried to pay close attention so he would always remember them.

There is some evidence that David had been on this continent before, as a small boy; yet, regardless, there is not even a small trace of remembrance of Europe in his brain, so this April day truly was a day of new experiences … and it was probably because Quimper was so quaintly European and so very beautiful in David's eyes that he felt good once he arrived there with Marc in the pale blue pickup.

The two men walked up to the train station and Marc helped David buy the right ticket, and find the gate where the Paris train comes through. Marc never saw the large envelope full of cash that David had on him. Things might have gone differently in this story had he seen the money. Then again, perhaps it wouldn't have made any difference.

With still an hour and a half before the arrival of the train, Marc decided to wait with David. He was actually happy about the delay because this allowed him time to write down some important phrases in French for David to use on his journey. Marc liked the young man a lot. For a fleeting moment, during their lunch that day, he caught himself fantasizing that David was his son, or that he would become his son – as he and his wife had never had children. Marc felt silly then for having this thought and he chased it out of his head right away.

Marc paid for David's train ticket to Paris, although the latter tried to refuse the favor as convincingly as he could without actually telling Marc that he had thirteen-thousand dollars American on him. Still Marc managed to pay the fare and he said to him, "Kid, if you ever change your mind about working on the piers, call me up. I'll send you a ticket back here right away!"

David felt ashamed for getting the free ticket while all that cash sat in his pocket, but he knew better than to pull out that envelope in the feverish state he was in. That envelope was the only thing that separated him from a bum on the streets. He couldn't chance losing it. He knew if he lost his money and couldn't afford to get to a doctor, and had to sleep on the streets, he wouldn't live another fortnight.

Then they saw the Paris train arrive in Quimper.

"You'll be alright kid. I've seen sicker than you, just remember. …And I hope your mother gets better – I'm really sorry about that."

"Thanks for everything, Marc. Thank your wife too for me."

"Will do. And you have our address and everything. If you wanna come out and stay and work, we'd love to have you. Concarneau would love to have you. It's really pretty country out here. And the boat work treats you right. The ocean keeps you strong. You'll get some color in your cheeks."

"Thanks, Marc. I'll remember your offer." David said this with appreciation, but his words were feeble from illness. He shook hands with Marc and boarded the TGV train to Paris. He walked through the train to the back, found a couchette to sleep in, and dozed off in his new, clean white suit – second class.

"Nice kid, that American. I hope he comes back someday. Dock work would do him good." Marc said to himself as he walked back to his pickup truck to return to Concarneau. Driving home, he thought of how he had to work a long day the next day, but he was glad that it was still early afternoon, that it was sunny and warm, and he didn't have to clock-in again that day.

On his way back to his wife, Marc stopped off at a pub, by the piers, where he went sometimes after his shift to have an afternoon beer.

He walked in and saw that Bertrand was working. This made him smile. He liked Bertrand, and Bertrand always poured him a little extra beer when his glass was half finished.

Marc sat at a bar stool and tasted the cold beer. The sun was getting warm and, although it was only the end of April, the day seemed to have that hot, stillness of a summer day. The beer tasted very good to Marc. And while he was enjoying it, his boss, the captain, came in.

"I was looking for you this morning, Marc. ...Forget to pull the parcels off the ship today?"

"I thought it was all just pallets of sturgeon," replied Marc.

"No, there were some important shipments on there that the workmen left behind. They were thinking that those shipments were to be left for you. ...Nobody unloaded them, so they went away with the ship."

"Man, I'm really sorry."

"You should be really sorry! ... by the way, was that you smoking up on that hill today?"

"I just had a smoke and ate my lunch. I looked around the ship and I didn't see anything but fish crates, so I left to go eat lunch."

"What was in the crate you took up there?"

"What crate, captain?"

"You left a dolly and a crate up on the hill. A crowbar too. ...Tell me, Marc, what was in that crate, and where did it go?"

"It wasn't anything ... I mean, captain, I...."

"Marc, do you work tomorrow?"

"Yes, sir ... at six in the morning."

"Come to see me at nine." said the captain. And with that, the captain turned around and left the pub.

Marc didn't sleep well that night. The next day, he went to see his boss at nine in the morning. After a while, he finally admitted to the captain that there was a stowaway in that crate found on the hill. He said that he had taken him up to the hill to let him out where no one would see, and to get him far away from the piers so as not to cause problems for the ship captain. He truthfully explained the situation and said that he told the stowaway to go far away from the piers and never to mention the name of that boat, or any boat, to anyone.

After Marc confessed everything, the captain told him he would have to find another job. Marc had worked those piers near Concarneau for more years than any of the others, but his boss wasn't going to risk going to jail and losing his captain's license for anyone; and sneaking an immigrant into the country illegally was a sure way for all that to happen. Marc left the meeting with the captain in shock. It was the first time he had ever been fired from a job – and this job had been his life for so long.

A few weeks later, Marc found menial work guarding the piers at night up north in Brest. He didn't like Brest. He thought it was an ugly town. It rained too much up there. But he had a wife to feed. So he took the job.

The two rented out their house in Concarneau and found a smaller place up in Brest. Then, while driving the pale blue pickup north with the back full of furniture to move into their new place, a gasoline truck weaved out of its lane on the highway and forced Marc and his wife off the road. Marc suffered a minor neck injury, but his wife – that little white haired lady with a nose full of grey freckles – died instantly.

Marc's grief was profound and he couldn't bare to stay even one night in the new house in Brest. As he had no real friends in Brittany – his only real friend had been his wife – he decided to do what he promised himself years ago he would never do again… and that is to go back to sea as a commercial sailor.

The ocean was cruel and the men were crude and they were all drunks. But the sea was his solace. The land just reminded Marc of his poor wife, whom he loved immensely.

He never returned to land again. His last days were spent at sea, drinking and working the hard labor of a sailor.

CHAPTER III

I'm afraid it isn't too pretty, but I must give you a brief account of David's arrival in Paris, so that you will better understand the strange events that occur later on in our tale – and so that you can see, first-hand, how a story that has started off so simply sweet, can turn so utterly scandalous. ...So here we have it:

The day was just ending, the twilight just beginning, when David's train entered the *Gare Montparnasse* in Paris. David had thought that he would sleep on the train, but the trip was a hard one. Once they departed Quimper, once he parted company with Marc, his illness intensified. He wasn't able to sleep for a moment, his fever was increasing, his abdomen cramped up severely, and his ears were ringing with migraine. A train attendant – a little plump woman who didn't speak English but could see that David was in poor shape, huddled up in a sweaty, clammy ball with a thin, wool train-blanket pulled over his shivering body – gave the young man a couple tablets of aspirin, a glass of soda water, and some sort of rotten lime to use as a poultice – all of which did nothing. Why had he felt so much revived when he was with Marc on that hilltop? Or with Marc in the pale blue pickup driving along the sunny country roads? Or waiting with Marc for the train to arrive in Quimper? Why didn't that relief that came gradually after being pried out of the pinewood crate on top of that sunny hill in Brittany last? Why was it that his illness had to return so suddenly and with such intensity? It was no longer the illness of dehydration and fever that had set in while David's boat was out at sea. It was that fierce and never-ending gut-stabbing pain that began before – long before, when David was in America. So weary, so worn, so dispirited and in such pain, David stepped off the platform of the train in the *Gare Montparnasse* and headed for the station doors, where the city of Paris lay on the other side.

Upon our hero's arrival in Paris, and his visit to the cathedral of St. Sulpice…

The sun had disappeared over the zinc rooftops of the great, ancient city of Paris. The twilight had come. Its ominous, dark light enshrouded all. We all dread the grim twilight in Paris, for here it never ends – or at least it never seems to. The twilight, this crepuscule, of Paris is fierce with its influence on the emotions and the spirits of the denizens of the city. It instills comfort in one, and threatens one, at the same time. It is powerful, this city's twilight. It can destroy all men and children with a sidelong glance.

David, however, didn't know any of this. It was his first experience with the twilight of Paris. He walked through the neighborhood of *Montparnasse*, looking for relief from his pain. His mind wandered not to thoughts of where he would sleep, neither to what he would eat. Deep in his abdomen, his body felt as though it were rotting away. His insides burned and his temples throbbed. His teeth clattered and his arms shivered. These were the symptoms he had had before, and had had for a long time; but they subsided a bit in Brittany – then the twilight of Paris brought them back. This evening was worse for him them ever. No American night had ever seen him so ill. No doubt, the journey in the crate across the ocean took a toll on his body. As he walked the streets of *Montparnasse*, not even aware or caring of the newness that surrounded him, his body was breathing what it felt to be its last breaths.

Paris loomed over him and he knew not where his wanderings would lead. Its mazes of streets deceived him. The shop-signs and streetlights deceived him. He knew not how to find a doctor's office in Paris and he knew not how to ask for one. Groups of people gathered at every corner. Dark-faced twilight wanderers and errant derelicts passed by him. He tried to accost some passers-by in English but his illness was too great to talk. He stopped some people, a group of teenagers leaving a café, and tried to speak, to ask if a doctor could be found nearby; but when he opened his mouth to speak, he felt and heard only a groan escape his lips. The teenagers laughed at him and walked away, jeering at this hapless foreigner, throwing back insults in French, as they disappeared around the corner.

The train station at *Montparnasse* is in the south and the river Seine is a half-hour's brisk walk to the north. It intersects the center of Paris. This river, though out of sight, must have been what directed David towards St. Germain. Bodies of water are said to have a gravity of their own which orientates people when they are lost – even if this body of water is out of sight. Yet, there was no way to guide David because he had no destination. True, while weaving through the mazes of streets, he gradually neared the river. But near the river he would be no less lost than if he were a hundred miles away from it.

After an hour of wandering in the twilit hell that he suffered during his first introduction to Paris, he came upon a cathedral. The magnificent seventeenth-century structure towered proudly over him and the rest of the passers-by. For a brief moment, looking onward at this cathedral of St. Sulpice, David felt an awe and freedom that alleviated his illness – but for only a moment. Then the bells began to toll.

The cathedral bells were tolling. He counted two and he counted ten. "Strange to hear twelve tolls of the church bells, and to still see the twilight linger," he muttered aloud, with sickness on his breath.

Then with the tolling of the bells, the people in the streets began to scatter, just as if bombs were dropping and guns were being fired. Men grabbed their women and led them off to where they disappeared together – through doorways, through alleyways, through gates and gardens. Mothers fetched their children from the birdbaths where they were playing – splashing around, soiling their white Sunday dresses.

Then David came upon Rue St. Sulpice: a little cobbled street lined with shops which were all closing up for the night. The young man hobbled down the little street, with a cold, sweaty migraine, which blurred his vision, and gave him vertigo. He knew he needed to focus on something, on anything, to keep his consciousness. He focused on the rivulets of dirty rainwater flowing down the gutters. He focused on a couple kissing in a doorway. He focused on a black car parked on the curb. He focused on some policemen who were hassling a bum. He walked down Rue St. Sulpice and focused his blurry eyes on the stone walls that lined the street. He then saw a most curious thing: pasted to these stone walls that stretched on for many blocks were hundreds of old-fashioned posters. Hundreds of copies of the same advertisement lined the stone walls of the buildings. David staggered over to the wall and studied one of these posters.

It was an advertisement for the Russian ballet – at the Bolshoy theatre in Moscow. It was a lithograph with a beautiful young ballerina executing a pirouette. She was tall and had fair hair and below the sketch of her figure, were a few sentences written in French. David's senses returned slightly while he gazed at this poster. He couldn't understand the French. He wasn't sure if the poster was advertising an event in Moscow, or if it advertised a Russian ballet that would be appearing in France, or if it was even an advertisement at all. This didn't matter to him. He couldn't understand the words that were printed on the poster, but this did not concern him. All he could understand was the great beauty of the lithograph drawing of the ballerina. She was the greatest thing David had ever seen. He thought of her beauty and thought of how she really didn't exist – she was just a drawing. "Lithograph girls don't exist," was all his feverish brain would let him think, and all his feverish mouth would let him utter, on the subject, "They don't exist, David, keep walking." Then he thought of Moscow and how he always wanted to go there. In all his life, he had never had a desire to go to France; but, for as long as he could remember, he had wanted to see Moscow – Moscow and St. Petersburg.

Then the pains began to toll in his body again. His kidney was flaming; he thought it was his kidney – wasn't quite sure where his kidney was but it sounded right. His kidney was ablaze, and his forehead was a hot oven cooking his brains that were black and burnt inside, no doubt; and his brain pounded with despair.

Like the church bells that tolled, his temples rang. He stepped back from where he stood, gazing at the poster, and continued on down Rue St. Sulpice.

Far off, he saw the flashing green, neon cross that he believed to be a pharmacy sign. It flashed bright green light against the nearby walls off in the distance and he knew it was probably a pharmacy and he knew it was probably still open and he knew the pharmacist would help him if anyone would. He paced quickly down the sidewalk. Every two steps he took, he passed another Russian ballet poster and he glanced at each one, just to look again and again at the beautifully drawn girl who didn't exist, as she made a pirouette.

When David reached the doorway beneath the green glowing cross, he saw the word "pharmacie" written on the windows and he saw the bright, white lights inside. He saw the customers waiting in line at the counter, and through the window he saw the women in long white coats who were obviously the pharmacists. As he opened the glass door, one of the pharmacists caught sight of David and ran up to the door that he was trying to enter through. He stepped one foot inside and kept pushing on the door that felt so heavy against his meek and trembling hands. When he stepped his second foot inside, the pharmacist seized him with a look of fear and anger on her face. She was speaking loudly and rapidly to our poor hero who just wanted to get inside to buy some relief from his pain. She then shoved him. She pushed him hard; and, weak as he was, he fell backwards, out of the pharmacy doorway, back onto the sidewalk. The pharmacist screwed up her face with repugnance on the other side of the glass as she quickly locked the door. David continued stumbling backwards, across the sidewalk, towards the street where the cars passed by, quickly navigating in the dark light of the crepuscule.

Next to the curb, facing the stone wall of the building, stood a man of about sixty years. He was quite overweight and not too tall. His face was ruddy and his dark, grey-streaked hair was wiry, like a mat of soiled steel wool draped over his skull. He was dressed like a foreign army general from the nineteenth century, wearing epaulettes of gold-colored tin. His appearance was quite comical. This man had been studying one of the Russian ballet posters that David had taken such an interest in earlier. When David stumbled backwards across the sidewalk, he narrowly missed falling into the road in front of a passing car. Instead he was saved by the cushioned belly of this hefty officer, whom he bumped into. The old man didn't flinch. He was planted firmly to the sidewalk and was as solid as a general. He took one look at David, the poor, sick young man who was suffering from pain and vertigo, a nausea and dizziness, of the worst kind, and he too shoved David – shoved him off into the other direction. The old general then tore down the poster of the Russian ballerina that he had been looking at, and rolled it up; then tucking it under his arm, he walked off, throwing David – who was stumbling to keep his balance nearby – a glare of the most disdainful and menacing kind, and continued on down Rue St. Sulpice with the lithograph poster tucked under his arm.

Then the twilight began to darken into night. David had been sick enough to begin with. The two strangers who pushed him in his weakness only made his recovery that much less possible. And so, the twilight fled, and night came forth; and David's sight went black. He could no longer tell if he was standing or lying on the ground. He felt himself spinning in circles. He felt the rush of some horrible chemical coming up from his gut. He tasted an acrid taste – like gunmetal on the tongue. He stepped off the edge of the sidewalk onto the street. He wasn't sure if he was going to faint, or die, or go to sleep, or what. Then all of his thoughts, all of his pain, all of his consciousness evaporated. David, in his nice, new white suit, dropped to the ground and rolled into the rain-filled gutter. The old army general, who watched this scene over his shoulder as he walked, chuckled to himself and continued on his way, with the rolled-up poster under his arm.

The pharmacist, who had been curiously watching David's disorientated actions all along through the window suddenly turned away when she saw his body fall to the gutter. Then all the passers-by vanished. And the cars, they too vanished; and there wasn't a soul on Rue St. Sulpice. And there, David lay, without the slightest consciousness, face down in the gutter as the filthy rainwater passed over his head and over his body with every intent to drown him.

CHAPTER IV

Meanwhile, at the Bolshoy Theatre in Moscow…

Our beautiful dancer of the lithograph that is strewn all over Paris to advertise the summer season at the Bolshoy theatre; with special travel packages and deals for the sensible, ballet-loving Parisian who wishes to see the sights of Moscow, take a tour of the city's historical monuments, and take in a ballet or two without spending a fortune; she in her real and glorious flesh is dancing at this moment for all of Moscow's society men and women. Her name is Anastasia Alexandrovna Mironova. She is called Nastasia, Nastenjka, or Nastya, has two and twenty years, and is blessed with a tall and slender figure, delicate and small, though strong feet and hands, and the most beautiful face that Moscow has ever seen.

Nastasia is not yet under contract with the Bolshoy theatre. In fact, this is her second time dancing on this opulently famous stage. Hitherto, she has been the prima ballerina of the Sunday afternoon family ballets at Moscow's less prestigious Gelikon theatre. It was there that she was chosen to model for the Bolshoy's famous lithograph advertisement that was pasted on every wall from Berlin to Paris, from Brussels to Barcelona. The director of the Bolshoy sought out an amateur dancer of great, immaculate beauty, since none of the dancers of his own Bolshoy have that real, undisputable and sensual beauty that Nastya has … that beauty that makes men feel lust and women feel envy and makes ballet goers feel like buying tickets.

So Nastya was chosen just over one month ago, to model for the artist who created this advertisement; and during her involvement with the Bolshoy company, the theatre director, and ballet master, *Monsieur Lavretsky*, as he is called, fell in love with Nastya in a most paternal and benevolent way and decided to give her a chance on the stage of the greatest theatre in Moscow.

It is only her second time dancing on this stage, yet the theatre goers – these Russian balletomanes – are already familiar with her and she is the subject of much talk among Moscow society. The men adore her, and the elderly women look on her as a young, promising fledgling who will achieve greatness if she is nurtured properly – and their way of nurturing her properly is to discuss her at social events and over private afternoon tea. The way the elderly society women speak of her, one would think Nastya is a newborn fawn that is trying to walk and, though very cute in her efforts to stand, needs the help of an older doe who has mastered the technique of walking. The younger women on the other hand, especially the commissioned ballet dancers at the Bolshoy, do not like her in the least. Many of them have at one time or another, in secret, wished and even prayed devoutly to God that she would suffer a serious bodily injury or death. …Such are the spectators of beauty.

Recently, there was even an attempt on the health of Nastya, by one of the established dancers at this theatre, one Varvara Fillipovna, about a week following Nastya's first performance at the Bolshoy. It happened after one confused, young reporter from Moscow got it into his head that Nastya had signed a contract to become a permanent company dancer at the theatre, and would be taking the job of Varvara Fillipovna – the latter to be dismissed. This young reporter published his misconception in many of the Moscow and Petersburg papers, as well as the international papers in several European countries. The article even reached the London *Times* and *Le Monde* in Paris.

When Varvara Fillipovna read the article she ran to the theatre in tears to find out if news was true – if she had, indeed, lost her job. And upon finding Nastya, who was repairing her slipper in the bathroom backstage, Varvara attacked her. She took a bottle of chlorine bleach from the bathroom floor and tried to force the poisonous fluid down the throat of our dear Nastya. Fortunately, Monsieur Lavretsky, the director, was strolling through the dressing room at the time and heard the commotion; whereas he ran into the bathroom and extracted the bottle of bleach from the hands of Varvara – no harm had been done. He then explained to Varvara that, although the rumors in the papers were just rumors, she would certainly lose her job and much more if she were ever to harm his precious Nastya. Varvara was glad to hear she still had a job but the whole ugly scene embarrassed her so much that she ran home crying and didn't return to the theatre for two weeks, thus missing two performances. Meanwhile, Monsieur Lavretsky was lamenting the words he used towards Varvara Fillipovna. For the two weeks she was absent from the theatre rehearsals and performances, Lavretsky's mind was in a terrible quandary. The conflict that was beginning to arise involving Varvara was certain, in his opinion, to cause many problems for the theatre – for reasons we will soon discover.

To go back to the present… Nastya has just finished dancing before the amorous audience and is now backstage changing into the clothes she will wear on her walk home in the mild Moscow spring evening. Although, she is glad that Varvara still has not returned to the theatre - for she is expecting another ugly scene the next time the two come in contact – there is still no peace for Nastya in the Bolshoy dressing rooms. The other dancers are full of glares and sneers and petty insults. Nastya is the most beautiful of the dancers and the least popular among them – two qualities which are, among women, usually well-woven together.

    Seated far away from the other girls, Nastya examines her foot, which is slightly bloody from a strenuous performance. The other girls are far-off, laughing and popping open champagne bottles. Some of them look over at Nastya and get great satisfaction from the fact that Nastya isn't laughing, or even smiling, and has no champagne of her own to drink. Nastya doesn't need a glass of champagne on this night. She is happy for the performance she gave and looks forward to going home and having tea with her family. On the inside she is smiling, though she makes sure to keep her appearance to the others one of cool reserve. She dresses as fast as she can to remove herself from the company of these feline girls backstage. And soon enough she is on her way out the door. But upon leaving the theatre, she runs into the director.

    "Nastasia!" Director Lavretsky calls out to her. "Nastya!"

    "Yes, Monsieur Lavretsky?" replies our Nastya.

    "Nastya, you were brilliant again! Don't worry about the other girls. I am going to do what I can to make you a permanent company dancer here. There are a lot of politics, you understand? And the problems with the other girls are only part of the politics. But you were great! A real beauty you are when you get on stage. Your right arm is a little stiff when you do the *croise derriere*. Try to let it glide through the air…."

    "Yes, thank you, Monsieur Lavretsky. I will work harder and…."

"...But, Nastya, you were great. And here ... here is..." the director reaches in the pocket of his navy blue frockcoat, "...a couple of letters for you. One is from Paris." He hands her the two sealed envelopes and looks at her while pushing his eyes out of his skull, and simultaneously lifting his eyebrows and dropping his jaw as if to express to Nastya that he has no idea what these letters are about, or why they came to her through the Bolshoy, though they must be interesting and well worth reading. Then he kisses her three times on the cheeks, in the Russian fashion, says goodnight and walks past her to speak with someone who had been beckoning him during this whole conversation with Nastya.

Outside it is a mildly cold, late April evening and the melting snow becomes a dark, murky deluge of water that runs down the gutter like a torrent. Nastya walks down Petrovka Street towards her home. She didn't care to shower at the Bolshoy after dancing. She will wait till she gets home. In the meantime, the sweat on her forehead and arms feels good in the cold evening air of Moscow. She has forgotten all of the petty girls at the theatre, and has forgotten as well the faces of the spectators; some of them were looking at her so strangely – or so she imagined. She forgets all of this now, and she is happy. Watching the smoking chimneys and the dimly-lit twilight that is lingering so late on this night, she is happy. Then, after passing down Strastnoy Boulevard, she comes to a safe little place near a well-lit park, where she can sit and read the letters passed on to her by Monsieur Lavretsky.

She finds a stoop and pulls out the first letter. It was sent from Petersburg. The stamp was dated the day after her first performance at the Bolshoy. She breaks the nice, expensive seal on the envelope and reads it over. It is from a little girl who lives outside of Petersburg. Her parents took her to see her first ballet at the Bolshoy and there she saw Nastya and how beautiful she was ... "And I decided that I want to be a ballerina like you. I don't know anything about it, but I am going to take classes ... I am still quite young," the girl writes, "but when I am your age I hope to be very famous and maybe you will even hear about me then and think that it was all of your doing that made me famous. You can smile and say that you made me a famous ballerina, all with your beauty ... and my father says...." And the letter goes on like that for sometime.

Nastya smiles, laughs a little and puts the letter and its nice envelope deep into her bag with her clothes. She pulls out the other envelope – the one from Paris – and begins to read:

Mademoiselle Anastasia Alexandrovna, forgive my impudence for writing to you directly. I discovered you and your unique brilliance through the reviews in the French newspapers. It was through my personal contacts with the Bolshoy that enabled me to contact you; however, I insisted that this letter remain confidential between you and myself and I trust that you will heed this instruction. My name is Monsieur de Chevalier. I live in Paris. I am an aristocrat and a patron of the arts; and I have strong influence over the "Opéra Garnier" and the entire French ballet. It would be in the best interest of our ballet – and in *your* best interest as well, I am certain – to have you join our ballet as the leading dancer, *la première danseuse*, in the greatest theatre of the city of Paris.

I have enclosed a railway ticket from Moscow to Paris and one thousand francs for your journey. This invitation shall serve as your visa for entry into my country. Please come at once. Your fame and your happiness in Paris is a promise!

Sincerely,

Le Monsieur de Chevalier

(PS: my address is on another sheet of paper enclosed in this envelope.)

This letter had a strange effect on Nastya. Her eyes flashed when she read it. One cannot be certain what she was thinking. All that is known is that this letter made a very strange and significant impression upon her. Unlike the other letter from the little girl, which she stuffed in her bag full of ballet clothes, this one she folds carefully, puts back in its envelope and places into the front pocket of her coat. She then stands from the stoop covered in packed snow where she has been sitting under the streetlamp, and she walks on, languidly, deep in thought, towards her home.

Nastya arrives on Sokolniki Street and climbs up the steps packed with snow leading into the building. It is now completely dark and the street is silent. Not even a drunk is yelling and swaggering down the road on this night. It is very quiet. Nastya climbs the stairs to her apartment where she lives with her mother, father and her little brother. She reaches the third floor and walks on the creaking floorboards to her apartment. She slides her key in the door and as she turns it, a faint commotion can be heard on the other side.

The door opens to the little flat and Nastya feels the heat from the stove pass through the room. It flushes her face and she drops her heavy bag by the door. A man and a woman seated at the little table in the center of the small room both look over as Nastya enters. The woman, who is her mother, – a short, graying woman with light eyes – remains seated. The man is her father and he jumps up when his daughter enters. His large, rough body is covered with hair and his beard is black and wiry and there is a great gentleness in his face, a great kindness in his eyes. He smiles when he sees his daughter as if he hadn't seen her for a year.

"Nastenjka! ... Dochenjka!" He cries as he embraces her, kissing her forehead and her cheeks over and over. Nastya goes limp in her father's embrace. She is tired from walking and is very happy to see him.

"Oh my Nastenjka! We heard you were beautiful!" He continues to smother his daughter's face with kisses.

"Oh Papa, I wish you'd been there!" Nastya tells him. The two continue embracing and the short little woman, Nastya's mother, rushes up to the two of them.

"Shhh! You'll wake your brother! He's just gotten to sleep. ...Shhh!" She taps Nastya's bottom lightly with a soupspoon. "Shhh! He's just gone to sleep, finally!"

She then taps her husband with the soupspoon and he turns to his wife. "Nevermind, dear," he mutters through his thick beard. Then he turns back to his daughter. He holds her face in his large hands, "Peter Nozdrev came by, just moments ago, to tell us about the ballet. He said you danced 'like a bird flying in a dream' ... 'flying in a dream' is how he said it. ...He said you were the most beautiful one. I am so proud! ...Nastenjka, my girl, I am so proud."

Her mother then jumps back in the face of her husband, shaking the wooden soupspoon at him. "Well, I don't see why you should be so proud when you weren't even there to watch. What should we care what goes on at the Bolshoy theatre? A place like the Bolshoy could at least have the honor of giving seats to the dancers' parents!" Nastya and her father, who up to this point have been looking at each other with great happiness in their faces, now turn to look at the old woman who continues talking, now addressing Nastya: "…Oh, it's not your fault, my dear. Even on what they've paid you to dance these couple of times, you couldn't afford to buy your parents' tickets to the Bolshoy! …But somebody should pay if they want us to be happy about your dancing there … yes, somebody should pay! Now quiet…" her voice turns back to a whisper, "…and come eat. And let your brother sleep."

The three walk over to the little wooden table at the center of the small room, where there are three wooden chairs. On one side of the table is the stove. Steam rises from a pot cooking on the gas flame. On the other side of the table, in the back corner of this little room shared by the family, there is a tiny bed where Nastya's brother is sleeping beneath a withered, woolen blanket. Nastya approaches the table with her head down. Before they sit, Nastya's father takes her delicate chin in his large hand and lifts it up so he can look at her face.

"I am so proud to have you for my daughter." he says, looking into her eyes. She smiles. Her father's words make her feel good.

The three sit down at the table. There is neither plate nor teacup in front of Nastya. Her mother and father each have a small teacup for themselves and two plates from which they had been eating before Nastya came home.

"The kasha is on the stove," Nastya's mother whispers to her daughter, "make sure to put the lid back on so we don't get bugs."

Nastya doesn't get up from the table. Instead she sits, still wearing her coat, in the room that is surprisingly warm on this evening. She guesses it is the heat from the stove making it warm. She looks at her mother, who slurps her tea. A piece of kasha is stuck on her lower lip. She looks at her father who isn't drinking his tea or eating his kasha. He looks deep in thought and every other moment he glances over at his daughter with a proud smile. Nastya doesn't feel like eating. So much is going through her mind. She looks at her brother's lump beneath the blanket, sleeping in the corner. She looks at every corner of the small room where the family eats and sleeps and does everything else together. She looks around the room – the room in which she has lived with her family for the last five years – as if she is seeing it for the first time. She speculates on every detail: how small the place is – just one room, with the exception of a tiny bathroom; how barren it looks and how unkempt, despite Nastya's and her mother's constant efforts to keep it clean. Their poverty is apparent. Nastya glances around the room for another moment, then lets her head drop down a bit as she thinks of all the things she loves and all the things she hates about living there. Her thoughts are interrupted when her younger brother coughs in his sleep; and, although no one is speaking, Nastya's mother makes a loud, "Shhh!" sound addressed to everyone.

Nastya feels in the pocket of her coat. She wants to pull out the letter from Paris but she doesn't. She realizes it would not be a good idea to show this letter to her parents. Her hand pushes it back, deep into her pocket and she lifts her head and says in a quiet but excited voice to her parents, "The ballet master says I am good enough to go dance in Paris...." She is then interrupted by her mother...

"Paris?! Why ever did he say that? The dancers in Paris I'm sure are all like painted dolls. You wouldn't be like a 'bird flying in a dream' there ... maybe a duck flapping in a pond! ...That's a crazy idea." She slurps her tea, and talks loudly, forgetting that her son is asleep just a few feet away, "Paris?! What a horrid place!" again she slurps her tea, "...Nastya, I'll need you to wake early tomorrow and help me with the washing" ... "now go and get some kasha so you don't starve!"

The light is warm and dim in the family's apartment. The little boy again coughs in his sleep. The mother continues to slurp her tea. The father slides his plate over to Nastya's place at the table, so she may eat from it; and he silently stands and walks over to the stove to get himself some kasha. Nastya is deep in thought. She has always wanted to go to Paris. She fears she could never be happy living far away from her father. He is her constant emotional and spiritual support. What he provides for her, she is sure she could never find elsewhere. In addition, she knows her brother is sick and he needs his sister. Yet, she knows that she is no longer a little girl and is becoming a woman more and more each day that passes in this little flat on the third floor on Sokolniki Street. She is not hungry. Her heart is weighed down by worry and there is even a little knot tying itself in her stomach. 'Who is this Monsieur de Chevalier? ...And why does he have such a ridiculous name?' she thinks to herself, 'I guess all aristocrats have ridiculous names,' she smiles. The thought of this rich horseman in Paris lightens her thoughts and lessens her worries. 'After all, he sent a ticket as well as money. I could always go tryout for the ballet and come back to Moscow if it doesn't work out,' she pauses in thought, '...Paris! What am I thinking? Petersburg maybe, but oh... to live in Paris - what an idea!' ... 'Even if I tried to persuade them, Mother would never let me go. Papa wouldn't have it either!'

Here we must stop and establish what kind of girl Nastya is. There are people who would receive an invitation to visit a foreign country and immediately laugh it off as an impracticality. There are those who yearn for the opportunity to move to a city like Paris – or even just the capital city of their own country – yet they would tremble under the enormous anxiety caused by even the notion of leaving their established lives, their families, and the things that are safe and familiar to them. Some people feel that one would have to be very brave to move to another country – even if the road were paved with as much security and promise as possible (though security is never a promise in this world – even with the smallest of decisions). Nastya, however, doesn't feel that such actions are acts of bravery. She sees life as a drama on the stage, a fleeting performance, or more accurately, as *a dance*: a glorious ballet, romantic in its progression and emotional flow of feats of daring, which are, to the dancer, often painful and scary; though to the spectator they appear to be graceful and beautifully delicate movements performed without the slightest fear or hesitation. It is this principle that propels her skill, making her a great dancer. For when she's dancing on the stage in front of hundreds of people who have come to see a beautiful spectacle, flawlessly performed, she anticipates the movements she must execute, not as risks, but as necessary actions which she *must* execute with the fullest attention paid to appearing graceful and carefree. Her leaps through the air on the stage are not risks to her, for she has no choice but to leap – it is the reason she is on the stage to begin with; whereby, a risk involves choice. The person stranded on the second floor of a burning building does not take a risk by leaping out. The drop may break the person's legs, but if he remains, the flames will engulf his body. It is not an act of bravery to try to save yourself from death by fire by jumping out of a high window – there is no choice in that situation. The coward and the brave jump alike.

Nastya is one who takes life very seriously. To her, all is a beautiful ballet that will soon come to an end. Although she is very young, we know that it is often the young who feel that life is the shortest and who feel it will end the soonest – such is the error of youth that leads the young to so many impulsive decisions. Yet, those who tremble fearfully with the thought of venturing out into the world and leaving their familiar homes on errant journeys, they too take life seriously – perhaps all too seriously – for theirs is a world where the slightest step off the path may pull them to a patch of thorns. And the point of the thorn is a threat too mighty to endure. But we all walk past the points of thorns and we all give our blood to them when we falter and stumble. And we all falter and stumble walking along, whether we walk close to home or far away.

Likewise, Nastya is one who doesn't take life *too* seriously. Her world is one of deep emotions and powerful romance. And all who lend their bodies to emotion and submit to romance are prey to deep loss and fierce pain. Those who shield themselves from emotion wear a cloth that resists pain and pleasure alike. Those who let their skin stay naked, allowing emotion to caress them, allow too the thorns to prick them and the swords to swipe them, spilling their blood. Yet, when a young woman allows every emotion of life to caress her naked skin, she must be ready to give herself to that which comes – and come what may; for she knows not the masks the future wears; and if he wears the mask of love but wields the sword of death, he will surely be free to strike her, whereupon she will fall – a death of body and a death of soul. So she laughs in the face that wears a mask. For, otherwise, she will perish of fear and die of fright.

To Nastya, the world is of eminent beauty and she consciously realizes she must not grasp it too firmly, or hold on too dearly; she must be ready to let it go if it decides to fly away. In this condition, she is safe in the world. For she knows that to attain profound glory, one must pay the highest price, and that price is the suffering of a wound – that wound which is made when that glory dies and falls to the profound depths. Nevertheless, this profound glory is the want of her, as it is the want of anyone who lives the romantic life. But glory comes to so few, and for so many this romance is destined for tragedy; so it was in the past and will be for always.

Nastya submits to her will to the romantic and the emotional life. She has no choice. It is her nature and it will be her nature for her entire life. This caprice of hers manifests itself in the form of grand decisions and bold actions that others look upon in awe and amazement. These are decisions and acts she *must* make, there is no choice; therefore, there is no risk, and no bravery involved. Nastya has never considered herself to be someone who is extraordinary in bravery and courage. She does what she *must* do, what her nature forces her to do, and she goes along in cool and devout submission. Yet she goes along with pride and grace, for it is just life, and life is nothing to cower beside.

On this night, there is a great change forming in the mind of Nastya. All this time, she has been sitting deep in thought, contemplating matters at the table seated beside her mother and father. Yet now she stands and walks over silently to the corner of the room where she sleeps each night. No one disturbs her as she pulls back the hanging gauze curtain that provides her bed with privacy. She sits down in the corner beside her bed, upon the wooden floor, so that she may be entirely alone.

From the corner where she sits, she can see the silhouettes of her parents sitting at the table through the hanging gauze sheet. She watches their silhouettes drinking tea together for many moments, until she feels herself drifting to sleep; she then decides to go from the corner to her bed.

On her bed, she drifts off momentarily, still dressed in her clothes and her wool coat. She is very tired, yet she doesn't want to sleep - she would rather stay awake and think about all of these thoughts which are swarming in her mind. But her eyes are too heavy, her head is too sleepy. She drifts off wearily, momentarily, and soon she again reawakens. Awake again, she looks to the sheet that hangs to separate her bed from the rest of the apartment. She no longer sees the silhouettes of her parents.

With her small and delicate hand, she gently pulls aside the curtain and looks across the room. She sees her parents now together bundled beneath a blanket on their bed – a bed which is much too tiny for the both of them, a bed that is tucked between the wall and the gas stove. The stove is now off and no more steam rises from the pot that sits on the cold burner. Nastya figures that she has been asleep for a long time, although it feels like she only drifted off for a moment. 'It must be close to dawn', she thinks; yet decides to dwell in thought no more for the night. The night is over and it is time to rest.

Nastya again falls asleep, still wearing her coat and clothes. Above her sleeping body, out the window, one can see the broad moon hovering over Sokolniki Street. One can see the shapes of the swaying trees, which appear black against the glowing crepuscular sky of Moscow. From her window, one can see the rooftops of the tiny buildings across the street. They have only two stories, these buildings, and the full moon lights up their roofs and reflects off the melting snow that covers them in patches. And, while the snow melts on the streets outside, while it melts on the roofs and on the branches of the fir trees, Nastya sleeps and dreams and sees many things:

Waking from a terrible vision, Nastya finds herself in her parents' apartment alone. Her mother and father have gone out somewhere; and even her brother, who is almost always lying ill in his bed, has left. The quiet of the empty room brings her anxiety and she feels that she too must leave the apartment as quickly as possible. She then finds herself walking out the door and down the stairs. Once outside, she looks down Sokolniki Street. There is a little fountain in a park, just near her home. The fountain spouts crystalline water and birds flutter around it, swooping down to catch fish from the fountain in their beaks. Then the birds cackle and fly off as they notice the coming storm. The clouds overhead turn dark and lightning starts to crackle in the sky. All the snow has long since melted and a violent spring squall has begun, flooding the streets with water.

Nastya finds cover in a doorway and watches the storm grow in intensity. Then she notices a group of balalaika players huddled across the street. They are playing a nostalgic Russian folk song. They keep playing, apparently, unaware or uncaring of the fact that they are already very drenched and the storm is beginning to flood the streets around them.

Nastya, seeing how quickly the deluge in the street is rising, fears that she will be swept away by the water; so, she begins to walk up Sokolniki Street towards a cathedral where she intends to climb the tower to escape the flood.

These balalaika players follow her up Sokolniki Street, laughing at her from afar while strumming sad songs.

She reaches the cathedral square and climbs the steps to escape the tumult of waves that are now filling the square. She is safe on the steps, but the balalaika players in the square are doomed. These drowning musicians float past her, one by one, playing their sad odes; all the while, their faces wear the expressions of terror, as they inhale the water and die.

The water level rises and the storm increases and Nastya surveys the cathedral, looking for a way to climb the high tower. She finds it strange that this cathedral should be here on Sokolniki Street. It doesn't look like a Russian church. It appears more like an immense gothic cathedral belonging to Western Europe. Its façade is comprised of several large Corinthian columns; and on either side of the façade, there are two immense towers – like the towers of a castle in a fairytale. It is perhaps a cathedral she has seen in a photograph, but more likely it is something from her imagination.

Nastya is unable to gain entrance to the towers and the water begins to rise up over the steps. Soon, the dark rainwater covers Nastya's head and she struggles to keep her head afloat, though it appears likely that she too, like the balalaika players, will perish in the flood. The whole cathedral square is now a violently flowing river and Nastya tumbles underwater, holding her breath. She is beaten by the waves and almost drowns. Just when she has no strength left to keep herself afloat, the flood subsides and the river flows out. The stone floor of the cathedral square emerges as the water passes away and Nastya surfaces, lying upon the ground, drenched, beaten and weary.

Now all is calm and the only sound that can be heard is the deep and faint roaring of the river as it flows on in the distance, continuing on its path through the city – away from the square. The noise is like the ocean as heard through a seashell. It is nighttime now, twilight has passed, yet the sky is lit-up. Nastya, fearing a return of the flood, finds a way into the cathedral and begins to climb the south tower. And, sure enough, just as she begins to climb, the cathedral square begins to flood again.

High up in the air, standing atop the tower, hundreds of meters above the lit-up city, above the dark cathedral square below, she feels the warm wind of a summer night blow against her uncovered skin. Now there is a man with her. She doesn't know who he is, yet she embraces him, and wants to embrace him. He, however, wants to jump. The two look down from the top of the cathedral belfry where they stand. The ground looms hundreds or thousands of meters below. As he urges her to jump, the ground becomes farther and farther away. Now the city is a cloud of lights miles away and the cathedral begins to sway in the air. They embrace to keep their balance on the top of the belfry, yet he wants to jump. For some reason she trusts this man, and she too, now wants to jump - believing that they will both live; that they will dive from the roof and fall to a peaceful river of water below where they will swim as calmly as dolphins.

They jump. And in the air they fall asunder, their bodies separate so as not to clash when they land in the water below. As the ground comes closer to Nastya, the terror increases. She now sees the ground clearly and it is not a deep abyss below, it is but a hard, stone cathedral square and it comes suddenly towards her as her body plummets.

Only seconds pass before she hits the ground in a sudden culmination of terror. She feels that she is no longer alive. The man, however, whom she was with, is still alive. The fall did not kill him, though Nastya died instantly upon hitting the stone square. As her soul lingers for a moment in her dead body, she feels envy – envy that this man, whose idea it was to jump, is still alive, while she is dead. She feels envy and terror. As it dawns on her that she will no longer be amongst the living, her terror rises to an apex and in immense fright she wakes up, covered in cold sweat, with a pounding heart.

Outside the tiny window with four panes of glass above Nastya's bed, the Moscow moon is still broad and shining over the rooftops. Nastya, now awake, lies trembling in fear. Slowly, as her eyes look around her, she comes to the realization that she is still alive and has only suffered a nightmare. She sits up in bed, still shaking slightly, and looks out her window. A wind has come and the trees sway – their dark silhouettes sway back and forth against the glowing night sky in the background. Nastya recalls every peace of her dream wondering how such a horrible dream could be dreamt. She looks again past her curtain and sees that all is dark and all are asleep. She hears her brother cough in his sleep. She looks again through her window, to the moon and the swaying trees.

She dreads going back to sleep, lest she has another nightmare so hideous and ugly; yet, if she were to remain awake, she would be haunted by her thoughts – some of which are equally as hideous and ugly as the nightmare just past.

While taking off her coat, and putting on her nightgown, which she will wear to sleep the rest of the night through, Nastya thinks about many things. She tries to force a lot of these thoughts from her head but she cannot. They are there and she knows she must think about them. There is nothing she can do and it frightens her. She knows now what is going to happen and it frightens her – but there is nothing she can do to change it.

CHAPTER V

The next morning, Nastya's parents awoke early and had a silent breakfast together at the round wooden table. Her father then left and walked up Sokolniki Street and took the tram to his job on the other side of Moscow. After he left, Nastya's mother roused her daughter to get help with the washing. She had all of the family's dirty clothes laid out in a pile in the center of the room. While the mother and daughter took all the clothes into the bathroom to wash them in the tub, they made sure to walk on their tip-toes, as Nastya's brother was still sleeping; and given his consumptive condition, they were very careful to allow him the longest and most peaceful rest possible, at those times when he slept.

Before lunch, while the two women sat in the bathroom scrubbing stains out of the clothes, at approximately eleven in the morning, a visitor came knocking at their apartment door.

Nastya's mother was alarmed most by the knock. "Who could it be? Who is it Nastya?!" she turned to her daughter.

"I don't know, Mother." The two sat paralyzed for a moment in the bathroom.

"Well go answer it. Don't keep them waiting!"

"Yes, Mother." Nastya stood and went out of the bathroom, and walked across the room to the front door. She opened it.

"Hello, Nastasia," came from visitor, who stood in hallway, where the air was stifling. It was unusually hot for an April day in a northern city like Moscow, and the hallway trapped in all the heat that escaped from the nearby apartments. The man's forehead was beaded with sweat. His frockcoat was of thick, navy blue wool with gold buttons. Underneath the coat, he had on a heavy, three piece suit. On his head he wore a nice, warm astrakhan hat, of the type which upper-class Muscovites find so fashionable to wear in the heart of winter. Who was this man wearing a suit and coat and a winter hat, standing before Nastya's door? It was the director from the Bolshoy, The man who had given Nastya the two letters the night before.

"Oh, hello!" said Nastya, surprised. She was embarrassed to see the director coming to her apartment. Her cheeks flushed red. She didn't know why he was coming and what he wanted; but most of all she was ashamed that he was, at that moment, standing in her doorway, looking past her into the apartment, obviously noticing her family's poverty. His impression of the place apparently embarrassed him as well, for his eyes glanced around to each corner of the room, then his own cheeks flushed red and he began to stutter, "I ... I'm sorry... I...."; but without finishing, he took Nastya out into the hallway to speak with her.

"Monsieur Lavretsky, I...." Nastya began. Then the director interrupted her...

"Nastya, I'm sorry to come by like this ... to come *here*, I mean ... I mean to have come to *your*...." His nervous fingers folded up the nice astrakhan hat he held in his hands, ruining its shape. "...I just wanted to say that you were great last night and I have every intention of getting you voted in as a permanent dancer. ...I think by next season, everyone at the theatre – the other dancers, I mean – will like you and respect you and...." his hat by this time, had become a crumpled little ball in his red, sweaty hands. He continued, "There're just these politics ... and they're just politics, you see. No one can do anything about them." He paused a moment, "Varvara Fillipovna seems to have some real strong ideas in her head, and, well, she's hot-headed a bit, you see ... yet her parents are great patrons to the Bolshoy. Her parents are patrons to a lot of the great artistic institutions in Moscow, but especially the Bolshoy – *especially, the Bolshoy!*" The director then uncrumpled his hat and put it on his head where it sat like a squashed pig. He then half-turned towards the staircase in the hallway as if he were about to leave suddenly. "It's just better for you and for the Bolshoy if you don't come back for a while. Let things cool off a bit. In the autumn, surely you can come to a rehearsal and see how things go with the other girls. I'm certain, by then, everything will be smooth and cordial. And you will be able to dance again with us; and the spectators, more than anyone, – with the exception of myself, of course, – will be delighted."

Then Nastya, who was aching all over, tried to speak but her words failed her. There was a large, burning knot in her throat that caused her much distress.

"Director … I… uh…." But her words were interrupted by Monsieur Lavretsky…

"Nastya, it's better this way." The director, with the squashed pig sitting on his head, took his hand and placed it consolingly, yet without the usual warmth he treated Nastya with, on her shoulder. Then his sweaty hand limply slipped off her shoulder and he turned and started down the staircase. Halfway down to the landing, he turned around and looked up at Nastya who stood frozen by the closed door of her apartment.

"And please, Nastya," he put in finally, "don't say anything to the newspapers about this. Can I trust you on that?"

"I would never…." she began. She had wanted to say more but her thoughts failed to become words. It was just as well, because the director was all too eager to leave Nastya's apartment building. By the time he finished his last sentence, he was already almost out of sight, down the stairs.

Moments later he was gone. He left the building and walked up Sokolniki Street feeling a strange anguish and embarrassment. He thought the meeting with Nastya went infinitely worse than he had planned. He had wanted to deliver the news with the paternal affection he felt for her, yet he hadn't had even the courage to look her in the eyes during most of what he'd had to say. Walking up Sokolniki Street, the director felt indignation towards himself for acting cowardly towards Nastya. He was more than fully aware that he had lied to her a little bit. He knew that things wouldn't be fine in the autumn. He knew the power that Varvara Fillipovna and her parents held over the Bolshoy and over himself – they had only made that too clear during their meeting earlier on this morning. He knew that Nastya would never be welcome at the theatre again. And he knew that he would never have the courage to look Nastya in the eyes again, if the two ever were to meet in the future – accidentally.

Back up in the hallway of Nastya's apartment building, next to her front door that remained closed, Nastya stood frozen. She felt sick and confused. She wasn't quite sure what had just happened. Languidly, without any emotion, she opened her front door and went back inside, whereas she seated herself at the round, wooden table, put her head in her hands, and tried to think about all that had happened.

Then her mother came from the bathroom…

"Who was that man?"

"The director from the Bolshoy theatre, Mother."

"Well, why didn't you invite him in?" her mother asked angrily, "Are you ashamed of your old mother?"

"No, Mother, of course not…." At this point, the emotions had begun to fall on Nastya and she could hardly keep the tears out of her voice when she said this. Her mother, however, didn't notice the turmoil that was starting to affect her daughter, she didn't notice the tears that began to run down Nastya's cheeks; she just turned back to the clothes in the tub, and muttering, "…ashamed of her old mother!" she closed the door and resumed scrubbing the laundry.

Nastya remained seated at the table. Her father was away at work. Her brother was sleeping, coughing every now and then beneath the heap of blanket on his tiny bed. No one was near. Yet still, had anyone been around, they wouldn't have been able to read the despair on her face. Nastya always had eyes that radiated something – radiated some fear, some happiness, some longing, or some sorrow – but now her eyes radiated nothing. If one had looked at her at this moment, they would have sensed a great emptiness in her soul – as if they were looking at someone who was no longer living. Such was the extent of the despair that filled our poor Nastya at this moment.

After the coldness drained from her body, after the hot flashes ceased, she looked around at her surroundings, her brother sleeping soundly in his bed, her mother behind the door of the bathroom scrubbing the clothes; and here in this room, the empty stove, the bare table and barren floor with dust gathered in the corners, and the dim noon light casting a small beam of sunlit radiance across the room that still looked so dismal – the room that she'd lived in with her family for the last five years. Such emptiness and dismal gloom corroded the normally vibrant and cheerful body of Nastya.

She retreated to her bed… then, drew the curtain closed around her and she took, from the pocket of her peacoat, the letter from Paris and again she read it. And while she read it, her eyes widened, her eyes beamed, and then they dulled and folded over in sleepy confusion.

Nastya fell into a dream. She fell into a stir of sleepy imaginings, and while she slept, that letter rested on her breast and rose and fell with each breath her sleeping body took. Then a bit of wind slipped through a crack in her four-paned window that faced out into the street, and the bit of wind blew that letter off her chest where it fell upon the barren floor.

When she awoke it was already dark. Her father had already come home from work, had eaten his dinner, and was now asleep for the night. When she drew her curtain back quietly after waking, she could see the large dark and shadowed form of her father's body in the lightless room sleeping heavily in the far corner near the stove. He had just fallen asleep when Nastya gazed past her curtain at him in his bed.

When he had arrived on this evening, tired and weary as usual from taking the slow and congested tram across the breadth of Moscow after the heavy labors of the day, he was angry with his wife for not only not having the supper ready, but for not having even started the tea water boiling on the stove. Throughout the tramway ride home, her father had been thinking of the hot soup and hot bread that would be waiting for him; 'At the very least, there will be some warm kasha and tea waiting', he thought to himself. But when he returned, his wife was still concerning herself with the washing of the clothes and she informed her husband in a most fed-up tone that he was going to have to wait an hour or two for dinner; and if he didn't feel like waiting, he would have to go and cook the dinner himself! Her mother explained to her husband that she'd been without help all day; as they had received a visitor that morning and, directly after his stay, which only lasted the briefest of moments, Nastya had taken ill and went to bed. After hearing this – it was directly after nightfall – Nastya's father went quietly over to his daughter's corner and drew back the curtain. The harvest moon, partially obscured by a cloud, cast an amber light over the sleeping girl. He felt her forehead, which was beaded with sweat; and he knelt down beside her bed to say a prayer for her health. After this, he went to his own bed, lit the lamp beside it and read from a book while dinner was being prepared.

At supper, the husband and wife spoke very little. They exchanged a few solemn words about their 'two sick children, asleep in their beds and missing dinner', but that was all that was said. After the last of the kasha was eaten and the tea was drunk to the dregs, the mother cleared the table and her husband went again to lie down with his book. After the dishes were finished. The mother went to join her husband in bed; and, minutes later, the lamp was blown, the room was dark and all were asleep.

Many people go through all or most of their lives without making or acting on a major decision. We could even say that most people bred on this earth fit into this category. They are the ones who live their whole lives in or near to the town where they were raised. They are the ones who marry young or do not marry at all. The former ones usually belong to families where marriage is considered the normal, sensible and most appropriate pursuit of all young people – often to the extent that to marry, or to marry not, isn't even a question open for discussion; whereas the latter – those of this category who never marry – are born of families where marriage is a serious step and a most important foot forward, requiring serious deliberation and the weighing of all pros and cons – among the groom the bride and their families and friends alike – and so, reluctant to have such a direct influence on their own fate, they side-step the issue with complete passivity until those around them too become indifferent and consider it a 'lost cause'. It is the people in this category who often have the same sensible job for many years, often for their whole lives; and change occupations only if a new one presents itself as something easily obtainable, with no emotional or psychological risk involved. Of course, every man and women has a complex fiber, relatively unique in its patterns of variants, though except for those who fall into the category of the extraordinary, all variants of people, no matter how random, still vary within a structure of closely-knit patterns and trends, which makes the practice of generalizing personality types not at all absurd. But we must note another type of person, a less common breed, and make note quickly that this type of person is the polar opposite of the first type expounded upon, yet there exists many people whose nature falls somewhere in between the two types.

    These people of the second type fancy themselves as decision-makers. They stand at the two-pronged forks that allegorically rest in every roadway and on every earthen path, and they deliberate amongst themselves to ensure that they are the ones, the only ones, who are making the grand decisions that decide their fate. "Shall I *pick* a plum from this tree?" ... "Shall I *marry* him?" ... "Shall I *kill* her?" ... It doesn't matter so much, the magnanimity of the question, as long as the one asking and acting on the question is allowed full control to decide what the answer will be. This second type of man, the *rational man*, can be seen standing at a crossroads, with grand options stemming off on either side, pacing back and forth for months. Finally, when it makes sense no more to pace, he will choose the road heading east, for example. Yet before he heads east, he will walk over to the road heading west, and tear it up. He will cut some trees to block its entrance and break the nearby dams to flood its trail in its entirety. This is just to make the choice of the westward path as absurd as possible. Then he will happily skip along his sunny eastward path as if it is the only way to go, as if he had never actually made a decision. "I made no decision! There was only one way to go. This eastern trail is lit by the sun and is smooth on the feet. That westward path was blocked by fallen trees and completely flooded with water. Only a fool would have ~~went~~ gone west!" this rational man says.

And still there is a third type – the rarest. Often they are called 'capricious' or 'vagarious', 'whimsical' or fickle', and some of those adjectives are more just and fair than others. This unusual type of emotional human being is governed by something more ethereal and less understandable than the 'fear and indifference' of the first type, or the 'rational ambition' of the second type. This third type is often called a 'dreamer'. They live according to a 'poetic method', an individualist's stratagem for living out something that can be considered – at least by themselves – a 'beautiful and purposeful life'. These dreamers act by what 'touches them' more than what is 'told to them' or even what is 'shown to them'. They can be marked by certain qualities, viz., as children, they were often the most imaginative, the most unruly, and the least understandable. Many of them had imaginary friends, or would go through bouts of prolonged existence living in the world of a story made up in their heads – or in a fairytale, which was read or told to them. As adults, they are the most inventive. They are more prone to cry, blush, or be stricken with sorrow – for theirs is an emotional world. And the activity that carries them through the hardships of emotional dejection is 'dreaming', as the ordinary world does not present rewards great enough and opportunities grandiose enough to make this life have the appeal that it needs to have to be worth living and bearing through. Thus, the ordinary world is augmented by the extraordinary possibilities that surface as dreams. And through these dreams, a poetic life is visualized and realized by the dreamer, whereupon the dreamer assumes this poetic life to be his or her fate. We must admit that schizophrenics may belong in this category just as creative geniuses, and 'sane' romantics can be classified here. We will not go into a treatise on 'schizophrenia and decision-making' in this story. If I live long enough, I may write on that subject someday, but *here*, we have more important things to get involved with. We are talking about the creative and the romantic people, for whom 'to live' is 'to compose a grand poem' where every step is in rhythm and every twist of fate turns with the beauty of rhyme – in tragedy, in love, in woe or in joy. These people are often called brave, for often the poems in their heads are heroic poems, and so, *thus they must live!* But people of this group do not choose their dreams anymore than a sleeping man chooses his nightmares, anymore than a poet chooses his words. The great poet is given his words, or he finds them, or wakes up with them in his bed; or he is attacked by them in an hallucinogenic state of madness – any of these, but choose them, he does not. So these dreamers do not choose their dreams – yet that they always act in accordance with them, is perfectly reasonable. A songwriter is not going to sing mediocre words to a song if he or she has written great words to accompany the melody, fearing that great words will make the song too beautiful. The songwriter's goal is to create the most beautiful and poetic song that he or she is capable of. Likewise, the dreamer's goal is to live out the most beautiful and poetic dream possible. They have no say in the matter. For not living their beautiful and poetic life, would mean to live out someone else's life – and their poetic souls can not allow this.

The dreamer often comes to the allegorical fork in the road right after the rational man has been there; and he sees the west is flooded with water and its entrance is blocked by limbs of fallen trees, and he looks to the east and sees the road is clear and even lit brightly by the radiant forenoon sun. So this person looks to the east and looks to the west and then, without a moment of consideration, without deciding to try one path for a couple of meters and then turn around and try the other path for a few, he realizes – and *to realize* is not *to decide* – but he realizes that he *must* travel this path or that. It may be the eastward, It may westward. It is not necessarily the 'one less traveled', though it often is most difficult of the two, for it is the most 'poetic' path. And so, off he goes in fear or in delight, in hope or in despair. Why would he take the path that is obviously going to bring him to despair? Because, *he must.*

For this third type of person: *the dreamer*, there is never a clear moment of a decision being made, when two or more tremendous life-affecting choices appear. It is rather that there is a realization that the options have appeared, an understanding that a choice has to be made, and a simultaneous knowledge of which option is to be taken, and finally, the execution of that choice, that option, without heeding the possible consequences, whether they be death or divinity.

David has the qualities of this third category of human. He is a dreamer. Our heroine, Nastya, she too is a dreamer. Both have very different dreams. They come from different parts of the world. David is male, Nastya is female, and both are extremely unique individuals; so there is originality in each one's approach on life. But neither of them are governed by indifference, nor by rationality. Nastya's approach to the poetic life is blessed with having more patience. Yet she also instinctively knows that the one who takes a great action, does so at the apex of the crisis. If one passes the apex of crisis, the chance of one taking this feared action becomes minute. And, as a dreamer in pursuit of the poetic life, Nastya knows that even if she doesn't want to take a certain action – if its consequences she dreads and fears – she may have to anyway. If here, romantic individuality is at stake, she *must* take the action, and so at the apex of the crisis, she leaps – for it is sure that at this moment she'll leap the farthest.

How to live the poetic life is the question squirming in Nastya's head as she lies in her bed, wide-awake, in the lampless room by the window, which lets in the soft glow of the Moscow twilight. While she ponders in great distress, her father wakes up and opens his eyes to the dark room in sleepy confusion. He puts his arm around his wife and remembers the troubles they had had that night. He remembers then that Nastya took to her bed with illness earlier in the day. He then rolls over to look to her bed to see if she is still asleep. He sees Nastya's dark silhouette through the gauze curtain that hangs before her bed. She appears to be sleeping soundly. Her father tells himself that he will check on her health the first thing in the morning before going off to work; then, he rolls back over and falls asleep again.

  Moments later, Nastya – now fully awake and alert with a clarity in her mind that she has not had for the previous day – goes into her coat pocket and pulls out the envelope from Paris. She takes the ten hundred-franc bills out of the envelope and courses over them with her hands. She has never seen French money before. She assumes that these thousand francs in her hand are equivalent to about one-hundred thousand rubles. She had no basis for this assumption, it just seems like the right amount to her – 'a decent sum of money'. Nastya then takes out the railway ticket and feels it in the dark with her hand. She sits up in her bed. She looks to the desk and there is a glass of water, which she guesses her father must have left for her while she was sleeping. She takes a sip of the tepid water and then, looking down on the floor, she notices the letter from Paris that had fallen there and wonders for a moment if someone else didn't find it and read it. She dismisses this suspicion and, picking up the letter, she puts it back in its envelope.

'I'll have to try,' she thinks to herself, 'I'll have to see what it's like and then that will be it.' ... 'I have a ticket and some money – probably enough money to buy a return ticket if I need to.' ... 'I have an invitation and it's obvious I have to go.' ... 'But do you realize, Nastya,' she continues silently, 'how far away Paris is? And you remember what it was like when you tried to go alone to Petersburg to be a dancer, two years ago? ... you were dragged back home before you even got out of Moscow!' ... 'No one's going to permit you to go. Try reasoning with them – it won't work. you won't be able to go.' ... 'Yet, you have to go!' ... 'have to, have to, have to!' ... 'if you don't, you are a failure and a coward, Nastya.' ... 'But should a girl be expected to do these things? ...These scary things? Should I have to go through all of this? Why can't I just remain here, being happy, dancing at the Gelikon theatre on Sundays, and washing the family's clothes? Maybe I'll marry a nice Russian man!' ... 'But I won't be happy doing that. That's not what I want. I know I have to go. I know I have to go and I hate it – as much as I love it. As strong as the excitement that fills me now, so strong is the fear that makes me tremble.' ... 'But I will not stop trembling by sitting here on my bed. I am going to do it, and I will think about what I have done later – once it is already done. Otherwise, I won't have the courage to do it, and I'll regret what I didn't do forever after.' ... 'But at the same time, I don't have to do it. I could stay here and not regret it – I could choose to not regret it.' ... 'Yes, but Nastya, that is not a choice. It's a choice but it's not *your* choice. You are going to do it and do it soon so the trembling will stop and your fever and shaking will stop, and then you can think about what you've done when it's too late to change it.'

From the same vein of these thoughts came the words that Nastya sat up in her bed writing for the next hour as she composed a letter to her father. The letter was slightly less consoling and comforting than she had wanted it to be; less so than her father wanted as well, he later noted with profound grief when he read it. But it said what it needed to say and Nastya demonstrated to him her self-will, determination and a growing maturity. This pleased the both of them, though her father summoned all of his courage and wisdom in order to let this please him. Nastya ended the letter with much affection, gave her regards to her mother and brother, as well; and she signed it "with love, I will return one day". Then she folded and sealed it.

Tip-toeing over to the large wooden table, she set the letter where it would be easily found once the plain light of day seeped in. Then she went back to her bed to get dressed.

The whole time she was dressing and packing, a part of her hoped that her parents would wake up, that her mother would come over to her bed and scold her for making so much noise in the night; whereupon her father would, of course, be awakened and come over to sit his daughter down and speak with her about what she was doing, about why she was packing up her suitcase in the middle of the night. "What reason could there be for all of this?" he would say; whereupon she would show him the letter from Paris and tell him what the director had come to say earlier that day; and he would, most compassionately remark, "My Nastya, you are too important to me – to us – to get swooped off by a train and flung in the arms of some strange man in some strange country....". While Nastya would interrupt, "But it isn't a strange country, it's France – a very civilized placed, Father ... and this strange man holds a great position in this city and he has agreed ... rather, he is hoping, to have me join their theatre." Whereupon her father would most rationally say, "Nastya, my dear, we will send him a letter, and if he's serious about all of this, he will first come to Russia to meet your family. Don't go into anything leading you by ink and paper alone!" ...And if he had said that and more – which he would, of course, have said a lot more – Nastya would have remained at home at least until the next development of our story. But the two of them, Nastya's mother and father, didn't wake up. They slept on through the night and her creaking dresser drawers opening and closing repeatedly didn't stir them in the slightest.

Once her ballet clothes were packed, along with some nice outfits for going out with Parisian society ... once Nastya had packed up her most sentimental possessions, like her tarnished silver pocket watch, which her father had given to her, which she absolutely could not leave without, Nastya pulled back the curtain as wide as possible, – so as to let her family know on first awakening that she was gone, – and she stepped out to the center of the room with her tan suitcase in one hand and a smaller valise that contained her ballet clothes in the other, and she then stood still.

"Goodbye, Papa," she whispered across the room to the sleeping body that rose and fell with heavy breaths in the night. "Goodbye...," she sighed again as she turned around surveying the room. Even if she had left something of extreme importance to her journey right there in plain sight, she probably would not have noticed for the clarity she had awoken with that night had by then left her mind, and she was in a particular fever at this moment and her senses were not what they usually were. Even if someone had come up behind her at this moment and, putting a hand on her shoulder, had said something to her, she probably wouldn't have responded or even noticed the disturbance. As she stood there in the center of the room, the sounds of the sleeping bodies faded out and all Nastya heard was the *ping, ping, ping,* of rain falling against a tin roof out in the hallway. But why this sound? It was not raining. And there was no tin roof in the hallway for rain to fall against. And, anyway, it could not rain out in the hallway – especially not on the third floor where their apartment was. So, why that sound? Nastya, at this point, disregarded everything except for her own plan. She surveyed the room quickly and walked towards her front door. She then set her suitcases down and opened the door. She turned around to look one last time at the small room where she had spent the last five years living with her family. She was twenty-two years old – it was time to move on. But like this? Silently in the night? She looked over to where her brother can normally be seen as a lump, sleeping beneath a woolen blanket in the corner on a tiny bed. This time, he was not the sleeping boy she normally saw, who coughed between silent snores out of sickness. This time she saw her little brother sitting upright in bed. He was looking towards her, towards his sister, who stood by the open door in the middle of the night. Oh, it was dark, but how the little boy's eyes glowed. They pierced through the still night's darkness like the flames of two candles. Her brother's body didn't move. He just looked on at his sister with a fiery stare. It was too dark to see his lips or the expression on his face, had there been any expression. He looked on towards her and she turned quickly and picked up her two suitcases; and then walked out into the hall, quietly shutting the door behind her.

Nastya descended the staircase with a flurry of fever burning in her mind. Could that really have been *him*? …Could that have really been her brother, awake, staring at her? and, like *that*? 'He didn't move,' she thought, 'he just sat there – and with *those* eyes!' '…It could not have been him … not with *those* eyes!'.

No one followed Nastya down the stairs, no one followed as she walked out into Sokolniki Street carrying two suitcases. Her parents remained asleep. All of Moscow was perhaps asleep as Nastya walked up the silent street and crossed over the tram tracks and turned up the sidewalk, which would eventually lead to Kurskyi station.

At the station, a few travelers slept in benches, a few others were in line buying or changing their tickets or asking questions. A train pulled up moments later, announced its departure for Poland, continuing on to Germany and France, and swept Nastya up. The conductor seated her in first-class and locked her suitcases in a tall, brass, barred compartment that looked like a very large birdcage. Nastya's brain didn't take in and process too much information during these moments on the train, at the station, or during the moments leading up to her being at the station. She had handed her suitcases to the conductor in a sort of feverish indifference, without even noticing, or caring too much, that he was the conductor. Had he been an ordinary swindler – of the kind that are so common in our train stations these days – she would have lost all her belongings. But fortunately, it had been a conductor employed by the railway who took her suitcases for her – out of chivalrous benevolence, mind you, not out of duty, for handling the luggage of passengers was not in any way this conductor's duty – and locked them up in the large brass birdcage. Finally, the train left the station and traveled on beyond Moscow, through the still night, on into the Russian countryside.

Nastya had had too much emotional pandemonium as of recent. Her poor body knew then that she needed sleep and it wouldn't let anyone interfere with that need. And as the train went on in the southward direction, Nastya's body rested, nicely-dressed, in a first-class train seat, her forehead beaded with sweat; and she slept there a deep and undisturbed sleep for a long time.

CHAPTER VI

Our hero's reflections upon waking up at Paris' Hospital St. Louis and his impressions henceforth... [thence forth]

'I awoke in the dark of twilight. I knew not where I was, nor how I had come to be there. I didn't realize that it was a hospital I was in until much later – perhaps it was hours or even days later. At the time, I thought it was a laboratory and I had been brought in, in fetters, by those apparitions who had been haunting my dreams. All I knew was that the needle I saw in my arm was facilitating the entry of an extreme poison into my body. I looked at the needle connected to a tube, which was connected to a plastic bag of liquid belladonna dangling over my laboratory bed. The only thing I knew I had to do was get it out of my vein. So, I pulled it out; and blood began to flow down my arm and over everything.'

To recall all of the incidences that occurred when David woke up in the hospital in the north of Paris, a couple nights after he collapsed in the wet twilit street, wouldn't make too much sense to you, the reader, for these incidences are quite strange and a little absurd. To have David to recall them to you, would be impossible; for when he awoke at the dark end of twilight in that hospital bed at St. Louis, he was completely disoriented – debilitated by the severe confusion caused by the medications that had been injected into him by the doctors – struck dumb by the days spent unconscious.

 It must reemphasized that David suffered a very severe attack of the nerves only days before, which caused a vertigo of the worst kind and resulted in his lying without the slightest consciousness in his brain in a dirty, wet gutter on Rue St. Sulpice in Paris; and, upon his awakening in the hospital, he was still in quite a shock. It would be accurate to say that when he awoke, and for hours following, he was still asleep in a dream, or perhaps a nightmare; he walked and spoke in a numb and confused, hypnagogic state.

But when his eyes opened that night for the first time in a couple of days, he did, in fact, see an intravenous needle penetrating his naked skin, which was connected to a tube, which was then connected to a plastic bag full of liquid dangling over his head – though the liquid was only vitamins and not 'liquid belladonna' as he mentioned when later recalling his impressions upon waking up in that hospital.

To give a brief account of the facts, from an objective point of view, is necessary to understand the chain of events that follows later on in our story:

When David awoke, he turned his head to the side in the dimly lit room and saw the needle in his arm. Tremendous fear filled his body. It was as if he had seen a poisonous spider crawling over his skin with the intent to inject him with its venom. In the quick movements of panic, he pulled the needle from his vein. Then, blood began to run down his arm and 'over everything' as he recalls. After enough strength returned to his body, he climbed naked out of the hospital bed and began searching for his clothes.

His brain, at this time, was not yet manufacturing thoughts on a consistent basis – he was still mostly delirious from the drugs he had been given; and his body, from whatever toll it had taken, was not responding well to the sudden bout of consciousness it was having. After getting out of bed, he stood alone, naked in the room, shivering with cold, and tried to piece together the obscure and dilapidated clues as to where he was and for what reason. His impressions on this looking back:

'I was plagued by nightmarish visions, by huge gaps in memory, and the most extreme and distressing confusion I had ever hitherto experienced.' … 'But one thing I remembered clearly is that the last time I had been conscious, prior to this horrid awakening, I was walking down some street called 'Rue St. Sulpice' … it had been raining … there were these posters of a beautiful ballerina on the sides of every building … the bells were tolling from a cathedral nearby … It was my first day in Paris – my *was it foreshadowed/ose mouth* [handwritten annotation]

first day in Europe, that I can recall – and I was wearing a suit, a white suit, given to me by an old dockworker in Brittany. And in that suit, in its pockets, I had a newly-issued French passport, as well as my journal containing some poetry I had written; and lastly, thirteen-thousand dollars, American currency, hard-cash, the most money I had ever known.' … 'And there I was standing, shivering naked in the dark room of some laboratory and I knew I needed to find that suit immediately.'

The consequences of losing these items suddenly became clear to David. The thirteen-thousand dollars that was last seen in the pocket of his white blazer, which was nowhere in sight, was not a trifling matter. He remembers trembling and shivering a violent shiver while looking around the hospital room for his suit, but he can't remember anything after that moment. A distinct gap in his memory follows. The next thing he can recall happened hours later: He was walking down the dark streets of Paris at night, fully dressed; and when he came to a train station he stopped and sat and thought for a long time about where he should go – with no money and no passport.

What ended up happening at the hospital was that he found his suit, moments later, in a wad on the floor of the closet. He searched through the pockets and found nothing except for some phrases in French, which Marc had scribbled on a piece of paper while the two were awaiting the train in Quimper. The journal was gone. The passport was gone. The money was gone.

Upon this discovery, David's fever burned with intense heat. He quickly dressed in his suit and left the hospital room.

Out in the hall, he caught sight of two nurses walking up ahead. He ran towards them like an angry animal and seized them by the shoulders. He asked them where his belongings were, where his money was. The two nurses didn't speak any English; and, both afraid by the angry tone of David's voice and the violent way his body trembled, they summoned a security guard.

The security guard approached David, who was by then suffering from an increasing state of fever. When he tried to ask the security guard to help him, his vision blurred, the blood ran from his head, and he fainted. The sick young man lay sprawled out on the floor in the hall until a stretcher was located and the nurses could collect him and put him back in his bed. Again David lay in a hospital bed, unconscious.

When he awoke the second time, he was calmer. The nurses had given him an injection of barbiturates to sedate him, lest he wake up angry and violent. This time, he awoke and pulled himself up in his hospital bed, calmly and without any fear or agitation. He looked to the linoleum floor at the figures who were gathered there.

Kneeling on the floor were two nurses and the hospital accountant. In front of them was a stack of papers. Among these papers was David's journal, also his hospital file. The hospital workers were ravaging through the papers like vultures, devouring whatever interested them. When the three saw that the patient had awoken, they looked over at him, whereupon, the accountant – who spoke good English – began to interrogate him.

She asked him his name, – which he could not recall at the time – and she asked him where he was from, and why he had a French passport if he couldn't speak French; and, most importantly, how he was going to pay for his hospital stay.

After a few minutes of being questioned, David pieced together enough of his memory to tell them that he had had the money to pay for the hospital stay, that it had been in his jacket pocket when he arrived at the hospital.

The accountant informed him that they had found nothing in his pockets when he arrived at the hospital except for a journal and a passport.

He then accused them, the nurses and the accountant, of stealing his money. They thought it was more likely that the men who had carried him across town and dumped him at the door of their hospital was the one who had stolen his cash. Yet, the accountant was not interested in the detective work surrounding David's lost money, "if he had ever had any to begin with." She was only interested in making sure the hospital got paid for their services provided to him. The accountant gave him back his journal with the green leather cover and said that the hospital would be keeping his passport until he returned and paid them the sum of forty-three hundred francs.

David, still sedated by the barbiturates, yet able to walk relatively straight, was escorted to the door. He asked them why he was being discharged and if he could possibly speak to the doctor to find out why he had been brought to the hospital in the first place.

"Did you run tests on me?" he inquired.

"Of course we did," replied the accountant.

"What were the results?"

"You'll have to ask the doctor. He, however, won't be in until morning," stated the accountant.

"But if I have to leave the hospital tonight, how can I speak to the doctor tomorrow?"

"Ugh," she said with annoyance, "you can come back to speak to him. You cannot stay here, since you cannot pay!"

"But where is all that money I had?" David asked in a voice of growing desperation.

"I can't answer that for you, young man," she replied.

"But where am I to go? ...in Paris, with no money?!" His words came out in despair.

"Oh, don't be so melodramatic, this is Paris, it's not Moscow, you won't freeze to death!" groaned the accountant as she led him to the door by the sleeve of his jacket – the way prison guards lead convicts to their cells.

Outside, the Parisian twilight loomed. David looked on the vast, deserted streets. He knew not where to go. He looked around, spat on the ground, and headed back to the entrance of the hospital. Again, inside, he asked them if there was someplace he could be treated without paying, as he knew that a hospital was where he belonged.

The accountant, after many attempts to get rid of him without helping him, finally acquiesced and wrote down the name of a doctor, *une généraliste*, near St. Germain who would treat him on a sliding scale based on the amount of money he had or was earning – which was nothing. She coldly handed him the address with a look of repugnance and reminded him to come back to pay the forty-three hundred francs he owed the hospital.

Our young man, dizzy from the hospital drugs and weary from a fever that lingered, fermenting in his brain, left the hospital, and walked out into the Paris night. He could not make a decision. The despair he felt over losing his money was greatly lessened by the barbiturates numbing his brain and he didn't fully grasp that he was now a broke and homeless man, in a new and strange city and country. After wandering aimlessly around Paris for hours in a confused stupor, he found himself standing outside a train station – the *Gare du Nord* – it was the time his brain began to record events again; it was a time of which he has recollection:

'All of a sudden I realized who I was, and where I was; and I pieced together as much as I could remember of the recent past to figure out what had led up to me being where I was. I stood in the street as a light rain fell, creating an amber mist in the glow of the streetlamps. A roar in the sky above suggested the presence of either airplanes or earthquakes or thunder or bombs. Cars slowly hissed by. The sky above was silver with the iridescence of the interminable twilight and all was becoming more eerie and more unnatural. I stopped outside of a train station and sat on a bench, thinking for a long time. When I fully realized my money was gone, I almost broke down in tears, but I could not cry. I just looked around with dumb stupefaction at everything' … 'I looked at the paper given to me at the hospital, which had the address of a doctor who would treat me for free. I looked then at the paper with the French phrases written on it, given to me by Marc. On the back of that piece of paper was his address. I remembered him saying to me that I could come and work on the boats anytime I wanted to. It hadn't made any sense when he had said it; for then, I had thirteen-thousand dollars in my pocket and was ill and on my way to Paris to find treatment. But suddenly I had become broke – completely penniless – and going to Brittany to work for Marc made the most sense. There I could get my body strong with physical labor. There I could have the clean air of the country and a dry bunk on which to sleep. There I could probably also see a doctor on a regular basis for treatment from my illness. What had brought me to Paris in the first place? Surely, there are doctors in coastal villages just as there are doctors in capital cities. Why had I told Marc that lie about my mother having suffered a stroke? Whatever it was, that same indefinable and noetic urge to go to Paris, which had driven me away from Brittany in the first place, was again urging me to drop my anchor in this city – no matter what the consequences. There was something in Paris I had to find. I wasn't sure at all what it was, but I had to find it. I sat on that bench and stared at the entrance of the station for a long time. I didn't think it would be hard to jump the train to Brittany. The conductors hadn't checked my ticket on the way to Paris. I was in a fever then, I just sat in agony and everyone left me alone. Some woman even gave me aspirin and soda water – a rotten lime to boot. ...All I would have to do is feign that agony again, keep to myself, ignore the conductors, and I would get a free ride to the coast where a job on the docks would be waiting for me.'

David knew that everything would be easier if he went to Brittany. He knew that his life was hard enough for the moment and making the safest choice possible would be in his best interest. He sat on the stone bench under a streetlamp facing the station for a long time while the rain came down in a cold mist dampening his body. He looked down at his body. His suit had been so gleaming white when Marc presented him with it a few days before in that sunny backyard in Brittany where a table was filled with food and flowers and the birds of spring were singing. The suit had become filthy from the mud in the gutter where he had fallen; there was blood on the sleeve, quite a lot of blood, from where he had pulled the needle from his arm. He looked again towards the station. He had nowhere to go in Paris. He could see the doctor in the morning, but it was a long time yet till morning, and every homeless night following would prove to be just as long.

 To stay in Paris would be his demise, of that he was certain. He had nobody and nothing in Paris. If he hopped the train to Brittany, he was sure that within hours he'd arrive in Quimper; and surely there someone would let him use their telephone. He would call to Marc, who wouldn't mind being woken up in the middle of the night by the phone – at least he'd understand once David had explained his circumstances. Marc, for sure, would be very happy to come pick him up in Quimper and take him down to the bunkhouse by the pier. David would probably get his old clothes back too – washed nice and clean by Marc's wife. No, David knew that if he were to stay in Paris, he would end up sleeping under bridges in a dirty, bloodstained suit. There are too many beggars to begin with in capital cities. There is a lot of competition for the coins that jingle in the pockets of the passers-by. David would have to join these beggars, yet he knew nothing of the trade.

 All the while, something was telling him to stay in Paris. David had grown up in the city. He was used to the city. The city was where he felt safe. He knew nothing of living in the country. Just the thought of it made him lonely.

 'I am too young and too ambitious to move out to the country. The city's good for my health, It's good for my mind.' ...But all these were just lies and pretexts that David told himself. The city would prove to be far worse for his health and his mind then the countryside would have been, had he gone there.

"I would just become nothing out there in that small, tiny little town on the coast, working on boats all day – unloading sacks of rice and cans of fish," David muttered aloud as he stood beneath the streetlamp in the cold mist of rain, staring at the entrance of the train station, "…But a more dreadful fate awaits me here in Paris, I know this." David felt the coldness of the rain on his face. "…I wonder who took my money. That was the only thing I couldn't afford to lose and I lost it – the moment I came to Paris, I lost it … It's pathetic really"… "Hey, watch out!"

Right when David was busy speaking to himself, a man carrying a large piece of luggage bumped into him on the sidewalk. By the time David turned towards him, telling him to "watch out", the man was already far up ahead, and had disappeared into the entrance of the station.

Then the mist of rain got lighter and people began bustling through the streets, crowding on the sidewalks – some with luggage in their hands, others with parcels and presents. One could hear some trains coming in, in the distance – their loud brakes sounded far off as they slowed to enter the station. People walked hurriedly past David, where he sat on a bench beneath a lit streetlamp in the dark of night, on the sidewalk facing the station. He decided to ask some passers-by if this was the right station to catch a train to Brittany. Despite his still feverish state and his self-conscious reluctance to talk to anyone at the moment, he accosted several people who passed him by. None of them were able to speak English, and none could help. Then a girl with her mother approached him.

"I can speak English," said the girl, who smiled and spoke excitedly with a heavy French accent. She was happy to get a chance to use the English she had learned in school. She stood facing David. Her mother stood beside her. The two of them were headed towards the station to meet the girl's older brother – the woman's son – who was just returning by train from Poland, where he'd been studying for the past year. The mother and daughter both radiated happiness. The mother had been longing to see her son terribly over the last year and now he was finally coming home. His train had originated in Russia and had traveled through Belarus and Poland, continuing on through Germany, and was bound for Paris' *Gare du Nord*. It would be arriving about ten minutes after the three's conversation ended on the street.

David was beginning to get tired and had to force himself to keep his eyes open. He looked at the mother and daughter. The mother had a nice, kind face and she wore a black wool peacoat. The daughter also wore the same black wool coat, and she carried a black umbrella as well. She seemed to David to be about sixteen or seventeen years old. She was pleasant to look at, but not pretty. Her eyes were blue and her pale face was covered in freckles.

"I can speak English," said the girl, grabbing her mother's arm to take her over to talk to David.

"Oh, I'm so glad someone can speak English, thank you," David spoke slowly. The barbiturates were still making him dizzy and he worked at making his words sound clear, polite, and not slurred, "I was wondering if you knew if trains going to Brittany leave from this station or not. I'm trying to get to Brittany."

"Brittany? Oh, *Bretagne*? Yes?" … "Umm…" "…You have to go to *Gare Montparnasse* to go to *Bretagne*. Just go into this station and walk down the stairs and you'll come to *line-four*. Take *line-four* towards *Porte d'Orleans*, then get off at *Montparnasse* and there will be trains to *Bretagne*." … "Are you going tonight?"

"Yes," replied David, "as soon as possible." … "Can you help me with one other thing?"

"Yes, sure!" replied the girl excitedly as she smiled at David and fidgeted with the handle of the black umbrella in her hand.

"I have this address on Rue du Dragon…." David showed the girl the piece of paper with the doctor's address on it. He asked her how to get there, and the girl, having a good knowledge of the city she grew up in, promptly explained to David how to best cross the river to get to St. Germain where he would have to walk quite a ways – past St. Michel and *Odéon* – to get to Rue du Dragon. She took great pleasure in explaining all of this, and wrote the directions very precisely on the backside of David's piece of paper. She even drew elaborate ornamental drawings of the various monuments he would pass along the way. After she drew the last curlicue on the Notre Dame, she handed the piece of paper back to him, whereupon he took it and thanked the two kindly; he said "merci" to the mother who hadn't understood a word of the two's conversation. The mother then turned to her daughter, reminding her that they would be late to meet her brother if they didn't leave right then.

"You can take down your umbrella," said David, "it stopped raining long ago."

"My what? Oh my *parapluie*... yes!" The girl took down her umbrella, blushing with embarrassment.

The girl then said a kind "goodbye" and *"bon courage"* to David as she took her mother's arm again and began walking towards the entrance to the *Gare du Nord*.

When they were far up ahead, the girl turned to her mother, "He was cute, don't you think, Mother?" The girl used the word *mignon*.

"Didn't you see the blood on his clothes?" replied her mother with an element of shock in her voice, "And his eyes looked strange."

"No. I thought he was handsome." This time she used the word *beau*.

David remained standing where he had been – under the street lamp, facing the station, with his strange eyes from the hospital drugs and blood on his clothes, while the girl and her mother went to greet the train coming from Russia. David looked at the doctor's address again, thinking it could be easy enough to find with the directions the girl had given him. He then thought about going into the train station and taking a métro to the other station where he could get a train to Brittany. He knew that's what he should probably do. His reason ~~and ration~~ told him that his fate would be easier – his future would be brighter – if he were to go right then, and not a moment later, into that station, which was just a few meters away, and head towards the trains to Brittany. He knew it would be foolish to stay in Paris, to wait out the night and see the doctor the next morning. Yet still, and we cannot say for certain why, David had this nagging feeling that it would not be best for him in the long-run to go to Brittany. It would be safer to go to Brittany. He would have a job and a dry place to sleep. But he felt there was something waiting for him in Paris. This feeling was based on noetic intuition alone and no visible outside element told him it would be good to stay in the city of wet concrete where the rain had begun to fall again. No doubt, his life would take a strange, new turn if he were to stay in Paris, with these odd, new circumstances that befell him. And, this strange turn might prove to be difficult, and it may end in disaster, but it could also end in glory. David had an innate desire to live a glorious life as opposed to the mediocre one he felt he'd have working on the docks and sleeping in a bunkhouse with other men. He knew he could go to Brittany and just work for a while, in order to save money. He could also see a doctor. Then he could return to Paris and seek out the glorious life. But something deep in him told him that his opportunity in Paris was right then, and he had to meet it right then. Yet, he knew that the sensible thing would be to go to Brittany, so he started walking into the *Gare du Nord*.

People flooded out of the ~~train~~ station, passing David as he entered. They were carrying luggage and all seemed to be happy to have arrived finally in Paris. Some were French people returning home from trips to Berlin or Warsaw. Others were foreigners traveling to Paris for vacation. There were Swedes and Russians and Spaniards among them. Some were old and traveled with their grandchildren. Many were young couples who embraced and kissed as they walked out of the station together to greet the foreign city of Paris.

David was walking towards the métro station in the *Gare du Nord* when all of a sudden he stopped. A big pressure had been growing inside him and finally he submitted to it. He could hold out no more. He knew it was useless to try to catch a train to Brittany. Although the thought of staying in Paris frightened him, he knew he had no other choice. He knew <u>it was fated to him to stay in Paris</u> and there was no use trying to fight it. He hated it that he couldn't take what he considered to be the "rational and safe path". He hated it but he had no choice. He *had* to stay in Paris. In that train station, David stopped, turned around, and began heading towards the street – the cold and wet street from which he came.

Holding the doctor's address in his hand, David started off on the hike that would take him through the dark and winding, cobbled streets of Paris, across the Seine, through the Latin Quarter, and eventually end at the doctor's office on Rue du Dragon. But the bank of the river was as far as he would make it on that night. He would settle on the quai, with a bridge for a bed and a river for a rug.

CHAPTER VII

A brief account of Nastya's voyage through Europe until her arrival at the Gare du Nord…

"Mademoiselle!" the train attendant shouts, "*Votre billet, s'il vous plaît!*" The sleeping girl in the train car is startled awake by the voice of the shouting attendant. She turns to him sleepy-eyed, not understanding why he has interrupted her peaceful sleep. Then, she looks out of the train window to try to figure out where she is. She sees the twilit countryside yonder. The sky is patterned with silver clouds, a twilit quilt, which the night sleeps beneath. The fields with their dark shadows and rolling hills stretch for infinity from Nastya's view. She turns back to the attendant, who is still shouting at her. She responds in English…

"I'm sorry? I don't understand."

"Your ticket, please," the attendant says, more calmly now, also in English.

Nastya fumbles through her handbag and finds her ticket, which she hands to the attendant.

"This is for second-class. You are in first class, Mademoiselle. You will have to move," says the attendant, studying Nastya's train ticket, "You can stay here, in first-class, but you must pay one-hundred and fifty francs more. Otherwise, come with me."

Nastya asks the attendant how much farther it is to Paris. If it is a long way, she'd rather stay in first-class. She thinks it's strange that this rich aristocrat in Paris would send her a second-class ticket from Russia to France. It's a long journey; and, based on the tone of the letter he sent, she would have thought for sure that the ticket he had sent was for first-class – so that she may travel in comfort and have a peaceful and relaxing voyage.

Not wanting to spend fifteen percent of her sole fortune on a first-class seat, Nastya decides to follow the attendant to the second-class car. He informs her that the train will come to *Gare du Nord* in only about fifty minutes. Nastya looks at her watch. It is ten after nine in the night. 'So late, yet the twilight still lingers outside,' Nastya thinks to herself as she looks out of the window of the train, 'How strange the twilight should linger this late.'

Meanwhile, the attendant has taken her luggage – her tan suitcase as well as her smaller valise, which holds her ballet clothes and slippers – out of the brass birdcage and he hands them to her; and then motions her to follow.

The second class car is a cacophony. Cigarette smoke hovers in the air above the ratty crowd of passengers who stand, holding on to the railings on the luggage racks, waiting for the arduous journey to come to an end.

All of the second-class passengers' eyes are bloodshot, their faces are sallow and their clothes are disheveled. The seats, which emit the smell of old, stale tobacco smoke, hold restless children and babies who perpetually cry aloud. The adults are standing up, as there isn't enough room for the whole crowd to sit in the packed second-class train compartment. The luggage of the passengers is stuffed overhead on the luggage racks. Bags and suitcases of all different sizes and shapes are thrown together and some teeter over the railing and look as though they will fall on the passengers' heads.

The train attendant forces his way through the crowd to help Nastya get her cases on the luggage rack. Nastya stands in the back, pressed against other passengers, while holding the only free space on the railing. The attendant pushes to the far-end of the car – to the only place where there is room on the luggage rack to put Nastya's two bags.

The rest of the journey is hard for Nastya as she stands in the back in the noisy and foul-smelling train compartment, but soon enough the train finishes winding through the fields of Northern France, and it arrives at Paris' *Gare du Nord* – at ten-o-five in the night. The loudspeaker broadcasts:

"Prochain arrêt: Paris, Gare du Nord" ... "The next stop: Paris, North Station." ... *"Paris, Gare du Nord: dernier arrêt. Avant de*

descendre, merci d'attendre l'arrêt complet du train." … "This is the last stop. Please wait till the train comes to a complete stop before deboarding." …And the train arrives in the French capital.

A Russian girl's impressions upon seeing Paris for the first time….

The train pulls in to the station and a crowd of people gather around the opening doors to greet their friends and lovers and sons and brothers and sisters who have arrived from a long voyage.

Inside the second-class train car, the crowd around Nastya begins to scurry. They are scrambling to get their bags off of the luggage racks and get off the train. Nastya is startled by the commotion, as she had just drifted off to sleep while standing up, holding the railing overhead.

People begin to push past her to get their bags and their children. Nastya focuses her sleepy eyes on the luggage rack. She sees her luggage at the far end of the car overhead – her tan suitcase and her clothing bag.

Right at this moment, Nastya and some of the other passengers are shoved hard and they turn around in surprise to see three young men – olive-skinned gypsies, of sorts – pushing past everyone as quickly as they can. These three men begin to grab bags and suitcases at random from the luggage rack overhead. The first piece one of the men takes is Nastya's small valise, which contains her ballet clothing and slippers. As soon as the three men have their hands full with other people's luggage, they push on through the protesting crowd to the open train doors where they exit quickly and run down the platform to escape.

"Help!" cries Nastya, in English, "Someone just stole my bag!" She runs as quickly as possible through the rest of the crowd in order to exit the train and run after the thieves. Some of the other passengers also lost luggage and, they too, run quickly to deboard the train and catch the thieves. They run off the platform screaming loudly in French. Nastya follows them down the platform, screaming in English.

On the platform, the thieves are nowhere to be found. The crowd outside waiting for their loved-ones to deboard doesn't take the three men running away, arms full of luggage, to be thieves. The crowd on the platform just thinks that they are honest travelers who are late to be somewhere, and thus they are running. One mother and daughter, both in black wool peacoats, the daughter holding an open umbrella – despite the fact that it isn't raining outside; and, even if it were raining, her being inside a train station with a covered roof would have kept any rain from falling on her head – both see Nastya run quickly down the platform, lugging her large tan suitcase behind her. She calls out in English, "Help! He stole my bag! Somebody help me!" The mother recognizes that the language Nastya is shouting in is English; and, as her daughter speaks English, she turns to her and asks what the girl is yelling about. The girl tells her mother that she is shouting because someone stole her bag, and she wants help to catch the person. The mother says, "Oh" while thinking to herself how great it is that her daughter of only sixteen years can speak English. Then the girl takes her mothers arm and leads her down the platform in search of the girl's older brother, who is supposed to be arriving from Poland on this train.

The girl doesn't see her brother on this night. The mother doesn't see her son. Upon arriving in Berlin, he had deboarded the train to have a quick look at the city, and was late returning to the station. His train had left without him; so he was forced to wait out the night in Berlin and take the first train the next morning, which would arrive in Paris the following day.

The girl and her mother both have that same sick feeling in their stomachs as they watch the last of the passengers – all of whom are strangers – deboard the train. It is a sick feeling of disappointment along with a feeling that is a lot worse.

Soon the train is empty and the platform is empty, except for the mother who paces up and down the platform, accompanied by her daughter, hoping that she will see her son appear. The daughter too looks everywhere for her brother but he is not at this station – not on this night. The platform is empty, the train is empty, the passengers have all left. The thieves have long since made their escape successfully with several pieces of stolen luggage.

Meanwhile, the owner of the bag of ballet clothes is looking around outside the train station for a policeman. 'I can't believe they took that bag!' she laments to herself, 'It had my Capezio slippers in it, the ones my father gave me. I'm sure he spent a week's pay on those slippers – I can't believe they are gone!' She lugs her tan suitcase around, looking for someone who might know if the thieves have been caught.

The thieves, however, are far from the ~~train~~ station by now. They have escaped and are walking down a deserted street in the north of Paris, examining their spoils. They find many valuable things: passports, currency, jewelry, et cetera; but they also find that one of the stolen bags only contains ballet clothing and slippers. The three men laugh it off with boyish jokes to one another while the man carrying Nastya's bag throws it into the edge of the sidewalk, where her ballet clothes tumble out and Nastya's expensive Capezio slippers sit in the dirty Parisian gutter. And the rain begins to fall again.

The girl and her mother soon give up looking for the young man who was supposed to arrive in Paris on this night. Both, with tears in their eyes, leave the station, and begin to walk silently home together. They live on the other side of Paris but they do not want to take the métro home. They would rather walk. Neither do they want to speak to one another. And so they remain silent. The darkest imaginings and worst fears in the world pass through their minds. For many hours they continue walking through the dark, winding and rainy streets of Paris towards their home. The mother had assumed that when she left the station on this night, she would leave with her son and her daughter – her two children. And the three of them would go to their cozy home where a feast was waiting on the table. The mother hasn't seen her son for a whole year and she spent the entire day cooking to celebrate his return. But the mother isn't walking with her son and her daughter, she is only with her daughter and there is a real sickness in her stomach. Eventually, very late at night, the mother and daughter arrive home. The daughter quietly goes into her room to lie down. The mother silently goes to the dinner table, where the feast is laid out, and starts to put the food and the dishes away.

Meanwhile, on this late night, Nastya has spent her first few moments in the city of Paris in a frantic and emotional state. Though she slept on the train, she is still very tired and the fact that her valise was stolen brings a flood of tears to her eyes. 'Don't be so emotional, Nastya, It was just your ballet clothes. They can be replaced. You're just tired,' she thinks to herself as she pulls the address of the Monsieur de Chevalier from her peacoat pocket. She studies the address, which reads: *forty-seven, Rue de Paradis*, and returns the piece of paper to her pocket, where it remains folded-up. Then she returns to the station. Inside the station, all is very foreign to her, but she manages to find a bathroom, which is empty, where she can change her clothes. She takes off the sweater and pants that she wore throughout her whole trip, the clothes she wore when she left her family in the middle of the night, and she puts on a black dress in the bathroom stall. She then takes some high-heeled shoes from the tan suitcase, which she holds closely beside her to keep it from getting stolen. Out of the stall, Nastya stands beside her suitcase, facing the large mirror. She applies lipstick, so as to look as classy as possible when she meets these aristocrats who are, no doubt, waiting for her on Rue de Paradis.

As she applies her makeup, two men, unkempt in appearance – both with black tousled hair, and dark, scarred faces that makes them appear as if their skin is really just patches of leather all stitched together – enter the bathroom and stare lustfully at Nastya. She sees the men and hurriedly gathers her things, placing them quickly in her tan suitcase, which she closes, picks up and lugs out of the bathroom, embarrassed and a little afraid.

Once outside, she shakes the embarrassment and fear out of her mind. She looks down at herself and takes a feeling of pride. She looks nice. Her fair hair falls on the sides of her face in gentle curls that were not made messy by the train ride – though, long it was.

She is a beautiful girl, a good dancer; she has just arrived in Paris at the request of an important aristocrat; and, after all, she is in Paris for the first time … so why not have pride and be happy? Nastya shakes the fear and embarrassment out of her head, and tells herself to be proud. She smiles, lifts her head, and confidently walks through the train station – her suitcase by her side. She goes back to the exit and with a light-hearted eagerness, she enters again the great city of Paris.

The first thing she notices is how narrow the streets are in this city. They are much wider in Moscow. She notices the peculiar street lamps, and she loves their shapes as they light the mists of rain passing by them making clouds of amber light.

She notices how friendly some people are, and how aggressive the others are. Several times, people accost her on the sidewalk as she walks around looking for Rue de Paradis – men *and* women. They approach and stand very close, first saying, "Bonjour," and then proceeding with long unintelligible phrases. Nastya doesn't speak French, though her English is good.

She feels the air on this mild, April night. The air feels thicker to her here than in Moscow. It feels thicker and it smells different. She notices fragrant smells of lavender and other flowers. She also notices the odors of garbage and decaying food that is scattered in the street. She finds it strange how so many people are gathered in the streets, talking. And how animated they speak, laughing, shaking hands. The women kiss each other on the cheeks. A man kisses a woman passionately while walking past the vendors on the corners.

The vendors are selling crêpes, and kebabs and sandwiches right on the street. Smoke pours from their grills and money changes hands – and young men and girls gather in lines talking to each other, waiting for their food to be made, and finally they leave, wandering into the dark horizons of the winding Parisian streets, disappearing together.

A euphoria begins to fill Nastya as she walks these streets. She momentarily forgets all the events of the recent past. She forgets about her mother's washing. She forgets about Director Lavretsky, having come by to tell her that she was no longer welcome at the Bolshoy. She forgets the form of her father's sleeping body, as well as the features of his kind and old, loving face, the way he looks at her with such pride. She forgets, too, that horrible sight of her little sick brother, sitting up in his bed, staring at her with those glowing eyes in the darkness as she turned to leave her home, to run away in the night to a foreign country. She forgets all of these things and a euphoria begins to fill her. She is in a new, strange wonderland where everything that happens is the unexpected. The signs are written in the roman alphabet. The tiny foreign cars hiss by, the passengers yell strange things out of the windows.

It is getting late but Nastya is not ready to meet her new… 'benefactor' … her new friend … the one who will make her a dancer at the city's greatest ballet: the Opéra Garnier. She wants to wander the streets for a while longer, gaping at the novelties, which present themselves on every corner.

Walking down a road void of streetlights, she notices how black the sky has become. It is now quite late and she realizes she had better go to this man's house, and meet him before it gets too much later. She tells a taxi driver, whom she hails and greets in English, that she needs to go to a house near the Opéra Garnier. The driver, who speaks basic English, drives down Boulevard Haussmann, on the orders of the pretty young lady in his backseat. He heads towards the Opéra.

Nastya, seated in the back, reads the address, which was enclosed with the invitation, the train ticket and the money, sent by the Monsieur de Chevalier. It reads:

I am easy to find – not far at all from the Opéra. 47, Rue de Paradis. Not far at all from the Opéra. ...and that's Rue de "Paradis", comme "Paradise!".

Nastya smiles and folds up the piece of paper. 'This Monsieur de Chevalier sounds like a kind man,' Nastya muses to herself, while riding along, 'I think he'll be a very kind, and very old man.' ... 'But what a ridiculous name he has!' she laughs aloud after thinking about his name and the taxi driver turns around with a self-conscious look to see what she's laughing at.

The car pulls up to the Opéra Garnier, and the driver opens the door for his passenger. Nastya steps out and looks at the grand monument – the ancient Opéra house, a magnificent palace in the center of a city. It's columns, like ancient pillars made of sand, extend into the sky supporting its green metallic dome that lights up the night. Winged seraphim and monstrous carvings of *moyen-âge* gargoyles protrude from the tiers of stones, stacked on top of one another, forming the arched entryways that lead to whatever spectacular things go on inside. On the outside, this palace is lit golden and green and sparkles like a gold crested hill in the sun, like a crown of diamonds.

"An ancient palace, built in the center of a city," Nastya mumbles quietly to herself, with reverence for what she is seeing, "It's so beautiful. So very beautiful! ...Even Mother would like it!" She smiles to herself and breathes in the thick, mild Parisian air, fragrant with flowers and garbage, and she then turns to the driver and asks him:

"I need to walk from here to Rue de Paradis. Can you tell me which way to go?"

"Rue de Paradis?" the driver responds, "That's back on the other side of town! That's near where we came from. Why did you have me drive all the way out to the Opéra?!"

"My directions said it was here...."

"I'll take you back for seventy francs." interrupts the driver with frustration in his voice.

"That's fine. I don't mind paying, just take me to *forty-seven, Rue de Paradis*, please."

Driving back through town, back to the place where Nastya began her introduction to Paris: the tenth arrondissement, which lies in the north of the city, the driver goes down Boulevard Haussmann and takes a left on Rue d'Hauteville. Nastya asks him where he is from. He tells her he is from Tunisia. Nastya thinks about Tunisia. It sounds like a beautiful place. She knows nothing about it and she believes it is very far away, yet she is sure that it's a beautiful place.

She asks him where he learned English. He says he learned it driving taxis in Paris. He asks her where she learned English. She tells him that she learned it in school, in Russia. He asks her if she is here to model. She laughs at this, yet pride beams in her cheeks at the flattering comment. "No, I'm a ballet dancer," she tells him.

"Oh, ballet!" he replies. The two continue on down the road. They pass the *Gare du Nord*, and after a few moments, the driver turns to Nastya: "We just passed Rue de Paradis."

"Well, why didn't you stop?" Nastya asks, surprised. The driver doesn't answer, he just turns the wheel and circles the car around to drive back down the road to Rue de Paradis.

The car stops in front of building number forty-seven on the 'street of paradise' and Nastya, excited to see where she'll be staying, squints her eyes and looks out the window to try to make out the forms in the darkness – but she cannot. It is too dark. She sits in the back, while the driver sits in the front seat. He waits for her, silently, to pay him. She waits for him, silently, to get out of the car and open her door for her. Many moments pass of silence. The taxi driver eventually breaks this silence:

"Seventy francs, please, Mademoiselle."

"Do you expect me to get it sitting down for you? Anyway, my money is in my suitcase – in the trunk." …Moments pass… "Will you please open the door for me?"

The driver steps lethargically out of the car and comes around to open her door. He then pulls her suitcase out of the trunk for her, dusts it off and tells her how nice she looks in her black dress and heels. He then tells her to profit from Paris, to enjoy her stay, and to not get "eaten up" by the city.

Nastya stands tall and proud. She is in Paris, on Rue de Paradis, just a few meters from the home of the great Monsieur de Chevalier. She looks down at the face of the taxi driver who is eagerly awaiting the fare. She smiles and hands him a hundred franc bill, and gestures to him to keep the extra thirty as is a tip. She doesn't know how much thirty-francs is, but she doesn't care – she is finally at her destination after days and days of traveling.

"Thank you, *mademoiselle… merci bien, merci et bonne soirée! …et n'oubliez pas, profitez de la France!*" And then he is off; and Nastya, with her head held high, picks up her suitcase and glances around at the neighborhood, which is to become her new home.

Though Nastya has always known poverty, she has had, in her past, no trouble assimilating into wealthy society. This is mainly because, as a child, as is the case with many children nowadays and back then, she believed that her family had money and was quite well-off compared to the rest of the Russian population. Her father taught her at a young age to take great pride in herself. Sometimes her mother and father could not eat three times a day because the money went to buying Nastya new clothes, or buying her the books she required for school, or it went to having her hair done by one of the fashionable hairdressers on Kuznetsky Most Street. She cannot remember ever going hungry as a child, though, all too often, she got to eat less than she wanted at dinner and was sent off to school the next day without a proper breakfast. At school, she held her head high and went through the day with a healthy young radiance and happy countenance. Her mother paid much greater attention to making sure Nastya's clothes were washed and mended when she was young than she has in recent years. This is mainly due to her having come to accept her 'low social status' as her lot in life, and, consequently, her daughter's lot too. When Nastya was very young, however, her mother still had hope for the family's acceptance in 'good society', and so, by the tub she scrubbed the clothes, and by the fire she mended.

Her husband, Nastya's father, had wanted to be a poet ever since he was a teenager. In school, instead of taking notes during a lecture, he would fill the margins of his page with magnificent verse and little pencil drawings. When out of school, instead of going on to the university, he decided to take a little flat in the city-centre of Moscow and begin writing verse seriously – for an audience. He sent his verse off to publishers, agents and magazines, but his luck never hit at the right moment. He always showed the right verse to the wrong man and those few times he ran across the right man, he showed him the wrong verse. The life of Nastya's father had been one unlucky break after another, though he eventually became happy and content with his life and even considered his luck to have changed for the better. He finally decided his life had become far better than it ever could have, had he became a famous poet. This happiness began with the birth of his first child, Nastya.

After failing in every attempt to earn a wage and reputation as a poet, and after many times losing so much money in his efforts that he was almost forced to freeze in the cold of his flat during the winters when he could not afford fuel, Nastya's father found himself a steady job as the assistant to a designer of artistic carpet patterns. Mostly, he was an errand boy and a pencil sharpener, but at the time, he felt this was the closest thing to being a professional artist that he would ever be – and, besides, it afforded fuel to heat his flat. It wasn't that he felt being an artist's errand boy was his destiny and the *only* thing he could ever do again. It's just what he did for pay. In his spare time he still wrote and compiled his verse and prepared manuscripts to be sent off to publishers. But no publisher ever bought a single line of his verse and he continued on running errands and sharpening pencils and the years passed on.

Eventually, his boss went out of business and Nastya's father had to find another job in the only industry he knew. He became a carpet layer, which is taxing physical labor; and he started working twelve hour days in order to support his new wife, and soon after, his newborn child as well. He soon completely forgot his dream of becoming a poet. Laying carpets all day took all of his energy and in the evenings, he had no motivation to do anything besides eat his dinner and sleep. He had lost the energy to stay up into the night, under a solitary lamp, writing poetry at his old maple desk. The verse that he had written before – when he was out of school, and later when he worked for the carpet designer – was kept in a drawer that no one in the family ever opened. Nastya's father became too afraid to open that drawer for the great sorrows of broken dreams that would, no doubt, be seen along with the sheets of paper, yellowed with age, containing his old poetry. His wife never had the slightest interest in opening that drawer, for she was never a lover of poetry. And Nastya was never allowed to open the drawer, so she hadn't the slightest idea what was in it.

When Nastya's father and mother met in their youth, they were both impoverished, but they married each other for love and completely overlooked the impact finances would have in the future. Nastya's mother was very pretty when she was young and she had several suitors who were well-off, – a couple of them were even wealthy, – but blind to the realities and difficulties money presents in life, and overjoyed with the love she felt for the man who was to become her husband, she married him, only a week after his proposal.

As a young couple they lived an intimate life in a small apartment – only slightly smaller than the one they occupy now. Their love for each other was strong and the room was always warm, for when they hadn't the fuel to burn, they had their bodies to warm one another. Then Nastya was born and they treated her with great adoration. Her father's life, especially, was changed by the birth. Nastya became his new creation. He had made that beautiful creature – his daughter – and had put her into the world ... exactly the thing he had always been trying to do with his poetry. He had created a beautiful poem in making his daughter; and the world, as well as he, looked on her as precious. Picturing his daughter's face – and later his son's too, to some extent – took the drudgery out of laying carpets for twelve hours every day. When he came home from work each night, he'd kiss her cheeks, which would always be red from playing outside, and he'd smile and eat his humble meal and be happy. He would sleep and be happy, dreaming the most pleasant dreams until five o'clock the next morning when he would have to leave his home to take the tram to work.

Nastya's mother, on the other hand, never saw her daughter or her son as being the 'great, beautiful creations' that her father did. She instead, and especially as the years progressed and their poverty became worse, saw the two children only as two extra mouths hungering after what little food sat in the cupboards. This bitterness grew as the years went by, yet was alleviated slightly when Nastya became old enough to help with the work around the house. It wasn't that the mother didn't love her children, she just had sorrows of her own to contend with. She had had dreams of her own which had been broken. Her dream was always to marry a man whom she loved, and live a luxurious life. She achieved the first part of her dream, but even that love waned a bit when the second part of her dream wasn't achieved. There were even sometimes, in recent years, when she felt consciously sure that she no longer loved her husband; though he has always continued to love his wife dearly. This conviction of hers, that she had fallen out of love, she always hid from him, hoping it would pass and the love would return. As the years progressed, and the chances of her dreams being realized became slim, she decided to wallow no more on the life she *could've had*. She became complacent and decided, once and for all, that it was indeed her lot in life to wash the linen and cook the kasha and hold her husband in bed at night. So on like this, family-life went in Nastya's home.

Later, growing up, when visiting the homes of her friends, Nastya would notice how nicely furnished these homes were and how many rooms they had. But her friends' families quarreled and, without an exception, their homes were cold with tension and bitterness. And Nastya would go back to her parents' one-room apartment after playing at a friend's house and immediately she would be picked up and swung around playfully by her loving father, while her mother would lay out clean and nicely pressed clothes for Nastya to wear the next day at school – in an effort to make her daughter appear to come from a 'good home'. And this affection that filled her family's apartment made the young Nastya feel that she came from the best home in the world.

Later, when she became an adolescent and her body took the form of a young beauty, all of the boys – rich and poor – followed after her. This attention didn't make her overly proud, however, for it was nothing new to her. Often, when a girl is disregarded at home, she – that is, if she grows to be very pretty – becomes overly haughty and snobbish later on when the boys begin to notice her. Rather than responding to the novelty of the affection with appreciation, she responds with mistrust and disapproval, which, though actually stemming from an opinion of low self-worth, comes across as an opinion of all too high value. But Nastya was always treated with love and affection, and her father always looked upon her as the most precious thing in the world; so when the boys at school, too, began to see her as the most precious thing in the world, she took this treatment to be normal and she appreciated it from them, as she appreciated it from her father. She walked around with the same great pride and confidence when she was sixteen as she did when she was six. And with this pride and confidence, she also displayed a nature of the most happy and high-spirited kind. She has never been known to put anybody down. If ever she acted haughtily towards someone, it was only an affectation, meant to cover a real and sincere appreciation felt for that person. In addition to her love for others, Nastya has always had a love for nature. She has always had a love for poetry too, though her father, unfortunately, never learned of this.

But even with the rationing of food and the dilapidated appearance of Nastya's home growing up, she has never considered herself poor – for everywhere there was affection in her home. She relates poverty to spiritual issues. Those whose parents yelled and spanked them were poor. Those whose parents ignored them … they were poor.

So, when Nastya was old enough to go to soirées where boys would be present, she started visiting the homes of the wealthy. And in every way she fit in. Wealthy parents with wealthy sons wanted their boys to court the young beauty. She had every desirable quality. She was feminine and pretty. She was well-dressed. She had great pride, yet was humble and nurturing to those less fortunate than herself. She always found a nice compliment for those who were injured. In addition, she was high-spirited and spoke her mind without hesitation; although, as a result of the great admiration she had for her father, she was always more than happy to let members of the male sex come forth with their opinions and make the decisions – so long as the decisions were reasonably sound. In short, she was seen as being the perfect young lady to marry: one who could submit to a man, yet still hold her own identity and keep her own beliefs – always holding her head up high. This pride and dignity of hers caused the young men to always want to please her with their decisions. They would lead her, but only in the direction she would want to go. Nastya's father looked on this aspect of Nastya's nature as a great possession; one which would result in her eventually finding a good man and having a happy marriage and a happy life.

Fortunately, however, the story of Nastya is far more interesting to you, the reader – and to me, as well – than it would have been had she run off after finishing school to marry a nice, sensible man who would love her and provide for her, as so many of her girlfriends had done. Finding someone, whom you can love, and who can love you in return, is a tremendously difficult task, compared to finding someone who will provide for you, whom you will be able to bear, and accept as the only halfway decent person you can find to spend your life with – a person you can like, yet whom you cannot love. Yet, to love and be loved is a necessity for Nastya. She will not leave the home of her father – who loves her so profoundly – to live in a man's house where there is merely acceptance, and no mutual love. But Nastya, with only twenty-two years, has never fallen in love; and so she remains at her father's house. …That is, she *remained* at her fathers house, until she recently ran away to pursue her other loves, viz., the ballet, and the adventurous mystery that awaits one expatriating to a foreign country.

So here she is now… in a foreign country, in the beautiful and romantic city of Paris; and she stands in the darkened cobbled street before the house of a rich aristocrat who is going to make her a star at the magnificent Opéra Garnier.

Nastya's meeting with the 'wailing man'…

She stands on Rue de Paradis, surveying her environment. Her family's street, Sokolniki Street, is perhaps only slightly cleaner and more beautiful than Rue de Paradis; but when Nastya looks around her, all she sees is poverty and misery. It isn't so much the rats lying dead in the gutters, half-eaten by those vultures that are so common in Paris these days; neither is it the garbage rotting in the drains of the gutters where the murky water is stopped up, flooding into the street and carrying the odors of the rancid trash and carrion. It isn't so much the dilapidated buildings towering overhead like great beacons of broken windows and misery, either. It is more the poverty that is so visible in the human form that she sees now on Rue de Paradis. It is the kind of poverty that Nastya recognizes as such – not merely a lack of money, but rather the despair and suffering that is usually caused by a lack of money. And here she sees it:

In a doorway, the gaunt, naked body of a man lies trembling in the cold. He has only a piece of gauze to serve as underwear and besides that, he is completely nude. His skin is pale and grey and covered with goose-bumps. He lies in the doorway, in the building next to M. de Chevalier's, and he is wailing. He holds his right eye and wails incessantly. With one hand he holds his eye and with the other he tugs at his pointy, grey beard; and from his trembling, white lips, and mouth of jagged teeth, he wails.

"They took my eye! They gouged it out!" he wails in English with a British accent. Nastya approaches him with great alarm.

"Who took your eye?" she asks with a look of the utmost concern on her face. The old man doesn't answer, he just continues shivering and wailing.

"Do you need me to get you to a hospital? or a doctor?" Nastya asks.

The man stops wailing to answer Nastya, "They can't do anything for me!"

"But, surely they can! You've just lost your eye, they'll need to fix it so it doesn't get infected."

"It's not going to get infected. I lost it years ago! It's too late to fix it! There's nothing anyone can do, little girl." Then he pauses for a moment. He then resumes wailing: "They gouged out my eye! Somebody gouged my eye out!"

"But if it happened years ago, why do you cry about it now?"

With this, the old man stops wailing and speaks to Nastya, all the while holding his eye socket, with a cupped hand.

"Ugh, I cried about it then too. But I cry about it now as well, for it's not gotten any better, my eye!"

"But wouldn't you get used to it by now?" asked Nastya.

"Oh sure, 'get used to it'! …I can get used to it. I have gotten used to it. It's been gone for nearly seven years. And it's not the worst thing. I've got another eye, you see! Ugh, it's not like they gouged my mouth out – or my privates!" … "I just can't get used to the fact that it was *them*… that it was *they* who gouged out my eye. Those dirty Russians – they're all crazy!"

"But I'm Russian." Nastya says, taking offence. And, with this, the old man looks at Nastya straight in the eyes, with a look of tremendous fear and hatred. He begins to tremble more severely. His single eye glares at her like a glowing, white stone. He nudges away from her, pushing his body back into the doorway as far as possible. His naked skin turns even whiter as he glares at her with a single, white eye – and his lips tremble…

"You are a Ru- …a Ru-ssian?"

"Yes," Nastya responds, "and we are not dirty."

"Listen, Comrade," spits the old man, "Ugh, you Russians are all crazy! …crazy, you hear?! You think a Russian girl has to marry a Russian man. Once, I met a Russian girl and she married me – an Englishman. The Russians found out about it and came to take her away from me … came all the way to Paris. They gouged my eye out and they took her away! They took her back to Russia and locked her up for good – she's still there as far as I know, locked up for good – put in the nuthouse!" … "See, I was coming home from drinking at a pub one night, and when I walked into my apartment, instead of seeing my little Russian wife, I see these big Russian men, fat men, with big furry hats. My wife was gone but here were these fat men, standing in my apartment, talking to a young couple – girl about your age. And the young couple, this bloke and this girl, were paying them money. Do you know *why* they were paying the fat, Russian men money?"

"No." replied Nastya, thinking that she would like to end the conversation with this one-eyed Englishman and go meet the Monsieur de Chevalier and relax a bit from her long voyage.

"…They were paying these men money," he continued, "because the fat, Russian men had just *sold* my apartment to them. They sold *my* apartment, without me even knowing about it!" … "The couple paid them a handsome sum. I saw the banknotes change hands, it was quite a stack. That's what kind of *connerie* goes on in Paris! Shit like that all the time! …So then, you know what I do? I tell the young couple to leave – to get out! – to give me my keys back and leave! You know what they said? You know what they said?! …Ugh, they said that they had just paid a lot of money for the apartment and that I was *trespassing!* Can you imagine? Trespassing in *my own* apartment?!

"…By this time the Russians had left – went outside – disappeared somewhere. I told the couple to give me back my keys or I'd give 'em each a mouthful of fist. They both stepped back surprised – scared even. Then the young bloke goes and calls the police – from *my* phone! …Now, I wasn't going to punch him then, nor his dumpy girl; what, after the police were on their way – but I wasn't going to leave my apartment either." … "Finally the police arrive, and you know what happened? Those swindlers – that con and his little dumpy wife – they show the police a *Bill of Sale* for *my* apartment… signed by those communists!"

"We are not communists," Nastya interrupts.

"…And the police," the old man continues while covering his right eye and tugging at his pointy beard, "the police they looked at that *Bill of Sale* and then looked at me and grabbed me. Then they threw me out the door – they threw me out *my own* door! The *flics* told the couple to have a nice life and enjoy their new apartment and they grabbed *me* and threw *me* out the door and down the stairs. The cops in Paris are like that, you see. They always get the wrong man." ... "So, anyway, I left my building and walked out into the street while the cops followed close behind me. Once I was out on the street, they too disappeared. I was thinking, 'finally those cops are gone!'. ...Then, who do I see parked in a car on the street? Those Russians! The fat men were sitting in the front of the car, and my wife, she was locked in the backseat. I started banging on the windshield, 'Hey!', I screamed, 'Give me my apartment, and give me my wife back!' ... Then, one of those Russians – the biggest and fattest one – got out of the car and gouged out my eye – my right eye – right in front of my wife!"

"I'm sorry." says Nastya, as she edges out of the doorway thinking of what she will say to get away from this man.

"So, if you're like those *other* Russians," the old, emaciated Englishman continued, "you should get the hell out of this city, right now!" He spits a couple times at the ground, in her direction, "Well, of course you're like those *other* Russians...!"

At this moment, Nastya turns around completely and walks off, in the direction of M. de Chevalier's building. The moment her back is turned to the old man, he begins wailing again. He wails and wails and Nastya tries to cover her ears from the sound – but it's hard because she is carrying a suitcase.

Nastya's meeting with the Landlady and the Monsieur de Chevalier...

Nastya takes a heavy breath and looks up at the dilapidated building, which is numbered forty-seven. It is a gloomy sight, but Nastya knows that some of these European buildings look old and run-down on the outside, yet have interiors which are extravagantly luxurious and big enough to jump a horse in. She once read about such interiors in a Russian design magazine. It showed pictures of run-down buildings in Paris just like the one she is looking at. Then it showed their interiors, which are lit by twenty-tiered chandeliers of crystal and gold. Beneath the chandeliers, paintings by the masters hang over elegant wallpaper that is handmade in Japan. And the doorknobs of all the doors are encrusted with rubies and the doorways gleam of emeralds. She has seen interiors like this. They are very common in Paris.

"I'm sure he will be very nice, I'm sure it will be very beautiful inside." Nastya mutters aloud as she walks up the steps to the front door of number *forty-seven, Rue de Paradis*, the home of the Monsieur de Chevalier.

She enters the door-code, which is scrawled on the back of the invitation she received, and the front door buzzes open. She enters into the apartment building hallway.

The sallow light from the lamps above shines down in a dingy yellow glow upon the tattered carpet in the hallway. Along one wall is a row of tin mailboxes. Against the other wall is a circular stairway leading up into darkness. At the far end of the dingy hallway, is a little elevator. Two apartment doors face each other in the hallway. She stands next to the front door, looking around.

On the mailboxes are the names of the tenants. She studies them for a long time, trying to find 'Monsieur de Chevalier'. Then, one of the doors in the hallway opens, and a dark pair of eyes peer out at her. They are the eyes of a man. She turns around when she feels the eyes on her back, and as soon as she turns around to look, the eyes disappear and the door closes.

Then the other door in the hallway opens, but this time dark eyes do not peer out at her. Instead, a stumpish looking old woman, with glasses and a cane, hobbles out, eyeing Nastya up and down as the latter tries to find M. de Chevalier's name and apartment number on one of the mailboxes.

"*Vous cherchez qui?*" the old woman asks in a voice made scratchy by decades of cigarette smoking. She taps at Nastya's legs with her cane.

"I don't speak French." says Nastya in a matter of fact tone.

"Who you are looking for?" the old woman answers in broken English – through a heavy accent.

"I think this can't be right." says Nastya, biting her lower lip.

"You are here for someone?" … "You speak English?" … "Me, I was in England once – for studies… many time ago…." The old woman is interrupted when Nastya hands her the letter and asks:

"I'm looking for the 'Monsieur de Chevalier'."

The old woman takes the letter with a quick grab and almost stumbles. She catches herself and scans the letter. Then she begins laughing. "Monsieur de Chevalier? …*non, c'est pas vrai!*" She begins laughing louder, *"Aah, ben, c'est pas vrai! Oo-la-la!"*

"What is it?" Nastya asks without humor in her voice.

"Fifth floor, to the right it says… It must be him! …We call him *Salaud!"* she says, still laughing hysterically, "I go show you the way."

And the two proceed to the shabby little elevator in back of the dingy hall. The old landlady punches the call button with repeated jabs with her cane. The ladies enter and the door closes. The elevator, just as dingy as the hallway, with the same sallow light, the same shabby carpet, and an ashtray next to the button panel overflowing with cigarette butts, begins to ascend. Then with a jerk, it stops in between floors. The door opens and the ladies look out with stupefaction to see that it is a long jump to the floor below them and a hard climb to the floor above. The landlady beats the ceiling on the elevator hard with her cane until the door again closes and the elevator resumes going up. Finally that shabby little elevator stops properly on the fifth-floor.

The landlady leads Nastya. The latter follows her down the musty hallway on the fifth-floor with a knot of anticipation eating away at her stomach. What has she come all the way to Paris to find? Who has she come all that long way from Moscow to meet? What is this Monsieur de Chevalier going to be like? She looks around at the wretched hallway she is walking down – a wretched hallway like this to greet her after arriving in Paris for the first time. She bites her lower lip and shudders a little. 'It will be all right,' she tells herself, as they stand before the aristocrat's front door.

Down the hall from the elevator, the two ladies stand by the closed door. Nastya stands tall, expectantly, and begins to bite the nail on her pinky-finger. Meanwhile, the landlady knocks on the door loudly, irreverently, with her cane. *"Salaud! Monsieur Salaud!"* she yells, "Are you home?!"

"Oui, oui!" comes from the man who has just opened his door and now stands looking down at the landlady who doesn't seem to realize that the door has been opened – she continues to pound the air with her cane, all the while yelling, *"Salaud? ... Salaud?!"*

"Quoi?!" says the man in an agitated voice, standing before the two ladies, eyeing the landlady with suspicion.

"Mon-sieur de Chev-al-ee-ay?" she says to the man, drawing out each syllable in a mocking jest, *"Vous-êtes là?"*

Then the man, who stands in the doorway of his apartment facing the landlady, turns to see who is accompanying the old woman. And when his eyes catch sight of Nastya for the first time, he looks into her radiant eyes and says: "*Mon Dieu!* My goodness! *Oui, c'est moi!"* ... "I mean, it's me, the *Monsieur de Chevalier!*"

Nastya doesn't smile, nor does she frown. She looks at the man standing in the doorway as he makes a clumsy bow, during which, his arm gestures to push the old landlady away.

He is a man of about sixty-years, quite overweight, and not too tall. His dark, grey-streaked hair is wiry, like a mat of soiled steel wool draped over his head. Nastya finds his appearance to be quite comical, especially with the round jolly cheeks he has all splotched with red stains. His face flushes as he looks at Nastya; the latter smiles at him, as though very pleased to meet him. He has that blushing and embarrassed innocence that is so common in young boys but not found often in men of sixty years. He is obviously trying to hide this puerile look by standing as straight as possible and thrusting his chest out. His chin, too, bulges out, and his flabby neck quivers slightly with nervousness. He looks rather like a large green stick with something dangling at the top of it. He wears a military suit with medals pinned to it. It appears much too small for him and it looks rather old fashioned. There are little brass bayonets pinned to his shoulders, beneath the epaulettes. Nastya wonders what war it was he fought in… 'It must have been a long time ago,' she thinks, 'he looks just like a nineteenth century foreign army general. He looks awful German.' Nastya looks the curious man up and down.

Then, the Monsieur bends forward to get a good look at the girl; and, as he is about the same height as Nastya, only a little shorter, their eyes almost touch. He studies her face with quick movements of his head – the type of movements that would be made by someone who is searching in the dark for a lost screw. Nastya begins to tremble slightly in the awkward moment. Then the Monsieur stops scrutinizing his young visitor, and he stands up straight, whereby he takes Nastya's hand –

which is holding tightly the handle of her suitcase – and he lifts her fingers up to kiss them – lifting the suitcase as well.

He kisses her hand, and says, "*Enchanté*, Mademoiselle." … "Very pleased to acquainteth you."

Nastya stands limp, as if in shock; it is too bad we don't know what wild thoughts are probably floating through her mind at this time. The Monsieur ushers Nastya into his apartment. The landlady remains at the door, swinging her cane to and fro, and laughing. As the Monsieur shuts his front door, one can still hear the landlady's muffled, scratchy laugh out in the hall as she walks back to the shabby elevator.

Now the Monsieur and Nastya are alone together. They enter through the vestibule into the salon, which is dim and cluttered with gaudy, inexpensive ornaments and furniture. At the far end of the room, there is a stuffed green chair – olive in color. In the opposite corner there is a stuffed green bird, perched on a carved wooden fish that the bird apparently has just caught. Against one wall there is a table, on which rest little porcelain military sculptures and other foofaraw. Against another wall, there is a glass shelf, which holds bottles of various schnapps, liqueurs and wines. Also, on this shelf are various glasses for imbibing these spirits. Above the shelf hangs a large, poorly painted portrait of the Monsieur de Chevalier himself. It has a poor-quality, over-ornamentally gilded-frame. On the floor, is a cheap tattered rug, to which Nastya takes an extreme dislike – as her father is in the carpet business, she has been trained to identify and appreciate fine carpeting. Nastya also notices some more striking and peculiar objects in the Monsieur's apartment – objects, which I will mention in a moment.

The two stand facing each other. Nastya drops her suitcase, and there is complete silence.

Then, with a slight tremble in her voice, Nastya breaks the silence. She pauses a moment, and then quietly says:

"You are the Monsieur de Chevalier?"

And with that question, the room begins to spin. Nastya begins to get dizzy. Everything moves around and around in circles, as the man has just grabbed her hand and is leading her in a dance around his living room. She follows his lead but waits for a chance to break away from him. All the while, they dance, and he says:

"I am indeed the Monsieur de Chevalier! ...At your service *très chère*," he spins her again, "Forgive me. I didn't know it was tonight you would arrive. I didn't know you would come tonight!"

And then, it is he who breaks the dance instead of Nastya. He takes a step away, and stands perfectly still. Nastya is glad the room no longer spins so fast. The dizziness starts to settle. And the Monsieur begins to address Nastya … then he stops. He has become flustered speaking to the young beauty that stands before him, and he gapes at her, as he wrings the palms of his hands in nervousness. Now the both of them are standing still … Nastya, all the while, holds her head to keep it from spinning.

"I had a little drink. Excuse me. Just a little drink – *a wink*, that's all! Just *a wink!*" The Monsieur then dances off on his own. He twirls over to the glass shelf and pours himself some schnapps.

"And I'm just going to have another little drink. I need just a little. Just a 'tad-bit' as they say in London, hee hee." … "A 'tad-bit' to ease my nerves. I have these nerves, you see." He spills a little schnapps on the shelf but finishes pouring himself a glass – and a glass for the young lady, too. He then twirls around, handing her a glass overflowing with apple flavoured liquor.

He continues, "Not for nerves. No, not for nerves! I have a drink to celebrate. And you have a little drink too … to celebrate! … hee hee." Nastya takes the glass; and, in order to ease her own nerves, which are trembling as well, she drinks the glass down quickly. Once her schnapps are finished, M. de Chevalier raises his glass in a toast…

"To our…" he begins, but stops when he notices that Nastya doesn't have a full glass to toast with. "Okay," he continues, "you can have another… but only to celebrate!" And then he sighs and smiles at Nastya, "…Oh, it is so nice to finally meet you. It is a splendour to have you in our humble city. Paris is grateful. Paris is *truly* grateful!"

That's basically how the first few moments of the meeting between the Monsieur de Chevalier and Nastya went. Though before we move on to the events which happened just after this meeting – events which have great relevance to the fate of our heroine – I must mention what those striking and peculiar objects were that Nastya noticed in the home of M. de Chevalier.

89

Right after Nastya saw the badly painted portrait of the Monsieur de Chevalier where he is portrayed as a general as seen from the profile, she looked around to the other walls; and, to her shock, she noticed many copies of that lithograph poster advertising the Russian ballet with the portrait of Nastya executing a pirouette posted all over the Monsieur's walls. When she saw them, that was the moment she knew something was wrong. That was the moment her intuition told her something was wrong with all of this. That intuition crept up on her like a fierce illness when she first noticed the posters of her pasted on his walls. She knew at that moment that she may be in a bad situation. But this she noticed right as the Monsieur was making his toast; and, the second glass of schnapps – which she accepted only on account of her frazzled nerves, after having refused it twice before – lightened her head, as well as her 'intuition', and she laughed it off as being just 'wild ideas' in her head. 'After all,' she thought, 'he is a most jovial man. I'm sure he is the aristocrat he says he is. No, he doesn't seem to have a lot of money, but he's endearing. And only aristocrats have oil-painted portraits of themselves on their walls – even if it is a badly painted portrait. I'm sure he's a moral person. I'm sure he has very strong morals. After all, aren't aristocrats bred to be morally sound?'

…Nevertheless, when she saw her lithograph portrait hung on every wall, except for the one where his own portrait is displayed, that was the moment she dropped her suitcase; and there was dead silence.

A few moments after their toast, Nastya asked him, while studying one of her Russian ballet posters hanging over the coffee table, "You didn't really find out about me through the Russian papers. You found out about me through these posters. Is this true?"

To which, he replied, "Through the posters, yes, yes… no, no, not through the posters… I mean, not through *these* posters… Through the paper, like I said, *Le Monde*. I have a copy right here.…" He picks up the newspaper and reads from the page that is already open: "Says here, 'Anastasia Alexandrovna to replace Varvara Fillipovna at the Bolshoy.…' You see?"

I implore you, dear reader, to be patient with me, as we momentarily leave the home of M. de Chevalier. The events which happen next surrounding Nastya and her host are dreadfully interesting, and I am tempted, no doubt, to present them to you this instant; however, I must resist… for now, it is important that we know how the life of David is progressing.

CHAPTER VIII

David's night beneath a bridge and his fateful meeting, the next evening, with Doctor Moreaux...

"A bridge for a bed and a river for a rug," David mumbles sleepily to himself as he lies outstretched on a metal rafter beneath the *Pont Alexandre III* on the river Seine. He had gathered some empty, tin fish cans to use beneath his head for a pillow. Then he crawled from the dark crevice of the embankment, out onto the rafters until her found a nice, solid beam beneath the bridge, above the river, that was suitable for sleeping. Now he lies there, pinching the fleas and swatting the flies from his face.

"Why did I stay in Paris?" he wonders to himself. He feels the anesthetics wearing off and the pain returns to his body. He hears the *ping, ping, ping,* of the raindrops hitting the iron lampposts on the bridge overhead. "Sounds like hail," he says aloud, "What are these things crawling all over me?" He scratches his body, while trying to fall asleep on the rafters of the *Pont Alexandre III*. Far below him, the river flows, and from the river's surface comes a scourge of mosquitoes. They have just hatched from their eggs and are taking flight for the first time. The males of the scourge go on to find plant nectar to feed on. The female mosquitoes, however, stop to drink blood from our poor hero's body, as he lies beneath the bridge.

"Why again, did I not take that train to Brittany? Some better destiny this is: sleeping soiled beneath a lonesome bridge!" ... "Well, David, boy... you'll find out your destiny sooner or later, you'll find out what it is that made you stay in Paris." ... "I just hope it ends well!"

...And with that, he falls asleep. His fatigue had been great and he now sleeps impervious to the bites of the insects, the noise of the rain, and the metal rustling sounds his tin-can pillow makes beneath his head.

When he wakes up, it is dark. But it is not the same night that it was when he fell asleep. He slept about twenty-hours, and now it is twilight on the next day. It is just after sunset. David, however, assumes that it is the same night, that he has woken up early, and that it is just before sunrise.

Upon waking, he looks over the edge of his bed and sees the dark river far below him. He suddenly becomes afraid that he is going to fall off the beam and plummet into the Seine. He slowly, carefully, inches up the beam, crossing all the rafters on the *Pont Alexandre III,* until he reaches the embankment on the Left-Bank, where he is safe. He then begins staggering down the river quai. His suit is filthier than ever and his mouth needs a brushing.

'It is almost sunrise,' he thinks to himself, 'time to see the doctor.' Although the sun won't be rising for another nine hours, the air has that cold, thin quality, accompanied by the light, wet fog so commonly found on spring mornings just before dawn. David pulls out the map from his pocket and walks on. He follows the girl's perfectly drawn map down the river quai, to Notre Dame, and back up to Boulevard St. Germain, where he then heads back in the direction he started from. He walks past all of the curlicue monuments that are marked along the way, and he thinks about that girl and her mother. He thinks about their neat, matching, black wool peacoats. He thinks about that train station. He wonders why he didn't try to hop a train to Brittany. He thinks about Brittany, he thinks about Marc, eating his lunch up on that sunny hilltop. But on this long walk, his thoughts keep returning like clockwork to the pains that haunt his body. The more he thinks about the pain, the more his anxiety increases. His pain is severe and it is chronic and he knows that it is caused by a serious ailment. And he believes now that it is going to kill him if he doesn't find the doctor soon. Why does he have to have these dying thoughts? He tries to think about peacoats and sunny hilltops as he continues walking. Anything to get those dying thoughts out of his head. He thinks about the mother and her daughter again. He wishes that he had a woman. Then everything would be okay. She would take care of him and he would take care of her, and everything would be okay. But no woman would have him now – not in the condition he's in. He knows this. Not with his sick body, and his dirty clothes, and their dirty, empty pockets. 'No,' he thinks to himself, 'now I have no money and no language and no home, and no woman would have me at all.'

David's anxiety is now at a climax. He feels that his pounding heart is about to explode. 'It's just a panic attack,' he tells himself, 'the best thing to do is just to stay calm and realize that it is not fatal. You start thinking it's fatal, and it will be. You worry yourself too much, and your heart *will* explode! But, you stay calm and everything will be fine.' David tries to think of placid things, gentle things, like lakes and squirrels.

He remembers *Dr. So-and-so* from the hospital in Seattle, coming in to wake him up to tell him he had a severe kidney infection – caused by tears made in the lining of the kidney from the passing kidney stones. He remembers how the doctor came back the next morning and told him they had been wrong – that he'd had no illness at all. Oh, how sick he felt then!

He thinks about that hospital with its long corridors lined with golden baby pear trees. How their leaves lit up like yellow sapphires in the springtime sun that came through the windows. David admired those trees as he walked down the hospital corridors in the morning, drinking his coffee.

He thinks about that hospital, and he thinks of the government people who came into his hospital room, one morning, to tell him he didn't have the right to receive government aid to pay his hospital bills. He remembers how they kept calling him *foreigner*, and *alien*. He'd been in America as long as he could remember – all of his life, he had thought – yet they kept calling him *the foreigner*. He remembers the government official, *Detective So-and-so*, grabbing his shoulder and shaking it – which made his insides rattle with pain – while he said to the young man: "You wouldn't be in so much trouble if your parents had only stayed in France in the first place … or at least had they been responsible enough to apply for a green card – like *honest* immigrants!" … 'Why didn't my parents ever tell me I am French?' David asks himself, 'It seems like too surreal of a story … perhaps, it's all made up … no, it couldn't be made up.'

"What horrible memories!" he mutters aloud through clenched teeth, "I just want to forget that whole horrible time." David continues on down Boulevard St. Germain. His heart slows its beating, the panic subsides a little, yet he still tries to keep his thoughts focused on something light. He thinks of the airplanes he saw when he was a kid – those large silver vessels shooting through the air, making the sounds of thunderclaps. He remembers their gorgeous, metallic bodies reflecting the rays of the sun off their silver wings, and how beautifully they flew! … and how they landed on that great, magnificent carrier ship, the *USS Enterprise*, which lay like a city on the sea, in the harbor of the great Puget Sound.

He thinks of the birds that used to land in his backyard when he was very young. In all memories he has of his boyhood, the sun is shining. That was back when his mother was alive, and in every memory he has of that time, there is the warmth of the sun. He remembers those birds that used to land in his backyard and eat the worms off of the rhododendron trees. He would run up to pet those birds, but they wouldn't let him come near. They were feral birds and would fly far away whenever he got to close. But then, they'd come around again and swoop down in the sunshine, picking up all the worms from the rhododendron trees in their orange beaks. 'Oh, how those beaks were brightly lit by the sun,' he remembers. He thinks about this as long as he can, but soon he can only think about the pain in his body again, which is growing stronger; and he remembers that he is a long way from the backyard of his boyhood. He is in Paris now, and it is a long ways away.

His breathing is shallow. His chest is constricted and he feels his heart as it tries so hard to keep beating. "Good heart," he says, as he rubs his chest trying to encourage his heart to keep beating. He is only twenty-eight years old, our David – much too young to die.

The girl drew her map well and David finds Rue du Dragon without any confusion. The sun still hasn't risen; and the sky, it seems, is only growing darker, which confuses David. He thought for sure the sun would have risen by now. 'Regardless,' he thinks, 'even if it is a little too early in the morning, I shouldn't hesitate to ring the doctor's bell. I am having a bit of an emergency.' David notes his shallow breathing and his constricted chest, and that persistent pain in his abdomen.

He walks down Rue du Dragon until he comes to number 'thirty'; and he enters the door code that is written on the piece of paper, which was given to him by the hospital accountant. The door *buzzes* and he goes inside. The corridor is dark and stifling with the heat from a furnace. The dark shadows shift like apparitions in David's view as he searches for the light switch.

Moments ago, when he was on his way here, to the doctor's office. He had been walking down Boulevard St. Germain. The rain had just stopped, and the people who had been inside the nearby shops and restaurants noticed this and began to leave their shelters, coming outside to enjoy the mild spring evening.

Under the clear, twilit sky, these people gathered and talked and laughed. Some had glasses of beer in their hands, and shiny black cars swerved around them as the raindrops gleamed on their hoods. The street was shiny and black from the rain that had fallen, but then it was clear, the sky, and no more rain fell. And the air began to get warm.

David continued on his lonesome way down St. Germain. He was damp and filthy and covered in dried blood, and partially dried mud, and dirt of all sorts; and the crowds on the sidewalk stepped aside to let him pass, without looking at him for more than a second. Looking back, he thinks that he must've appeared as a derelict – a drunk clochard, or a wretched hobo. At the time, however, he didn't feel any different than the other people who were gathered in the street and on the sidewalks, except for the fact that he was in so much pain and needed to get to the doctor's; whereas, they were free to drink their beer and laugh and be happy, in the springtime, evening air.

He wanted so much to join these people – but this was not to be his night. He was a lonesome traveler... sick, and filthy, and seeking help; and he followed the girl's map down St. Germain with his head down, so as not to see the expressions on the people's faces who noticed him.

St. Germain is the street of the lonely, errant Parisian. Young people from *La Sorbonne*, from the *lycées*, from their side-street offices, from their countries far away, from their nearby solitary apartments; young people from the jails and the all-night *boites* ... all these errant Parisians wander St. Germain until they find love or ecstasy, or home, or a friend's flat where they can crash – always someplace to go, or something to look for. ...And then there are those with no place to go, and nothing to look for. These are the hopeless ones.

As David stood outside the doctor's door – at thirty, Rue du Dragon – studying the medical plaque on the wall, which is engraved with the name: *"Odette Moreaux – généraliste"*, he thought to himself that this is what separates him from the hopeless. The hopeless, like him have no home to go to, and no lover to find. They have no friends to meet and no money to spend. They may speak the language, and they may be in perfect health – that they have over David. But what they don't have, which may be more valuable than health, is someplace to go and something to look for. Health is often considered the prime possession, the greatest possible thing one can have, but is Hope not Health's twin brother? Can one remain healthy very long without Hope? Nothing deteriorates a man like the loss of Hope. Without something to look for, or someplace to head towards, the human body eventually shuts down. The heart stops beating. The blood ceases to course the veins. And the soft, delicate human body collapses to the ground, where it remains: lifeless.

But this would not happen to David. He was sick, yes. He felt like he might even die on this night, but he did not want to die and he had someplace he wanted to go, there was something he was looking for. He had lost everything, but he was in a new city and a new country and his Hope was alive. So, his poor heart kept beating and he kept on living. He kept on living and he kept on walking and when he buzzed the door of the doctor's office, an older woman answered and welcomed him into the dry and comfortable warmth inside.

"Il est un peu tard, non?" came from Doctor Moreaux, whose first name is 'Odette'. Her hair was wet from showering in her apartment, which adjoins her medical office, and she dried it with a towel when she answered the door. She wasn't at all afraid or surprised to see a sick man wearing a blood- and dirt-stained suit standing in the doorway of her medical office. Though it was late, Doctor Moreaux is used to getting all kinds of strange patients off the street coming to her door at all hours. Such is the life of a croaker: in this case, a government paid physician, providing sliding-scale services to a cast of recovering drug-addicts, who, more than occasionally, augments her wages by dispensing additional relief on the sly. She is good at her trade, and she is good at coldly turning these people away after-hours or at any other time she doesn't feel like dealing with them. She doesn't mind throwing the riffraff back out onto the street to sleep in the rain after they've walked all the way to her office to petition for medicine. Sometimes, they will find a hundred franc bill somewhere – steal it, or borrow it from someone – and give this to her, whereupon, she may, or may not, give them a couple of morphine tablets wrapped in a little piece of foil paper before turning them back out onto the street. But she did not turn David away, though it was after-hours. It was already ten o'clock when he arrived, but Odette let him in, without fear for her safety. She had no reason to fear for her safety. David had no intention of harming her. He just wanted medicine, and she knew this.

"*Il est un peu tard, …non?!*" she repeated her question, this time speaking louder.

"I don't understand," he said, in response to her question in French.

"It is a bit late, isn't it?" she repeated herself in English. She had just come from the shower, and was wearing a robe, with a garish pattern – some kind of orange kimono – and she wore bracelets and bangles on her thin, aging wrists. As she spoke, she waved her hands, and large, ceramic bangles clacked together on her wrists, mimicking the sound of horse hooves walking on pavement. Odette had bought those ceramic bangles in Barcelona. They were very expensive, yet she has never received a compliment on them – although she wears them everyday. Their clacking seem to inspire only insolence from her guests and patients.

"Are you English?" she asked, "…No, you must be the American that the Hospital St. Louis told me about, yes?"

"I am not American, I am French."

"Oh yes, they told me. You had a French passport. Yet, you can't speak French? … curious, indeed!" Odette surveyed the young man up and down.

"I've been in America all my life," replied David, "That's why I don't speak French."

"So what are you doing here?" she asked, laughing for no apparent reason. As she laughed her arms waved more and more, and even started to flail about, which made her Spanish bangles clank together like a stable full of horses running loose.

"I'm sorry to come at this time, Doctor … I should have waited a few more hours."

"In a few hours I'll be sleeping," she said as she knitted her brow together and eyed David suspiciously, "Anyway, it's okay, sit down." She directed him to a chair facing her desk. She then went around to the other side of the desk and took a seat, all the while staring at the odd looking patient who had just arrived at her office late at night in a blood-soiled suit.

"You are a curious looking thing, aren't you?" she asked him, still drying her thinning, dyed hair with a towel. David sat opposite her, slumping in his chair like an invalid. He asked her for some medicine for his pain. She asked him what was causing the pain. He told her it was his kidney. She believed he was probably in pain of some sort, judging from his appearance. She opened her desk drawer and pulled out a wrapper of foil containing two morphine tablets. She gave these to David and he swallowed them without water. Then as she spoke, his mind wandered and he began to look around at her office.

tenses

Odette's medical office is cluttered and the décor is noxious. Expensive and opulent furniture sits beside cheap fold-up chairs, tin standing ashtrays, and biohazard refuse containers. An examining table stands near one wall and a shelf of medical devices stands on the other. The desk is made of fine rosewood, yet its surface is covered with papers and books and various trinkets. A few amateurish, abstract paintings hang on the walls in gaudy, overly-ornamental gilded frames. Signs are posted everywhere in French. The only beautiful thing David saw, besides the rosewood desk, which was then covered with clutter anyway, is the window directly behind Odette when she sat at her desk. The window panes form an arch, and a beautifully carved bird nests on top of the arch, in an intricately carved, wooden eyrie. Through the window, David could see the twilight lighting up a little stone courtyard with a stone fountain. In the fountain, the broad leaves of tropical plants catch the falling water, whereupon it drips down the green stems, shimmering with silver in the twilight, and the water continues on its course, landing in the stone basin of the fountain. Trees could be seen through the window as well, their branches swayed with the light April wind. The moon began to show through the clouds and it shimmered on the water of the pond, reflecting lights of various hues.

David looked past Odette's head, staring out her window for sometime while she filled out some forms regarding this new patient. The morphine tablets soon began to take effect and David started to feel dreamy. The pain in his gut had vanished and he felt calm and peaceful and all he wanted to do was watch the water from the fountain drip off the broad leaves of the tropical plants outside in the silver twilight.

He mused on how close that fountain was. 'It's strange that her office is in the city," David thought to himself, "and it's on the ground-floor, yet she doesn't have bars on the windows.' ... 'It's better without bars,' he decides, 'that way, one can see the fountain.'

"What is wrong with you?" asked Odette at that moment.

"What?" replied David.

"Why are you here?"

"Oh, I...."

"Wait," she interrupted, "I can't look at you anymore in that bloody, filthy suit. Look!" she exclaimed, "You're making my chair all dirty." At this moment, Dr. Moreaux leapt from her own chair and ran around to where David was sitting, in a panic, as if she had just discovered that David's clothes were filthy. David quickly stood and began to brush the chair off.

"This is a very expensive chair! I had it sent from China!" Odette exclaimed to him. Moments later, she calmed down and asked, "Do you have anywhere to go tonight?"

"No," he replied.

"Okay, you can bathe here and change; and you can sleep on the sofa if you want," she told him. He looked around the room for a moment.

"I don't see a sofa," he said; yet, by this time, Odette had already left the room and was in an adjoining room, which served as her apartment. She beckoned David to follow her, and so he did.

The apartment of Dr. Moreaux is one large room, also opulently furnished without regard to taste. It only has two doors and one large window. One of the doors, the one David entered through, is the only door leading to the outside. And to get to the outside from Odette's apartment, one has to pass through her medical office. The second door leads to the bathroom and at this moment it was ajar and steam was pouring out from Odette's shower.

The window in the Odette's salon is somewhat larger than the window in her medical office, and it too has an arch crested with the beautiful carving of a bird. From the window in the salon, one can also see the same fountain in the courtyard outside, as is seen from the window in the office – though from this room it is somewhat farther away and the tropical plants catching the water are partially obscured by some white lattice. This window also doesn't have bars on it and David thought to himself that it must not be a very dangerous neighborhood where the doctor lives. 'True it is very calm outside,' he thought, 'one can't hear so much as a car, or a person's voice, or anything. This must be a very quiet neighborhood.' He stood and stared, and looked past the desk in the salon, through the window. Meanwhile, Odette went to the closet to get some clothes for him to wear after his shower.

'It's a good thing for her there are no bars on the windows,' he thought, 'because I see there are some latches on the window-shutters. Those latches probably unlock so that the shutters can be opened, and the doctor can go right out her window and sit by that beautiful fountain in the summertime. She probably also leaves the shutters open in the summer months so that the hot wind can blow in here … hmm,' he continued musing, 'It must be nice to have a home … If I ever have a home, I am going to take good care of it – and I am going to take good care to make sure I enjoy it. I'll never let a hot summer wind blow outside without having the windows open to let it in….' David continued thinking in this manner for sometime. His thoughts were made somewhat lighter and more foggy from the morphine that stirred softly in his head. He even forgot that he had been in so much pain only a half hour before. Now, pain was the farthest thing from him. He felt nothing but numbness. Then the doctor returned with some clothes.

"You can wear this suit," she said, handing him a dark brown, nicely tailored, double-breasted suit. David's eyes gleamed upon looking at it. He loved it – even more than the white one.

"Thank you! Thank you…" he started.

"You can't have it!" she interrupted, "It's my husband's. He's in Strasbourg on business. He'll be away for a couple more days. You can borrow it until he comes back. By then, you'll have to find a job so you can buy your own suit." … "Now come this way, I'll show you the shower."

"Thank you, Doctor."

"Call me 'Odette'."

"Thank you, Odette." David was at this moment, and for several moments after this – that is, until he fell asleep and had a most startling dream – very happy. Losing his fortune, of course, had been a stroke of the worst kind of luck there is. Yet, once again, after only being in France for a few days, he was being helped by an older person who didn't want his money; someone who only wanted to make sure he that he was clean and healthy. …And when he bathed and put on his new suit, he felt like a king. He was the poorest, most destitute, king that ever lived, but he didn't need money, for he had the help of the kind, older strangers who felt that he was a good person. David couldn't see any selfish motives for what Marc had done: feeding him, and clothing him, and taking him to the train station, and buying his ticket to Paris; and he couldn't find any selfish reasons for what Odette was doing. She could have given him the morphine tablets and sent him on his way. But she didn't. She lent him nice clothes and let him bathe, and later in the evening, after the two talked and David told her his story – about his coming from America, and about the pains he was suffering from – she gave him some tea and told him he could sleep on the leather sofa, which is right next to the bed upon which she sleeps.

Sitting on the leather sofa, David and Odette talked for quite a while longer… That is, until the tea came. While drinking the tea, David became very sleepy.

"What is this tea?" he asked, "It's good, but it is making me so sleepy."

"Doxylamine succinate," Odette replied.

"Oh," he said as he slumped on the sofa. Within moments, his heavy eyelids folded over his tired eyes and he fell into unconsciousness. And, as soon as he was asleep, he was swooped into a dream:

David sees himself as a young boy, and there is a carnival around him. No more than four, maybe five years old, he stands by the merry-go-round at the *Hôtel de Ville* in Paris. He had passed the *Hôtel de Ville* in the night just recently, while walking from the Hospital St. Louis to the bridge under which he had slept in a nest of fleas. But in this dream it is daylight. It even looks like morning. He doesn't ever remember seeing the *Hôtel de Ville* in daylight, yet he imagines it perfectly in his dream. Every detail of that vast ornamental palace is carved out to precision.

He holds his mother's hand. The colors are light and vernal and airy and the sounds of the carnival continue, making the young David laugh. He watches the horses spin around slowly bobbing up and down with little children grasping on to their reigns, also laughing. But their laughter turns to hysterical fear when the merry-go-round begins to spin faster and faster. The circus music too begins to get louder and more shrill and the young David becomes frightened. Panic takes hold of every muscle in his body. He wants to run away from there but his mother keeps holding his hand, squeezing it hard. He looks up at the young, pretty face of his mother – who seems to be no older than twenty-five in this dream - and he speaks to her in French, using words he never knew that he knew, *"Maman, j'ai faim!"*

"David," she replies to him, while the carnival music gets louder and louder, "you say, 'I am hungry' ... 'I am hungry', remember? When we get to America, they will only speak English. So we must *only* speak English, too. No French, okay?"

"But... but... *j'ai faim!*" the young David says pulling his mother's arm, so as to get away from the merry-go-round, which is spinning now even faster than before.

Then one of the painted horses leaps from the merry-go-round and bites David's leg. He cries out and tears stream from his eyes. The horse gallops away, taking the young David off by the leg, dragging him through the city square, off to devour him as spoil.

Then all is dark for a moment. David wakes up to find himself not at the *Hôtel de Ville*, nor anywhere in Paris. Now he is on the deck of a large boat – a pirate ship – which is rocking fiercely in a stormy sea. Despite the tremendous waves, the sailors manage to bring the boat in and dock it ashore. The men begin to unload the cargo while the dark rain pours down. Soon, night enshrouds all, and little David cries and looks everywhere for his mother.

Then the rocking of the boat ceases and all is calm, though it is still night. David sees his mother and his father, both very young, the latter in the handsome uniform of an officer, holding hands and walking down the pier towards the boat. David's mother takes her child's hand as the captain yells from bow, "Untie the ropes, or we're never gonna sail!"

Then the boat begins to sail and the land starts moving away from them. David's father picks him up and holds him, as his mother points to the land. She is smiling and saying to David in a cheerful voice...

"Come on, David. Say goodbye to Europe. Take Daddy's and Mommy's hands. We never have to see this country again. We're going to a new place to be happy."

"But I forgot *quelque chose, Maman!*" he says as he wakes up.

Lying on the sofa, he is alone. It is late and quiet. David looks over and sees the dark form of Odette sleeping in her bed, under a light sheet, just a few feet away. David looks to the ceiling and thinks quietly to himself. The vivid pictures of his dream resonate in his mind. His body is tired, his body is weary, but his mind is wild and pensive. 'It was a strange dream,' he thinks, trying to piece together every part of it from his memory as he lies there in the dark, on the sofa, with some sort of woolen rag for a blanket thrown over his body. He pulls back the woolen rag and sees that he has been undressed – not a stitch of clothing upon him except for a solitary sock on his left foot. He looks at his gaunt, naked body in the light of the moon, cast through the window, and he muses to himself: 'Doctors and nurses … they are almost magicians in the way they can undress someone who is sleeping, without that person waking up.'

He is no longer tired. The dream of his mother and father, the boat and the carnival, flashes through his mind, mingling with the startling memories of his recent past. He thinks to himself for a while, in the dark; and then, with his gamy thoughts, he gets up from the sofa and quietly walks over to the large window facing the courtyard.

Through the window, he sees the fountain. The water still pours from the spout to the basin, although it appears to be the middle of the night. Above the wavering trees outside, above the rooftops and over the chimneys, the moon floats broad and full – casting a beam of silver light through the courtyard, through the panes of glass, and across the surface of the wooden desk in front of the window. David looks at the desk. It is a fine one, also made of rosewood, but unlike the matching desk in Odette's office, this one is uncluttered. On its surface is a stack of writing paper, some loose stamps, and a sealed envelope with a Montblanc pen lying beside it. In the center of the desk there is a candle, a box of matches and a brass letter opener that looks like a tiny sword. Next to the sword is a hairpin with a jade leaf at one end. The other end is pushed into a wine cork. Next to the cork there are two wine glasses and a heavy cruet made of thick lead crystal. In the cruet is some red wine.

David takes the matches and lights the candle. He sits down in the desk chair with his back against the large window. He watches the candle flame dance on the facets of the crystal cruet, that elegantly shaped vessel that contains wine instead of vinegar. He muses on the beauty of the crystal cruet and watches the hypnotizing patterns of the flame skip across the illuminated facets. In the room, so dark, – except for a moonbeam that enters through the window, and a candle which flickers on the desk, – the young man kneels by the window. He hears the soft, feminine breathing of the old doctor lying naked beneath the thin sheet on her bed. He smells the odor and fragrance of mildew and lavender wafting over from a pot of dried flowers in the corner of the room; and he sees that candle flame dancing like a Spanish woman in a red and yellow dress on the facets of the cruet. He stares for a long time at that light shimmering on the crystal vessel. And, kneeling there upon the floor, he falls again to sleep.

About that which has happened meanwhile at the great aristocratic home of the Monsieur de Chevalier…

It has been a full day and night since we were last at the home of M. de Chevalier on Rue de Paradis; and, lest we let anything slip by that might be detrimental to the development of our story, we mustn't go anywhere else, right now, except back to the tenth arrondissement of Paris, to see the events that occurred over the last day and night, as they pertain to Nastya – the heroine of our story:

While David was sleeping with his harem of fleas beneath the *Pont Alexandre III* on the Seine, Nastya was being entertained in the three-roomed apartment of the man who had sent her the letter inviting her to come to Paris to begin a career as a dancer in the city's finest ballet. The train ride from Moscow had been interminably long, and Nastya was obviously very tired from the voyage; thus, after arriving, she only wanted to make a brief, polite acquaintance with the man, before seeing her room and going to sleep in the bed he had provided for her. The Monsieur, on the other hand, was so happy to have this young beauty in his home, that he urged her to stay up with him and toast to their health, and toast to their future, and toast to the ballet and anything else he could think of. He had no desire to let the poor girl get any rest, and so the commotion continued late into the night. Take this instance, for instance:

"I know what it looks like to you, coming here," says the Monsieur as he parades around his apartment in his French army uniform, pointing at all the rubbish that is piled in the corners. "It must look like I invited you here from Russia to live in a swamp." He is beginning to get a little drunk, and his cheeks flame with bright red spots, "It isn't a swamp though, my dear; and I don't know what Russia looks like, because that may be all swampy too! But this here is not a swamp. It is my apartment... and there is much *love* in my apartment. Even when I am alone – and I am, mostly, or always, alone, mind you! – that is, except when I have a good friend visiting; because I have often a good friend visiting from some foreign place or from right here in Paris, and as I was saying... yes! There is *love* here! And for *that*, it is not a swamp!" ... "But I know how it must look to you. Though, it is really a nice apartment. The foundation is solid. It was built during the reign of Napoleon – Bonaparte, I mean: the *good* Napoleon. ...And the neighborhood is very lively ... very ... well ... *different*. You'll see. Always a commotion outside. But here there is no commotion ... in *here*, we have *love*!" The man holds his heart with both of his hands as he appeals to Nastya who is seated on the sofa in her elegant black dress. Her legs are crossed, the schnapps have worn off, and she is completely sober. She bites her lower lip and looks up at this man who is twirling around the room, holding his heart and toasting his glass against the windows and the vases on the shelves.

Then Nastya speaks... "It's cold, Monsieur de Chevalier. Can you close the window, please?" She begins to shiver slightly.

"Not *Monsieur de Chevalier!* No, not *that!*" he clasps his hands and stops twirling to speak to the young lady, "...We are friends now. Call me *Jean Salaud*... no, don't call me *that!* Call me... let's see. You are Russian, yes? You have a Russian name, yes? Well, give me a Russian name too." ... "Call me *Salochka!* No, no, better yet: *Salaudski!* ...It's a great Russian name isn't it?"

"It sounds more Polish than Russian." Nastya eyes him strangely.

"...I'll be *Salaudski* and you be my *Naski!*" he continues, not listening to Nastya.

"But what is your name?" she asks.

"Well it's... it's the *Monsieur de Chevalier*, of course; except that's awful long, so you just call me *Salaudski*. It's shorter. More frrrriendly" he rolls the word 'friendly' over his tongue as he sips his schnapps, "I want us to be great frrrriends, here. *Bons amis!* Two members of the same...." Then Nastya interrupts him:

"Well, what do your other friends call you?"

"Why, *Monsieur de Chevalier*, of course; except that's a little long. Don't you think that's long? You can call me something more friendlike, more...."

"Okay, *Sal... Salaudski*," Nastya agrees. She thinks back on all that Salaudski has been saying. Some of the words slipped by her. Her English is very good but Salaudski speaks too fast, and his accent is heavy. At first, she felt that what he was saying was important; but now she decides that it probably isn't too important, after all. All she wants to do now is change out of her nice clothes and go to sleep for the night.

"...I can speak a good gentleman's English, don't you think? I pick up languages faster than a parrot, I assure you," Salaudski continues, feigning an Oxford accent, "Just you watch, after a few weeks of your being in Paris, I'll even be able to speak Russian – just like a regular Pushkin...." At this, Nastya laughs without restraint. Perhaps because of her extreme tiredness, his statement seems to be one of the funniest things she's ever heard. He scoffs playfully at her and continues, "...I learned English when I was stationed in Wales, during the war ... the hillsides were being shelled at night; and all morning long, we had to clean up the men who had fallen. And as we walked around with those wheelbarrows, picking up the men who had been hit by shellfire in the night, I would speak to the other soldiers. They were all English. Everyone was English. I was the only Frenchman stationed in Wales at that time – and for that, my Motherland awarded me the *Croix Rouge*. Have you ever seen a *Croix Rouge?*" He asks Nastya while pointing to a tin medal on his breast. Meanwhile, instead of paying attention to the old man's stories, Nastya gets up and goes to her suitcase to retrieve a coat that she has packed away. She puts on the wooly black coat over her light black dress and returns to sit on the sofa.

"But you're getting your coat on, you're leaving already? You just got here. Oh, stay and have one more drink!..."

"I'm not leaving, I have nowhere to go," she says to him, shocked by his last statement, "It's just cold."

"It's cold." reiterates Salaudski, "It is cold, I know. They took the heat." ... "You know, my dear, I am an aristocrat." ... "It may look as though I'm not, but let me educate you to French history" ... "The aristocrats have never had any money in France. We have no money, no... But we have influence!" ... "Influence, I tell you, we do have, my dear!" ... "Don't worry about that!" ... "They took the heat, but in my room it is warm. If you want you can go sleep now, I'll be along later.

No heat in here, but my room is a furnace! 'Hotter than Hades' – as they say in Athens!"

"It's all right, I'll stay here on the sofa, I'm used to the cold," says Nastya.

"Of course you are. I didn't mean to suggest otherwise. I implore you to forgive me if I made to seem like you were not used to the cold – you are Russian, I am sorry." ... "But you will need to sleep well tonight. You know, you are a great dancer, Anastasia; this is why I asked you to come to Paris. Tomorrow night, we have a dinner party with none other than the director of the grand Opéra Garnier!" ... "That, my little lamb, is the influence of my good blood!" ... "A meeting with the director of the Opéra Garnier! Tomorrow night, *we dine together* – the three of us!" ... "The *four* of us, I mean. His wife, too. She will be coming. She is lovely – a real plum! You will need to look nice, too. You'll need to sleep well tonight. You shouldn't look tired. Are you tired? You don't look as bright and shiny as you do on the poster...."

Nastya, who has been listening with great attention ever since Salaudski brought up the meeting with the director of the Opéra Garnier, now looks at the posters of herself, pasted all over his walls.

'He's right, Nastya,' she tells herself, 'when you modeled for that silly poster you were a lot brighter and a lot shinier. Now you are tired – tired and wrinkled from traveling.'

Then she begins to speak, interrupting Salaudski, who is beginning to go off on another subject... "But how can I look bright and shiny in that poster? It's just a lithograph!" she laughs playfully, looking straight at him. He then stops talking and gesturing his hands, and dropping his arms, he stands very still for a moment, looking carefully at Nastya's expression – as if to understand if she is making fun of him or not. For a moment he has a look of fear on his face. Then he realizes that she is just playing with him and he too starts to laugh...

"Yes, a bright and shiny poster, that's a funny idea! Ha!" ... "But really, Anastasia, it is important that you don't look tired tomorrow night. Come! Come to my room, it is warmer."

"Don't you have a separate room for me?" she asks.

"Well, yes. Of course. It's just not as warm, that's all. The air is a little cool. But I guess you have a body to warm it up, so I'll take you there." The liquor Salaudski has been drinking begins to make him feel weary. Either it is the liquor or it is Nastya's request to sleep alone. One of these suddenly dampens the mood for Salaudski and he wipes his brow that became covered in sweat during the excitement of the two's meeting, and he huffs a bit; and then he helps the young lady up from the sofa and shows her to her room.

"May I just kiss the tip of your hand, before I leave you, my fair?"

"Of course," says Nastya in a tired voice, as she sits on the edge of the bed. She holds her hand out to be kissed. Salaudski kisses not just the tip of her hand, but the palm of the hand as well. Then he sits on the edge of the bed beside her. She throws him a questioning glance – one of slight disapproval.

Salaudski eventually leaves Nastya's room – but only after several minutes of hand-kissing and fervent protests against her sleeping in the cold guestroom all alone when she has 'the opportunity to come to sleep in a warm furnace'.

When finally she successfully asserts that he goes to bed alone, he stands and bows and entreats her one more time to allow him to kiss her hand – but 'just the tip!' After the third entreaty, she forbids further enjoyment of her hand and orders him to go to bed, promising that the two will have plenty of time to see more of each other, starting the following morning.

Alone in a tiny room that is half-occupied by a tiny bed, no bigger than Nastya's bed in her parents' home on Sokolniki Street, Nastya sits with her coat on, waiting to take her clothes off until all is quiet and no sounds can be heard on the other side of the door. Finally silence arrives, yet moments after it is broken, as a clamoring begins in the kitchen where Salaudski is apparently making something to eat. She can hear pots banging and tin-cans being opened behind the closed door. She sits on the edge of the bed and waits.

As soon as all is still again, Nastya undresses and folds her black dress, placing it on an empty shelf above the foot of the bed. She then puts on her white nightgown, which she had packed in her suitcase; and she slips her body beneath the tattered, wool blanket on the bed. Nastya then turns off the lamp by the bed and the room darkens. She listens again for sounds in the kitchen – all is quiet. The moon comes through the window in a broad beam that casts itself across the bed. The tattered, wool blanket is too warm. The room isn't cold as Salaudski said it would be. She is very tired but she spends a long time watching the moon out the little window above her bed. As a little girl, she sometimes wondered if the moon looked the same in France as it does in Russia. Now she sees that it does. The clouds soon cover up that moon and Nastya falls into a deep and silent sleep.

CHAPTER IX

Through an innocent death, the songbird heralds the coming of spring. With his death, Nastya's life in Europe began. She didn't ask for a sacrifice; nevertheless, he gave his life to wake the sleeping girl.

This is how it began. A bird, flying from the north-east, at nine-thirty in the morning, crashed against a pane of glass in the window of M. de Chevalier's guestroom, in the fifth-floor apartment, where Nastya had been sleeping. The collision had no effect on the window, except to dirty it slightly. The effect the impact had on the bird was fatal – its wishbone snapped in two. The only effect it had on Nastya was to wake her up with a loud *thud* – the sound of its body hitting the glass – beyond that, she didn't even realize what had happened. A moment ago, she was asleep, dreaming of something taking place back home in Russia. Now, she is awake and alert, sitting up in a tiny bed in a foreign country.

For a moment, she longed to be back in her dream – back in Russia. Now, when she realizes that she is in France, that she is awake, and that this is reality and not at all like a dream, she becomes very happy and very excited and immediately, she crawls out of bed to go explore the curious world she has entered.

After climbing out of bed, she takes off her white nightgown and dresses in a light-colored shirt and a pair of linen pants, most fitting for a vernal day in a city such as Paris. She then tiptoes out of her cramped little room, in an effort not to wake her host, in the event that he is still sleeping. Her efforts though are useless. He is not still asleep. When she enters his salon, she finds a note from him and sees that he is not home at all:

"My little lamm [sic] ... hope you slept well ... out on urgent busyness [sic]... back for lunch ... there is a grapefruit on the counter ... Gros Bisous!" ... "- Me."

This note is scrawled in shaky handwriting on the back of a horseracing ticket; and is not at all similar to the invitation that was mailed to Moscow, which was far more eloquent in style and form. Here, even the handwriting is different. Nastya looks around in the corners of the flat, in the man's bedroom, in the kitchen; and, seeing that no one else is home at all, she feels happy. This happiness is intensified when a little beam of sunlight penetrates the far window, illuminating the dust that floats in the air of the salon. Nastya runs to the window and, turning the latch, lifts it open wide.

Smiling, she sticks her head out of the window, taking a breath of the spring morning air. It is that Parisian air of the warm, springtime mornings in the tenth arrondissement, which is so fragrant with lavender, offal, saffron and carrion. No other quarter in Paris balances these smells so evenly.

Outside, the sky is a pasty blue like the frosting on a cake and all the little buildings on Rue de Paradis are gleaming with the golden glow of the morning sun. Down below on the street, little Arab boys and Persian cats can be seen playing with the garbage that lines the curbs. They all look so happy.

One little solitary car putters down the road and young men in the backseat whistle out the open windows to a woman who stands on the corner, adjusting her bootstrap; and little birds – robins and cardinals and bluebirds and sparrows – flit through the sky, catching the morning light on their flapping wings, bathing their little bird heads in the sun as they fly. One can tell that the sun has just risen over the buildings and everyone in the neighborhood is just now getting used to it being here.

Nastya feels the warmth and the brightness on her face for a few moments; then she closes the window and skips over to her suitcase off in the guestroom, where she gets her little white shoes and laces them up; and, putting the invitation from M. de Chevalier in her pocket so she will have his address in order to find her way back, she skips out the front door and leaves the apartment. And off she goes, down the circular staircase, from the fifth to the ground floor, and out onto the street, to take a walk in the nice light of day.

near Gare du Nord

Nastya walks down Rue de Paradis and looks around at all the novel sights that wait to greet her: the grey, zinc rooftops atop buildings constructed with sheer, white stones; the children running through the streets, chasing their cats, and calling to them in French; the young fathers and mothers, chasing after these children, pushing babies in little carts, while the cars chase after them.

She sees lost tourists looking at maps of the city; and men wheeling wagons, selling maps of the city, along with balloons and bubblegum. She sees shady cutpurses and dealers hiding in the doorways; and she passes by 'the wailing man', and walks quickly so as not to be forced to hear his wailing for too long. Then she comes to <u>a sort of river.</u>

The waves on the river flow and cascade with glimmering sparkles of sunlight on their tips. These jewels of sun dance like a handful of diamonds thrown over the golden sand of a dessert or the light green grass of a meadow. Nastya dips her hand over the edge of the white stones, which form the bank of this river; and as cool alluvion flows up against her hand, the alluvium settles on her fingers, in little dark specks. So the all<u>uv</u>ion flows and the alluvium grows on the hand of Nastya which caresses the river's surface, as she dangles over the edge, laughing in the new experience.

?

Once her hand is all covered black with the sediment from the water, she waves it around in the tips of the waves, to clean it; and then she pushes herself up from the stone embankment and looks out at far as she can over the river.

On the other side, apartment houses and cathedrals shoot up into the pasty blue sky. They are built awfully close to the river and Nastya wonders if they ever tumble and fall in.

She looks again to the river, and its cascading waves that catch the sun. How happy she is to see this. How happy she is to be here. Despite all her worry and all her fear, for what may or may not happen. That will all come later if it ever comes. Now she is under the kind warmth of the sun and now she is beside the peaceful flow of the river, and now everything is fine and all is glorious. Now it is springtime, and all is fine, and the only thing she knows she mustn't do is waste the spring.

She sits on the white stone embankment of the river, watching the crystal facets of the blue water and their sunny jewels encrusted in them. She watches this and thinks to herself: 'So this is the Seine ... it is so much smaller than the Volga or the Neva or all the other rivers in Russia.' ...While she muses on this, a man approaches her. He is walking like a marionette on strings and his face is pale – deathly pale – yet he is not dead, nor even near death. He is just a mime, and his face is made pale with makeup.

The mime puts his face in front of Nastya's and bobs it back and forth like the pendulum on a clock; all the while wearing a silly grin, he blinks his eyes with the tick of the second hand. Nastya smiles at the mime and points at the river, *"La Seine?"* she asks.

"No," says the mime, in English, "It's the *Canal St. Martin.* The Seine is a long ways away." The mime sits down beside Nastya on the bank of the canal, but Nastya doesn't seem to notice that he wants to speak with her. She just looks out on the water of the canal, watching the shimmers of light. The mime looks at her intently, yet she does not notice. Finally, after a few moments, she stands and continues walking down the road.

Nastya comes to a vendor selling chestnuts. He roasts them in a large metal basin that looks like a steel drum. She puts her face close to the drum and stares at these chestnuts with the utmost curiosity. She has never, hitherto, seen anything like them. The vendor smiles at the young beauty, and speaks...

"Bonjour, ma belle! ...Qu'est ce que vous voulez?"

Nastya looks at his dark round face, as he says these nonsensical words. She smiles a great smile – a great, sincere smile – and she shakes her head back and forth to let him know that she doesn't understand of what he is speaking. Then, as happy as can be, in the light of the morning sun, she walks off, continuing on down the road.

Thus, the morning went on for Nastya – a parade of new sights and innocent discoveries, and when she finally wanders back to forty-seven, Rue de Paradis, she has still the happy air of someone who has just been born to a new a wonderful world.

It was so bright on the street – so fresh and clean, despite the carrion. But when she enters the lobby in M. de Chevalier's apartment building, the atmosphere is dim and the air is musty. Once Nastya closes the main front door – once she is inside the lobby – she is overcome by the mustiness of the air, and she sneezes. After sneezing, she hears two doors creak open simultaneously. The one on the left is the landlady's door. She looks to the one on the right.

Peering out of the door on the right, she sees those same eyes from the night before looking out from darkness at her. She cannot see the face, only the eyes. They are the eyes of a man, and they have mystery in them. She is frightened by them, but she doesn't know why; she cannot read them or even question them, for as soon as she looks at the eyes, they disappear and the door closes. Nastya turns around quickly and puts her hand on her chest, over her pounding heart. She then notices the landlady peeking her head out of the other door – the door on the left. She also wants a look at Nastya, as the latter enters the building. The landlady's door creaks open and the short, old woman, peering out into the hall, erupts with a kind and scratchy laugh. "Eh, hee hee!" she laughs.

"Oh, good morning!" Nastya says, turning around, with a happy and innocent tone in her voice. The landlady opens her door wide and hobbles out in the hallway.

Meanwhile, on the fifth-floor of the same building, Salaudski, or the *Monsieur de Chevalier*, if you'd rather, is standing in his kitchen, making himself a sandwich, and wondering where that 'pesky ballerina' went off to. He is not truly afraid that she has left him for good, although the terrible possibility of that keeps nagging at him. He has become slightly worried, though he has the feeling that everything will be fine. He knows she will come back, 'she has probably just went for a walk … and besides, her suitcase is still in her room'.

Downstairs in the foyer, Nastya is thinking about that man who just kept staring at her. His door was open a crack and he just kept staring out at her, with those strange and frightening eyes; those eyes that carried, at the same time, so much intrigue, and so much mystery…

"Who is that man? Why does he look out like *that?* …With *those* eyes?" Nastya asks the landlady in a hushed, secretive voice – the kind of voice which is only used among girls, when conspiring together in a mischievous plan. The landlady watches Nastya's eyes grow big and roars with laughter at her question…

"Oh, *ma chérie*, you must think horrible things about the people who live in my building Yes, that man's a creep," the landlady says this while brandishing her cane in the direction of the man's apartment across the hall, "he scares all the people, it's true, – well, all the girls, – but he stays in his apartment, and he pays me on time each month, so I let him stay." … "Ah!" she continues speaking to Nastya, "you are a pretty girl, yes? *T'es vachement belle!* You should meet my grandson. His name is Patrick Schwarz. *Schwarz*, I know – but his father was the German. I can't help that. But he's my grandson, *cent percent*, and he's a genius. You two would fall so much in love, I know it! … He's working for the *Institut Pasteur*. He's getting his PhD, you realize? He just cuts up mice all day … cuts them and gives them diseases, you see. But soon he'll have a Nobel Prize. He's my grandson … smart as a whip!" … "*Mais, ma chérie*, you must get away from that *salaud* upstairs … he's a real *salaud*, and he'll do you in … he'll do you in, I tell you…!"

This whole time, Salaudski has been cutting up pieces of gruyere cheese to put in his sandwich, while turning over the possibilities in his head of where Nastya went off to all by herself. He spreads the mayonnaise on his baguette and puts thin slices of gruyere inside the bread, with cornichons and tomatoes. Then, he folds the sandwich together and takes a bite. Just then, his front door opens quietly…

Nastya walks in on tip-toes with a radiant smile on her face; and when she sees the old man standing there with tousled hair, and a long sandwich sticking out of his mouth, she laughs aloud…

"Hell-o, Sal-o!" she giggles, pointing at the man with his mouth full; whereupon, he takes the sandwich out quickly, and sets it down on a small, square wooden table in the vestibule.

"What?! 'Sal-o'? … Why do you call me *that?!*" demands the man impatiently, while spitting bits of sandwich out of his mouth. The happiness he felt upon first seeing the young lady walk into his house disappears and his face flushes red with an expression that suggests that he **is** quite angry.

"The landlady called you that just a minute, ago … when I was downstairs. She said that was your name…." Nastya says, while rubbing her fingers against the palms of her hands out of nervousness. Seeing how red his face has become, how distorted with anger it now is, she worries that she has just accidentally insulted him to a degree that can't be lessened with an apology. While nervously rubbing her fingertips against her palms, she continues to speak… "I'm sorry I came back so late. I am sorry. It is very pretty outside, and…."

"She calls me that?! … *'Sal-o'?* … *Bastard?!!*" Salaudski continues on, "…That witch! Doesn't she realize I served in the army of her country?!" … "When she was hiding in her raggedy culottes, in her raggedy apartment for twenty years, I was marching over Paris with our French flag! I was marching to Weimar – to Berlin! …while bombs were raining down! I took a bomb in my leg for France – for *her* country and she calls me *what*?!" At this point, he has the leg of his trousers lifted up to reveal an old man's pale white leg covered in little light curly hairs. He slaps his leg with his hand, while looking at Nastya with a face flushed bright red from anger. His leg wobbles like confiture when he slaps it.

"Is there no more honor for the aristocrats of France?" he demands of her. Nastya doesn't answer but rather just stands there, with a worried look on her face. Salaudski then repeats the answer while throwing his fist down against the surface of the small square wooden table in the salon; but instead of his fist hitting the table's wooden surface, it lands square in the middle of the sandwich that he had set there – and mayonnaise shoots out of the sandwich, splattering on his belly. Nastya sees this and begins to giggle. Salaudski then looks at her intently, as if trying to find out why the girl started giggling again. Just then, he too begins to laugh. He throws his head back and chuckles … but then he stops and grabs his bare, pale leg again with both hands.

"Oh, my poor leg," he cries, "we must give respect! …If not to me, at least we must give respect to my poor leg!" When he says this, his leg starts trembling even more than before, and the old man loses his balance and falls to his knees. He looks up at the girl who towers over him. She bends down to help him up. As she helps him to his feet, he – who is exhausted from the stumble and the flagrant display of emotions – says to her…

"You look very beautiful today! Oh, yes, quite a beauty. Nevermind my aristocratic leg. Let's go to the Opéra to see that they make you a dancer!"

Nastya nods her head to Salaudski. Then a broad smile begins to form on her face and she turns around and skips happily off to her room to change clothes.

A few moments later, Salaudski is also changing his clothes. He stands before the long mirror in his bedroom – beside a bed heaped with clean but wrinkled clothing. He is tying a tie and humming an old French marching tune: "dee, dahl, ee, dum! … dee, dahl, ee, deeee!" Then Nastya's voice comes from the other room. She has finished putting on her black dress from the night before, and now she slips into her heels.

"But I thought we weren't meeting the director until tonight?" Nastya asks loudly from the other room, "…at dinner, I mean?"

"No dinner. No, not tonight, anyhow. We'll have a social dinner with the director and his wife in a few days – maybe next week. But that will be a *social* dinner – after they've already started you dancing. Today is the *business* meeting. Today you go to meet the director at his office."

"But you told me last night that we were having dinner together tonight … you, me and the director and his wife!" She walks into Salaudski's room to say this; and, at his request, she starts helping him to tie his tie.

"…But I don't know how to tie a man's tie," says Nastya.

"Well, who does, really?" replies Salaudski. He then answers her question from before, "…That's what the 'urgent business' was about, today. I was at the restaurant, making sure our table is reserved … the best table … the one with the fish tank full of carp … and, so you know, the owner of the restaurant filled me in on the whole story. We're to have a social dinner later on … today is a business meeting, down at the Opéra … Anastasia, you are choking me!"

"Well, I told you I don't know how to tie a tie!"

"That's okay, I'll do it." He grabs his tie, and Nastya backs away. Then Salaudski turns to look at Nastya, who is all dressed and made up, "Oh, Anastasia, you look like a star! …A shining star! The kind that do not fall out of the sky…!" his eyes begin to glimmer a little with emotion when he looks at her, "I'm very glad you are here," and he pauses a moment, "Did you get to see a little of Paris, today?"

"Oh, yes, I did! …Me too, I am also glad that I am here!"

Salaudski offers his arm, on which dangle brass military medals adorned with various colors of yarn, and Nastya takes it, happily. The two walk out of the man's bedroom and pass through his entryway. He takes his ring of keys from the table where his sandwich still sits, and the two walk arm in arm down the stairs, out the door, and down Rue de Paradis, on their way to the Opéra Garnier.

David's last, brief meeting with Odette before the incidences occur which dramatically change our story…

This last night, David enjoyed a cup of tea, chez Odette; and during the tea, unconsciousness came along swiftly and quickly swept him up. Now it is morning and he wakes up alone at the fault of the sun shining on his eyelids through the large bay window. His head is groggy and his thoughts are foggy. It feels as though he has only slept for a moment – or as if he has been sleeping for eleven years. Now sitting on the edge of the bed, he tries to collect his thoughts. He wonders why his head feels as it does – as if, instead of brains, it is stuffed full of lint. He wonders why he is again naked in this old doctor's bed – and where is the old doctor? The room is all quiet. He has never been in the habit of sleeping naked. What happened this last night, before going to sleep? He tries to piece together the little bits of his memory, which run astray. He stands and looks for some clothes to cover his body with. Then the usual pain, his everyday enemy, recommences in his gut; and his skin beads with sweat. He can feel the fever starting. The pain starts fluttering in his belly, as if a bird is inside him, trying to catch flight; and every time one of its wings hits the lining of his stomach, it sends a twinge of pain and nausea all throughout his body. He could use some of the doctor's medicine. He could use a cup of coffee, too.

David wraps one of Odette's husband's white bathrobes – monogrammed with the initial, 'H', embroidered in gold thread – around him and walks over to the door leading to Odette's medical office, which is, no doubt, where the doctor is hiding.

Standing next to the closed door, David hears a loud commotion in the adjoining medical office. He tries the knob but the door is bolted from the other side. He knocks loudly so as to be heard over the cacophony.

The fumbling of keys is heard on the other side of the wall. Then, the door opens and Odette, wearing a white medical coat and a stethoscope, stands in the open doorway looking up at her patient dressed in her husband's bathrobe.

"Well, good morning," she says to David, almost shouting so as to be heard over everyone. There is a large group of people gathered in her office and they are all grumbling about something.

"Dr. Moreaux? *Venez vite!*" comes from a man seated in a fold-up chair, in a low-pitched, quivering voice that sounds like a lamb baaing – a voice that is so commonly found among junk addicts. With one hand, the crying lamb holds his arm, where he has just tried to self-administer an injection – until he was stopped by Odette's intern. His other hand clasps his gaping mouth and unshaven chin with anxiety as he calls to the doctor, asking her to come quickly.

Odette turns her back to David for a moment and looks at the patient who is glancing skittishly around him in confusion and anguish. The other patients call out to the doctor, competing for her attention. Right then a girl, dressed as a nurse in a gleaming white coat, rushes over to the doctor who is standing near David in the open doorway. The girl is Odette's intern, and she is quite young – about twenty-one or twenty-two years of age. She has light blonde hair, bright blue eyes and tawny skin. She is a very beautiful girl and David watches her admiringly as she approaches.

"*Docteur....*" the intern begins, but she is interrupted as a dwarfish looking man, with a fuzzy orange beard and straggly long dirty hair, jumps in front of her – it is the man who tried to inject himself. He stands before the doctor, begging her…

"*Docteur, j'ai besoin d'un autre comprimé!*"

Then the intern regains her position beside the doctor and informs her in a voice of urgency: "*Docteur Moreaux, il a tenté de se faire une injection – donc, je lui ai confisqué son comprimé!*"

"*C'est vrai, Luc? Vous avez fait ça?*" Odette turns to the patient, alarmed that he has just tried to inject himself with his medicine.

Then Luc responds, in nervous agitation, as he clasps his trembling jaw in anxiety, "*Ben, oui … mais … le medicament n'est pas assez fort! Et, je fais des cauchemars depuis une semaine. …J'ai l'impression que je vais mourir comme ça!*" … "*S'il vous plait, Madame? S'il vous plait… je vous en supplie … ah!*" …he finally screams out, gasping an imploring gasp. He repeats, over and over, that he has had nightmares every night for the last week and he is afraid he is going to die with this sort of medical treatment. He is sincerely afraid.

Luc is just going through the withdrawals of a ten year junk habit; and, like most patients with an old habit, he feels like the medication isn't strong enough and that the doctor is making a grave mistake by not encouraging him to keep shooting-up. In such cases, the patient feels that the doctor just isn't aware of his or her unique circumstances, which call for a treatment that differs from that which is given to the others. Patients such as Luc truly believe that they will die if the doctor's orders are followed.

"Du calme!" Odette looks down at her dwarfish patient, using a firm voice, *"Combien en prenez-vous par jour? ...8 mg?"* She sets her clipboard down and walks over to her desk drawer. Opening it, she takes out a blister of tablets, *"Je vais augmenter votre dosage à 16mg pour l'instant. ... Approchez! ... Sous la langue!"* Odette puts the large, white opioid tablet in the dirty, outstretched hand of Luc, and she watches him to make sure he puts it under his tongue and keeps it there, until it dissolves. Then Odette turns to her young intern…

"Assure-toi qu'il n'ait pas de seringue," Odette orders her, assuming that Luc has more syringes hidden in his pockets. Odette has been in this business for many years, and she knows all of the junkies' tricks.

"Entendu, Docteur Moreaux," replies the intern, in a respectful, subservient tone. Then the pretty intern walks away, bringing Luc along by the sleeve. She sits him down and checks his pockets and checks under his tongue to see that the tablet has dissolved. White pharmaceutical saliva ferments on his lips and he licks them. Once, his tablet has dissolved, he opens his mouth and lifts his tongue to show the intern. He licks the specks of white and the creamy saliva off his lips; and the intern, satisfied, moves on down the line, dispensing the opioid tablets to rest the hungry, fiendish patients who line the walls, rocking back and forth in their chairs, wrought with anxiety and despair.

In the medical office, the intern is asked by Dr. Moreaux to handle the patients for the rest of the morning. Dr. Moreaux then ushers David back into her salon and asks him to have a seat in the chair facing her desk. In a few moments, after locking the door so the two have privacy and setting some water to boil so the doctor may have her tea, she comes around and sits in her leather desk chair, facing David.

"Please don't come into the office wearing just a bathrobe again," she begins, "…at least not when there are patients in there, okay?"

"I'm sorry … I couldn't find my clothes this morning … when I woke up, I wasn't wearing anything … it was a little strange." David says this, curious of Odette's response. He watches her eyes while he speaks, though halfway through his sentence – as the pain in his stomach grows worse – he loses interest in speaking and begins to hunger for her medication.

"Yes, I had to undress you. It was not a pretty sight. You were in a terrible fever last night and you were pale and covered with sweat, don't you remember?" … "No?" … "Oh well, if I had left you in your clothes, you would have burned up in the night!" … "Why are you looking at me like that?" … "You laugh, but it's not funny, your fever was really high. I did a great thing for you, undressing you and pressing a cold washcloth to your forehead for the whole evening."

"I didn't mean to laugh," David responds, "I mean … well … thank you, I don't remember anything from last night."

"Well, you were quite a responsibility last night. It's seems that you are feeling better today, I'm glad…!"

"Actually, Odette, I'm not doing so good today. Do you think I could have some more medicine – for the pain?"

"You know, David … Luc, that patient I was just talking to, he sleeps at *Gare de l'Est* – right out in front of the ~~train~~ station. You could join him, you know. It's still cold enough outside to suffer…"

"But, I didn't…" David tries to interject, but she continues speaking over him:

"…In fact, most of those patients out there in my office sleep outside, someplace or another."

"But why do you say these things, Odette? What did I do to make you…."

"Nothing," she interrupts, "you did nothing. I just want you to understand that I am going beyond my duty as a doctor by letting you sleep at my house, bathe at my house, wear my husband's clothes; and don't forget the medications I have already given you. They are not free. Somebody has to pay for them."

"Odette," David protests, "I never asked you to for a bathe – neither for a bed. And if you don't want to give me medication for free, then I'll pay for it. Though since I cannot pay for it, I just won't take it. I never asked for…." Yet, he is then interrupted as Odette waves her hands in annoyance…

"Stop, please stop! This is annoying. I just have to make it real clear that what I am offering you is a special privilege. It is not your right to receive my services – and what I am doing for you is indeed a service.

I am doing it because I like you. I think you are a nice young man and you deserve to be better off than those other junkies in the other room."

At this point, David stops talking. He doesn't see how anything he could say could benefit him at all. He decides to just sit and wait. He folds his hands in his lap and looks beyond Odette to the arched window behind her. From where he is sitting, he can clearly see the fountain outside. The morning is bright and he watches the sunlight shimmering on the water dripping from the broad leaves of the elephant ears that catch the flow of water from the fountainhead above. It is the first time he has looked out at this fountain during daylight. 'It is prettier at twilight,' he thinks to himself. The increasing pain in his body is robbing him of the ability to see anything as being very beautiful at the moment. Not even picturing the face of Odette's intern brings him joy.

After a moment, Odette arrests his wandering mind: "I spoke to the hospital where you were the other night," she informs him, while scanning a clipboard in her hand, "They got your test results back from the lab."

"And what were they?" David asks, shifting all his attention to the doctor who addresses him with a blank face and the tone of indifference. He scoots his chair forward, with a sudden, nervous unease.

"Well, first of all, they would like to be paid their forty-three hundred francs. Do you know when you will be able to do that?"

"You know I have no money ... what were the results?"

"Well, they would like to be paid soon – then they will return your passport to you ... Anyway, your tests showed nothing. ... No liver damage, no kidney damage, no stones, no irregularities in white or red blood cell levels. Your thyroid is fine, your glucose levels are fine ... basically, no abnormalities." ... "Physically speaking, you are a perfectly healthy young man..." Odette relays these results in a reserved, almost rueful, voice; and David assumes that the bad news has just yet to be relayed. He waits in nervous agitation for the death sentence.

"I don't understand," David breathes through trembling lips.

"I don't either," Odette responds, "Why exactly did you go to the hospital in America?"

"Because of kidney stones, which caused a severe kidney infection as a result from the stones cutting the tissue as they passed. At least, that's what *Dr. So-and-so* told me...."

At right about this moment, David is suddenly overcome by a pleasurable sensation, which eases the pain in his body and stops the sad thoughts in his mind. The origin of this sensation and the reasons for it are not known; nevertheless, David is momentarily relieved of all pain and malcontent. He spontaneously throws his head back in a peal of laughter.

"Why are you laughing?" Odette asks, with impatience.

"I don't know," David responds, with a wide smile on his face, "Suddenly I just feel a lot lighter, like a great burden has just been taken off me...."

"Are you finished?" Odette asks.

"Yes," David replies, no longer laughing, yet still smiling with bright eyes.

"...And *Dr. So-and-so* also told you," Odette continues on the subject of the hospital in America, "that *their* final tests, *also*, showed you as having no ailment at all, isn't that correct?"

"Odette, why do you speak such good English?" David asks, spontaneously.

"Because my husband is English. Don't change the subject, please."

"I'm sorry... what did you ask? ...Oh, yes, about *Dr. So-and-so!* ... and yes, that's what they said ... eventually, right before they deported me to France, they said I was fine ... that I have no illness, at all. But test results can be wrong, and the first results said that there was, indeed, a problem."

"But the test results from the hospital here in Paris also said you are fine – it looks as though the first results were wrong.'

"But that can't be!" exclaims David, as he jumps up from his chair. A moment after, however, a sharp stabbing pain in his kidney forces him to sit again. That brief moment of pleasure, and sweet relief from the aching torment is over. Dissatisfied with the course of this conversation and annoyed by the results of the tests, David no longer feels like laughing. He appeals to Odette earnestly, "The pain is real. The pain is so real and so intense and it comes everyday without fail." A feeling of desperation begins to flood David. By discrediting the existence of his illness, by denouncing the validity of his pain, this doctor is dismissing his need for a cure. This is exactly what all the doctors before her did; this is why he was never successfully treated. This is why he always was sent on through to the next leg of the race, to a point where he'd be further broken down and much closer to death. By finding nothing wrong with him – by declaring his blood free from fault, and his bones free from error – these doctors drove his body on towards the blind man's death…

"…Free the hospital bed!" they all say, "this boy can't pay!" … "Make room for the rich man who's coming in with a broken pinky! He needs it cast in gold!" … "This guy can't pay, so send him off to die in the gutter. Let him fall in the stone square, or out in the street, and drown in his pneumonia. There's nothing wrong with him, anyway!" … "Had he even a little kidney stone – the size of this rich man's heart – we'd let him stay … wouldn't even make him pay! That's the beauty of a government like ours! Even our *non-citizens* get treated with *dignity!*" … "Yet, when the man hasn't a dime… suddenly, test results show up blank! Meanwhile his body may be riddled with cancer and his brain may be rotten with tumors, but he hasn't got a dime! So, say the boy's fine! … let him go out and die in the street! …no blood on our hands!"

"Are you finished yet?!" cries Odette in extreme annoyance as she, too, jumps up and runs around the desk to pull David down in his chair. "Please stop!" she says, "No one's going to make you die in the street! *Mon Dieu,* what a lot of strange ideas you have!"

By this time, David has settled down and is back in his chair, recovering his breath from the flagrant display of his frustrations with the world's medical system.

"I'm sorry, Odette. I don't know why I got like that. I guess I'm just sick of everyone saying I'm fine when the pain is so real and so horrible. If I had had a heart attack, or some other indisputable illness, they would have never kicked me out of the hospital or sent me here to France in the way they did. If they kept me in the hospital, I never would have collapsed on the street and lost all my money. I wouldn't be in the position I'm in…."

"Okay, enough! I don't want to debate your little … um, 'issues' … they don't concern me. I have a dozen lunatics out there in my office who all have there own little tragedies," she gestures to the closed door leading to her medical office where a cacophony can still be heard coming through the walls.

"Yes, I worry about your intern in there, with all those men." David says, with sincere concern in his voice.

"Oh, she's fine," Odette replies, throwing her pencil down on the desk, "…listen, David, we don't have time for such chatting, alright? We're just going to decide your treatment and end matters here."

"But why do I get a treatment if there's nothing wrong with me?"

"Who said there's nothing wrong with you?" … "I just said there's nothing wrong with you, *physically*."

"Oh," David responds, sitting very still, looking at Odette with rapt attention. After a moment, Odette continues…

"I mean, you definitely have an illness, if you are in such pain. One could even say it's a *physical* illness – if that makes you happier. But it's one involving your *brain chemistry* as opposed to your *organs*." Then Odette pauses, picks up her pencil from the desk and begins biting the eraser. For several moments, the two people – the aging doctor in a white coat with dyed hair pinned up with ceramic peacock clips, and the young patient, dressed in a bathrobe belonging to the doctor's husband – sit facing each other, thinking. The former thinks about an appropriate treatment for the young man, and the latter wonders when the former is going to give him some tablets to ease his pain. Finally, the silence ends…

"Why are your hands shaking, David?"

"I don't know," he lifts his hands and looks at them curiously, turning the palms over, "I didn't realize they were."

"Hmm." Odette jots something down on the clipboard with her pencil. "Well it looks like your ailment is psychosomatic … meaning that you are suffering from a phantom illness. It's a *maladie imaginaire*, nothing else."

David listens with great interest.

"Have you ever suffered from depression?" she asks, "…lasting at least two weeks or more and marked by an excessive fatigue or restlessness?"

"Probably, but I don't remember."

"How did you feel before you entered the hospital in America?"

"I was in a lot of pain. The same pain that I'm in now."

"But how did you feel *emotionally*?" Odette asks.

"Fine. I had a couple good friends. I had a place to live and some savings. Things were alright."

"Take this piece of paper," Odette says, handing David a blank sheet of paper and her Montblanc pen, and continues, "I want you to draw a box of apples … one box, and maybe five or six apples."

David takes the Montblanc pen and draws a small square in black ink in the center of the sheet of paper. Then he draws five little balls clustered together on one facet of the square. He only spends about twenty seconds on the drawing, and then he hands the piece of paper back to Odette.

"I see," says Odette. She studies the drawing as if she were deciphering a secret code. "You've certainly got the megrims!" … "What worries me most is your shaking hands … see how they twitch?" David again looks at his hands and shrugs his shoulders. All the while he asks himself, 'What kind of doctor is this? …the sliding-scale kind, I guess. Shaking hands? My hands have always trembled and they're the least of my worries now. What about this pain in my gut? That's what worries me. I wonder what Odette wants with me? …Letting me sleep here in this rich apartment with expensive things all around, bathing and clothing me? …holding a washcloth against my forehead at night? …It can only end badly, I'm afraid."

"Do you feel an impending sense of doom in your day to day life?"

"Quite the contrary," replies David. "Every time I get a meal I feel like that meal will sustain me. Each time I sleep, I know that that sleep is going to revive me from weariness. Every time I feel the sun, or see it's magnificent rays shimmering off of a shiny object or a wave on a river, I feel like that is the reward and the grace of living. I think I know what you're getting at, Doctor, but I am not that person. My mind is healthier than my trembling body lets on. I feel no sense of impending doom. My mind is happy, no matter what becomes of my circumstances. As long as I am alive, I will be able to sleep, and thus be revived. As long as I am alive, I will find food, and if my eyes don't go blind, I will be able to reap the reward of enduring life: to see the light of the sun. If I do go blind, I will be happy with its warmth. And if I am thrown into cold darkness, I will, no doubt, find another reward for enduring such pain. …And, I am in pain, you must understand. It is chronic. At times, I feel I will die from it. But now I feel I will not. I came to you for relief from my pain – only, for chemical relief. You cannot offer me any other relief. If you offer me a warm bed and a bath full of warm water, that is your kindness and I thank you. But that is not the relief I seek. Beneath a bridge on the Seine, I can fall asleep. And if shivers wake me up –

making me clatter my teeth in the damp cold night, I will fall asleep again. And always the sun and the warmth will return. ...Not every day, no. ...But every year, yes. ...And if I don't live to see the next summer, so be it! ...But this is no doom. It is just life. Anyway, I think I will live a long time. My mind is healthy...

"...And if you refuse me chemical relief from my pain, I will go without. And I will be in great pain, but I am not afraid of pain. I have felt every sort of pain there is and I am not afraid of it. At times I even revel in it, which may be difficult to understand. But, you see, if I can lose everything, and go to a strange country where I haven't any friends, and sleep beneath a bridge, and be tormented with pains of the worst physical sort, yet still be happy! Well then, that is a success of the noblest kind. Is it not? ...I feel that every sad man wandering in loneliness and darkness, is only separated from happiness by one moment, one purposeful change of the thoughts...."

"Still, there are those," Odette interrupts, "whose minds do not allow them to 'purposely change their thoughts' ... those who cannot make the bridge from misery to happiness no matter how hard they try. There are many people plagued by such tremendous illnesses of the mind that they cannot, no matter how much they want to, find happiness or joy or purpose or anything. ...And for them, doom lies ahead."

"But it doesn't, for even misery passes," says David.

"True, misery does pass," agrees the doctor, "But their minds cannot conceive of this."

"Well, fortunately, I am not one of these people. Yet if I become like this, if the disease in my body spreads to my mind and I become one of these such people, I pray I will realize that the misery will pass, and...."

"But, you have no disease in your body," Odette interjects, "this disease, I must inform you, is purely in your mind. It is a *psychosomatic* disorder. And you are not going to die from it, so don't worry about that, but it will worsen if you do not accept treatment."

"But I am here to receive treatment. ...And mind or body, it doesn't concern me. Anyway, I acquiesce to your treatment, whatever form it takes. You are, after all, the doctor."

"Yes, well, I am going to start you off on some medications to return the balance to your brain. I am going to start you on 800mg of L-dopa per day, in order to raise your dopamine levels. Then we have the problem of the opioid dependence. You have been taking a lot of morphine for your pain, I see." ... "I have given it some thought and I am willing to let you stay here for one more week. In a week's time, my husband will return, and he certainly will not approve of your staying here; so you will have to find another place to stay in one week. During this week, you cannot take any other medications besides the L-dopa. Do you understand? am I clear? Unless I give them to you, that is."

"Yes, it's clear." David replies.

"I am also going to give you injections of a drug called S-X. It is a revolutionary new treatment that only exists in France. The molecule is very similar to that of morphine. But it doesn't urge the body to yearn for an increased dosage. In fact, increasing the dosage causes many unpleasant effects, such as nausea, vomiting, and hysteria. Because of this, the patient opts to diminish the dosage rather than augment it. Yet, because it is similar to morphine, and has almost the same analgesic properties, it prevents the symptoms of opiate withdrawal when a steady, slowly diminishing, therapeutic dose is given." ... "I will give you 16mg today and tomorrow and reduce the dosage by 2mg every other day. In a week you will be at less than two-thirds the initial dosage. After that, we can work out an outpatient program to reduce the dosage until you aren't taking any medications at all – other than the L-dopa. But you must agree to not take *any* medications unless I give them to you. Do you understand?"

"Yes, doctor, I do."

"Okay then, please undress, I'm going to give you your first dose of the treatment."

PART II

From flophouse bed, to poorhouse bread,
all outhouse sorrow, I thee wed.

CHAPTER X

The sordid events that led up to the glorious present where all is a teeter, and all fates waver in the incalculable caprice of the crepuscule...

Nastya was alone in her room at Salaudski's place trying to kill a large cockroach that had crawled into a crevice in the floorboard to eat some vermin that had died beneath the floor. She could see the back legs of the hideous insect waiving in the air as it dug its nozzle into the groove in the floor to get at the food. She attacked its legs with the heel of her shoe, and managed to crush them. Horrified by the sight of the crippled cockroach flailing its front legs in the air as its back legs remained mashed against the floor, she ran out into the salon to get Salaudski to come and help finish killing the creature. Salaudski, however, would take no part in it. He was passed out and snoring with an empty bottle of Anjou balancing on his large belly.

Nastya tried to wake the man and failed, afterwards she sat in the chair across from him, and watched him sleep and snore for several minutes. His face had grown long yellow whiskers from a week of not shaving. She had been staying at his house for a full seven days by this time, and for the previous six, Salaudski had not moved from the sofa, except for his midnight strolls into Nastya's bedroom each night to wake her up by caressing her hands – entreating her to come to sleep beside him. Each time she would refuse and ask him to leave, whereupon the old Salaudski would hobble back out to his sofa, swill a few drinks, and pass out for the night.

On this seventh night, she sat in the chair across from the sleeping old man with the empty bottle rolling around on his belly and she bit her lower lip. She didn't believe he was still injured – the cut had healed. It was visible and obvious that the cut had healed and she didn't understand why he was lying down like this all the time. And, if he could hobble into her room every night to disturb her sleep, drunkenly begging her to place her 'soft, young and sweet body' next to his for the night, he could certainly hobble around for other things. He could certainly hobble into a taxi to go to the Opéra Garnier.

When we were last with Nastya and Salaudski, it was the day after the former one's arrival in Paris and the two were dressed nicely and heading down to the Opéra Garnier to interview with the director. Salaudski had insisted that the two walk instead of taking the métro – as he professed that paying for the métro only put money in the public transportation department's pocket, which was an 'evil thing'.

"I won't give a bloody sou to the RATP! Not even if I have a million sous rotting away in the bank. They just use that money to build more ugly, noisy things: buses and the like. Soon they won't be happy with a métro underground. They'll start their jackhammers and build bullet trams in the sky! They'll build them everywhere! Then, I'll wake up one morning and find a tram running right through my living room!" Salaudski was raving, "...They'll have run out of places to put those damned tramways so they'll run one right through my apartment! They may even build a station in there with a ticket-stand. Then if I want to use my bathroom, I'll have to wait in line behind a bunch of strangers.

I'll have to pay two francs to get into *my own* bathroom… that will just be *more* money going to the bloody RATP!"

So Salaudski insisted the two walk all the way from his dingy neighborhood to the beautiful area in the ninth where the Opéra is. This was a mistake because Nastya, who can normally walk gracefully in heels, no matter how uneven the sidewalk is, accidentally managed to catch a heel in a crack of the pavement. The shoe split and she took off the broken heel, and also took off the heel of her other shoe. She then continued walking; though, she insisted that the two stop at one of the many shoe stores on Boulevard Haussmann to buy her a new pair.

Salaudski said it wasn't necessary to buy any new shoes. He told her that the director wouldn't mind in the slightest if her shoes were broken. In fact, he even told her that the director would most likely be impressed by the broken shoes, saying that a girl who can walk the Parisian streets with less than adequate foot apparel must be excellent at adapting to any adverse conditions that may be present on the ballet stage. He told her that if she is to become a dancer in one of the world's greatest ballets – perhaps *the* world's greatest ballet, she would have to show off her ability to do remarkable things with her feet. And walking in Paris with broken shoes is one of the most remarkable things one can do with one's feet.

To all this nonsense, Nastya laughed, imploring Salaudski to buy her a new pair of heels before they reached the Opéra. Salaudski still refused, saying that "giving money to shoe vendors is almost as bad as giving money to the damned RATP", but in order to put himself on the 'same footing', so to speak, as Nastya, he took off his own shoes so that he, too, would be forced to walk in "less than adequate foot apparel".

He even took off his socks, despite Nastya's protests that what he was doing was absurd. He then forced the girl to take his arm – which she did not want to do, and took reluctantly – and the two continued on their way… she, in broken heels; and he, in his bare feet.

It was only two blocks later, when the two came to the rubble that paves the way down Boulevard des Italiens, that one of Salaudski's blackened, bare feet struck a large shard of glass from a broken wine bottle that lay on the sidewalk. Blood began to fill every crack in the heel of his foot; and, as he bounced up and down, holding his ankle in his hand, blood dripped down all over the sidewalk, making a trail of incarnadine splotches on the pavement.

One could hear the old man crying from blocks away as he hopped around the Boulevard des Italiens, holding his bloody foot. Nastya was too angry with the man for taking his shoes off to begin with to go and offer her support; but finally, seeing how much blood there was and hearing how loudly he cried, her sympathies soon gave in and she went over to the little, round man and put his arm over her shoulder for support. And after using her nice velvet scarf for a bandage, she helped the crippled man back home. They never made it to the Opéra that day.

Once they returned to Rue de Paradis, Nastya nursed the old man's wound, which consisted of a long gash up the center of his foot. After rubbing it with iodine, she wrapped gauze around it and elevated his leg by resting his ankle on the arm of the sofa where he lay. Then she cooked him some broth and took his temperature – as the invalid began to complain constantly of an "approaching fever from the shock of such a horrid wound". When his temperature showed normal, he began to brag to his nurse about his body's excellent ability to handle shock: "I've taken shrapnel from German shells," he exclaimed, "a broken bottle of Bordeaux is not going to ruin me!".

Then, Nastya sat in the little chair opposite the sofa as the light of day dimmed into twilight; and she sat by the wounded man and listened to his stories – which he told with fervor – so that he would not get lonely, lying by himself. She had wanted to go out and see more of Paris, – as it was then only her second day in Europe, – but he told her that if she left his side, his health would go to ruin and he would die of loneliness…

"But I will just go take a walk for an hour or so. I'll be back by twilight. You'll be fine for an hour or so, won't you?" she asked, imploringly, as she looked out the window in the salon at the clusters of buildings across the street, wanting so much to go explore around them.

"No, my dear, not *an hour!* Don't do that to me! The loneliness will kill me! It's not that I haven't been alone before – I've been alone here more hours than one can count – it's just that I'm trapped here like a rat caught in a highchair! …And an invalid's loneliness is the worst, you know. Oh, please!" cried Salaudski in protest.

"But just *one* hour?" she replied, "Don't be so melodramatic!"

"Well, if you leave, I'm going to get so bored that I'm going to want to get up and walk around," said Salaudski in a matter-of-fact tone that had a tinge of a threat in it, "and if I get up and walk around, surely the bandages will fall off and dirt will get in the wound and I'll get an infection. Then, surely, they'll have to amputate my foot! I've survived sixty years of wounds without an infection. Oh, don't make me get one now…!" his words trailed off in an imploring tone of despair, as he closed his eyes, and let his head drop to the side, in a dramatic attempt to show Nastya how grave the matter really was.

Nastya rolled her eyes at this show of drama but she really didn't want him getting up and walking around in her absence and she believed he would do it. So in the chair she stayed – watching him by day and waiting on him by night. She made him his favorite verveine tea, which has a nice grassy taste that cannot be compared to any other taste on earth, and he drank large cups of this while eating madeleines. At dinner, he drank his broth in one swallow, and when Nastya took the bowl back to the kitchen to wash it and put it away, he snuck a couple 'winks' of whiskey from the Jameson bottle he kept under the sofa. Then, with the whiskey swirling in his brain, he began to tell her tales of his life.

He told her about how he earned his epaulets on the German front. He told her how he had fought at Dunkerque when the French army disbanded and "how all those sissy Frenchmen ran home! …the Brits too!" he told her, "…but I remained!".

"…I was the last of the French army at Dunkerque and I had already established a friendship with General Marshal because of the English I had learned while serving in Wales. It was just me, General Marshal and a bunch of Polish refugees who were camped out in any old manner, along the quais in the port. All the French inhabitants fled to the south. There were American soldiers too but they were ill-informed of the situation in Europe, and were all under the direction of Marshal who was, as well, at the time, not at all informed…

"…I sat with General Marshal in his tent and talked to him every night before he went to bed. He said I was a 'young man with a good rapport and a lot of sense'. General George Marshal said this … to me … and I was still quite a young man at the time…

"…And so every night I'd go back to his tent and give him encouraging words to ease his anxiety and to make him sleep well. Each night, when I came to his tent, he sent his American guards away, saying, 'It won't be necessary to guard me tonight, men … I have the Monsieur here with me, I'll be just fine.', and the American guards would go off to sleep and it would just be General Marshal, myself, and that solitary oil-lamp that made the inside of his tent glow with a warm amber light, which, he said, also helped to calm him down – that and my soothing words…

"…He told me his fears, his apprehensions, regarding the relationship America was to have with the war in Europe. He didn't know what decision to make. He was cut off from Britain and none of the American forces in the area could communicate with the French – or the Polish, either; so he had to count on me to be his translator…

"…During the day, I met with the Polish refugees and their leaders and I met with my own people, the French, too – who were slowly diminishing in numbers as they retreated to the south. Then, every night, I'd sit at the bedside of the worried General as he grinded his teeth and rubbed the palms of his hands against his thumbs in nervousness, and I'd tell him what he needed to know about the situation in Europe…

"…'General,' I said, 'I know you don't want to have to make this decision but I'm afraid there's no other choice. *You must!*' …And he immediately sat up in his sleeping bag when I said this. He looked into my eyes with this look of great epiphany. He knew what decision I was talking about. Although, he hadn't thought about the decision himself, he could, as he told me, somehow read my mind by listening to the calming and wise tone of my voice – these were his words. He sat up in his tent and looked right into my eyes. His face was firm with resolve. He looked at me and said, 'Monsieur de Chevalier! You are right! Why did I not think of it before? Surely, Europe will disintegrate if the Americans don't amend the Neutrality Act. If we remain neutral, and don't act, Germany will acquire all of Europe!'…

"…The American General didn't sleep at all that night. He left the tent right away and told me to sleep in his sleeping bag. He said he wouldn't be needing it and that I deserved a good night's sleep after my 'great diplomatic brain-storming', as he put it…

"…But I didn't sleep, no! I didn't reward myself at all. No, I stayed on duty and watched out of the flap of the tent; and I watched

General Marshal as he stayed up all night in the dispatch shed, wiring messages to the American President. The next day, their Congress gathered in an emergency meeting on the other side of the Atlantic; and, almost immediately, America amended the Neutrality Act and began sending arms and ammunition to Europe!...

"...General Marshal had to return to United States to engage himself in the offensive plans that were being made in America, but I stayed at Dunkerque. Later, when he saw how successful the allies were becoming, as a result of America's help with arms, General Marshal came back to Dunkerque to thank me. He flew all the way from Washington, just to thank me..." By this point, Salaudski's eyes had welled-up with tears, and he related the story to Nastya with growing nostalgia, "...You should have seen his eyes when he pinned the epaulets on my shoulders! How proud he looked! 'You're the real General,' he said, 'General de Chevalier – *the knight who saved Europe!* ... he even cried! There were tears in his eyes, and they glistened in the light of my oil lamp, which I kept in my tent at Dunkerque. It was the light that blazed as I lay awake at night thinking about the war and wondering if my advice on the war would spell our victory or our defeat...

"...This time, it was the General's turn to sit up and ease *my* anxiety as *I* was the one lying in the tent, lit by the oil lamp, weary and trying to sleep. '...Your advice,' he told me, 'is going to save Europe. Do not rest badly tonight, not tomorrow and neither the next... You, Monsieur, are *the knight who saved Europe!* Wear these epaulets with pride.' And after he pinned them on my shoulders, he left and boarded the cargo plane that had flown him in from London, and off he went to continue the war."

Salaudski's story went on for that like some time. He had had many more adventures in his life than that. That was just the 'crest of the arch', so to speak. His life had had several great and heroic moments like the one at Dunkerque. And, although Nastya knew that he couldn't possibly have been more than about two or three years old when that event at Dunkerque supposedly had taken place, she laughed it off as being the innocent, post-shock raving that is the result of the trauma caused by receiving such a deep wound on the foot.

'He probably wasn't even able to talk yet when America got involved in World War II,' she decided, 'The poor thing is raving. Look at his forehead. It's starting to turn bright red. I bet he has a fever now.'

She shook her head slowly at him and got up to go to the kitchen to get the thermometer again.

"Not good, you poor man," she said, "You have a little fever. Not much of one, but you should lie here and rest until you are completely well. I'll bring your meals. And no more drinking from that whiskey you hide under the sofa, okay? ...I'm just going to take this bottle and... hey, give that to me!"

So, Salaudski let himself be coaxed and pampered like a sick child. He whined to her when his forehead was too hot or too cold, or when his belly hurt, or when the cut on his foot was flaming up again; and she brought him all the necessary supplies to encourage his return to health, viz., vitamin tablets, bandages, iodine swabs, hot broth and cold juice ... also, extra pillows for under his head, copies of *Le Monde diplomatique*, and so on.

She stayed by him all that afternoon and evening, and half of that night; until sometime after midnight, he suddenly flopped off of the sofa, and onto the floor, clutching his head, and roaring with agony. This was his way of complaining to her that his headache was becoming unbearable; so she, wanting to help as much as she could, agreed then to rub his forehead with calamine lotion. It was while she was rubbing his flabby, red forehead, with the creamy pink lotion that he took her by the shoulders and pulled her soft, young body towards his – feeling her breasts against his chest. Then he pressed his lips against hers.

"*Nyet!* What are you doing?!" Nastya screamed in great alarm, while trying to pull her lips away from his and free herself from his grasp.

"Mmm," he gasped, "Just come here, my dear. Mmm, yes ... no, please don't push me away, I'm a poor invalid and all I need is...."

"No! Stop it!" she exclaimed, managing to break away from him. She stood up and looked down at him as he lay there on the sofa, rubbing his belly with one hand, and twirling the hairs on his head with the other; all the while staring up at her with a look of cool indifference – indifference mixed with the sly expression of a trickster. Then he folded his hands over his belly and changed his expression to what appeared to be a look of disgust. He looked at her as if she were his one-legged dog who had just bitten his hand – her master's hand – and is therefore going to be shot because no mistakes at all can be made by a one-legged dog. He looked at her as if he wanted to shoot her and her face flushed red from anger – anger and another dozen sordid emotions. There were tears in her eyes and her lips quivered as she tried to find words to say to him. But there were no words to say to him – or at least she couldn't think of them. Finally the tears overpowered her and began dripping from her eyes. She turned her back to the old man on the sofa and ran off to her little bedroom. She shut the door behind her and tried to lock it. It was no use – there was no lock on the door. She pushed her suitcase up against the door to keep the old man out. This too was a futile effort and was done as more of a gesture; the suitcase was much too light to keep even a child from opening that door. Anyone trying to open the door would just fling the suitcase aside; but Nastya needed a psychological lock at that moment, and the suitcase against the door provided that lock, and lessened the fear that was aching her body fiercely at this moment.

Nastya then tucked herself in the little bed beneath the window where the midnight moon was hovering gracefully over the strips of dark grey clouds in the sky; and she let herself cry.

Meanwhile, Salaudski, heaved himself off the sofa and, once standing, tried to hobble on his one good leg over to Nastya's bedroom, 'to put things right again' – but he could not make it. He got as far as the chair that sits in the hallway before her bedroom door and he flumped down hard in its wicker seat, moaning from the stress put on his wound. He sat there for many moments while Nastya was silently crying in her bedroom, her face buried in the pillow. Salaudski sat in the hall and held his head in his hands. He held the flaps of skin at his temples with his thumbs and forefingers and began shaking his head back and forth, gasping every now and then from the pain in his foot. Finally, he managed to stand and get a bottle of *eau de vie* from the kitchen cupboard. He took a heavy pour of the strong liquor and drank it down quickly. Then, with the alcohol acting as an anesthetic, he managed to hobble, with almost no pain, over to the sofa, where he flopped on his back and fell asleep for the night in a sea of snores.

Meanwhile, Nastya cried the night away in her bedroom. After some time with her face ensconced in the pillow, she managed to get up and get her nightgown from her suitcase. Halfway through changing out of her clothes to put on her nightgown, however, she stopped. 'I don't want to sleep in my nightgown, tonight. I want to sleep in my clothes. I want as many clothes on as possible.' And with this, she started putting on her pants and her sweater again. Moments later, she was lying fully-clothed under the wool blanket on the tiny bed in Salaudski's guestroom.

'I have to leave,' was the conviction that entered her mind, 'I *must* leave. I don't care if he can get me in the Paris ballet, or not. I'm not going to pay for my place at the Opéra in this way – he is dreaming, that horrible, old ... ah! I need to leave and go back to Russia. But how can I leave? Where am I going to get the money to leave? I've seen the prices in Paris and a thousand francs is not even enough to buy a pair of shoes – let alone, a train ticket to Moscow!'

But she was still determined to leave this man. She was two and a half thousand kilometers from her home. She needed to get back there as soon as possible. She remembered the awful feeling she had had before, when she first arrived at Salaudski's home, and saw hundreds of posters of herself pasted on his walls. And she knew the awful feelings she was having then – and the disgusting feeling of his cold, old lips forcing themselves against hers. She knew they would only get worse, these feelings. She knew that even more terrible things would happen if she were to stay in Paris. If she stayed, everything would certainly get worse and worse. This was her conviction: she would be ruined.

While laying awake, sobbing quietly and staring at the yellow moon out the window, Nastya made plans. The next morning she would wake early – as early as possible – and slip out Salaudski's front door, with her suitcase in her hand. She would get on the first train to Moscow. Even if she had to sneak on the train and hide in the filthy bathroom for whole voyage. If that was the only way to go without paying for a ticket she would do it. Perhaps it even crossed her mind to steal the money from Salaudski to buy her ticket. She would have done it. But Salaudski is on a small pension and has no money lying around. She would try to pawn the military decorations on his jacket, except she knew they were all made out of tin. 'Some general,' she thought, 'He's no general! ...It was just a guess, but her guess had been right as Salaudski never came close to being a general. His rank stayed at second lieutenant for all forty years of his military career, and when he was dishonorably discharged for injuring himself with his own landmine during mine-laying practice, he was given a small pension. Because he was injured in uniform, he was guaranteed a disability pension check every month from the French government.

But enough about Salaudski; at this point, Nastya was through with him. She had her mind made up to go get the first train in the morning back to Moscow – under all circumstances.

Her plan flowed through her head as clear as pond water while she lay in her bed. But that was at night - when the anger was fresh and the sadness was new. By morning, after she had slept, after her pillow had absorbed every tear, and once that bitter and shame-inducing clarity of morning fell on her, she had a completely different outlook on the situation. Of course, she was still going to get rid of the odious Salaudski, but she wouldn't fall a coward in the city of Paris just yet. She still needed to make a success of her trip to France. If she went back to Russia, and told her family that the monstrous Monsieur de Chevalier didn't want a dancer, but was only looking for a foreign concubine, she would never be able to have pride in her home again. She would be a failure. She would be worse than a failure; because, most often, failures go off on their lonesome, solitary ways to some remote crevice in the earth, and it is there that they starve to death – completely alone, without having any company to burden with their wretchedness. But Nastya felt that going back to Russia would create a situation where she'd be a failure of the most nocuous sort. All the grief she had brought upon them, with her leaving in the middle of the night. She had thought that making it as a ballet dancer in Paris' most prestigious ballet would certainly make her parents proud to the extent that they would forgive her for running away – not just *forgive her*, but *be glad* about her running away to Paris. They would look back on it and laugh, saying…

"Well, our daughter is a star, just as she said she would be someday, back when she was a little girl. I couldn't be more proud! Whatever misfortune she was forced to curse us with, is no misfortune at all. It was just a necessary rung in the ladder that she climbed to her success. The important thing is that she is happy and has achieved her dream. What I had to suffer, for the sake of my Nastya's dreams coming true, I will happily suffer again, and ten-fold worse, if that's what it takes to make *all* of her dreams come true. I am not a martyr, but I am a father – and the differences between the two aren't always clear." …That is what her father would say, when finding out that Nastya was hired on at the Opéra Garnier. …Her mother would say something more like this:

"She did it! She made the ranks! Now millions of girls all over the world are jealous that they aren't her. That's just the way it is, though. I made Nastya to be great! … carried her around for a whole nine months, just to make something better than the other parents were making. All the other parents' children are half-cooked, half-spoilt pigeon eggs. But my Nastya is a pedigree ostrich. Just try and find fault with her breeding when she's dancing on stage at the Opéra Garnier in Paris. She's a perfect bird. And all the rest of those girls are just eggs!

Eggs that will *never* hatch! Why won't they ever hatch? Because they're spoilt, that's why!...

"…Even if she doesn't help with the wash anymore, she at least sends a handsome check once a week so we can have good meals on our table each night. *What if* she is in Europe – that despicable continent? *What if* she broke her father's heart by running away to that horrid continent in the middle of the night, one night, while he was sleeping a worried father's sleep because his daughter had taken to bed sick that day?" …We remember the last time Nastya's father saw her, he placed a glass of water by her bed and kissed her forehead, tenderly, praying that her good health would return soon. Then he went to sleep in his own bed, and as soon as he woke up the next morning, he saw his daughter was gone and he truly believed, though it was the hardest thing on earth to bear, that she would never return – that he would never see her again…

"…So, what if she broke her father's heart pulling that stunt?" her mother would say, "Let his foolish heart be broke! He deserves a broken heart for the mere scraps he buys for our dinners. My Nastya, however, - the new star of the Parisian ballet, – she puts hare on the table!" … "Fresh hare with truffles and pomegranate confiture. She can break her father's heart any old time she wants just as long as she's putting hare on our table!"

To Nastya, it was certain, the only way she could return to Russia, to her parents and her brother, with any dignity at all, would be if she first succeeds in doing what she set out to do, that is, if she becomes a ballerina at the Opéra Garnier. Nastya cannot leave France after only a few days and one horribly unpleasant event. She has too much pride and takes her ambitions too seriously to cower back to Moscow like that – and so soon. The only way she will permit herself to return to Russia, is if she goes back a success. Such is the nature of Nastya. If she tells herself that she is going to do something, accomplish something, she will either accomplish it or she'll remain trying, with a fixed concentration bordering on monomania. This nature of hers has always, in the past, blessed her with generous rewards. This perseverance resulted in her becoming the prima ballerina at Moscow's Gelikon theatre. This nature also resulted in her being discovered by the Bolshoy. But this nature also reveals a side that may not be so healthy. On the day of the night she boarded the train to Paris, she had been most politely dismissed – or fired, rather – by the director of the Bolshoy. Now, the Bolshoy is a prestigious outfit, and most any other girl aspiring to become a professional ballerina would feel honored to be hired as merely a ticket vendor for this theatre. Most any other girl would not let her pride be damaged by a dismissal from the Bolshoy, had she ever been honored to dance there in the first place. Any other girl would see the dismissal as an appropriate, albeit not too pleasant, ending to the fairytale of dancing at the Bolshoy. Other girls would tell their mothers:

"Mother, the Bolshoy fired me today!"

Whereupon, their mothers would reply, "Well I knew it would happen sooner or later. But you can be very proud of yourself that you got to dance at the famous Bolshoy theatre for two weeks, at least … what an accomplishment!"

But Nastya chooses not this 'normal role' as the daughter who failed at her extraordinarily lofty goals, yet succeeded at her only moderately ambitious ones. Who is, therefore, extolled for those moderate successes, whereas the extraordinary failures remain in view as reminders to the girl, and her family and everyone else, that she is normal, average, and nothing too remarkable. Some parents prefer to shield themselves from any suggestion that their kids may have a touch of the extraordinary in them. Likewise, many children are careful to hide any evidence, whatsoever, pointing to the fact that they have a bit of the extraordinary in themselves. To these children and these parents, life is seen as difficult. People who attempt outlandish feats and then succeed are seen as exceptions to the human race, whom only God can fathom. Someone, for example, who flies a full-circle around the world in a zeppelin with no fuel, no compass and its bladder full of holes, is seen as a phenomenon that should not be emulated. These children do not want to risk their lives or their wives or their sanity, for the possible attainment of something lofty and noble, they would much rather live as erring mortals, dwelling in the safest cubbyholes of the earth.

Most parents, we are quite sure, want their children to abstain from lofty ideals and noble feats to a degree that is higher than that which is wished by the children. They do not want their children – whether they are fourteen years old or forty years old – to go attempting any around-the-world trips in popped balloons. 'There is a reason why it has never been done before,' they say, 'because it is dangerous! Just the thought of it makes me nervous! Get those ideas out of your head. If you want to be the hot-air balloon champion of our little, unknown town in an unheard of region of our almost non-existent country, that is fine. That is great actually! I'll even help you buy your balloon. …But if you want to be the champion of the world? Well, it's a huge world filled with an insane quantity of human beings and there is no way that you – my child – can compete against billions of other people who, no doubt, have a natural advantage over you, because they are from China or Italy or Peru or Canada ... while you are just from this nothing town in nowhere land and anyway, it is a ridiculous idea so get it out of your head!"

Parents like this would be content if their child was dismissed from the Bolshoy theatre. That brings them closer to average marker. Few parents truly want their children to surpass the mean average. Of course, they would disagree with this notion of mine, swearing to me that they want nothing less than to see their children grow up to be Presidents of their countries; or, at least, factory owners, architects or plastic surgeons. But they do not really want this, if there is a risk. They want their children to reach these high levels of success only if it is safe and easy for them to do so. First and foremost is that their children each are born with two eyes and one head, the right genitals and ten toes. Anything more than that is a threat to the family unit as a whole. Zeppelins crash. Eyes get poked out. And how humiliating it would be to have a genius child with only one eye! ...Now you may not think this way; but I assure you, most parents do. When they say otherwise they are only pretending.

But back to how this all pertains to Nastya: She is a girl who seeks to be extraordinary, or at least to live an extraordinary life. There is no way that a girl like Nastya is going to, first, tell her parents that she was fired from the Bolshoy theatre, second, accept this dismissal, and third, resume a mediocre life – such as dancing on Sunday afternoons at the Gelikon theatre's family ballets. No, a girl like Nastya would not allow herself to consciously regress. If she gets kicked off the Moscow stage, she's off to Paris to dance on the Parisian stage!

In the clarity of morning, following the evening that Nastya lay awake in her little bed at Salaudski's crying, Nastya decided that she would go through many more difficult things – face hunger, homelessness, and countless brushes with death – before she would go back to her parents' home in Russia with the news that she failed in her aspirations abroad.

It was settled. Nastya would not be hopping a train to Moscow. She would stay in Paris no matter how perilous the situation. 'Come hope, come despair, come what may, sweet serendipity – a life of chance in the bustling city; let me be sorrowful, let me be merry, while I risk all to be extraordinary!' ...Those are the eyes with which Nastya sees things on the matter. She is not to be average. Yet it is normal that Nastya is like this; for average people are not worthy of having their lives illustrated through hundreds of pages of novel paper. That she is so skewed from the average, this is what entitles her to hold the position of the heroine of our story. But is she extraordinary because she is the heroine of our novel? ...or is she our heroine because she is so extraordinary? ...Oh, how did you get me off track? This is the second time you have led me away from the story I am trying to tell! Do you purposely want me wander on strange subjects and chew an illiterate cud for pages on end? Do you want me forget exactly how this story goes? ...Or how it *went*, rather?! Sometimes you really aggravate me! ...But since you are devoting *your* precious time to reading that which I have spent *my* precious time writing, I will forgive you and even thank you once again. *Thank you, dear reader!* ... I'm sorry I said you 'aggravate me' ... that was rather childish of me ... but let's move on...

So, when Nastya awoke the next morning, she did not go running off to the train station to go back to Russia. Instead, she awoke first with shame and uncertainty – her mind was full of doubts; and, not wanting to see the Salaudski, she walked straight from her room to the door, to go for a stroll around the neighborhood. While walking, the city of Paris loomed over Nastya, imposing its strangeness and unfamiliarity on her. While walking, her shame and uncertainty grew. She was in a terrible quandary when she returned to Salaudski's apartment building. She wasn't sure if she should go up stairs and take her suitcase, or not. But as soon as she reentered Salaudski's apartment building on Rue de Paradis, she was greeted by the landlady who had a letter for her. It was from her father – sent from Moscow to the address Nastya had given him in her farewell note – the note, which she had left in the center of the round wooden table on that night she snuck away to Kurskyi Station and boarded a train for France. This letter from her father made it all too clear that going back to Russia was a notion she couldn't even consider. The letter gave Nastya courage. She took the letter and read it while walking again around the block. And, after reading this letter, she decided she would no longer entertain the idea of returning to Moscow. She decided her opinion on matters and she chased away the shame. The farther she walked, the more times she read the letter, the more firm grew her determination and her resolve. On her way back to Salaudski's, she had not a drop of weakness in her. She was ready to deal with the lecherous man and she was ready to deal with Paris. And, soon enough, we will see how she deals with Salaudski, and how she deals with Paris;

but first, we must not forget that we have another extraordinary life to illustrate… the life of David.

CHAPTER XI

The Cat, the Cage, and the Concubine...

Odette had David subjugated on the floor of her apartment. He was not responding well to her suggestions, however, as he could not see the sense in what she was doing. When he had agreed to follow the 'doctor's orders' he had trusted her – feeling that she would not harm him. Still at this moment, he trusted her; and that is when she had him pinned to the floor, where she gave him his first injection. She injected him with a chemical called *L-dopa*, which was a grave mistake on her part. David's body could not tolerate the effects of that potent drug. He should not have allowed that poison to circulate his system, yet he had no say in the matter. He had promised her that he would take all the medicines she prescribed. And, above all, she is a licensed physician, and he didn't know that that chemical is a poison – at least it is at such an extreme dosage.

When David was pricked by the point, and injected with L-dopa, he began to climb the walls. He began to speak to the spiders in the corners. He tried to drown himself in the sink basin. And finally, he latched onto the ceiling and hung there for many hours, until it was time for his next injection. This second injection was given to him without his awareness. This second medicine was the chemical *S-X*. S-X is used for its analgesic and sedating properties. It also suppresses breathing and induces nausea. At high doses, it can cause hysteria, tremors, and mental disorders of varying severity, which can be permanently debilitating. It is a revolutionary new medicine in Europe.

After the S-X was shot into his system, his trembling hands – frantically grasping to hold on to the ceiling anywhere he could, tearing chunks of plaster out with his fingernails – immediately released and

David fell from the ceiling like a dead bug dropping from a window pane; and he remained there, on the floor where he landed, for some time – curled-up in the fetal position in an opiate-induced stupor.

Dr. Moreaux either didn't put to much thought into David's condition, was badly trained in medical school, or just had ill-intentions towards the young man, for the L-dopa was not an appropriate drug in his condition. Each time Odette administered the medication –and she began to administer it regularly – his body would react in the same way:

Directly after the injection, he reacts like a cat reacts to being pummeled by a waterfall… His eyes turn bloodshot and they bulge out of his skull. His skull turns bright red and tenses with blue veins that streak his forehead like lightning bolts. Then, like clockwork, he pounces on the ceiling and remains fastened there until the chemicals in his body are metabolized to a less then toxic level. The drug changes his thoughts. When he is on the ceiling, he no longer thinks as a human does. Instead, he is like an animal, a predator, hunting on the vast plaster ceiling for those hallucinations that serve as his prey. Once he catches and devours a few of these hallucinations, his body begins to calm down. But this doesn't happen for several hours after the injection. Immediately after being injected, and clear up until the moment when his body relaxes enough to unlatch itself from the ceiling and drop to the floor, – where it then continues hunting the illusory beasts that roam the wooden floors of Odette's apartment, – David's poor body undergoes a panic of the worst kind, lasting several hours. The drugs hold him at the threshold of seizure and push him towards the brink of suffering a fatal ischemic stroke. His heart pounds and the constricted veins bulge on his inflamed forehead trying desperately to push blood through to his organs. Then, in an acute state of panic, he begins clawing with his fingernails at whatever object is around, – be it real or illusory, – while his mind, though lost in the instinctual realm of a primitive beast, is fully aware that his body is about to explode, implode, or in some other fashion, disintegrate. It is the worst feeling David has ever experienced. Being under the influence of that medication is like having a noose around your neck and an executioner standing behind you, ready at any moment that his caprice will strike to kick the stool out from under your feet and watch your neck break in the yank of the noose.

He has been at Odette's now for almost a week and every morning the torture treatment begins at half-past eight o'clock. As soon as Odette has finished her tea, she fills a syringe. Then comes the needle through a crack in the sheets where David's bare body is exposed as he sleeps in the bed of Odette. Then, before he has even a moment to grow accustomed to being awake, the gasolinic L-dopa is circulating in his system and up he is on the ceiling, fastened like a cat in terror.

He feels the anxiety and the fear that he will die when his body will burst open after the explosion of his heart, but there is nothing he can do about it, except wait it out. He doesn't even realize why he feels this terror, for Odette always injects him at eight-thirty in the morning, while he is still asleep. The drugs wake him instantly but Odette is quick to remove the needle and take a step back, for instantly his eyes open, turn bloodshot, and bulge out of his trembling skull with a look of the most profound fear and panic. And then, he jumps.

This medicine transports David to a world so instinctual and animalistic that there is not much, while in this state, that separates him from a wildebeest. His thoughts diminish, his awareness that he is at that moment a free-willed, sentient being vanishes, and he begins to hunt around the room, automatically almost – incapable of restraining himself, unaware that restraining himself is even possible. Then a fever mounts, and, when he cannot find any creatures to prey on, his panic reaches an apex. With the apex, comes the vertigo and the nausea and explosions of light on the retinas of his eyes; and then his brain begins to manufacture hallucinations: a sort of self-defense mechanism. His pulse rate skyrockets, his heart pounds at incalculable speed and his temperature rises to the point where his brains are about to boil – and why? ...all because he cannot find food. The L-dopa dopamine stimulation robs his brain of its ability to reason and stand aware of the present moment; and it sends him into the timeless, thoughtless and instinctual realm where only nocturnal, carnivorous beasts belong – a realm void of all that makes one human. But the human body has an amazing talent for reacting quickly to anything organic or inorganic that poses as a threat to the survival of that body. Poisons that are so volatile that they can burn holes in the ocean floor are no match for the antidotes created by the beautiful human body. When David's body is reeling on L-dopa and his heart rate and body temperature are both rapidly nearing fatal levels, - and all of this because his animalistic mind is reacting to an adrenaline rush of panic produced by the need to hunt for food and the inability to find any, - his brain instinctively saves his life by producing vivid hallucinations of food that yield to all of the senses.

At the apex, the moment the hallucinations begin, he feels a pleasant, most euphoric, sensation that tells him that he is saved. His life is spared. Food is abundant and plentiful.

Little hallucinatory rabbits hop over the lamp chains that hang from the ceiling. Illusory squirrels hide in the cracks in the walls with imaginary peanuts stuffed in their cheeks. Birds of all varieties: storks, pigeons, robins, bluebirds, crows, vultures, touch down on the ceiling, so that their beaks may pick for seeds, or fish, or rotting flesh in the plaster; and they touch down long enough for David to pounce on them and slice through their thick clusters of feathers, tearing into their soft, poultry flesh that rips so easily, causing bird blood to gush out and form a pool around the animal's collapsed carcass and mess of bones and cartilage that David tears through, as he devours all but the bones and feathers. By four or five in the afternoon, he has usually caught, killed, and feasted on several different types of birds, a few varieties of rodents and at least one large mammal or marsupial – all of the hallucinatory kind. If these hallucinations didn't create themselves, David would have, without a doubt, died by now from a brain hemorrhage caused by imaginary starvation. But, since he is able to calm himself slightly, and preoccupy his panicked mind during the L-dopa rush by finding little creatures to prey on and nourish the body, the perfect machine of his body has managed to regulate temperature and blood pressure during these drug episodes, keeping David alive these last several days where, each day, Odette's eight-thirty medicine resembles more and more a lethal injection.

The only thing that pulls David out of this hysteria is Odette's opioid shots – the infamous S-X. It is as if she times these injections not by when the patient seems to need the shot, but rather, whenever she herself grows tired of watching the frantic beast pouncing on invisible animals in her apartment. The first couple days, she was intrigued by the patient's behavior on L-dopa. She even spent the first thirty-six hours of his treatment, taking copious notes and observations with the ambition to write up a scholarly article on this strange phenomenon, which she could then publish in any of the reputable medical journals.

But after two days, her interest in the subject waned, and as soon as she had heard enough of the patient's noises each afternoon – the scratching at the walls and the licking of the chops after a kill was made and the flesh was devoured – she'd scream out, "Enough of this!" and run to fill up a spike with the opiate injection; and *pop!* she'd pounce on the patient's naked rear just as if she were hunting vermin as well, and in it'd go: the spike and the whole load of S-X; and moments later, the white, opaline liquid would be coursing his veins, overpowering the L-dopa, and the patient would drop from whatever he was attached to, e.g., the ceiling, the light fixtures, the houseplants, et cetera, and into the fetal position he'd go. His eyes would roll back slightly in his head and his lips would take on a foolish, drooling grin, and once the shudders caused by the rapid chemical change passed through his spine, he would decontract his muscles, unravel his body, and let out a great sigh, whereupon, he'd begin scratching himself fervently all over his body – paying special attention to his armpits, his chest and his genitals.

Why Dr. Moreaux continued this absurd treatment for almost a week now, one can only guess at. She must have known that these daily injections were pushing the patient's body into toxic conditions where death is not necessarily the most grim result. David could have easily suffered a hemorrhage or a stroke on any one of these last few days. He could have simply gone psychotic, or neurotic, or insane in any of the other popular ways. He could have suffered paralysis and be doomed to spend the remaining years of his life as a drooling invalid. One must assume that Odette, a licensed doctor, was aware of all this. David, however, had no say in the matter, as the hypnotic qualities of these two medications confused his poor brain into not being quite sure what, if anything, was happening in the world.

Dr. Moreaux may have seen his new behavior – with the torrents of energy surging through him as he gives up his human ways to take on the role of a beast – as an improvement. He was a bit sluggish before … always complaining of the damned pains in his abdomen – *that damned kidney!* Perhaps Odette saw this increased vitality and lustfulness as a change for the better; however, this is not so.

The most likely scenario is that Dr. Odette Moreaux belongs to that strange sect that flourishes so abundantly in Paris – a sect that has almost altogether died out in America. I'm talking about the sect of the lonely, aging women of less than adequate beauty, who are often sharp and domineering, and in this generalization, are almost always Parisiennes; who in addition are always marked by one necessary distinguishing quality, which is their uncontrollable sexual desires that manifest when they are able to 'abduct', so-to-speak, a young man of half their age who is in a weak position – usually of the financial sort, but often enough who is also in poor physical or mental health.

These women seek out and find men young enough to be their children. Men who are suffering from some ill-luck, or are, in another

150

way, locked into a compromised position, whether it's money problems or emotional despair, and they proceed to adopt them. The old woman adopts the young man in order to amplify his ill-luck, exaggerate the degree of troubles he is suffering from in order to force him into the feeling of utter hopelessness and dependence on her (the latter being the prime objective of the woman). Then, once she deflates the already weak young man to a debilitating state, she holds up a mirror to him – *her mirror* – which shows him an image of himself that is far worse off then he really is in actuality. All of this chips away at his self-esteem and makes him feel that he would be lost without the help of the older woman. Once she has devalued him to this extent, she is ready to go on to her next conquest, viz., having her way with him sexually.

Why this disease affecting aging woman is more prevalent in Paris than in other cities of the world, one can only speculate on; however, wherever these women come from, whether it's Paris or Palo Alto, Seattle or Sao Paulo, they all conduct this business in the same way. They all take the same steps and use the same snares to entrap their young men. There are no cultural differences in this disease. This disease affects not the culturally trained brain – it bypasses that channel and aims straight for the *animus pravus*, which it takes with severity, spreading it's infection throughout all of the tissues of the body.

Another unifying element of this disease: it runs the same course in every infected woman. In the midcourse of the disease, the woman is filled with elation, sexual friskiness, hope, and faith that she will attain her ultimate goal. Seeing a woman in this stage of the disease is like watching a woman whose brain has been eaten away by syphilis – it is often a delightful and interesting experience, (that is how it is seen, anyhow, by third-party onlookers – uninvolved spectators). It is neither delightful nor interesting in the mind of the young man who falls victim to this infected woman, not at this stage anyhow. He feels that his power has been lost, and is in the disillusion that he is dependant upon the woman for his survival. Of which power the man has been robbed, he is not quite certain; for when he first was enslaved by her disease, he went into enslavement willingly – for he was then, already, in an abject and disempowered state. He was void of the power of which all *humans* are entitled. By the second stage of the disease, however, when the infected woman is at the height of her influence, the young man subconsciously attempts to gain back this lost human power. But the woman gives no gifts, she only makes trades, and the hand that gives is smaller than the hand that takes. So, subconsciously, he begins to trade the power he has retained up to this point: the power of which all *men* are entitled, in exchange for diluted driblets of this lost human power. It is a foolish exchange and the young man soon finds out that losing his humanness is a bearable enough dilemma, one from which he can recover. Even the most bedraggled pauper can reinvest in human power. But once a man loses that power peculiar to all men, he is without the strength or the will or the means to regain this – and at this point he is truly lost.

At this second stage of the disease, when the woman is robbing the man and thanking him with a few filthy centimes thrown at his knees, the woman feels empowered, giddy, and playful – and she exudes this, wearing a golden halo of power. If she were to know that she had the infection – though complete unawareness of the disease's presence is a marked symptom during this stage – she would, most certainly, resist taking the cure, (just as women with neurological damage as a result of syphilis often resist treatment), for she wouldn't want to lose the mental derangement that results in gaiety of spirit, and a new found happiness. She suddenly has a big sword in her hand and she wants to swipe with it.

It is after this stage, however, that the disease takes a sharp turn, driving the infected woman down a path of confusion to a physical and mental state of pain and misery. It is in this final stage that the woman realizes she never got what she wanted to get from the young man. She realizes that he will never give her what it is she really wants; nor will she be able to take it from him against his will. What was it she wanted from him? What is her ultimate goal? She seeks not merely his power; and anyhow, in human relationships, power must be shared, not robbed, in order for it to have a tonic effect.

The infected mind, in this stage, is hindered by a derangement that causes the woman to obsess about how she is going to take what she wants from the young man without his consent. This is, however, a pointless endeavor for the woman, for the infection, by this time, has most certainly spread throughout the brain, prohibiting her to remember or discover or somehow realize what it is she exactly wants. This stage reveals the pathetic condition of the infected woman to a third-party observer, for she appears like a clochard, digging petty coins out of a fountain filled with pigeon feces. The coins add up to nothing, so she must eventually abandon the fountain and dig through the poodle feces in the park. She has no clue what she's looking for, yet seizes every opportunity that arises to take something from the young man; however, it never even occurs to her that she must know what she wants in order to be satisfied. Women in this stage are headless, and go down like crippled chickens in a cockfight.

To the second-party observer, the young man, she appears at this stage to have lost the halo of power she used to boast. Her flesh shrivels and the wrinkles in her jowls deepen. When she tries to speak, it seems that her gizzard can only utter a feeble *squawk*.

The young man does not feel victorious while watching her blindly swaggering towards her demise. On the contrary, he feels like he is going with her – and he is. He props the crippled woman's arm over his shoulder and helps her walk to the edge of the cliff. By this stage, the presence of an awful disease is all too apparent to him, and he knows that he must pull the plug. He must kill her or help her kill herself, even if he too dies in the process.

So the limping, old woman squawks in the ear of her young beau as he carries her to the edge of the cliff; and, as they near it, the ground crumbles under their feet. He looks into her eyes, searching for the glittering light in her retinas that sparkles with the jewels that she has stolen from him. If she goes down with his jewels, he thinks, he must go down too – though the drop is a hundred meters long and at the bottom lies a ravine of jagged rocks that flash in the sunlight like the jaws of a wolf.

So he looks in her eyes and he sees none of his precious jewels sparkling. In her eyes there is an absence, a void; they are two artificial balls of clouded glass. The woman is already dead, she has poisoned herself with his power and it turns in her stomach with the diseased bile and cankerous detritus, and there is nothing he can save of what was his. So he musters what little strength he can and heaves the woman's body off the cliff, where it cracks asunder in the ravine below.

That is just one culmination – yet the most typical culmination – of this disease when it runs its course. The infected woman's mind deteriorates and her host, the young man, is released – though he may remain in a psychological muddle for years following.

To say that Odette, herself, is infected with this disease is a loaded statement. The symptoms of this pandemic can be caused by other, more benign, diseases. It would be unfair to label Odette as a carrier of this disease without first drawing her blood. But she doesn't allow her blood to be drawn, she only draws the blood of others, such is her profession. So, before we can safely conclude that it is this disease, and not syphilis, or a mangy tapeworm, which is eating at her brain, you must be aware of the events that have transpired over the last week that David has been staying at her place:

The first few mornings, at precisely eight-thirty, David would awaken to the startling rush of the L-dopa injections, and for the rest of the day, he would race around her house in panic trying to kill the imaginary vermin that infests her apartment. Only in the evening would he get relief from this unbearable intoxication, when she herself would grow tired of his hyperactivity and shoot him up with opiates. Then he would lie on the ground for hours in a drooling stupor until Odette would help him into her bed, undress him, and take pleasure savoring with her tongue all of the crevices of his naked, half-conscious body. She cursed him for not being able to get an erection when he was drunk on the opiates. She beat him with a soupspoon, and jabbed him with a scalpel. She was in love with his beauty. But he would not share his beauty with her willingly, and so she took it.

    She cut his hair while he slept, and chewed on the dark tresses. She scratched him and she sipped the drool from his sleeping mouth and dressed in his underwear and his filthy socks. She liked the filth. She liked to make him dirty. She enjoyed destroying his young beauty with scissors and scalpels. She spared his face, for the nonce. It was his handsomest possession, and she would only take it when nothing else of his satisfied her. But she helped herself to everything else and she reveled in it – for a bit; that is, until it lost its newness and ceased to bring her pleasure. If she disfigured his face, she knew, he would no longer be appealing, and she would have to throw him out in the gutter to sleep.

    On the fourth day, David awoke naturally. Odette had neglected to give him his eight-thirty injection. She was angry with him. She considered those injections as a great service paid to him – paid to his health. She wasn't going to give away any more free services. She was going to let him wake up naturally and beg for the injections. She wanted to be paid. She was tired of his listless, naked body limp in her mouth, not reacting to the nibbles of her incisors. She was weary of his half-closed eyes and his limp genitals. She wanted his eyes open. She wanted his teeth to sweat. She wanted him to hunger for her like a proper man. So, she deprived him of the juice.

He awoke at about eight thirty-five on the fourth morning with a terrible headache and no clue as to where he was. He pulled back the sheets and saw his naked body covered with fingernail scratches and small puncture wounds. His first thought was that again he had woken up on the examining table in some laboratory where he was a specimen. But unlike the time he woke up in the Hospital St. Louis, completely disoriented from shock and barbiturates, on this morning he awoke with a clarity of mind that was uncharacteristic for him, as of late. No doubt the residues of toxic medications still mingled with the blood in his veins, yet they seemed to have left his brain alone; – his thoughts were sober, his vision was clear. But he caught sight of his damaged body with the abrupt shock that one might experience when waking up sober in a public toilet after passing-out drunk there the night before. He looked at the ceiling, at the chandelier, at the tops of the drapes. It was clear that he wasn't in a laboratory, or in a hospital, or in a public toilet; he was in somebody's apartment, in somebody's bed. And when he turned his head and saw Odette sleeping nude beside him – her withered breasts resting on the muscle of his arm – he leaped from her bed in shock.

"What is going on?!" he demanded of her, as she rolled over, apparently just waking up.

"What do you mean, 'what is going on'? …Did you sleep well?" She rubbed the sleep out of her eyes and yawned like a coquette.

"I mean, *what is going on?!* Why am I here, and why was I naked in your bed?"

"You fell asleep here. You took off your clothes because you were hot, remember? I don't like the fan on at night. The noise keeps me awake." While Odette spoke, David pulled the sheet up to cover his groin and looked around frantically for his underwear. Then he responded, pointing at the sores and scratches on his chest and belly…

"And I suppose your bed is crawling with bedbugs?! What are these scratches from?"

"Oh, those… I explained to you last night but I guess you don't remember." … "I'm going to stop your opiate treatment. You have had some kind of reaction to the medicine. You kept scratching yourself. I almost had to put you in restraints. Finally, I managed to get you to drink some doxylamine succinate. You went right to sleep after that. You stopped tearing at your skin and fell right, fast, asleep. But honestly, no more S-X for you. You have been suffering the uncommon side-effects."

"If I went 'right, fast, asleep', how then did I take my clothes off?"

"What are these questions, accusations? ...Are you accusing me, David? Because your tone of voice sounds like you are accusing me. For your information, you went right to sleep after drinking the medicine, but you kept whining in your sleep about how hot it was. I didn't want the fan on. I don't like it on at night. So, finally, you – while half asleep – took off your clothes ...satisfied?" Odette spit her words out, while covering her breasts with the bed sheet. Growing angrier, she continued, "...And do not accuse me! I'm the one who is letting you in my private space. Do you think I want your smelly body next to mine? You haven't showered in days. I'd actually prefer to sleep alone. I think it's kind on my part to offer my bed, so you don't have to sleep under a bridge, or on a bench."

"I just took a shower yesterday." said David, accidentally leading the conversation away from where he wanted it to go.

"I'm sorry, that was five days ago."

"But how long have I been here? I couldn't have... what day is it?"

"You've been here since last week. I'm afraid the medications have affected your memory. You know, almost every pharmaceutical carries potential, rare side-effects that are serious. When such side-effects occur, the doctor cannot be blamed." ... "But don't blame *yourself*, David; it's not your fault either. The only thing to do when a body reacts like yours did, is to stop the medication. Once I saw that your scratching was causing bleeding, I stopped the medication and sedated you. That's the proper procedure in that situation. Ask any doctor."

David didn't know what to think. His stomach hurt and his head pounded, but his thoughts were suddenly clear. He didn't understand how so many days could have passed without him being aware of it. Had he been unconscious the whole time? Or was his brain merely not recording the events that occurred? He decided not to dwell on it too much. He wanted to clean his skin and he wanted to eat. He wanted his head to stop pounding but more than anything, he wanted food.

"I don't have anything in the house, unfortunately. I'll have to go to the *épicerie*," was her response to his request for food.

156

"May I take a shower, please?"

"Yes, please do. I'll go to the *épicerie* and buy groceries."

"Nothing with meat, okay? No fish either, I don't eat it," David said walking off towards the bathroom.

"Demanding, aren't you? Who would eat fish in the morning, anyway? ...They must do that in America, yes?"

"Just please hurry, I'm really hungry. When was the last time I ate?"

"Well, it's been days. But you wouldn't eat on your own, and I wasn't very well going to force you! ...Anyhow, I'll come back as soon as I can. But I'm not going to hurry. I think you need to know your place here – you are a guest, and a patient ... and, you are indebted to me."

"How so am I indebted to you?" One could tell by David's tone of voice that he was shocked at what he was hearing.

"You know that forty-three hundred francs you owe the hospital? Yes? Well, I paid that to keep your credit good. Now you don't owe the hospital anything. Does that make you happy? I paid forty-three hundred francs for you, and I've given you a place to sleep. I have tried to care for you, David. Can't you see that?" At this point her eyes welled up with tears, whereupon she hid them from David by pushing her face into the pillow like an ashamed little girl.

David scoffed at her crying and began to speak in a demanding tone: "Did they give you my passport back? I'll need that to find work."

"Yes. I have it," said Odette, pulling her face out of the pillow, revealing red, puffy eyes, "It's locked up safe. I'll give it to you when your health is stable. I don't want you fainting on the street and having someone take you for it."

"Smart precaution, Odette, may I take a shower now?"

"Go ahead."

After David went into the bathroom, Odette got up and dressed in a light, spring dress that was altogether too girlish for someone of her age. Then she took her purse, her wicker shopping bag, put on her Spanish bangles, and left, passing through her medical office, to the only door leading to the outside. She knew David would not leave while she went shopping. If not for the fact that he had no money, he would at least remain so long as Odette was the keeper of his passport. It was hidden away somewhere in the apartment. She has a lot of little cabinets, drawers and chests situated around the room – all of them were securely locked.

There are two deadbolts on the door to Odette's medical office – one on either side. When she left the salon, David heard clearly the sound of the bolt being locked on the other side of the door. He wondered why she was locking him inside.

In the bathroom, David found the clothes he'd been wearing scattered across the floor. He dressed quickly and left the bathroom, returning to the salon. He surveyed the room with quick, furtive glances. Then he returned to the bathroom, pulled back the shower curtain and turned the hot water on. A steady jet of water streamed down from the shower head, and steam rose up from the tub. He felt the hot water with his hand. It felt good, and he could think of nothing more pleasurable than a shower at that moment – a shower and a meal. But he didn't have time for a shower. At least he figured he didn't. He put his head under the water to wet his hair, so as to give the impression that he had taken a shower. He ran his fingers through his hair, as he watched a stream of dirty, blackened water run down off his bangs. Something was wrong. He reached for a towel and left the water running.

When he turned and looked in the bathroom mirror, he was horrified. His hair had been cut – badly cut. Sprigs of wet, black hair stuck out in the sides, and on the back. His head resembled the feathers of a crow, a crow with its wings clipped. 'Did I do this?' he wondered, 'What kind of hysteria was I in these last few days? Why don't I remember a thing?' … 'Why didn't she tell me about this when I woke up? Did she…? No, I must have done this to myself. But why?' … 'And these scratch marks, they are more than a few hours old. Some of them must have been made two or three days ago. They are already getting infected. If I scratched myself like this two days ago, why only last night did Odette stop my medication and sedate me? …I just don't get it….'

He was thoroughly confused, yet he decided to let matters go. He didn't have time mull over his hacked hair and battered body. He had things to do. After searching for iodine in the medicine cabinet to treat his wounds, – which he did not find, – he left the bathroom, leaving the shower running.

Back in Odette's salon, David walked quickly over to the desk next to the window. He knew exactly what he wanted from the desk. Though his memory of the last few days was naught, he remembered clearly seeing a hairpin and a letter opener on the desk, at some point in time.

One night, about a year ago, when David was living in Seattle – on Belmont street, in a modest, little apartment with tattered wallpaper and crumbling, plaster walls; which he chose to take solely for the quaint, little courtyard out front with the gurgling fountain that was enclosed by a tall brick wall that kept out the traffic noise and the sight of the cars passing down the busy street; which he chose, as well, for the beautiful empress tree that could be seen from the kitchen window – he was sitting on the edge of his fountain, watching the water spew out of the stone spout and fall languidly into the base of the fountain below.

It was after midnight and the courtyard was empty, except for David and his fountain. He couldn't sleep and he didn't want to be alone in his quiet apartment. Not with how he was feeling. A hollow loneliness ached in his body. He didn't have a friend in the whole city and he felt empty and alone. He pondered on his future and reflected on his past as he sat on that fountain edge, watching the silver light of the full moon over the courtyard reflecting off the stream of water, which cascaded out of the fountain into the basin below. That full moon was reflected so bright and so clearly in the pool of water, turning into tiny ripples of moonlight when the irregular flow of water came splashing down in the basin. No diamonds he had ever seen, in all the jewelry store windows he had ever passed, glimmered as clearly, and purely, and as bright as that moon did glimmer in the wavelets of water in the fountain. He had no one – not a friend, neither a lover – but he had the moon and its precious gems that coursed through his own lonesome fountain and for this he felt happy. With the palm of his hand supporting his chin, and his eyes glowing with the light of the moon, he sat and watched his fountain, and he pondered the heavy questions that ached inside of him. Then, there was a disturbance.

He lifted his head quickly and looked around. He saw nothing but he heard the loud footsteps of someone, a man, running quickly towards him. A moment later, the running man emerged from behind the high stone wall that gave his courtyard its privacy and David stood up quickly, more startled than afraid.

The man was breathing heavily, panting and sweating. He was wearing torn pants of a heavy dark green material – the kind the dockworkers wear to work down at the piers. His shirt was torn as well and covered in sweat. His face was scarred and appeared old, though the man was young – about the same age as David. His hair was tousled and blond. It was shaved on the sides revealing a small, homemade tattoo etched behind his ear.

It was clear to David that the man was running *away* from something; he wasn't going to attack David, on the contrary, he gave David a beseeching, almost helpless, look as he ran around the fountain to hide behind the trunk of nearby tree, enclosed in the courtyard.

As the man heaved to catch his breath, trying to do so without making an excessive noise, David approached him, slowly, cautiously. He didn't say anything.

"Do you live here?" the young man asked, wiping the sweat from his forehead with his damp shirt.

"Yes," replied David, "what's going on?"

"Do you mind if I come inside for just a minute? I'll explain everything. I really need help. I'm not a thief or anything. I won't stay long. I just really need help."

David thought it over for a few seconds and decided that the man seemed sincere enough. And if David could help him, why not? Anyway, he himself needed someone to talk to in this sprawling city where he knew no one.

"Sure," said David, "let's go out this way and around." He began to lead the man out of the courtyard to the street, where the two could enter David's apartment through the backdoor. But the man stood firmly rooted to his spot, hiding behind the trunk of the tree.

"Is there anyway we can get inside from in here, in the courtyard?" he asked, "I can't go out onto the street."

David then understood, getting a sense of the man's urgency; and he quickly led him through the shadows, along the wall of his apartment building, all the while, walking on the man's right side, to shield him from view from the street. The two walked quickly through the shadows and climbed the flimsy, metal stairs, leading to David's front door.

Once inside, David shut and bolted the door. He made to apologize for the unkempt appearance of his apartment, but the man didn't care. He walked right past David quickly and shut the blinds on all of David's windows. He then went back to the front door and double-checked that it was bolted. Then, he took a deep breath and sat

Indian-style on the cream-colored carpeting that was bare of furniture, thin and stained. David went to get a glass of water for the man who sat on the floor, trying to catch his breath. Then David took his own seat on the thin carpet, and stared at the stranger.

"My name is Milo."

"David."

The two shook hands. Milo's hand was very rough and calloused. His grip was firm. He took his paranoid eyes off the closed blinds for a moment to look into David's eyes when the two shook hands. David appreciated this.

"Do you have a cigarette? The cops took mine," said Milo.

"Yes, I think I do." said David, getting up to get his cigarettes from a drawer in the kitchen. He then returned with a box of good English cigarettes, "555s", which he didn't smoke very often, and a glass of water for himself. He sat again in the same place, facing Milo, who had, by this time managed to catch his breath. David looked at the man's wrists. There were red handcuff marks on them.

"They put them on tight, don't they?"

"What?"

David pointed to his wrists.

"Oh, yeah," he replied, "and they took my cigarettes and my gun. But I got away. Whew! Shit, did I get away! It was beautiful." … "Don't worry, I'm not dangerous, I'm not going to try anything weird."

"What happened?" David asked curiously.

"I was popped with a friend down on Pike Street. He was carrying twenty-five grams of black, and they got me with an unregistered handgun." … "Man, I knew we were going down hard. I already had a warrant and I wasn't looking forward to spending the next five years in the clink." He spoke fast, as the adrenaline was still coursing his body, "…So they cuffed us and drove us down to King County. They booked my friend first. It wasn't even his tar, he was slinging it for someone else – poor guy. Anyhow, they booked him first. I was still cuffed to the bench in the hall. Then, you should've seen it – it was great! I did the hospital trick and it went beautifully!" … "I started faking a seizure right there on the ground … and can I fake a seizure, let me tell ya! I almost pulled the bench out of the ground, see, I was still handcuffed to it. Then, the bitch cop ran up to me. She didn't know whether I was epileptic, or withdrawing from junk, or what. It was obvious it was more than junk withdrawal, I mean, you should've seen it! I was flailing my arms, clenching my jaw, my face was, no doubt, bright red, and then the bitch cop and one other came up to me and uncuffed me. They picked me up – at that point I was pretending to be chocking on my tongue, spit was foaming on my mouth. I couldn't turn blue, like an epileptic does, but I was limp and my eyes were back in my head." ... "Anyway, they threw me in the paddy wagon and drove me up to Swedish hospital...

"...A hospital is a lot easier to escape from than a jail, let me tell ya! The second I was alone – and they thought I was out, and didn't bother cuffing me to the bed – although they had a cop standing guard outside. I could see the back of his pig-head through the little window in the hospital room door." ... "Three minutes later, I made my move. The pig's head was gone from the window and I knew he was probably standing right beside the door, but I had to move then. There is no way I am going back to prison – no way!" ... "So, I bounced. I just took off and slammed through that door so hard! ...And I don't even know if there was a cop behind me or not. I didn't even look back. I just ran my ass off down that hall and down the stairs. I know all the exits at Swedish, and every street leading away from it by heart. I ran out on Broadway, but Broadway is the last place I wanted to be. Sirens came from all around. They might not have even been after me – maybe I was just paranoid ... anyway I got off Broadway, ran down Madison, to Summit, then to Spring, and soon I was running down Belmont, and I saw your little courtyard, and that's it! ...I saw you, and you look like a nice enough guy...."

"Whew, I'm glad you got away!" David's eyes grew big from hearing the story. His jaw dropped. Milo's breath grew more rapid while telling his story, animated with hand gestures; yet, he had to stop a moment to catch his breath.

"I'm glad I got away too, you don't even know! I am never going back to prison."

"It's too bad about your friend, though."

"Yeah, it's too bad. But prison is good for him. He was tired of running. He'd been running even longer than I have ... was even thinking of turning himself in. He'll probably be happier in there." Then he looked at David imploringly, while taking a drag from his cigarette, "Listen, if I go back out on the street now, they're going to catch me. The street's too quiet. Is there anyway I can crash here on the floor? First thing in the morning, once people are out in the streets, I can get down to the bus station...."

"Yeah, sure. That's no problem," replied David, "if you want, you can sleep now, I'll turn the light off. There's an extra blanket in the closet."

"No, I'm fine. My heart is beating too fast to sleep now. Just as long as the blinds are closed."

David wasn't tired either. He had had a lot of thoughts pressing on his mind that night and it was pleasant talking to Milo. He enjoyed his story, and thought that Milo was an interesting guy.

So, the two sat up and talked. Milo told David of his life and David told Milo of his. Then Milo began to give David a few tips on how to be a criminal (which is the whole reason I am flashing back to this event in David's life, as you will soon see for yourself). ...First he explained to David what to look for in a handgun:

"My gun was beautiful," Milo went on, "it's too bad they took it!" ... "It was a .38 – perfect. A .22 won't work for shit, but a .40 is too big. Mine had a snub nose, nice and small – easy to hide. But you put hollow point bullets in a .38 and it works just as good as a .40 You'll stop anyone cold and dead with hollow points." ... "Double action, too. You don't want single action, you have to cock it after every shot. Automatic's the best. I only knew two guys who sold automatics out of their basements, but they both went down a while ago. Anyway, last thing is, you don't want to keep it with the factory grip. That metallic shit will slip right through your hands when you're all sweaty, running with the thing in your hand. So what you do is take some tubing – the surgical kind junkies use to tie themselves off, that yellow shit – and you cut it and hot-glue the handle of the gun, then you wrap that rubber tubing around to make a nice grip – then you've got yourself a weapon!"

The two young men, continued on smoking and talking for several hours. Milo was entertaining, and David knew he was genuine. He told David that the only thing he'd ever shoot at is a cop, and David believed him.

Then Milo told him how to pick a lock nice and proper. David, coincidentally, had the two things that Milo needed to demonstrate: a letter opener, and a hairpin. The letter opener was a gift from his father. It was monogrammed with David's initials: "DSS".

The hairpin was left behind by a girl that David used to be with. They had had a falling-out and, already, six months had passed; but David hung on to that hairpin – not thinking she would ever come back, or anything; he just kept it to remind himself of her, now and again – even though the memory always brought sadness and pain to him. Even handing over her hairpin to Milo seemed wrong to him. That was probably the most private of all his possessions … the most sentimental thing in his apartment. He thought of this girl as Milo went over to the bathroom door and summoned David to come watch how to pick a lock. He wondered where she was on that night. It was already three in the morning. He figured she was probably sleeping. He wondered where she was sleeping and whether or not she was sleeping alone.

David stood by Odette's desk, running his fingers over its fine, polished rosewood surface, feeling the soft grain. He thought of that girl, and he thought of Milo. He had told Milo to come back anytime to visit. The two had parted, the next morning, on the best possible of terms. Milo said he was off to the bus station to get away from Seattle until the heat cleared. Then, he said, he would return and pay David a visit. He never returned.

David hoped Milo got away and found a nice quiet life somewhere where the authorities weren't looking for him. Yet, his intuition told him that he had been caught and was put in prison. Otherwise, David was sure that he would have come back to visit. David remembered his face, the fear in his eyes, when he had said that there was no way he would ever go back to prison. Prison is a bad place, and David truly hoped that he hadn't been caught.

He quickly picked up Odette's hairpin, which looked nothing like the one that his old girlfriend had left at his apartment in Seattle. He thought for another moment about her. He wished that the INS had let him take some things from his apartment before shipping him off to Europe. He would have taken the hairpin. 'No,' he thought to himself, 'It is over with her. I must let go, those things of the past.'

He realized he was killing precious time with his reveries. She would be home soon, and he had to hurry. He held her hairpin and letter opener in his hand, and quickly walked over to a locked cabinet, on which there was statue of an odalisque carved in wood. He admired the cabinet, also of rosewood. The lock was brass, plated in gold. He hoped his passport was inside.

He jammed the letter opener in and before he even tried to slip the hairpin in, the lock gave. "Poorly-made lock," he muttered, opening the cabinet lid. Before he had time to examine the contents, however, he heard someone or something approaching him. He turned around.

There was no one else in the room. He could hear the shower water running in the tub in the distance. Steam was pouring out of the open bathroom door. He passed off his anxiety as mere skittishness and focused his eyes on the contents of the cabinet.

Mostly it was rubbish: official looking papers, which were probably tax forms; and romantic looking letters that reeked of perfume. They were all written in French and David didn't understand a word on any of them. He closed the cabinet lid, but heard no click – the cabinet didn't lock. He tried to lock it by forcing the latch that had sprung back into the hole as hard as he could, but it would not catch. He had broken the lock. A little bit of sweat began to run down his forehead. He couldn't let Odette find out he had been going through her things. Not while he was staying with her, at least. But why not? She admitted to having locked up his passport. It was his passport, after all; and, if she wouldn't give it to him, had he not the right to look for it, himself? Still, the proper way to do it would be to tell her he was leaving her place for good and demand his passport back. Then she would have to give it back. He could have the police come if he needed to. The important thing is not to do anything illegal. But where would he go? Why this talk of leaving her place for good? He was still ill, his kidney burned with intensity, his back felt like a piano had fallen on it, his headache pounded so much that he was sure he had meningitis, or a brain hemorrhage of some sort. He couldn't leave. She was his doctor and he needed her. Besides, he was starving and she was, at that moment, shopping at the market for him.

He abandoned the rosewood cabinet but not the hunt. Next he went over to that old, beautiful desk by the window. There was one drawer without a lock. This one contained files of papers and other useless junk. The center drawer hadn't a lock either, but it only contained paperclips and morphine tablets – the tablets were all divvied up and wrapped in foil wrappers. David swallowed two of the tablets, and deposited four foil balls, each containing two pills, in the pocket of his trousers. Then he stopped for a moment to examine a sore on his bare chest that was causing particular pain. It looked as though red streaks were beginning to show up in the area surrounding the sore – that is a sure sign of infection. The sore itself was deep – it didn't appear at all to be a scratch – the surface was developing a puss, and the irritated skin had become white. This self-examination, however, was interrupted abruptly when David heard a loud *thud* behind his head. He jumped up suddenly and turned around to see what had happened.

He looked at the large window facing out to the courtyard. Apparently it had been a mere bird, he saw a flash of it bouncing off the window out of the corner of his eye a moment after he turned around when hearing the *thud*.

He turned the latch on the window shutters and looked down to the ground below. Sure enough, there was a bird, a robin, twitching in its last moments of life. It had clearly broken its neck on the impact with the window. He then looked up at the laurel trees swaying over the fountain in the courtyard where the water bubbled down over those broad, tropical leaves, which looked so green on this morning. Paris can have such an innocent light to it in the morning – a soft, pastel, and innocent light – and a peaceful quiet too. By crepuscule, however, you realize she's no more innocent than a black, hooded executioner, or the whores on Rue St. Denis.

David pulled the latch of the window and pushed the shutters open, letting in the thin, mild air of the sunny morning. He gazed outside again at the sunny courtyard. A gardener was trimming the rhododendrons near the fountain; he looked over at David when the latter opened the window. He almost forgot that he had a nervously ticking clock to race. It was time to draw the curtains and get back to work.

After closing the shutters, David located the pin in the window latch, which allowed the windows to be locked; and, with a firm jab of the letter opener, he freed the pin and slid it out, placing it in his pocket. The window latch was then loose and he shut the window, taking care to make sure the latch appeared as normal. Then he drew the crêpe curtains closed and got down on his hands and knees beside the desk – in order to open the last locked drawer.

The lock on this drawer gave quickly with the hairpin tucked inside and one quick jab with the letter opener; but the sharp, brass letter opener bounced back towards David after opening the lock and sliced a nice gouge in his hand. He sucked at the blood that dripped down his fingers as he pulled open the drawer and peeked his head over the desk, one more time, to see if anyone was entering. The room was quiet, though the shower water could be heard running in the distance and the clippers of the gardener could be heard sheering the deadheads off the rhododendrons out in the garden.

All interest in these and other things flit away in the instant David looked inside that left-hand desk drawer belonging to Dr. Odette Moreaux. Gamblers deal a million cards, archeologists dig a million holes, and trained thieves work their entire lives, in hopes of coming across a treasure such as the one David found on this morning. And this was his first time putting Milo's lock-picking tricks to work.

David slid open the drawer and saw a beautiful future: stacks of banknotes – all fifty, hundred and five-hundred franc bills; travelers' cheques; bank cards; loose sapphires; set diamonds; Tahitian pearls; fire opals, so on and so forth.

Skittish and nervous, his eyes darted around the room as he pulled out a stack of bills and flipped through it. He checked again to see that the drapes were drawn. They were. He looked through the drawer for his passport. It wasn't there. The passport didn't so much matter to him, when he thought about all the other precious contents of the drawer. He studied again the stacks of bills. A few ten-franc notes were thrown in, but mostly they were hundreds and five-hundreds, all neatly stacked, and wrapped in manila rubber bands. His eyes widened and his heart raced as that immense fortune coursed through his hands. He picked up a loose fire opal and turned it to catch the light, whereupon fragments of bright orange, yellow and blue light danced the dance of wealth and luxury. David then slid the drawer back in, leaving it ajar a few centimeters. He then returned the letter opener and hairpin to the exact places on the desk where he had found them – first wiping his blood off of the letter opener with his sock and bending it back into shape.

He then stood up and walked over to the bookshelf beside the door leading to Odette's medical office. He had his eye on a bag on the top shelf – a large medicine bag, made from dark brown American leather, with two leather handles and a zipper. The bag smelled funny – as though it hadn't been cured. He pulled the bag down and examined the contents. There were a few dozen boxes of morphine tablets inside – enough to ease his pain for six months, maybe more. He didn't want to steal the doctor's pain medication; besides, all he could think of was that drawer full of cash and jewels. It was still ajar. What if Odette returned at that moment, and saw that he had picked the lock and left the drawer containing her immense fortune open? He would be finished. He didn't want the gross of morphine, yet he had to look out for himself. He took five boxes of tablets, a couple week's supply, and put it in a plastic bag that was lying on a table near the bookshelf – it was too much to carry in his trouser pockets. He then zipped the leather medicine bag shut and placed it exactly where it had been on the top shelf. Then, he carried the plastic bag containing the five boxes of morphine tablets into the bathroom.

The mirror was steamed and tub was full of water. He pulled the drain plug and turned off the water. He then crouched down on the floor by the toilet and stuffed the plastic bag far back behind the toilet, between the pipes, where it was out of view. Then, remembering the cabinet drawer he had left open, he sprang to his feet and went back into the salon.

He pulled the drawer out wide and flipped through the banknotes again. All was quiet and still at first; but then, he heard a sound, which he believed to be the gardener tapping on the window. He disregarded the sound and paid full-attention to the money. He saw a beautiful future, alright. But it was not his future. It was the doctor's future. He considered her very lucky to have such a fortune, and a home as well – shelter from the rain and a place to be alone – away from the world – whenever she wants.

David kept looking at those jewels and those banknotes in a kind of dazed reverie. And all the while he thought, how ridiculous it would be for him to steal that money. How absurd. On the one hand, it most certainly would not ruin her. He was sure she had an even larger fortune in the bank; and, anyway, she had a profession. She could, in due time, earn it back. Perhaps the jewels were sacred to her. Perhaps they were gifts from her husband, but David could do fine with the banknotes alone. And banknotes rarely carry any sentimental value. Taking them, however, would be unfair to her. But, was it not unfair to David when someone, the nurses, the men who carried him to the hospital, or whoever, stole his sole fortune – that thirteen-thousand dollars? Did they not rob him of every chance he had of making a good life for himself in Europe? Shouldn't he try to get that money back in anyway he can?

But it wasn't *he* who stole his money. He had never stolen anyone's money. Is that his strength? Or is that his weakness? He obviously has not been a master of survival as of recent – losing everything he owned and ending up without a home. But what would be a home to him now? It would be warmth. It would be his place to be alone. But to be alone in a home built from the bricks of someone else's misfortune? He would rather sleep in a field of grass; at least then, he would have the dreams of an honest man.

'If I were doing it for my family… if I were doing for the woman I love… I would do it,' he thought, 'I could sleep comfortably in a home built on the misfortunes of others, if that home was also giving warmth to someone I love. But my mother is dead. My father may be as well, for all I know. Wherever he is, in America or not, he is far away and I will probably never see him again. And there is no woman I love and no woman who loves me…

'I could kill all the odious doctors of Paris and all the merchants and bankers and whores and priests, and the butchers' and politicians' daughters, and build a home from their bones – use their skulls as bricks, and burn their fat to heat the rooms – if it meant keeping the one I love warm and dry and happy – but for myself, alone? I would not even build a hut from the hairs that fall from these people's heads.' … 'My conscience is heavy, and maybe it is skewed, though I don't think it is. A man who has killed has right to live, so long as there is someone whom he loves and gives to. But even the pettiest thief should die from shame if he steals for no one but himself.'

David realized Odette may not return for sometime yet, and he had a terrible hole in his belly that needed food to fill it. He decided to take a ten-franc bill, the smallest bill in the drawer, out from the center of a stack tied up in rubber bands.

He put the ten-franc note in his pocket. It would be enough to buy a small meal – some bread and cheese, perhaps. The rest of the money – those tens or hundreds of thousands of francs – and the precious jewels, bank cards and travelers' cheques, he arranged in the desk drawer, exactly how they had been arranged; and he carefully slid the drawer back in, until it clicked. The drawer was again locked. The lock had not broken this time.

Why hadn't Odette returned yet? Why had she allowed him so much time to prowl through her things? Surely, it never occurred to her that he would go through her things. Not that she naïvely believed that he was too honest to break into her locked drawers and cabinets. In Odette's mind, no patient is honest. She believed any patient capable of robbing her blind, would do so at first opportunity. The reality is, she just considered David a half-wit, incapable of opening a locked drawer. Even if she had given him a key and pointed to the lock the key fit into, she was sure he'd never be able to figure out how to get it in. It's surprising that she even bolted him inside her apartment. Just closing the door would have been enough in her mind; for surely 'if he's French and can't even speak French, he must be too dumb-witted to know how to turn a doorknob!'

Unfortunately, dear reader, we don't have time to wait for Odette to return. I've already spent far too long enumerating the events *chez elle*, and too much time expounding on the relationship between our doctor and her patient. Please note, that I was careful not to waste your time with too many flowery images and watercolor descriptions. All that has preceded in this chapter, you will soon see, plays an enormous role in bringing clarity to what is about to happen to you, to me, to Nastya, Salaudski, David and everyone else. We have weaved the blanket, so-to-speak, and now it is time to lie under it. ...And, you know the kinds of things that go on, when two or more people are gathered beneath a handmade blanket and the lights are out! ... well, it is about time to get back to the life of Nastya, which has been progressing on the other side of the Seine, all the way across town. But first, we must be aware of one more event...

Upon David's meeting with Marick, the junky from the quai, and the great hope that is born along with it...

Since David had found no iodine in the medicine cabinet, once he had put the ten-franc bill in the pocket of his trousers and closed and locked Odette's drawer of fortune, he took the heavy crystal cruet, which sat on Odette's desk, half-full of table wine, and poured the sanguine alcohol on the nearly-infected wounds on his chest, dousing them liberally. There was a slight burn, but nothing too intense. Afterwards, he had to go change into another pair of Odette's husband's trousers, as the ones he had been wearing were covered in red wine. He also put on a cream-colored shirt – also her husband's – which he greatly fancied. The shirt appeared to be handmade silk; the texture was uneven, the buttons were abalone, and it fit beautifully. David admired himself in the mirror of the armoire. All of his cuts and scratches were concealed by the clothes; and his hair, which he or someone had hacked at pretty good, didn't look so bad once it had been combed back.

He put on the old husband's shoes and smiled at himself smugly in the mirror. The morphine had begun its mild, yet satisfactory, effect and his pain ceased. His head felt more clear than it ever had since his arrival in Paris. He felt good, happy, without a care, just as he had felt riding in the truck with Marc, with a large sum of cash in his pocket – a new visitor to a foreign land. He once again had money in his pocket. It was only ten francs, but that would be enough to cure his hunger for the time being. And, still, he was a new visitor in a foreign land. Odette was nowhere to be found, and he was off to see a little of Paris.

David walked with the confident strides one has when wearing clothes that one feels handsome in, over to Odette's desk, where he took, once again, the letter opener and hairpin from the desktop; and, whistling a happy tune, he walked right over to the door leading to Odette's medical office – the one bolted from the outside – and slid the letter opener through the doorjamb; and, within seconds, the bolt slid and the door opened wide.

He tossed the hairpin across the room and it landed right on the desk, next to the crystal cruet now empty of wine; then he deposited the letter opener in his pocket. He shut the door to the salon behind him and bolted it – just as Odette had done. Then he walked to the front door to exit into the hallway.

With a quick turn of the bolt on the front door, the door flew open. David took a step into the hall, where a man in the shadows touched his shoulder.

David gave a start – he jumped back in alarm. The man didn't budge. He just kept standing there, in the shadows, wearing dark clothes that smelled of sweat.

The man's eyes were alight with a sick yellow glow and they gazed unflinchingly as the man held on to David's shoulder. David felt in his pocket for the letter opener, with its sharp brass point, it could stab like a dagger. He prepared to extract it, as he backed away. Then the man began to speak…

"*David,*" he said, "*Docteur Moreaux est là?*"

"Who are you? How do you know my name?" David said, slightly bewildered, yet no longer afraid.

"Can you speak French? ...That's alright, I can speak in English. Is Doctor Moreaux here? I have been waiting outside for an hour?"

"Um, no. She isn't. She went shopping."

"And she left you here alone? Who was that in the shower until just now?"

"That was me in the shower; and yes, she left me alone, if it is your business."

"But your hair isn't wet."

"It was. I dried it." said David taking a couple steps back through the open doorway in the medical office.

"Well, it doesn't matter. Anyway, my name is Marick." He extended his hand; and, after a moment of reluctance, David took Marick's hand and shook it.

"How did you know my name was David?"

"Everyone here knows. You are the patient who has been staying in Odette's apartment. Don't you remember introducing yourself to us while we were all getting our doses of S-X the other day? All you said was your name, in the French pronunciation: *Dah-veed* ...I thought you were French."

"Ha! you thought I was French? That's funny. But no, I don't remember that at all. I really don't remember anything that's happened lately...."

"Listen," Marick interrupted, "I'm not really in the condition to chat, David. I've come for medicine and I was hoping the doctor would be here. Do you know when she's coming back?"

"No, in fact, she should have been back a while ago. What medicine do you need? Maybe I can help?"

"I don't know, some S-X, some morphine, something... some junk of some sort. I'm feeling like hell, and the doctor was supposed to be here to give me a dose."

"I have some morphine," David said, reaching into his pocket and pulling out one of the foil balls he had taken from Odette's drawer. With these words, Marick's eyes lit-up – and not with the sallow sick glow they had had in the hallway a moment before; they lit-up bright white with happiness, as though David was his savior... and apparently he was.

Marc unwrapped the foil ball with avarice and looked at the two, small yellow tablets contained within. "This is all you have?"

"Yes," David lied.

Marick took a deep breath, "Well, it's not enough to swallow. I'll have to slam it. You don't mind?"

"I don't understand," replied David.

Marick smiled at David's naïvety. "Can you wait in the hall, and knock on the door if Odette comes? I'm going to shoot it."

"Okay," agreed David.

"You won't tell the doctor, will you? If I shoot these tablets?"

"Um ... no. No, I won't tell ... No, of course I won't!"

Marick eyed David suspiciously at first and then smiled a trusting smile. After that, David went out into the hall and closed the door most of the way, leaving the heel of his foot in the door, preventing it from locking - just in case.

David hated the sight of injections. Even at the hospital, whenever he saw someone else receiving an injection it was unbearable. The blood ran from his own head and he'd clench his white fist and chew on his knuckles until the horrible procession was over.

Behind the door, he could hear Marick crushing pills and getting water from the sink near the examining table. He could hear him tying himself off and then there was a moment of silence....

Then Marick, made a loud cough, which was followed by a deep sigh. Then he pulled the door open to the hallway and David took a step back. Marick's face was calm and contented. He untied the tube around his arm, and put his works back in his pocket. Then he smiled at David and began to scratch himself, and rub his forehead.

A few moments before, his voice had seemed so strained, so unhappy, so deeply wrought with pain. His back too was stiff and his movements were jerky. In short, Marick had been a mess when David first saw him. But after taking the shot, it was as if a completely new man stood before our David. A happy, jovial fellow whose lightness of heart showed in the gaiety of his eyes.

"It was only sixty milligrams," Marick told David, smiling happily, "But it will help for a few hours, anyway."

David felt happy that he was able to help Marc get relief from his pain. He felt sad that Marc needed to get relief in that way, but that wasn't David's business. Anyway, David knew the human body's potential for torment and suffering and it is nothing to scoff at. At least, Marick had found relief.

The two walked down the hallway together and out into the street on Rue du Dragon – David in his silk shirt and wool trousers, and Marick in his dirty corduroy jacket and pants. They walked on down Rue St. Benoit and the two could see the Cathedral St. Germain in the distance. Its tall, pointed tower ascended above the buildings that lay on their right. David looked at the cathedral tower, with it's crude, grey stones, stacked up to the dark conical roof; it looked as though it had been built by apes instead of men. David slipped into a daydream, momentarily, as he walked past the medieval relics in the golden light of spring.

"I'm headed down to Quai Voltaire," said Marick, 'You can come. I live down there."

"Oh, yes? I'd like to," replied David, "How long have you been living there?"

"About a year. It's a good life. A view of the river, no one hassles you. I like the streets in my neighborhood. And it's close to St. Germain."

"How much do you pay? …If you don't mind me asking."

"Not a thing. I have a good situation."

"Really?!" David's interest peaked. He was starting to think that meeting Marick was the best thing that could have happened to him. 'Good thing I didn't stab him with a letter opener,' he thought, "Are there other places for rent over there? I mean, something where I won't have to pay?"

"There's a whole quai of them; however, you have to be lucky to get a good spot. Otherwise you end up in some dump with bedbugs, and lice, and roaches, and people pissing on your house, and that kind of thing. But you helped me out, David… I'll help you out. If you come tonight, I'll cook some rice and vegetables and we'll have a picnic by the river. I'm a pretty good cook, I think you'll like the dinner. Then you can stay with me, and tomorrow we'll find you a place of your own."

"Thank you, Marick, I really appreciate it. I've needed a break like this. Since I've been in Paris, my hopes have dried up a bit."

"But you've been lucky enough to stay with the doctor...."

"Yes, but that's been more of a problem than you know."

"I think I can imagine. I wouldn't stay with Doctor Moreaux, myself. No way in hell!"

David laughed at Marick's comment, and laughed at much more. He laughed and looked up at the light blue noontime sky and the soft springtime sun and he laughed with happiness at his great change in fortune. He had made a new friend and this friend was going to help him find his own place to live. This was, no doubt, what his health needed. A good friend and his own place to live. Then he could get his passport back from Odette, and he could find a job. He could work an honest job and enjoy the strange and beautiful adventures that meet anyone new to a foreign country. 'A view of the river … close to St. Germain!' he thought, 'What a great life! Maybe my health problems will disappear completely. Maybe, I'll make other friends, too. Surely I will. Maybe I'll find a girlfriend! …Well, one thing at a time. Now, I have to go back and say goodbye to Odette. I'll slip the ten-francs that I stole into her pocket – without her knowing, of course. Then, I'll enjoy the nice meal she's probably preparing right now. The nice French food, fresh from the market … then I'll have yet another meal with Marick, by the Seine.'

David's thoughts made him drunk with happiness. He looked up at the sun sparkling yellow so tenderly, with its mild, spring warmth, in that pastel blue sky that is so peculiar to Paris, and he mouthed the words, 'Thank you. Oh, thank you so!'

David told Marick that he had to take care of something right away, something that could not wait, but he wanted to see Marick's place as soon as possible. Marick shook David's hand in the most amicable of ways, and said that it was not a problem. He would wait for him down on Quai Voltaire. He drew David a little map of how to find him and asked him to hurry, so that the two could enjoy a little bit of the sunshine together out on the quai where the boats are docked and the pretty girls walk by.

With great, mutual friendliness, and much hope for the future, the two parted ways – for the moment anyhow. David would return to visit Marick later on this night.

CHAPTER XII

Now that we have illustrated the life of David, as it has been lived over this last week chez Odette, we must go back and peer into the life Nastya has been living these last couple days. To be chronologically specific, we'll resume the life of Nastya, starting yesterday morning and follow-up until the glorious present moment.

You may have been worried about Nastya, as we haven't seen the lovely girl for quite some time. But she has been handling herself well at Salaudski's.

In fact, the last we saw of her, was the morning after the wounded "Monsieur de Chevalier" tried to take advantage of his "nurse" by forcing the young beauty to embrace and kiss him while she was rubbing lotion on his feverish forehead.

If you recall, she spent that evening crying in her little bedroom, while Salaudski took a nightcap and passed-out in a 'sea of snores', which brought dreams so light and carefree. Nastya thought the best thing to do would be to leave Salaudski and Paris as soon as possible and get on a train to Moscow. She would not let her lack of funds be an obstacle. She was prepared to hop the train and stowaway.

The next morning, however, she felt differently about everything. She would, under no circumstances, let Salaudski have his way with her; yet, she was not giving up on Paris so easily. She had been in France less than a week and she wasn't about to run back home a failure.

Upon waking, she took a long walk to both get away from Salaudski, and plan her next move – plan the next step necessary to move towards her goal.

As soon as she reentered Salaudski's apartment building on Rue de Paradis, she was greeted by the landlady who had received an envelope covered in Russian characters, addressed to: *forty-seven, Rue de Paradis.* It was obviously for Nastya, and the landlady had a good intuition about the situation upstairs on the fifth-floor, and knew better than to give the letter to Salaudski; so she waited for Nastya to pass by her door and then she popped her little wrinkled head out of her front door and said, "Pssst!"

Nastya turned around surprised. She had been deep in thought and the old woman calling to her caught her off-guard.

"Pssst! ...Mademoiselle!"

"Hello!" said Nastya amicably, while watching the old landlady hobble out into the entryway with her cane, while tapping at the envelope.

"I think this is for you. It comes to me yesterday. I can't read it so it must be Russian...."

Nastya took the envelope with a trembling hand. Emotion began to seethe in her body. She looked down at the little woman and then looked at the envelope. The address was in her father's handwriting. The two stood silently in the hallway for a few moments – the landlady looked to Nastya expectantly. She wanted to hear the gossip in the letter. Nastya just looked at the envelope for many moments, in tender and emotional introspection. Then the door opposite the landlady's creaked open and the dark, scaly face of the man, with the eyes of a pimp, could be seen looking at the two women through the crack in his door. The landlady noticed him right away and hobbled over to his front door, brandishing her cane at him. She tapped his door two times, sharply, and said in English, "Go on! Get back in there, you creep!"; whereupon, he pulled his head back inside, just as a turtle pulls it's scaly head into its carapace when it is aggravated. Then he closed the door.

The landlady turned back around to where Nastya had been standing with the intention of making the young girl spill the gossip. But Nastya was already walking out the front door of the building – going back the way she had come; and her silent and introverted manner, the way she looked down at the envelope while taking slow, languid steps to the front door, gave the landlady the impression that the girl wanted to be alone. Before the landlady had a chance to tap Nastya's behind with her cane, the latter had already left the building and was headed down the sidewalk on Rue de Paradis.

A letter from a loving father in Moscow, to his only daughter in Paris, – translated into English (for our benefit)…

My Precious Nastenjka,

I feel I have so much to tell you. A lot has happened since you left us. But now is not the time to tell you all about it. I will save some news for a future letter.

I am not angry at you, Nastenjka. You are an adult and can make your own decisions. Your leaving without saying goodbye to your mother, your brother and myself, left me torn and bewildered, but I soon realized that that was the only way you could have left. I have always trusted you to take actions with regard to your love for us and your respect for yourself, and I trust that your leaving, unannounced, heeded this love and respect – and I am not angry with you.

Mother was angry for several days, but now she only cries. Yet do not harm yourself with needless worry. She is strong, your mother. She knows, as I know, that you did what you had to do, and that you will take care of yourself.

I worry about you, my little girl, in some strange country, where you don't speak the language and you don't have your family. Oh, Nastenjka, if you only knew how a father can worry about his daughter – his only daughter. There is a pain I cannot describe … but the last thing I want to do is make you feel badly for what you have done. You are a free-spirit, like your father. You have big ambitions for your life and I am proud of you for your strength and determination. …But still, I worry I will not see you again. Will we see you again, Nastenjka? And will it be a long time, yet? Oh, it will be a blessed day given to me by the Lord when I see you again! But please don't grow up too much. I want you to remain my little girl … Oh, I know that's foolishness. If the Lord is kind and you return, you will return a woman and not a little girl. That is the natural order of life. All I pray is that someday you return. As you know, we have not a lot of money; but if you ask, I will send you a train ticket without hesitation. But I will wait that you ask.

Moscow is lonely. It is sad and lonely and it is cold, very cold. But the letter you left behind for us has helped our spirits and continues to help our spirits. It warms the cold nights and eases the loneliness.

Now I send this letter to you and pray, and pray, that you receive it in good health – and in safety. How is this aristocrat with whom you are staying? He had better treat you well – my only daughter!

Well, God bless you. You are in all of my thoughts, hopes and prayers. Please be safe and know that I will always remain,

Your Loving Father

PS: I have just read over what I've written to you and I don't want it to seem that your actions have brought senseless misery to me and your mother. I don't want you to feel any guilt, Nastenjka. We are sad, yet we are strong. And this is life, and life must be confronted. You did what you had to do. I know that you had no choice. Your strong and ambitious character would allow no other fate.

So go on in Paris and give it all your best. Work hard and you will achieve what you want to. You are out in the midst of the world now, so go forward and be strong – do not be afraid. You are a great dancer and I know that you will be a success. Try hard, but above all remain happy and have respect for yourself. Try to learn French, too, while you are there. It will be a good asset to you throughout your life. And enjoy the beauty of Paris, not everyone gets the chance to go there. But remember, if things go badly and you need to come home, do not hesitate for a moment to ask me for a train ticket. I will have you one within the hour. I will always look after you, my girl, and the Lord too is with you.

By the letter's conclusion, Nastya's eyes are wet and her cheeks are stained with tears. She wanders through the empty streets, reading again every word her father wrote. Then, after reaching the Canal St. Martin, she folds up the letter and puts it into the pocket of her coat. She then sits on the stone wall and looks out over the canal. The sun sparkles on the tips of the wavelets, and the water, remarkably clear on this day, reflects the blue of the sky and the tiny, white puffs of clouds from the sky overhead. Nastya sits and thinks for a while. She thinks over the line her father wrote: *...You are out in the midst of the world now, so go forward and be strong – do not be afraid.* She sits there on the stone wall, knowing exactly what she needs to do. Then a cold breeze comes and one of those tiny, white clouds eclipses the sun, throwing a cold shadow over everything. Nastya suddenly stands up and starts walking back to the home of Salaudski.

Anastasia's entrance into the Opéra Garnier…

The front door creaked open timidly as Nastya entered Salaudski's, more than a little afraid of what he may say or do. He was still asleep on the sofa, when she entered. Again, he had a an empty bottle of wine rolling around on his large belly in the rhythm of his loud, crackling snores.

Nastya tip-toed into her room, and sat on her little bed beneath the window while she thought about her father's letter.

The last part of his letter reinforced her decision to stay in Paris and to put great effort into becoming a success – though without compromising herself. It made her happy, and more secure, knowing that at any time she could ask her father for a ticket home and he would send one 'within the hour'.

Nastya pulled her suitcase close to her. She opened the latch and took from her purse a pair of scissors, a needle and thread. She then took her father's letter from her coat pocket and set it on her knees while she examined the lining of her suitcase, where she had made a hidden pocket to hold her passport. She took the scissors and trimmed the threads in the lining. She then tucked the letter into the suitcase lining, next to her passport, and sewed the lining shut again. Then she looked around the little room and made sure nothing of hers was lying around. Everything she had, was either on her body or in her suitcase. She shut her suitcase and closed the latches; and then set it beside her door, as if she were getting ready to move out.

In the next room, Salaudski was still snoring like an old gasoline engine when Nastya entered and walked up to stand beside him. She looked down at the old man.

"Excuse me," she said in a loud voice meant to wake him, "I am going…." Her words were cut off when Salaudski choked loudly on his snores and jumped up with wide, startled eyes.

"Oh my goodness! Anastasia. You scared me!"

"Salaudski… I am…."

"No, Nastya, I am sorry about last night. I thought you wanted it, I mean, I thought you wouldn't mind, I mean, you were giving those signals, and…."

"It really doesn't matter, I…." and again she was cut off by Salaudski…

"Anastasia, my first goal, my only goal, is to make you a dancer at the Opéra Garnier. And that is what I am going to. You will see me in a new light, once I make you a famous dancer. I don't expect you to love an old codger like me. But maybe you will, one day, love this old codger once he makes you a star in Paris." … "But realize, I do not force you to do anything…

"Nastya, please. Come with me right now down to the Opéra Garnier. I know the director is there now. We will not walk. We'll get a taxi. Okay? We'll go straight there and have our meeting and that will be it."

"I don't think it's going to work out with the Opéra Garnier. I've been here a week and we haven't even gone there once. I don't think I should stay here with you and be your kept-woman…."

"But how can you say that, Anastasia? How can you? I'm not keeping you anywhere. And it's going to work out with the Opéra Garnier – I promised in the letter I sent and I promise you now. The director is probably just as upset about not having met you yet as you are. I know he would love to see me, and he is so excited to meet you – we've talked about you a lot. He really is a kind old man, that director. Always running around with busy things going on. Oh, I'm a fool Anastasia, and I'm sorry. Because of my foot, I've kept you waiting … and then, I made the mistake of doing what I did last night. I'm sorry, Anastasia. I just thought maybe you … I don't know, I guess I really thought that you appreciated me. I didn't want to … I didn't want you to…."

"To what?" asked Nastya, tapping her fingers with impatience, while looking down at the man lying on the sofa.

"…Just what I did was foolish, and I promise I won't try that again and I promise to do what I said in the letter. You'll stay here and I won't try to get you into my bed – unless of course you want to come, because then … but I won't try that and just like in the letter, I promise you happiness. The Opéra Garnier is going to make you a dancer … the prima ballerina, I'll bet you anything."

"Okay," Nastya responded, "one last time – but you will hire a cab, alright?"

"Yes, my dear, five minutes and I'll be ready," said Salaudski, jumping up excitedly from his sofa, "and you go get ready too. Five minutes and we'll leave.

The two didn't speak the whole cab-ride down to the Opéra. When they were getting out, Salaudski almost asked Nastya for some money to pay the driver, but he saw the rather unsympathetic look on her face and decided to keep his mouth closed and pay the driver out of his own pocket.

The two headed up the steps towards the front doors of the Opéra. Salaudski led the two, hobbling up the steps with his wounded foot, and mismatched suit.

"Someday you'll own this place, m'dear!" he shouted back to Nastya who walked up the steps behind him, coolly, with pride; her high-heels clicking on the stone steps. She held her dress in a bunch on her thigh as she walked so as not to trip over it. She did not pay Salaudski a response to his last statement.

The two entered the unlocked doors; and, once inside, they stopped and gazed out into the stunningly elegant and empty room. It was all quiet inside, that is, until Salaudski started tapping his foot to call attention to someone. Nastya was quiet. She stood there admiring the gilded mosaics on the walls.

Then, from across that immense room, came the *click, click, clickety, click* of a high-heeled woman approaching. Salaudski and Nastya simultaneously looked up to greet the woman who wore a white business suit and a white hat that looked like an upside-down candy dish perched on her head.

"Bonjoo-er?" came from the woman who spoke with a distinct English accent. She had that annoying gnarl in her voice that is so common amongst English people – even more so amongst Americans – when speaking French; it sounded like she was saying 'bonjour' with a wad of taffy in her teeth. She looked the visitors up and down with eyes that reflected haughty disdain. Then Salaudski made a low, clumsy bow, saying, "*enchanté*, m'dear … a pleasure to meet you!" during which the gold-colored medals on his uniform clanked together like a tin-can weathervane.

"Yes, can I help you?" the English woman disdainfully asked Salaudski, after which, Salaudski beamed in his most faux-aristocratic English accent…

"We are, herby, here, my dear, to audition for the director. The young miss shall like to dance for him." Salaudski nodded to Nastya who then tugged at him, trying to remind him that she didn't have any ballet clothes to audition in. "It's okay, my Anastasia, certainly the Opéra Garnier has enough slippers lying around," he whispered in her ear.

"I'm sorry," began the English woman, "the director does not come out to see people. Especially not just anyone."

"We are not *just anyone*. I am the *Monsieur de Chevalier*, and this is the *Star of the Bolshoy Theatre*!" Salaudski said proudly, patting Nastya's head, and flicking a little tin medallion on his breast.

"I see," said the English woman, completely unimpressed, "…well, then, you have an appointment?"

"I always have an appointment with the director! …As he said years ago when he and I were on the Italian front together … I was pulling shrapnel out of his leg – he was mortally wounded – and he said, 'Monsieur, *my most noble hero and savior of my leg*, with me, no matter how important I become – for I will become important – just as you, too, will become important – with me, my dear Monsieur de Chevalier, you always, always, have an appointment!' …Later I took a wound myself," said Salaudski, pulling up his pant leg to show the English woman his scars. He then made his leg wobble fiercely to demonstrate the seriousness of the wound.

"I see," replied the English woman, not caring to watch the leg wobble. She paused and then continued, "The director isn't here. Pray, tell me, did he ask you to come? …to come *here*, I mean?"

"My oldest, most closest friend, the director? …Why, young miss, he asked me to come here or there or anywhere where he could see me again! When we were on the front, and I was pulling shrapnel out of his leg – you see, he was mortally wounded – he looked at me deep in my blue eyes. You see these blue eyes?" Salaudski lifted his eyelids with his fingers to make sure that the English woman had a good view of his eyeballs, "…he looked into my blue eyes and said, 'My most noble hero. Just one promise. Promise me one thing…' By this time, the leg of our dear director was getting gangrene and the whites of his eyes were turning yellow from the pain, '…promise me one thing! …that, wherever I am, you will come to see me. And if this wound proves fatal, that one day – though pray not before your time – you will come to see me in heaven.' …He said this to me! And since his wound did not prove fatal – which is so fortunate for all of us! …for this young miss, as well!" he motions to Nastya who stands beside him listening intently to the conversation. "So, I now come to see him. Not in heaven… no, not in heaven, mind you! …but in the Opéra Garnier!"

"I see," replied the English woman. She then turned and walked away, with the *clickety-click* of her heels on the floor.

A moment later she returned with a small card in her hand. "Here is the address for the office of the director – *nine, Rue Scribe*." Coldly, and not without contempt, she handed Salaudski the card, "You may send him a letter requesting a rendezvous. You must, however, send a letter. His office does not accept visitors. …Is that clear? …Anything else?"

"No, Madame, this is all very fine – all very fine. Though I worry for you that the director may be angry at your delaying our reunion. I'm sure he's very eager. It has been many years. I may be forced to admit to him your name."

"All right. Is that everything?" the English woman said while turning to walk away.

"Um, what is your name?" asked Salaudski.

"Worthing. Madame Worthing. …You will see yourselves out, I trust." And with that, the English woman turned around, without so much as a nod of the head to say goodbye, and off she walked, going: *click, click, clickety-click.*

Nastya then pulled Salaudski's sleeve, motioning him to leave and they both began walking towards the front doors of the Opéra.

Once outside, Salaudski took Nastya's arm, but she let go, and walked slightly ahead.

"She must be new," Salaudski started, "She has obviously never met the director personally. It is also obvious that she's had no experience talking to aristocrats before." … "Fortunately, Rue Scribe is quite close. Shall we walk?" Salaudski asked, trying again to take Nastya's arm. Again, she let go and replied…

"I think we had better send a letter, as the woman asked us to do."

"Send a letter?!" Salaudski began to flare up, "We don't need to do any letter-sending! That's nonsense, Anastasia. Come on. Rue Scribe is quite close." He tried once more to take her arm, but Nastya quickly ran ahead and began walking several feet in front of Salaudski in the direction of his house.

"I'm not going without an appointment!" she objected in a loud voice while looking straight ahead. At this point, Salaudski became angry with Nastya for walking far ahead of him; and he started running to catch up with her. When he reached her side, he tugged at her…

"Anastasia! I paid for a taxi ride down here … I paid for your train ticket here, all the way from Moscow, so that you would work with the Opéra Garnier, and now you won't even go to meet the director? He is right in this neighborhood, damn you! I paid for your train ticket, and this is how you treat me? How can we make you a ballet dancer if you won't even go to an interview?!"

"You are talking nonsense," Nastya replied to all of this. And, as soon as she said this, Salaudski reached out and grabbed her hand, which then made a fist, and he began pulling her in the direction of Rue Scribe.

"*Aye!*, that hurts! What are you doing?!"

"Come with me, Nastya."

"You're hurting my hand." … "Let go, please!" …And Nastya broke away and crossed to the other side of Boulevard des Italiens, where she quickened her pace to get away. Salaudski chased after her, roaring reproaches and entreaties, which Nastya ignored; but soon he grew winded.

Eventually, Salaudski either gave up or lost sight of Nastya. Once she turned down Rue Vivienne, she stopped a moment by a boulangerie and looked around. Salaudski was nowhere near. She was relieved. With a deep breath, she resumed walking, but in a slower pace, down Rue Vivienne, in the direction of the river.

After passing the *Palais Royal* and the *Comedie Française*, she noticed the river in the distance. She saw several small bridges traversing the Seine and she decided that a walk alone in the sun, beside the river, would do her some good. She was angry at Salaudski … angry at him for dragging her along to this ridiculous farce at the Opéra … angry at him for treating her like she were his concubine for the whole week, while he lay around whining from a cut foot … angry at him for basically molesting her while she slept and forcing her to kiss him while she was awake, while she served him broth! 'That lecherous fool!' she thought to herself, 'I want to be so far away from him. …And yet, where I am to go? I know nothing of Paris – and what's worse, Paris knows nothing of me. I have no friends here to take me in. I might as well become the concubine of this old pauper. What other choice do I have?" … "What a hideous thought!" Nastya began to cry from the wretchedness of it all, then she laughed from the absurdity of it all, and sighed from the strangeness of everything; and then she bit her lower lip in worry and uncertainty. She walked past the *Louvre* towards the river and stopped a minute to gaze at the beauty of the structure. She had never seen this part of Paris before. The stone steps and the fluted Corinthian columns of the *Louvre* looked to her like a postcard from Athens. She had never been to Athens but she hoped one day she would go. Nevertheless, Athens looked beautiful in Paris and the sight made her happy and not worry or think too much about Salaudski. She looked in wonder at the building, while walking to the riverbank. Then she came to *Pont des Arts*, which was filled with pedestrians walking back and forth across the bridge, while taking in the sun. She too, walked across the bridge and stopped in the center of *Pont des Arts* to look out over the river at the *Pont Neuf* and the *Place du Pont Neuf* with it's little grassy park, enshrouded with the immense canopies of trees, that splits the Seine in two. It was the most beautiful view she had yet seen in Paris. She stood on *Pont des Arts* for a long time, in the afternoon sun – gazing out over the island in the Seine – and she thought.

After a while spent on the sunny bridge, she continued wandering aimlessly; she crossed over the bridge to the Left Bank. She then descended the stone steps that lead down to the cobbled walkways lining the Seine down by its banks.

The high stone wall that blocked the streets and buildings of the Left Bank from Nastya's view as she walked along the riverbank also cast a pleasantly cool shadow that gave respite from the heat that was starting to swelter. This day had been much hotter than those previous in the month. Nastya thought about the heat and suddenly she realized it was no longer April. It was now the second of May. 'I am so glad it is springtime.' she smiled to herself.

Nastya helps a poor stranger in need, whereupon she is repaid generously…

When she came to the cobbled walkway a little further down where the boats are docked, Nastya noticed a man leaning over the stone wall, trying to pull a large piece of green tarp in from the Seine. The current of the Seine was pulling fiercely in opposition to the man and he was gasping and groaning to try to get this tarp ashore.

Nastya ran up to the man, and, leaning over the wall herself, she asked if he needed help.

"Oh yes," he replied in English, "I can use help, thank you." His accent was good, unlike a Frenchman's accent. He groaned and pulled and tried to catch his breath again before talking to her. "I just went to get some oranges at the *épicerie* and I come back and somebody's thrown my tent into the river. These horrible kids! They think that somebody doesn't need to live in this tent? What if someone took their parents' cushy apartment buildings and threw them in the Seine? Would they think that's funny? I don't understand these horrible kids!" The man had a firm grasp on the giant green tarp that was being pulled by the river current. Nastya leaned right beside him and helped him pull the tent in. With the two's strength combined, they managed to slowly bring it over the stone wall. Once they got it out of the water, they spread it out in a part of the quai where the sunlight hit, so that it would dry.

Then he looked over at Nastya as they spread the tarp out on the cobblestone bank of the Seine; and he smiled at her with a kind, benevolent smile that revealed an innocence that seemed strange on the wrinkled face of middle-aged man. His face was dark and weathered, and looked as though it has seen a lot of life, and has experienced many things; but the innocent guise was not a false one, this man truly had the gay and harmless expression of a young boy. Nastya found this to be an attractive quality. She liked his face. Moreover he was interesting to look at because of his ethnicity. He was Moroccan and his skin looked like milk chocolate or light-colored leather. She smiled at him and her eyes beamed; to this, the man became very happy and smiled even more so.

Nastya agreed to help the man set up his tent once it was dry; and the two sat on the edge of the wall, with their feet dangling just over the river, to wait. And while they waited, they spoke.

The man started: "I live here, you know, so it's terrible when I come home and find my house floating down the river."

"I can imagine," said Nastya, "How long have you lived down here?"

"Well, I came to Paris when I was eighteen – so, a long time."

"How long have you been here?" he asked.

"A week." Nastya responded, "I'd like to live in Paris. It is so beautiful. But, I think I will go back to Russia."

"Oh, you are just a tourist?"

"No, I came to live here, I was offered a place to stay with this man but we are having a lot of problems – or he is having a lot of problems, rather. So I think I'll have to leave."

"Is he French?"

"Yes."

"That's the problem, right there. Frenchmen always create problems for women, it seems. They're either too effeminate or too jealous or too insecure or too abusive."

"Yes!" laughed Nastya, "He is all of those! Except he's not too effeminate. He's kind of boyish though, although he's sixty-something."

"Oh, he's too old for you. You two aren't *together* though?"

"Oh, no! He wishes we were."

"And since you are not, he's giving you problems."

"That is part of it. Still, it's more complicated than that."

"Anyhow, he sounds like a typical Frenchman. You need to get away from that. You're a pretty girl, you know. Very pretty."

"Thank you," blushed Nastya with a little uneasiness.

"But I didn't mean… I'm not trying to, you know, say that in a sexual way. I'm not like these French guys."

"I know you didn't mean…."

"I'm just saying, you need to be careful because there are a lot of guys in Paris who go out and meet young pretty girls and then ruin them. Not just French guys either. Americans and Germans and North Africans do it too, but the Latin men are the worst!"

189

"Thanks. But there are also men like you who warn us girls about these guys, right? There are also good men in Paris."

"Oh, but I am not a good man. I mean, I would never hurt you, or any woman. But I can't have a woman. I can't support one. I live in a tent on the river. I borrow money from friends for food and eat on credit at the cafés that allow me to. I used to have a drug problem too...."

"But, you shouldn't say those things about yourself," Nastya interrupted, "If you used to have a drug problem, you don't anymore."

"Right, I don't anymore."

"And you like to live on the river, I thought."

"Yes, I do like it. I have a beautiful view and I get to fall asleep looking at the lights on the river through the flap in my tent."

"It sounds beautiful. ...If you like to live on the river, there must be nice women too who would like to live on the river."

"But if I met a nice woman, I would want to give her a beautiful apartment, let her have a clean bathroom – a place to keep her things nice. I would want to be able to take her out to eat. And buy her clothes." The man looked into Nastya's eyes, trying to gauge her thoughts on what he was saying, "I just hate it because the Frenchmen and those others who treat woman so badly in Paris always have homes to take them too, and money to buy them drinks and dinners and clothes; it's the *Parisiennes* – they are always so absorbed by money. I don't have any money, yet I would treat a woman well, but they won't give me the chance."

"Well, that's their loss, I think," said Nastya, "If these *Parisiennes* just want a man who will buy them things and give them a luxurious place to live, they deserve it when they're not happy. ...I'm sure you'll meet a woman who will think it's romantic to live in a tent by the river. I would, if I met the right man. I would live by the river in a tent and eat on credit at cafés!" Nastya laughed wholeheartedly, dangling her legs over the river. She looked at the dark face of the man, who had a pensive, thoughtful and serious gaze.

"Well, a girl like you deserves more than a tent on the river. I don't even know you, but I have an intuition about you and I think you are too precious of a girl to be living outside, and begging food from friends."

"Well, if your friends give you food, it's because they want you to eat and be healthy. Anyway, you're lucky to have friends. I don't. I am alone here."

"Yes, I have friends, and I should feel good about that – I mean, I do feel good about that. Money can destroy bad friendships all the time, but good friendships can always destroy money."

"That's nice. I think it's true."

"I guess it's true. I couldn't imagine what it would be like to have no friends here. ...So you came alone? ...To live with this man?"

"Yes, but I'm going to stop living with this man. I may have to get a tent to put next to yours," Nastya laughed. The man couldn't tell if she was being sincere. He decided she probably was. She sounded sincere.

"Well, if you ever need a place to sleep, you can come here. My tent is big enough and there are other places around here to sleep. A lot of people sleep down here. Not just clochards, but artists too, musicians, poets, travelers – a lot of travelers, like yourself. Well, not like you actually...."

"Thanks," interrupted Nastya. "I'll keep that in mind. I may go back to Russia in a couple days though."

"Oh, I didn't mean, 'my tent is big enough' like 'we would sleep together', just so you know. I would never try to do anything sexual to you. I would never try to disrespect you or make you uncomfortable."

"I know you wouldn't. I didn't think you meant that. I believe you are a good man. ...Thank you for saying it, though."

The two sat silent for a few moments beside each other, watching the orange sun start to dip lower in the sky, making the waves on the Seine look like little glowing flamelets from a campfire. The both were a little stirred inside emotionally from meeting one another; they liked each other. The man thought that Nastya was one of the rare girls with beauty as well as a tender and romantic soul. Being a man, he naturally respects physical beauty in women; but he also gives high esteem to women who are not snobbish, but who are altruistic – those who care more for romance than for money.

And Nastya liked the man. She liked his aged and weathered face that also showed a youthful kindness and innocence. She believed that she could sleep in the same tent as him and that he would not touch her.

She didn't know why she trusted him after only knowing him for less than an hour. Maybe it was because he had showed his weakness and helplessness when his tent was being dragged by the river, while he was frantically trying to save it. Maybe it was what he had said to her: his warnings about the men in Paris. Maybe it was something else: his eyes, or his smile, or the way he nervously fidgeted with his hands, rubbing the cuticles on his fingers as he talked. Whatever it was, she felt she could trust him, right away.

For a few more minutes, the two sat together, silent, each thinking their own thoughts – with their legs dangling over the river. Then Nastya said…

"Do you think the tent is ready to go up?"

"Oh, the tarp!" replied the man, turning around, as if he had forgotten completely that Nastya had been waiting with him until his tent was dry so that she could help him set it up again. "Yes, thanks for waiting with me this long. I think it's probably dry." He walked over to the patch of sun where it lay to dry, and felt the sturdy, green material that was already dry and warm with the rays of the sun. "I'd almost say that it was a good thing those horrible kids threw my tent in the river. It needed a bath – it was so dirty. Unfortunately, the Seine is probably the dirtiest bathwater in the world."

Nastya laughed at this comment and jumped up from the stone railing where she had been sitting; and went over to help set up the tent.

The man weighted the base of the tarp with cinderblocks and Nastya tied the ropes to the large, round iron hooks that jutted out of the stone walls surrounding the little enclosed area down on the river bank. After a few minutes, the task was done and the tent was built. The two stood back and admired their accomplishment. Then, the man climbed in his tent and disappeared. A moment later, he stuck his head out smiling.

"I'm going to take a little nap," he said, "if you are around later, come back and we'll eat some oranges and drink a bottle of wine. I have some Anjou and fresh oranges from Spain – got 'em at the *épicerie*."

"I would like that," Nastya replied, "I'm not sure if I can come back tonight, but I'll see."

"But please try," said the man, climbing out of his tent to kiss Nastya's cheeks. "I'll wait for you, but if you don't come, I'll just go to sleep and wait for you to come tomorrow, okay?" The two kissed each other's cheeks four times.

"Okay, I'll try to come for dinner."

"I hope you make it," He smiled, "By the way, what is your name?"

"Nastya. What is yours?"

"Marick," the man replied, with a wave goodbye.

CHAPTER XIII

Nastya walked back down the cobblestone walkway near Quai Voltaire, past the evenly planted trees that line the walk. She passed under the labyrinth-like tunnel beneath the *Pont du Carrousel*, which is walled and arched with old stones and is lit by neither candle nor lantern. The dark tunnel is lined with small coves dug out of the stone where old mattresses and small tents have been laid by squatters who make their homes along the river Seine. Nastya walked quietly through the dark cavern, not wanting to wake those who had gone to bed early on this evening.

Once outside the tunnel, the last light of day came down and Nastya squinted her eyes from the brightness. She climbed the stairs leading up to the *Pont des Arts* and looked out again at the river lit by golden ringlets of light. The sun had disappeared over some trees that lined the bank of the Seine, but the river continued to sparkle with some golden shimmers of mysterious light that appeared to have no source. It was the last light before the crepuscule.

Odette's secret and David's farewell…

The same evening, David returned to Odette's with a happy and hopeful air about him. He was going to start a new and independent life among the creatures of the Seine. He thought Odette would be glad to receive the news. He hoped that all would go well. He just needed his passport and a kind farewell and he would be off.

There were other doctors in the city and he could visit them to receive treatment – a lighter treatment – something less violent than the treatment Odette had given him. He would soon enough be able to find a job, and get some pay coming in. He was optimistic. He took his meeting with Marick to be a pivot in his life. When the two had walked along the narrow, sunny roads west of the Latin Quarter, when David had caught sight of the Cathedral St. Germain, during this whole promenade, in fact, the air was perfumed with hope. It was the only time, hitherto, he had walked the streets of Paris free from pain, free from restraints of any kind – and in addition to all of this, he had been with a friend, his new friend ... a fellow man who walked with him because he too wanted a friend. They were two men and they didn't want to play games with each other, or rob each other, or take the other person's soul ... they just wanted to be friends. And all the air of Paris was perfumed with hope and a promising future.

When David reached Odette's, he found the door wide open, but he didn't see anyone in the medical office; nor did he hear anyone beyond there, in Odette's apartment. There didn't appear to be anyone at all. He noticed two shopping bags filled with groceries from the market lying on the floor beside the open doorway. He also noticed Odette's keychain dangling from the lock in the door. David wasn't so much worried by all this as he was curious.

Quietly, he slipped inside. When he entered Odette's apartment through the door that stood wide open, he saw the form of the old woman half obscured by the curtain, which hangs near the bed. He saw her backside, the cloth of her dress, the back of her head, and its dyed, thinning hair. He saw her tremble slightly as she stood facing the wall in the corner. He stood silently and watched her. She held the telephone receiver to her ear. She had apparently dropped the groceries and left the doors open in a hurry to catch this telephone call. David stood silent and went unnoticed.

"Yes, I got it," Odette said into the phone, as she faced the wall, smoothing the fabric of her dress in nervousness. Then she continued, her voice notably affected by grief, "...and I think you said all you needed to say." Her voice became angry... "But how could you have?" she asked the person on the telephone as she choked on her tears. Then, to mock her tears and grief, she took on a sharp tone with an affectation of sarcasm, "Oh, I'm sure the bitch is wonderful!" And then she paused, and said more quietly, in voice of melancholy, "No, I don't want you coming back here. Not if it's only for that." Then there was a long pause where she just stood there, trembling noticeably from fear and sadness.

Her head nodded every now and again as if to make a silent response to the caller's words. David stood by the doorway and listened in silence. Then Odette began to laugh a nervous laugh, a maniacal laugh, a laugh mingled with wretched despair… "Oh, yes, your suits are gone. All your clothes are gone! No use coming back for that. I took them all to the *Jardin de Luxembourg* and set them ablaze in a big bonfire – together with your pathetic letters!" She laughed again, even more maniacally this time. Then her laugh was cut short, she was silenced. She listened a moment and then said quietly, without the menace she had before, only with sorrow, "I loved you, Howard." Then a pause. Then a moment later, "No, something, something…." The last words were undecipherable through her tears. At this moment, David slowly backed up through the medical office and started for the front door, which still stood wide open. When he reached the front door, he heard Odette hang up the phone receiver. She could be heard crying. She thought she was alone and she cried for a moment without restraint, choking on the tears in her throat. Then she stopped and there was only muffled, silent sobbing. Then David knocked loudly on the wall next to the open front door.

Odette stood frozen a minute and David knocked again, pretending to have just arrived. He stood by her front door in the dark brown suit belonging to her husband. David liked the suit, he was glad it hadn't been burned.

A moment later, Odette appeared by her front door and stood looking at David, trying to mask all emotion – her eyes were swollen.

"How long have you been standing here?" she asked.

"I just got here … you left your groceries on the ground." He pointed at the bags next to the door in the hall. Odette picked them up and carried them into her apartment, David followed.

"I had to run to catch the phone. I thought it was you calling."

"But I don't have your phone number, Odette."

"Anyway, I bought you food. Have you eaten?" she asked, as she took some items out of the bags, putting them in the cupboards in her little kitchenette.

"No. What would I have eaten?"

"Well, I thought that's why you left." She turned the dial on the oven and then stood by the cutting board, slicing onions. "Anyway, I'm going to cook you dinner, and then we can go to bed early tonight, okay David?"

"I have plans tonight. I can't," David said, in a reserved voice, whereupon Odette dropped her knife and the shallot she held in her hand and she turned to face him. She wore a look of deep longing and sorrow. Her makeup was smeared.

"But I am cooking for you. I bought you a fresh *tarte provençale*, with onions and cheese and ham inside. It will be good. We'll drink wine."

"I don't eat ham, Odette."

"Well, damn it! I'll go back to the *épicerie* and buy something else. How was I supposed to know you don't eat ham?!" Her voice blended sadness and anger and desperation. She didn't try to conceal the solitary tear that rolled down her cheek.

"I'm going to eat with a friend. He lives down by the river. That's where I went. I waited a long time for you, but you didn't come back. It took me a while to get that door unlocked. I was trapped in here."

"I'm sorry, I didn't realize I'd locked it. It was just out of habit. Listen David, we'll go together and buy something else to eat. I didn't know you didn't eat ham. That's all I have is that *tarte* – and these onions. But we'll get something else and have a nice dinner." She approached him and put her arms over his shoulders, looking into his eyes beseechingly… "…We'll have a nice dinner, and we'll go to bed early tonight."

"I can't, Odette, I am planning to stay at my friend's. He offered me a place to sleep. That's what I wanted to tell you. Now I don't have to burden you anymore for anything. You don't need to give up your shower or your bed or your time anymore. I'm going to stay down by the river and get a job and make a life for myself – become independent."

"Ah but David, please, just stay tonight. I don't mind giving up my shower and my bed. Just don't leave me tonight. Okay?" With these words, the tears resumed and Odette's voice became rather pathetic sounding. "Just don't leave me tonight," she repeated again, while blinking her eyes and trying to pull David closer to her – to which, David's response was to back away. When she tried to kiss his neck, he seized her forearms, which were rested on his shoulders and he forcefully held them, while he backed away from her.

"Odette, don't. I never asked for this. I needed a doctor, that's all. A place to sleep, yes. But not this. You have put me in an awkward position and now I want to leave." He let go of her arms, and once she had control of them, she put her hands to her face, to cover herself and hide from him. She wept softly in her hands, muffling the sound. Her crying was stifled and affected, as if she were only testing his sympathy.

"I'm not the one to take your husband's place...." He stopped himself before finishing. He didn't know why exactly he had thought it was a good idea to say what he had just said. Upon these last words of David, Odette broke into a reel of tears; and then she took her hands from her withered face and looked at the young man with a torn look of anger. Her eyes were swollen from crying.

"Get out," she said, "please just go. I want to be alone." Her voice quivered as she spoke.

David walked past her, towards the other side of the room, looking around as though he had left something in her place. "May I have my passport?" he asked.

"Just go," she responded, "I'll get it later, I just want to be alone." She turned to face him and noticed him pulling from the pocket of her husband's suit, the monogrammed letter opener. He set it on her desk next to the crystal cruet that was empty, except for a little puddle of red wine in the bottom.

He noticed that she saw him taking the letter opener from his pocket and, before she could speak, he said, "I needed it to get the door unlocked."

"You drank my wine?" she asked, looking at the crystal cruet on her desk. The light of twilight began to seep through the window. The curtains had been drawn open again. The light reflected off the facets of the large, lead crystal vessel. It reflected a strange quality of light – light of pure silver.

"I couldn't find any iodine. I needed something to treat my sores."

Just then Odette began to laugh a crazed and maniacal laugh. her swollen lips quivered and her eyes, glassy with tears, flashed at the young man that stood across from her. "Take off the suit, please. If this 'friend' is giving you a place to stay, he can give you clothes to wear as well."

To this, David replied spitefully: "I have nothing to change into. I'll bring old Howard's suit back tomorrow."

Upon hearing David utter her husband's name, Odette growled, "Oh, you are an evil young man!" She snarled, spitting, "Take it off now. It belongs to me!" Her anger grew to an apex.

"I'll give you the suit back. First give me my passport back."

"I'll give you your passport back when you pay me the forty-three hundred francs I gave the hospital on your behalf." She laughed as she said this, flipping her tongue around. Her laugh was intoxicated by her feverish anger.

David stood frozen, looking at Odette with a look of shock and disbelief. His jaw dropped to express his amazement at the gall she showed. The two stood frozen in their places, looking at each other, locked in a power struggle. Odette was visibly examining the arrows in her quiver, fishing for another weapon to use against him, in order to get what she wanted – whatever it was that she wanted.

David ended the struggle with the only weapon he saw fit and appropriate to use. He turned around and walked out of Odette's apartment, slamming the door to her medical office, and slamming the front door leading out to the hall. His footsteps could be heard on the stairs. Soon he was gone … away from Odette, away from her apartment, away from Rue du Dragon. Hurriedly, he headed through the crepuscule down St. Germain, past the cathedral and down Rue St. Benoit, towards the Quai Voltaire – to go find Marick.

A brief account of David's stay on the twilit quai, where the gamin lay, and boats pass slow and wonton…

David was starving when he reached the Quai Voltaire. He located Marick's tent through the map that Marick had drawn for him. It was exactly where he said it would be and it looked exactly as he said it would look. The green tarp, weighted with cinderblocks, was hoisted with ropes tied to iron hooks on the stone walls and formed a point about six feet off the ground. A swarm of gnats hovered over the tent and the air appeared thick, like the air of a summer night, though it was only May and night had yet to fall.

Marick had promised David some rice and vegetables, and when David came to the tent, he saw a pan sitting on a small stove, right outside the flap of the tent. The lid was on the pan, and David lifted the lid, putting his nose down to smell the food. It was only half cold, the food, and smelled good; and David looked around for a fork to eat with. He also looked around to see if Marick was near. He then heard a rustling in the tent.

David smiled when he heard Marick inside, and he closed the lid and stuck his head through the flap of the tent, and saw, in the darkness, Marick's body lying down – he was taking a nap.

"Hiya, Marick!" he yelled, "It looks good, what you cooked."

"…What do you want?" came from the man lying in the tent. The voice sounded irritated – irritated and sleepy.

"Is that you, Marick?" David asked, surprised at the coldness of the greeting.

"Yes, it's me. What do you want?!"

"You asked me to come back, remember?"

"I'm sleeping," Marick grumbled back in a voice that showed no humor. Suddenly, David felt as if he were an uninvited guest in someone's home. He backed out of the tent, which he had crawled halfway into to greet his friend, Marick.

"I'm sorry," David put in finally, as he sat on the stone ground outside the flap of the tent, "Is it okay if I eat some of this food? I'm starving."

"Yes, I don't care," said Marick, "just leave me alone. I'm sleeping.

David now felt out of place sitting by Marick's tent. He felt out of place eating his food, as well, although Marick had told him he could. Earlier, when the two had parted on the best possible of terms, Marick had told David that there was plenty of room in the tent for the two of them to sleep. David had not actually seen the tent, he just went on Marick's word. The latter told him that he could spend the night in the tent and the next day he would help him find his own place down near the quai. There were plenty of places to squat, Marick told him. Plenty of nice, clean places. And if they didn't find anything right away, there would always be the little holes dug into the walls in the cave that formed the base of the *Pont des Arts*. Anyway, Marick had said that there would be room in the tent for the both of them. Now David saw that it wasn't so. Even if there was a small space for David to squeeze into beside

Marick, to pass the night, he was not welcome inside the tent. He even felt unwelcome to sit even near the tent. Marick was irritable and tired and didn't want to be bothered.

David sat for what felt like many hours outside that little green tent, on the rough cobbled ground. He again took the lid off of the pan and picked at the lukewarm rice and vegetables with the fork he had found lying on the ground next to the pan.

In his hunger, he ended up eating more than half of the food that remained. After, he put the lid back on and stretched out his legs; and there he remained sitting, a few feet from the tent, looking out over the dark, glassy waters of the Seine that carried the silver shimmers of twilight on its few and tiny wavelets.

Every few moments, a boat would pass by. Some were dark and quiet. They looked old and were low in the water – their bows bobbed up and down languidly as they passed by the quai. David assumed that these boats were taking commodities to the refineries in the east. These boats passed by without a sound – they were strangers, as was he, unnoticed in the Parisian twilight.

Other boats belonged to the police. They shone their lights on the quai when they passed, lighting up the walls and the cobbled walkways, looking for the gamins who sell hashish, and for the drunks who fight along the banks of the river.

Then there were the boats that passed also slowly, but merrily and wantonly as well. People could be heard and seen carousing on their decks. The voices of young girls were heard, laughing, giggling – they wore nice dresses and heels; they wore their hair in flamboyant styles; their skin shimmered from glitter and gloss as they sipped their champagne on the decks of the boats. Oh, how David wanted to be amongst them.

The men, they talked freely, wantonly as well, all slightly drunk, all in French. They drank beer and talked to the ladies. Some of them were alone with the girls on the decks. Others gathered in groups and laughed loudly like the drunk and carefree young dandies they were, enjoying a night on the Seine.

On one of these boats that passed, a young man with combed, black hair, wearing a grey suit, sat alone on the stern of the boat, – away from the others, the guys and girls, – while he played a classical guitar softly and to himself. It was *Recuerdos de la Alhambra*, a song that David had heard in his youth. The young man played it masterfully – beautifully. Its notes, its slow and melancholic rhythm, its continuous tremolos cascading in the minor key, resounded over the river and swept David with profound feeling and nostalgia. He no longer wanted to be with those pretty girls, dressed in silks and heels, their golden heads of hair curled and flowing down over their bare shoulders – those girls who left a sweet trail of perfume as they passed by, down the Seine. He no longer wanted to be laughing and drinking beer with those young Parisian men – who cheered and drank with such wanton merriment, such carefree delight. He had wanted both those things only a few moments before. He had wanted to be with those men and to be with those ladies. He too wanted to drink and laugh and kiss and watch Paris pass by from a boat on the waves of the Seine. But then he heard that young man – maybe just a boy even – playing that Spanish song alone on the stern of the boat and then he no longer wanted any of those things. Then, all he wanted was for that song to keep playing – to never end; to fill his body and carry it upon its tremolo for eternity – down the French river, and into the Spanish sea.

But as all things end, so did that song. And soon the boy and the boat and his beautiful classical guitar were out of sight, beyond the river's bend – and the *Alhambra* could no longer be heard. And David felt more alone and more sad than he had in a long time. He sat by the tent of the sleeping man who did not want to be disturbed, the man whom he did not know, and he watched the twilit river shimmer with colors of gold and silver and copper and bronze. He sat alone and let the shimmers of light dance in his eyes – his eyes that, for no reason he could think of, welled up with little tears … tearlets that sparkled with the light from the river.

And so, David sat and watched and waited and hoped that that sad song in the minor key would come floating again down the Seine. But the boats stopped floating by, and the quai became very empty, and the night began a-falling.

What happened to our heroine's plans to return to see Marick, and how Salaudski, in his peculiar manner, managed to spoil everything…

When David had been overhearing Odette's conversation with her husband, earlier on this night, Nastya had just arrived back at Salaudski's and was washing her clothes in his sink so that she might have something clean to wear to go visit with her new friend, whom she had just met and who had offered her a dinner of wine and oranges, served fresh on the cobbles on the quai of the river Seine.

Salaudski was not at home when she returned, and she was glad of this. He had left a key for her under the doormat and a note saying he was sorry for how the events of the afternoon had gone. The note said that he was out on 'urgent business' and that he would return in the evening time. Nastya hoped that he would not return before she had had a chance to wash her clothes and dress to go visit Marick. She had put the key to Salaudski's apartment in her purse and she felt she had the right to take it and let herself in when she returned later in the night.

She stood in the dim and drear, sallow light of the kitchen scrubbing her blouse with soap. 'It is silk,' she thought to herself, 'it will dry quickly.' … 'Anyway,' her thoughts continued, 'Salaudski and I have a *business* relationship. Or at least, that is what we *should* have. That is what would be appropriate to have. That is what we *must* have. If he is going to be too childish, too vile, to set the boundaries of our relationship to keep it businesslike, then I must take the initiative to set the boundaries. If I must be the older and more responsible of the two, then so be it. He must learn that he cannot order a concubine from a foreign country on the pretext that he will make her a star. If he tells her that he is going to get her in the ballet, then such is a business offer. I will compensate him for his help, once he has helped. Until then, I don't feel like I owe him anything – after all, I was invited. My happiness, he said, was "a promise" – no one owes me happiness, but if he makes a promise like that, he should take care to try and follow through. My happiness does not depend on this man, but it would sure make things easier if he would just let me alone, not come into my room at night, and help me get into the ballet. It seems more than fair to me that I should have a key and be allowed to come and go as I please....'

Just then, her thoughts were interrupted by Salaudski himself, who had barged in through the front door, raucously, merrily, smiling with delight upon seeing Nastya in his kitchen.

"Oh, I am glad it is you, Anastasia! You know, the door was left unlocked, I thought my house was being robbed!"

"You left me the key," replied Nastya, leaving her clothes in the sink and turning to face Salaudski. The latter was holding a pastry in his hand.

"I know I left you the key, I'm so glad you came back! Did you get my note? I bought you a *tarte à la fraise*." He set the pastry on the little wooden table in the vestibule and fetched a knife from the kitchen, with which to cut it. While getting a knife, he noticed the clothes in the sink… "You are washing your clothes in the sink? But, you shouldn't be washing your clothes, my Anastasia! You are no *washerwoman!* You are no *soap-scrubber!* You are no *silk-scratcher!* you are a *dancer*, my Anastasia! Come and *dance* with me!"

Whereupon, he took Nastya's hands, which had resumed scrubbing the clothes, and he pulled her out into the salon where he started twirling her around. At first she was startled by his fervor; then she began laughing; then she became dizzy from being twirled around so many times.

Then, suddenly, Salaudski ended the dance and took two steps back from Nastya. He looked at her aghast, "But why were you washing your clothes like that?"

"Well, how else are they going to get clean?" laughed Nastya. She held her head in her hands to keep the room from spinning.

"As soon as we get you a contract at the Opéra Garnier, my dear, we'll hire you your own *femme de chambre*. You'll have a different outfit for every day of the year!" roared Salaudski, throwing his arms in the air to illustrate the grandiosity the future holds for them. "Now come eat some *tarte à la fraise* – it has real *fraise* in it!"

"Oh, I'll eat some later – maybe tomorrow. I have plans for dinner to…." Yet, before she could finish, her words were halted by the extreme look of shock on Salaudski's face. His gaiety turned to horror as he looked at her as though she had just sentenced him to death.

"You have plans tonight? Tonight, you have plans? …for dinner?!" He stood across from her, wringing his hands together, looking at her with a plea for mercy. "But you can't! … not *tonight!* Not on *this* night! No!"

"But, why not?"

"Anastasia, don't you realize that on *this* night – not tomorrow, mind you! – but on *this* very night, tonight, we have a dinner with the director and his wife?"

Nastya stood silent and looked into Salaudski's eyes, searching them, trying to see by his gaze whether or not he is joking with her. He continued...

"Yes, tonight we have a dinner. He wants to give you a contract. You can sign the papers tonight." Salaudski looked at Nastya with a disconcerted expression, as though he were hoping that she wouldn't say anything to spoil the plans to finally meet the director, for certainly she would not be granted another interview with such an important man.

"...You see, after you left me on the street today, I went to number nine, Rue Scribe and I talked to the director. He let me into his office right away. Right when he saw me, his face beamed. We hadn't seen each other in years. I told him what happened earlier at the Opéra Garnier and he said he would fire that stupid English woman right away. He begged my forgiveness for over an hour. I told him there was no reason to beg my pardon, 'It's really too much,' I said. But he said, 'No, it's not too much, my dearest, my Monsieur de Chevalier, *savior of my leg!* You deserve all the apologies in the world, you deserve the *croix rouge*. I will get rid of that English *salope* right away! Don't worry, my most honorable friend...'." ... "And then we talked about you. He knows you more than just from what I've been telling him all along ... he saw your picture on the lithograph, strewn all over Paris, advertising the Bolshoy theatre. He loves the Bolshoy. He's been there many times. I didn't know it was such a great theatre. I didn't think such a great theatre could exist in Russia. But he, the director, seemed to think the Bolshoy was a palace for dancers of magnificent skill. He told me that if you are great enough to be a poster-girl for the Bolshoy theatre, you deserve a chance at the Opéra Garnier. You don't even need to audition first. What I mean is that he'll *try you out!* First comes the contract, then the tryout; but this means, Anastasia, that you are in ... you don't need to audition, you are already in! ...We are to meet tonight at nine o'clock at the *Bistro d'Hiver.* That's in just an hour and a half. We'll have to get ready quickly...."

Such joy filled Nastya upon hearing this. This Salaudski – *the Monsieur de Chevalier* – had actually done what he said he was going to do. Nastya looked at his face that so often had a look of self-mockery in it; but this time she read nothing but sincerity, earnestness, and hope in his expression. He appeared to be as happy about this contract as Nastya was – and Nastya was overjoyed. She would be a success in Paris, after all. She wouldn't need to sleep down by the Seine. Soon she could move away from Rue de Paradis into her own apartment – something in a nice neighborhood. Soon she could dance again, too – in a world-class theatre. Oh how she missed dancing. She thought about her last performance at the Bolshoy. How beautiful she felt. How beautiful the whole ballet was – the music, the costumes, how the crowd adored the show, how they loved it!

Nastya reveled in the memory for a moment and thought about the good turn of fate that came when she had finally given up all hope only a few hours before.

Then, Salaudski dropped a dirty lead weight on Nastya's light heart… "And when you get this contract, my dear… you will know it is because of me, right?"

"Yes, of course," she laughed.

"And will you sleep with me, then? …instead of sleeping alone in your tiny little bed. I mean, will you love this old man? I trust that you will love me."

"I can't believe you just said that!" Nastya took a few steps back and surveyed Salaudski, questioningly. 'Why did he have to ruin such a good moment?' she wondered.

Salaudski took a few steps closer to Nastya – the latter, just stood there in amazement. He then put his hand on her shoulder and she flinched a little. Then he caressed her shoulder, beginning to move his hand down towards her small, round breast that was well-formed in her light spring shirt. "I just want to make love to a dancer at the Opéra Garnier, that's all."

"Stop it. Please, stop it!" she cried, throwing his hand off of her chest. She then covered her face in her other hand and hid her eyes. Salaudski backed up a step, realizing that he had really offended her. Then she took her hand from her eyes and threw him the most angry, menacing glare she could. And then she stomped off to her tiny, little bedroom and shut the door.

Outside her door, Salaudski could be heard stamping his feet and entreating her for forgiveness for many minutes: "Oh, Anastasia, what have I done? I am a worthless man. I can't even stand to be in my own skin sometimes. But you, okay, I leave you alone, but forgive this old man. I know I don't deserve your great, illustrious forgiveness. Me, I'm an old man … my blood is great but my skin is dirty. Even when my skin is clean, I can't stand to be in it sometimes. Oh, Anastasia? Are you in there? You didn't fly out the window, did you? Oh, okay, I'll leave you. Farewell!"

At ten minutes before nine o'clock on the evening of the dinner with the director and his wife, and all the moments that follow...

Salaudski was standing at the door to Nastya's tiny little room, which was closed. He put his ear to the door and heard nothing. All was silent on the other side. Suddenly, he became very worried that she was no longer in her room – although an escape would have been impossible, for her window is on no less than the fifth-floor, and Salaudski had been pacing this whole time through the vestibule back and forth before her closed door. He was getting worried that she had gone to sleep, was crying, or some how had flown away. At ten minutes to nine – the time when the meeting with the director was scheduled – there was still no sound from Nastya's room. The plan was to go to *Bistro d'Hiver*, which is in the fourth arrondissement, - Salaudski lives in the tenth, - that is at least ten minutes by taxi.

Finally at ten minutes to nine, Salaudski opened Nastya's bedroom door. To his surprise, she wasn't in there sleeping or crying; on the contrary, she was dressed up, and stood by the mirror, putting on a necklace. She wore her famous black dress and heels. Her hair and makeup was done. She wore a fine perfume. She was ready to go.

Nastya turned and glanced at Salaudski, who stood in her doorway looking on her with adoration, and she beamed him a smile – a radiant smile. Her lips glistened with gloss, her hair was elegantly curled and her fine dress revealed her soft bare shoulders, her long white neck and her delicate, feminine arms … though most notably, her eyes beamed with that radiance that only Nastya has. Her eyes like jewels shone like flashes of sun lighting the specks of gold on the bed of a stream; and there was no light in the room to reflect off her eyes. They radiated on their own. She looked at Salaudski and said, "We must hurry if we are to be on time, no?"

"Yes, my dear – on time! If we are to be on time, we must go. But I must dress! … dress and drink … drink and dress!" And with that, Salaudski twirled out of her doorway in joyous delight and retrieved a glass of *Ricard* he had waiting for him on the little wooden table in the vestibule. A moment later he twirled back into her doorway… "No time to dress and drink! I am already dressed enough – and you are dressed enough for the both of us. You are a queen! My Russian Queen, most beautiful thing I've ever seen!" … "Come, my coquette, the troika is waiting – we must hurry, our troika is waiting!"

And with that, the elegantly dressed young ballerina and the old Monsieur de Chevalier were off – and down the steps, and out the door and through Rue de Paradis, where they quickly found a taxi and got inside.

At five minutes past nine, they stopped in the fourth arrondissement. Salaudski paid the driver, leaving no tip because he failed to drive as fast as Salaudski had ordered him to; and the two entered a little café on *Rue de Turenne*, near *Place des Vosges*.

"I am the Monsieur de Chevalier, where is the service? Where are our drinks?!" Salaudski called out in raucous merriment after the two had been seated for a mere two minutes.

"Is he here?" Nastya asked, "Is he the one over there with the black frock coat on, with that woman?"

"No, of course not," replied Salaudski, squinting to make out the elderly couple seated at a table in the back, "That man is a nobody … and that woman he is with, she is a moose! The director would not have a moosy wife like that. The director's wife is a real beauty, forty years younger than himself, mind you!" And he eyed Nastya, putting particular stress on the last phrase he uttered… "forty years younger than himself, mind you!" …He was already a little drunk from the anis he drank back at the apartment. While Nastya had been dressing, he had drunk four glasses of *Ricard* and his face had become quite flushed. He looked around for the barmaid – finally she came and took their order.

"Why did you order white wine?" Salaudski asked after the barmaid left their table.

"I like white wine."

"My dear, Anastasia… white wine is what they drink in Alsace. Here in Paris, our ladies drink red wine. It makes their hearts swoon and their thighs tremble." Salaudski grabbed his heart passionately with both his hands as he said this.

"I think you are crude," said Nastya, rolling her eyes and blowing a breath of disbelief towards Salaudski, "Where is the director?"

"He will be coming, my little pheasant. His wife takes a long time to ready herself. A long time indeed. …Oh, good the drinks are here."

The barmaid, who was a rough peasant-looking woman with broad shoulders, set a glass of white wine in front Nastya carelessly, so a little wine spilt over the rim of the glass onto the table. She then set down two glasses of scotch in front of Salaudski and collected seventy francs from him.

"The wine is good, my little pheasant?" Salaudski asked Nastya, as he drank down one of his glasses of scotch in one swallow.

"I don't know, I haven't tasted it yet."

"Oh," said Salaudski, "…that is a word in English isn't it?"

"What word?" asked Nastya.

"*Pheasant.*" he replied.

"I'm not sure, I've never heard it before."

"Well, you are my *little pheasant*, anyway."

"It's cold in Moscow, right now," Nastya informed Salaudski, after taking a sip of her wine – which had a bitter taste and made her wince.

"Mmm," mumbled Salaudski, not having anything else to reply to her statement.

"…I always thought," continued Nastya, "that if I ever made money dancing in the Parisian ballet, I would take my family to the south of Russia – to the Crimea. It's warmer there. It's better for my father, and my brother – for my brother especially. The climate in Moscow is not good for his health."

"Hmm," replied Salaudski, "I'm going to get another drink." He tapped his two empty scotch glasses and stood up from the table to go order directly from the bar. Nastya took another sip of her bitter wine and looked over to the door. An older couple was entering and she was trying to decide if it was the director and his wife or not.

A moment later, Salaudski returned to the table with a fresh glass of scotch. "Did you know that this place is called the *Bistro d'Ivrogne?*" he asked Nastya, in a conversational tone.

"Oh," replied the latter, "Did you know," Nastya began, "that *bistro* is a Russian word? The French have adopted it, but it is a Russian word. It means 'fast'."

"Yes, that's all fine," said Salaudski, in a voice of growing impatience, "but you didn't understand me." ... "This place is call *Bistro 'd'Ivrogne'*. We're supposed to meet the director at the *Bistro 'd'Hiver'*!"

"What?!" exclaimed Nastya in alarm, grabbing her purse and jumping up from the table. Salaudski also stood up and as Nastya hurried away from the table, towards the door. Salaudski called after her:

"You didn't drink your wine!"

"You drink it, let's go!"

And Salaudski guzzled his third glass of scotch, and Nastya's bitter wine as well, and the two were off.

They walked quickly down Rue de Rivoli. Nastya lagged behind slightly as she was wearing heels – but this time, unlike the last, she didn't break a heel on the sidewalk. She eventually gained pace with Salaudski. He told her that the *Bistro d'Hiver* was not far enough away to take a taxi to. It was only a few streets down – on Rue du Bourg-Tibourg, in a little square, blocked off to traffic, where innumerous little tables and chairs are set out on the stone floor of the quaint little terraces.

"Look, we can sit outside, it will be warm enough. The braziers are lit," Salaudski said, upon arriving at the terrace of the *Bistro d'Hiver*.

"Well, shouldn't we go inside and look for the director and his wife first?" asked Nastya, in an appalled voice, "...I mean, we are already quite late!"

"Yes, inside first! First we check inside for the director. Then we sit out here together under a warm brazier. What do you want to drink?"

"Nothing, thanks," said Nastya, sitting at an empty table on the terrace.

A few minutes later, Salaudski returned to the terrace with a glass of red wine for Nastya and another scotch for himself.

"What is it, snowing in spring?" he asked as he sat down at the table in the outdoor square littered with people.

"It's not snowing," said Nastya, wincing at the tall glass of red wine Salaudski had set before her. She looked up at the sky above, which was clear.

"Was the director inside?" she asked after Salaudski situated himself in the metal chair beside her and took a drink of his whiskey.

"Is he here? …Are they here?" Nastya asked again, growing more and more impatient.

"Shhh! Listen…." Salaudski unfolded a piece of paper that he had been holding in his left hand the whole time. Then he explained to Nastya:

"The director called and left a message with the bartender. The bartender wrote down the message only a few minutes ago – apparently, he had just called. There has been a problem. It says…."

Salaudski finished unfolding the paper and began reading aloud:

"'My most honorable friend, and savior of my leg,'" he looks up to see if Nastya is paying attention, which she is, and he continues, *"'My most honorable friend, and savior of my leg, …You won't believe the misfortune we have had. The best dancer at our most illustrious, Opéra Garnier, has just taken a bad fall while performing tonight, and has broken her ankle….*

'As I take the utmost concern for the health of my dancers – treating them as if they were my own daughters, mind you, - I have gone to the hospital to see that she is properly taken care of … I am calling right now from the hospital … I will rush to meet you and the beautiful Anastasia I have heard so much about, just as soon as a cast is put on our poor girl's ankle…'

'…Please wait for us. My wife and I can't wait to meet the Russian dancer; and, even more, I can't wait to see you again, my most illustrious, long-time aristocratic comrade….'

'PS: If I don't make it tonight, enjoy yourselves, the two of you, have a few drinks, and be merry; and we will see each other tomorrow at two o'clock at the Opéra Garnier. We will go over the contracts and make sure everything looks okay; then we'll start Anastasia dancing right away….'

'Your humble servant, Monsieur So-and-so.'"

211

Thus Salaudski finished the letter, mumbling some incomprehensible words at the end, after 'Monsieur'. He then looked up at Nastya, who sat across from him at the painted metal table under the hot brazier erupting blue flames on the terrace on Rue du Bourg-Tibourg, and he tried to gauge her reaction. Nastya stared at Salaudski, with her little eyebrows furrowed, in a face that concealed what she was thinking.

"I think he will come later, once he's finished at the hospital," muttered Salaudski, setting the letter down on the table, "And, if not, we drink our health – we drink our health like the good man suggested – and we go to see him tomorrow at two."

"That's terrible she broke her ankle." Nastya said, without a trace of concern in her voice. She was not thinking about the injured dancer. She didn't care about this dancer. She was thinking of one line in the director's message: '...treating them as if they were my own daughters, *mind you*.' The '...*mind you*' part especially struck her.

"Is the bartender French?" Nastya asked.

"What, here? At this place? ...Of course he's French. I mean, I don't know where his blood originated from – he could be a Turk for all I know. But he speaks French – just like a Frenchman. Some Turks speak French just like Frenchmen, you know...." Salaudski rambled on until Nastya interrupted him:

"And the director, he is French?"

"Of course he is French! We fought the Turks together! ...Oh, why did I say the Turks? I meant the Germans. It was all this talk about the Turks that got me confused! ...Why do you ask me that?"

"I just don't understand why, if the director is French, and the bartender is French, and *you* too, Salaudski, are French; I just don't understand why that message is in English?" Nastya tapped the paper on the table and looked in Salaudski's eyes – waiting for a response.

"This message, Anastasia, was obviously meant for the both of us. The director knows that you don't speak French. It is for your benefit, no doubt, that he left the message in English" ... "By the way," he continued, "why aren't you drinking your wine?"

"I don't care for red wine. Why didn't you get white wine? You know I prefer it."

"I told you, we don't drink white wine in Paris. Try your wine, you'll like it. It's a very good one. It will make your heart red and your thighs swoon, remember? Or, your heart hot and your thighs red, I think it goes...."

While Salaudski went on speaking, Nastya noticed something on his right hand. Between the thumb and index finger on his right hand were fresh smudges of blue ink – as though he had been writing with a leaky pen. Curiously enough, the message that had been 'taken by the bartender over the telephone' was also written in the same hue of blue ink. Nastya noticed this and her eyes fixed on Salaudski's ink-smudged hand. Thoughts raced through her mind upon seeing this. She sat there, staring at the man's hand and thinking distressing thoughts as he went on talking about the influence red wine has on a lady's heart and thighs. Then she cut him off, most blunt and direct:

"Maybe I should go see if the bartender speaks English ... because I don't think he took that message. I don't think it was a message from the director at all." Nastya's face flushed red when she spoke to Salaudski, and her anger mounted. Salaudski, felt a tense situation arising and drank down the last swallow of his whiskey in order to prepare for the tension.

"Are you calling me a liaaar?" he finally asked, poorly enunciating his words due to the puddle of whiskey that sat beneath his tongue, "Are you calling me a liar, Anastasia? Because I have never lied to you. I have never, ever lied to you. You don't think the director went to the hospital to accompany that poor dancer who broke her ankle? You don't believe that? ...Well, we'll go to the hospital and see for ourselves. We'll go to every hospital until we find him. But ah! We can't do that! What if we went around looking for him at the hospitals and he were to come here and miss us? That would be tragic. He asked us to have a few drinks and wait here for him. Any moment, his driver will pull up to this very terrace. We can't not be here. That would be a tragedy!"

"I don't think he's coming here, tonight," Nastya interjected.

"You *are* calling me a liar, *Mon Dieu!* I don't believe it!" Salaudski, threw his fist onto the table, and his empty whiskey glass shook; Nastya's mostly full wine glass teetered, spilling a fair amount of wine on the table, at which point Nastya stood up from her chair and looked down at the old man, whose face turned into rage...

"It doesn't matter, Salaudski... I'm going now. Goodbye." Nastya's tone revealed the contempt she felt for him at this moment. She then stopped, took a breath and chose her words... "I'm going out tonight and I'll be back tomorrow or the next day, then we can talk. Okay, Salaudski? Goodbye."

These words of Nastya pierced through Salaudski like a sharp pin. Each syllable she uttered was another stab to his gut. His face clenched up in frustration. His forehead throbbed, and his lips quivered. He then got up from his chair and stepped towards Nastya. She stood firm, looking at him with indignation. He reached towards her. He tried to take her hands; he wanted to appeal to her, to make her stay.

"But, how can you?" he asked in despair, "'Tomorrow or the next day' you say? But that's an eternity for me to be without you, my Anastasia! *Tomorrow* or *the next day*? …Why, we'll miss the meeting we have with the director. It's tomorrow at two o'clock, you remember? Don't you remember? Oh, please!" He begged Nastya. His voice trembled with worry and high-pitched, drunken entreaties.

"I don't think we have a meeting tomorrow at two o'clock. I don't believe you, Salaudski." Nastya spoke firmly as she pushed Salaudski's hands away from her, "I don't believe any of it – not a word you say." She held her purse close to her and looked around the terrace, deciding which way to walk away from this man. Some of the others seated at the tables on the terrace looked over in their direction, taking interest in the scene that was arising. Most, however, took no interest and continued drinking their aperitifs and talking amongst their own company.

"Nastya, you cannot leave. If you want to go, come home with me. Come home with me now. Here, I'll get us a taxi." Salaudski turned his head and looked upon Rue de Rivoli, hoping to see an empty cab waiting around. There were no cabs. His face shriveled in a pathetic look of longing and frustration. He wrung his hands and turned back to Nastya, appealing to her, while she stood tall and looked down at him, without the slightest sign of sympathy.

"Salaudski, go home!" she instructed him, "I'm not coming with you, tonight. We'll talk in a couple of days. Okay? Goodbye!" And with that, she took her purse and walked off the terrace, through the aisle, past the tables and chairs and the eyes of the people seated in them followed her – their mouths gaping at this young beauty who had spoken loudly and with indignation towards this quivering old man dressed like an army general, whose face wept with drunkenness and frustrated sadness. But his sadness turned to anger as soon as Nastya proudly walked away from him, her heels clicking on the terrace. Her face wearing an expression of haughtiness and disgust. This expression enraged Salaudski, and he walked quickly off the terrace catching up with Nastya on Rue de Rivoli.

As he followed Nastya down the sidewalk on Rue de Rivoli, she increased her pace, and looked back at him with anger and annoyance. But Salaudski kept on her, his own pace increasing, until he finally caught up with her.

"Listen my coquette, you come with me this minute! Do you understand, girl?!" He yelled this to her, as he followed closely behind. Finally he grabbed her bare shoulder with his large hand whereupon she turned around, faced him, and pierced his eyes with a sharp and angry glare…

"No, you listen," she said, "do not follow me, and do not talk to me! I am going by myself; so leave me alone, right now! Do *you* understand?!"

She stood still on the sidewalk, looking at Salaudski's eyes in order to see that he had understood her clearly. He did not flinch from her words. Instead he himself grew more angry, and seized the opportunity with Nastya standing near him, facing him, to grab her hands.

He grabbed her delicate fingers with his large, rough hands and he squeezed them.

"Where are you going to go?" He laughed at her, sardonically, "You have no money! You're going to go begging on the street? You're going to sleep in a doorway in a black evening dress and heels?" …And with this last phrase, he squeezed her fingers so hard that she cried out.

"Stop it!" She cried as tears instantly formed in her eyes from the pain. "Please stop!" she cried loudly; and, at this, some passers-by took sight of the two and one man, a stranger, approached Salaudski to make sure he wasn't harming the young lady. Salaudski noticed the man approaching, and to avoid confrontation, he immediately dropped Nastya's hands.

Nastya put her hands to her face, waiting for the pain to leave them. Salaudski began to speak again. The stranger did not come any closer; after Salaudski let go of Nastya's hands, he went back on his own way. And Salaudski continued…

"You have no money, Nastya. What are you going to do in Paris, all alone, with no money."

At this, Nastya took her purse from her shoulder and pulled the zipper to open it. Out of the one-thousand francs Salaudski had sent to Nastya when she was in Moscow, a couple hundred went to cab-fare, on the night she arrived. A couple hundred more had gone to paying for medicine, bandages and ointments for Salaudski's foot, which he had cut almost a week prior; and a few hundred additional francs had been spent on his food – which Nastya bought and cooked for him, while he was laid up with his injury. There should have still remained, however, two- or three-hundred francs in Nastya's purse. But when she unzipped the purse and opened it, she saw that the money – which she had tucked in the little side-pocket on the inside – was gone.

When Nastya realized the rest of her money was gone, Salaudski laughed cruelly... "You see? You have no money! What are you going to do? Walk around like a little gamine? A little coquettish tramp?! Ha!"

Tears streamed down Nastya's cheek as she looked at the man in anger and disbelief. She did not understand why he had taken her money from her, or when he had done it.

"But that was my money," she protested through her tears, "Why did you take it?"

"It was not *your* money. It was *my* money!" Salaudski looked smugly at Nastya, apparently very satisfied with himself. Nastya, could not bear another moment of the confrontation with Salaudski. She felt such indignation – almost hatred – towards him. She clenched her purse and her hands trembled slightly. Her lips, too, trembled, as she knew not what to say. From her eyes streamed tears, rolling down her cheeks. And not wanting to look another moment longer at this old man who had suddenly become so cruel, she turned around and walked as quickly as she could away from him, down the crowded streets of Paris. She walked on and on, ever so quickly, not looking back, but looking ahead at the unknown chaos in the streets of Paris, where she would take refuge from this old man. And only when she was sure that he was not following her, and that he was nowhere near, did she stop. And by that time it was already night and the streets were dark, and she was far away from where she had left Salaudski. She was on an unknown street in an unfamiliar quarter and the heavy darkness of night enshrouded all – yet she felt safer still for being away from Salaudski.

CHAPTER XIV

That which is found when a confused and distraught Nastya goes to find Marick – in search of refuge and nothing more...

Nastya, alone and crying, but better off still for being on her own and away from the cruel man Salaudski turned out to be, found herself finally near the river Seine, where numerous bridges spanned, each lit-up with the resplendent glow from the red night's sky overhead and the streetlamps planted on its bow. She saw this light on her dark path; it quelled her heart and eased her woe.

She walked on in joy and sorrow and relief. She escaped from that man, but now she'd need another, for surely she would soon grow hungry; and she is no hunter. Besides, pigeons and rats are the only game around. The fish in the Seine would poison any fisherwoman.

'A washerwoman is what I'll be. I'll scrub other people's linen if I have to,' Nastya thought to herself as she walked on by the Seine, 'I just can't go back to *that* man – not to *him*, I can't.' ... 'I'll go and be Marick's kept-woman if I must. At least Marick would never force his lips upon me, or force his hand upon my breast. He will feed me, and give me a warm place to sleep, and he won't try to make my "thighs red with wine"' ... 'And if our home blows in the Seine, or if some kids throw it in the river on a prank, Marick will pull it out – and I will help – and we'll dry it in the sun, and set it up again. I will pull our house out of the Seine and be Marick's kept-woman ... oh, it sounds horrible though: my fate! What am I going to do? Father, I may need you to come rescue me. Your little girl might not be able to handle this!' Tears streamed from Nastya's face as she walked along with these fearful thoughts in her head, 'No, it's okay, Nastya ... you will go and become

217

Marick's kept-woman. Even if he does turn into a Salaudski, at least he will fetch your home if it falls in the Seine.'

Nastya quickened her pace, and cried heavily as she walked, determined to find Marick right away; yet, when she came to a bridge arched over the Seine, she stopped and leaned against the copper rail, so she could rest a moment. She looked down the length of the river. It stretched off into the horizon like a giant, black snake slithering in the night. A deep red, sanguine glow of light billowed in the sky above the river and the rooftops, over the trees and the cathedral towers; and she looked at this deep red, dark night sky and wondered if this light she saw, was a sign of hope or a sign of despair.

Tears fell down her cheeks; and once they all drained out, and she'd no more tears to give, she dried her eyes and continued walking – crossing the bridge, arched over the Seine – and descended the stone steps that lay on the other side.

For a long time she walked down the cobbled path on the Left Bank, along the river, without finding anyone or anything. Then, after passing through a dark tunnel and walking past a row of evenly planted trees – whose bodies, strong and grand, stood heroically in a line against the stone walls of the quai, like giant soldiers with weapons against their shoulders, guarding a fortress in the night – she found herself in a place she recognized.

It was the Quai Voltaire, and she saw in the distance, that little green tent – the one belonging to Marick, which she helped him construct earlier on this day. It stood far off, and alone; a lonely tent, she could see its fabric flapping in the wind. She could see the trees around it swaying against the dark red sky.

When she approached the tent, she saw a man sitting beside it, on the hard stone ground, with his knees pulled up to his chest and his face buried in his arms; his arms were wrapped around his knees and it appeared as though he were sleeping. A half-empty wine bottle stood by his foot. There was a pan of food beside him too. Nastya, thinking it was Marick, decided to call to him. The man, who actually had been sleeping, gently awoke upon hearing her voice, and he lifted his head as she called to him again:

"Marick?" she asked, "Is that you, Marick?"

"No," replied David, "Marick is in his tent. He's sleeping."

Nastya looked at David curiously, strangely. This man also spoke English... 'With a nice accent,' Nastya noticed, 'he doesn't have a French accent at all. He also knows Marick.' ...And Marick, the one who was sure to help her, was, she was informed, sleeping in his tent. Nastya flashed David a kind smile, a shy smile, and got down on her knees to look inside.

"Marick?" she whispered into the tent. He did not answer. His body did not stir. "Marick?" she called again, this time a little louder. Still his body did not stir, it did not even move a little. It was as still as stone. Meanwhile, David remained seated on the cobblestone floor outside the tent. He remembered the dream he had been having before this girl came and woke him up. It had been a nice dream. He thought of this girl who was shouting at Marick inside the tent. He liked this girl. He liked the way she smiled at him just before climbing in the tent. He thought of his dream and he thought of the girl and his sleepiness went away. Then, suddenly, his body began aching with its usual torments. While Nastya called to Marick, David took a drink of the wine from the bottle beside his foot to quell the pain, but his body did not take it well. He winced at the acrid taste and set the bottle down. The swig of wine had only made his stomach hurt more.

"Is he alright?" Nastya asked David, after pulling her head out of the tent, "He doesn't look alright."

"He's been sleeping all evening," David responded, "I tried to wake him earlier but he was not happy about it."

"He doesn't look like he's sleeping. He's not moving at all. It doesn't look like he's breathing."

At this, David jumped to feet, his face took on a look of tremendous concern. Nastya stepped back, also with a worried look on her face, giving David room to crawl in the tent and check on Marick.

"Marick!" he said loudly, almost in a shout. He shook the still man's ankle, which rested next to the flap on the tent. The body did not stir. "...Marick!" he called out again, this time shouting; again he shook the man's ankle. "Marick, wake up, Marick!"

"Leave me alone... I'm sleeping. Go away!" grumbled the man inside the tent, and he rolled over, changing the position in which he was sleeping.

David and Nastya both let out sighs of relief upon hearing that Marick was alive. Nastya had no particular reason to fear for Marick's health. David, however, knew that Marick had injected himself with morphine earlier in the day; and, after the girl informed him that he wasn't responding and that she didn't think he was breathing, he became quite worried that something terrible had happened. After Marick told David to 'go away', David slipped out of the tent, and sat back down by the half-empty bottle of wine. Nastya, however, remained in the tent and called out to the sleeping man once again…

"Marick! It's me, Nastya!" she said in a loud but gentle voice, "Wake, Marick! … it's Nastya – you asked me to come see you tonight."

"Go away, Nastya!" roared the man in the tent. "I don't feel good, I want to be alone!" After saying this most coldly, Marick crawled over to the flap in the tent, which was open, and shooed Nastya away with a look that revealed torment and profound irritation. He then closed the flap and tied it shut with a shoestring, so as to be left alone. Nastya, dispirited, backed away from the tent and walked over to search for a cinderblock to sit on. While she was looking around, David stood up and found an unused cinderblock behind the tent, leaning up against the stone wall; and he dragged it around to the front for Nastya to sit upon. She took off her heels, which were causing pain in her feet, and sat down carefully, trying not to ruin her black dress.

She looked over at David once again and smiled: another shy smile that is so uncharacteristic of Nastya. She thanked him and then she put her head in her hands, as if she were about to break into tears.

Our young man looked on her with great interest. Who was this curious girl who spoke in English? Who was this elegant beauty who knew Marick – the junky who sleeps in a tent by the river?

"Would you like an orange?" David asked her, in an attempt to console her. Nastya looked up from her hands. She hadn't been crying, she had merely hidden her face in a sudden fit of despair.

"Yes, thank you. I'm starving," she replied, smiling at David. He too smiled at her and his lips shimmered under the streetlamp as they were wet with the red wine he had drunk.

He pulled the burlap sack of Spanish oranges, which Marick had left outside of the tent, in front of him and handed one to Nastya. She peeled the orange and ate it with avarice. She hadn't eaten since the day before, and it was already nighttime.

"Do you want some wine?" David asked, handing her the half-empty bottle.

"Sure," she said. She took a drink of wine from the bottle and sighed. Her lips too now glimmered with the wet wine, caught by the light of the streetlamp. "I normally don't like red wine," she continued, "but this is good."

"Marick has good taste. He's a good cook too – not much of a host, though."

"Yes, not much of a host. How long have you been waiting for him?"

"Hours now. He invited me to come eat with him. He said he would let me sleep here, or he would at least help me find another place to sleep nearby." After David said this, he regretted it. He didn't want to let on to this girl that he was without a home or a bed for the night.

Nastya, looked at David in bewilderment. He was nicely dressed, in a dark brown suit that looked like it had been made by an expensive tailor; and his hair – though it looked like he had just had a bad haircut – was combed nicely, and Nastya thought it looked cute with the short sprigs of hair sticking out funny. So, she wondered why this nicely dressed and attractive young man had come to depend on Marick, the man who lives in a tent by the river, for a place to sleep. She thought he must be one of those many American travelers who come to Paris for a short time with decent clothes and big ideas, but no money to eat or rent a room.

Nastya took another drink of the wine and laughed, "Me too ... I was invited for dinner and he said he would offer me a place to sleep as well. How funny." ...After she said this she blushed and regretted saying it for the same reason David regretted what he had said.

David looked on Nastya with bewilderment. He couldn't think of a reason why this beautiful girl, who was dressed as if she were staying at the *Hôtel Crillon*, would be sitting on a cinderblock at nearly midnight, with no place to sleep."

"But you are French?" David asked, searching for clues.

"No, no. I am Russian."

"Really? From where?" David grew interested. He sat up straight and perked up his eyes, forgetting that he had been hunched over to ease the pain in his abdomen. He had always been interested in

Russia. As he loved poetry, he had read a lot of Pushkin in the past. He had also read everything Gogol had ever written. But above all, he loved the drama involved with Russia and everything Russian. He loved the stories about the Tsars and Tsarinas. And especially he loved the story of Rasputin – this great Russian peasant who seduced his way into the culottes of royal Russia and then proceeded to discredit the tsar and tsarina to their people, which ultimately led to the Russian Revolution. He loved the excitement of the 1917 Revolution but, moreover, he loved the old romance of the Tsarist Russia of the nineteenth century… Her stories, and songs, strummed on a balalaika; all he knew of Russia, he had read in books, he had never hitherto met a Russian in the flesh. This excited him.

"From Moscow," Nastya responded to his last question, "Are you French? You sound American."

"No, I'm French … but I grew up in Seattle – in America … in fact, I don't even speak French. I've been back only a week or so…."

Nastya's mind drifted to thoughts of America. She had read many travel books about America. She knew a little bit about almost every city in the United States. She thought about Seattle. "Someday," she told him, "I would like to see the Space Needle, and Mount Rainier, the San Juan Islands, and…."

"How do you know about those places?" David asked, surprised that a girl from Moscow would know anything about the West Coast of America.

"It was in a book I read. I've read a lot about America," Nastya went on, taking another Spanish orange from the burlap sack. "May, I?" she asked, holding up the orange.

"Sure, they're not mine. They're Marick's. But he said we could eat here tonight, right? …Do you want some rice and vegetables? It's probably a little cold but it's good." David pulled the little pan out in front of him and took the lid off – stirring the food with a wooden spoon that had been on top of the pan.

"Yes, he did say that – and thank you. I am really hungry."

"Well, eat! Eat it all and the oranges too, and drink some wine if it will help."

Nastya took the pan and ate the rest of the rice and vegetables with the wooden spoon. Then she washed it down with a healthy swallow of wine. She then started peeling another orange, and laughed…

"I feel so much better. When I came here, I was in great despair, I thought my life was ruined. Now I feel … well, maybe it's the wine – though I didn't drink too much … but I feel happy. Hopeful. I was really counting on Marick to help me out…."

"There's a pomegranate too! Only one, you can have it." David pulled a ripe pomegranate out of a bag that had been next to the sack of oranges, and handed it to Nastya. Nastya beamed a giant smile. Her radiant eyes flashed and she looked at David with delight.

"How did you get a pomegranate? I thought they weren't in season until the fall?"

"It's Marick's – he's a magician!"

Nastya set the orange down and peeled the rind off the pomegranate, revealing the lush, sanguine seeds that looked like little red rubies scattered in the albedo. She ate one of the rubies and reveled in it. "It is a great luxury to eat a pomegranate," she laughed, handing a bunch of seeds to David.

"Yes, I love these too," he replied, and a moment later: "What is your name, by the way?"

"Nastya."

'So Nastya is to be her name,' David thought to himself, 'it is a beautiful name – a perfect name … Nastya!'

"What is your patronymic?" he continued.

"Alexandrovna," she told him, amazed that a foreigner would know to ask a Russian for her patronymic. "My full name," she went on, "is Anastasia Alexandrovna Mironova, but I go by 'Nastya'."

"I can call you… 'Nastenjka'?" David asked, coyly.

"You can. It's cute. No one calls me that except my father. Hmm. You certainly have read a lot about Russians! …But what is your name?"

"David."

'So, David is to be his name,' Nastya mused, "It is a nice name," she said aloud. David then blushed, and feeling himself blush at such an innocent compliment, he felt silly, and hid his face in his hands. Yet, it wasn't the compliment on his name that made him blush. It was the way Nastya had looked at him when she said he had a nice name. Those eyes like emeralds, that hint of a mysterious smile she gave him, the way her eyes looked at his twice, and darted away twice, and how her little mysterious smile then turned into a big grin, and how she laughed then, a benevolent laugh – that was what had made him blush. Had his eyes not been buried in his hands, however, he would have noticed that Nastya, too, was blushing.

Just then, there was a commotion. Nastya and David both looked up and over at the tent that was beginning to shake. A groaning sound came from within. It was as if a hungry animal were trapped inside. It began to scratch at the inside of the tent. David and Nastya started laughing. They had both been helping themselves to the wine and they were very happy talking to each other and their hearts felt good and their spirits were light.

Then they heard Marick untying the tent-flap and a moment later he stuck his head out, surveyed the two people sitting in front of his tent, and then he climbed out. The Moroccan man with the dark, weathered face threw both Nastya and David looks of annoyance as he paced in front of his tent, scratching his belly and armpits. He paced like this for many moments, while Nastya and David watched him, waiting for him to address them.

But Marick just paced the cobbles back and forth, scratching himself all over. Every few moments, he cast an unfriendly glance in their direction.

"How long have I been sleeping?" Marick finally asked in a scratchy morning-voice.

"I don't know," David replied, laughing a little, "A long time, though. It's already after midnight."

Then Marick walked over to the pan that was set on the stone ground between David and Nastya. He crouched down and took the peeled orange off the lid. He then took the lid off the pan and was horrified. "What?!" he cried, "where is my dinner?" He then reached over and found the burlap sack that had been filled with Spanish oranges. It was empty and he held up the bag, waving it with anger in the faces of his guests. "One peeled orange is what you leave me? One goddamned peeled orange?!" … "You two have a lot of nerve, eating all my food! You know that?"

At this point, David stood up and stepped in front of Marick, who was also standing. "Listen, Marick. You invited me … you invited us … to have dinner at your place. You even said that you would give me a place to sleep. You told Nastya that as well! Now you are yelling at us about the food. We came for dinner and you wouldn't wake up, so we ate.

"But you ate everything! Do you think it's easy from me to get food? Do you think I can just walk to an *épicerie* and buy more food? Do you think my tent is wallpapered with French francs? Do you think I have an ounce of gold in my pocket? This means I'm going to starve! And what the hell are you going to do about it? Go get me some more food!..."

"We'll go find you some more food, alright?" Nastya interjected. She was by this time standing and had put her heels back on. She clutched her purse tightly, making it obvious that she was ready to leave. She then went on, "I'm sorry, Marick, I'm the one who ate everything – I was starving. I hadn't eaten all day. I'll find you some food."

"Yeah, well, there's an *épicerie* just up the street." Marick's voice calmed down a little, though not much, as he pointed up from the quai towards the streets of the Left Bank. Go down towards the *Institut de France* – that building with the golden dome, and take a right on Rue de Seine. Halfway up Rue de Seine – before you get to *Buci*, there is an *épicerie*. Make sure to get me some bread, and cheese, and some more wine...."

"But I don't have money with me, Marick," interrupted Nastya, speaking softly and shaking her head, "but I'll go now and find you some food."

"Girl, I think you have plenty of money in that purse. Don't lie to me … you're dressed like a...." Marick was about to finish what he was saying, but David, growing angry, interrupted him…

"It isn't any of your business if she has money or not, and it's no concern of yours how she's dressed either. And comments like that to her are just going to provoke me," David walked up to Marick and looked down at him, firmly, "...and I don't think you want to provoke me." Marick backed off and looked away, but David continued speaking to him, though in a calmer tone… "Anyway, Marick, the food was lying out. It probably would have been stolen if we hadn't been sitting here. And by morning, the bugs would have gotten it anyway…." But David's words were cut off when Nastya came beside him and slipped her arm through his in a gesture suggesting the two leave together.

225

"That's alright, we'll find some food, Marick, and bring it back," she said while turning away with David.

After walking a few meters away from Marick's tent, Nastya let go of David's arm but continued walking beside him. These two strangers walked away together, down the quai of the Seine; and Marick could be heard in the distance shouting nasty things.

CHAPTER XV

And on we walked as clandestines,
through foreign streets, with stains of wine
on our lips, and stars glistened overhead;
cathedral steps, and ancient squares,
we fled from the past, in warm embrace,
...and never once thought of our homes.

The two walked on languidly together down the quai. Nastya looked at the stars overhead, and David looked on at the boats that passed slowly by. Upon the boats where music played, were again those revelers, drinking and laughing – young men with their girls, kissing. 'Was it this same night,' David thought, 'that I watched those people gathered on the decks of the boats, in a grand, twilit orgy, laughing from love and drunkenness?' David had slept a little since then; he had dozed off for a while in front of Marick's tent, and it seemed like a long time ago that he was sitting on the quai alone, watching those boats go by.

'What jealousy I felt, back then, watching those people together, feasting and fancying each other. How restless and uneasy my spirit had been then, but now I am filled with a gentle peace … for then I was alone; and now I walk with Nastya…

'And though we do not kiss or drink, and poverty has quelled our hope, I could laugh and sing more merrily than all of those aboard. …For they feel merely pleasure, but I feel happiness…

'And as I walk with Nastya, for a reason I can't understand, all the illness that has hitherto riddled my body, all the sickness that has torn at my gut and ate at my head, has now lifted. An illness I have had for months, which has never shown mercy except for those times I have been given a pill or a point, is now gone. And not a tonic have I taken, save a swallow of acrid wine, yet still the pain is gone.' David felt all of the illness in him evaporating as he walked beside Nastya down *Pont des Arts*. All the drug-induced confusion that began at the hospital, and continued on at Odette's – that too disappeared. And all his sorrows and worries of being lost and penniless in this new country – they all vanished.

"That was terrible how Marick treated us, wasn't it?" came suddenly from Nastya, who had been quiet for quite some time, "I can't stop thinking about it. I don't feel that I should try to find him food. After all, he invited me to come for dinner, and I go out of my way to come and he is passed-out when I get there. He also invited me to stay with him, but now it looks like *that* won't be possible." … "And he was so kind too, you know, David? He said that I could stay as long as I want and he would never try to 'dishonor' me by laying a hand on me. 'Dishonor' was the word he used. He said that I could sleep in the same tent as him and he would never even touch me – he was so polite earlier." … "And now I go back, and he's a cruel monster. Just like the men in Paris he had warned me about."

Then David turned to Nastya, and looked into her eyes that shone with sadness, "So, you have no money and nowhere else to go, besides Marick's tent? …If I may ask."

"Well, I have a place to stay, or I *had* a place, rather, with an old man whom I trusted; but I shouldn't have trusted him, for he.…"

Nastya explained to David her story of Salaudski. She explained why she left Russia and what she experienced this last week after coming to Europe for the first time. She told him how he grabbed her hands on the sidewalk of Rue de Rivoli, and how he squeezed them so hard that even her head throbbed with pain. She explained everything to David as they walked by the river and she told him that she was going back to Moscow as soon as possible. Under no circumstances would she stay with that man again. She had been cowardly, she said, when she told him she would return the next day to talk things over. She would return, but only to get her suitcase. If it didn't have her passport in it, she said, she would just forget it, and leave it behind. But since she needed her passport, she would return – but only for that.

David then explained his similar situation. He told her of his coming to France and losing thirteen-thousand dollars, and being ill and having to accept the charity of a certain female doctor whose goal it was, as he saw it, to keep him poor and make him dependent on her drugs so that she may have him for a slave – an unclothed slave who would caress her on command. He also said that he would never again stay with her. But he too needed to return to get his passport. He would return – but only for that.

"I bet Salaudski and this Odette woman are a lot alike. Both very lonely … we should introduce them!" Nastya laughed for a moment, and then stopped and said in a voice more sullen and serious…

"I think there are probably a lot of lonely people in this city. I don't like it very much here. When you are far away in Russia, you think Paris is the most romantic place on earth – the most beautiful too … but I don't think it's very romantic or very beautiful. I saw its ugly side quickly." Then she paused, and continued…

"But your sickness, it is not too grave?"

"No, heavens, it's not too grave," David said in a grand and melodramatic voice, as if mimicking a character in one of those romantic novels that are so popular nowadays, "In truth, it is gone! …I was cured by a benevolent angel who flew down and woke me from my sleep upon the bank of the river."

"Oh, don't joke. Your sickness worries me."

But then it dawned on David that he is not the character of a romantic and popular novel; and so, his voice returned to its usual serious tone and sullen timber…

"Fortunately, nothing is a joke to me right now. What is fortunate is that I am serious beyond measure. This moment is the first moment in a long time that I have felt well – truly well – without the help of medicine." …Nastya listened and walked on beside him, biting her lower lip and thinking many things.

The two arrived at *Pont Neuf* and looked at the clusters of ancient buildings and monuments lit-up against the dark sky on the island in the Seine. They paused for a moment, standing close to one another, leaning on the stone wall of the bridge. They watched the fluidity of the river and the gracefulness of the clouds, as both the river and clouds changed shape, and drifted off into the horizon.

"I've only seen the ugliness of Paris as well. I haven't seen any beauty in this city, until now," David turned his attention from the view of the island and looked at Nastya. "You know, Nastenjka..." he began, and she laughed at hearing him call her this nickname. He laughed too, and continued, "...when I lost my money, I almost returned to Brittany to work on the docks. I met a nice older man and his wife out there on the coast and the man said he would give me a job, working on piers, bringing in cargo. I'd have a place to sleep, three square meals and coffee in the morning, plus wages. I even went to the train station, *Gare du Nord*, with the intention to return to Brittany. If I had gone, I would right now, no doubt, have a dry bed and a full belly, some cash, and the company of this great man and his wife – though his wife doesn't speak any English. ...But, anyway, I couldn't allow myself to go. I knew it was the sensible choice, I knew staying in Paris with no money, in poor health, would probably destroy me. Capital cities offer no mercy to the down and out. But, I couldn't go. Standing at that station, I knew no muscle in my body could be forced to get on a train to Brittany. There was something in Paris I had to find. I didn't know what it was, yet I knew that my life and happiness depended on it. I knew that I had to remain here." ... "And, I know that fate is sometimes cruel and merciless. I know the trick of the intuition: nine times it will lead you right into the pastures of pleasure; so by the tenth time, you trust it blindly, and as you are blinded you cannot see where you are led, and so intuition takes this opportunity to lead you off the edge of a cliff."

"That is so pessimistic," Nastya said, as she pondered what it was that David had experienced in life to put an idea like that in his head, "...So you never trust your intuition, because you think it is out to destroy you?"

"That my intuition is out to destroy me, I would say is true. That I never trust it, or follow it, that is certainly untrue. In fact, I *always* follow my intuition. Consequently, I have fallen off many cliffs. Yet, I have also spent long sojourns in the pastures of pleasure. Those who make decisions through rational processes are much safer in life than those who heed only intuition; for rational processes tend to lead one into the forest, where the canopies of trees give shelter and their branches give fuel to burn for heat. But those who sit by campfires under a parasol of pine never venture far enough to reach the pastures of pleasure."

"I think you are a lot like me, David. I feel that way too, though I've never consciously thought about it in those terms ... Yet, intuition is the reason I am in France right now. And I will stay until my intuition tells me to leave. ...A ballet dancer who doesn't follow her intuition would break an ankle in every performance. ...But what was it you were going to say?"

"...Just that, if I had done the reasonable thing, I would be with old Marc and his wife right now, living the safe, comfortable life on the seaside. But there was some reason I had to stay in Paris, so fortunately – yes, fortunately – I stayed!...

"...Please know that I am not blinded by every woman I meet. I am twenty-eight years old and I have been led to many a crucifixion by women whom I trusted. I am not jaded though, for I still believe in love and the goodness of women and men...." ... "But, what I want to say is that I have a presentiment that soon I will be in a place completely different from right here. I will be in a completely different situation. It *must* be so. For things cannot remain the way they are. This is chaos. But I won't take the safe way; and if I am led off a cliff, I will fall to my death knowing that I knew that was a probable outcome all along." ... "My intuition told me to stay in Paris. And so I did. And now my intuition tells me that I have just found what I remained here to find." David turned Nastya and put the palm of his hand on her soft cheek. She felt his palm to be soft. She closed her eyes, when he touched her face. She inhaled deeply, and began to think about the things David had just said:

'I don't know this man. And the things he says are strange. He implies that the reason he remained in Paris was to meet me. That is what he meant by what he just said... *I have just found what I remained here to find* ...and then he puts his hand on my face.' ... 'He doesn't know me either. He could be a dangerous man. He could be a crazy man. But how do you feel, Nastya? ...I feel good. His hand upon my cheek makes my lips swollen, it makes my eyelids heavy – and so they close. His hand on my cheek does not make me want to pull away, to fight him or to run. On the contrary, his soft palm, warm against my bare skin makes me want to pull closer towards him. I don't want to fight him, at this moment, I want to love him. And this could be very dangerous, for I really don't know him....'

Then David took his hand from her cheek. He was worried that he had possibly frightened her with his confession, for was he any more to her than a stranger? He stepped back, whereupon she opened her eyes and looked at him questioningly. He suggested the two sit upon the stone bench, in the middle of a patch of lavender that had been planted on the quai. Ivy grew on the stones all around them, and its leaves glowed a phosphorescent green in the light of the moon, which rose broad and full over the city. The pleasant, sweet smell of lavender rose up from the patch around the bench and they both breathed it in with great appreciation.

David sat far away from Nastya on the bench. He felt ashamed of himself for admitting those feelings he had for her, after knowing her for such a short time. It was the boyish admission of a saccharine romantic – that was all. David's nature *is* romantic – this he cannot change. He merely hoped he hadn't frightened her.

He sat for many moments, thinking of what he should say to break the silence. He felt ashamed and silly for what he had said: that *she* was the sole reason he stayed in Paris … that he was looking for *her*. What fever was boiling his brains when he said this? He couldn't have possibly meant it; after all, he had only just met her. But he knew that he had meant it.

'Shame is a terrible thing,' he thought to himself, 'Guilt is fine, for it condemns the action. Realize the action was bad, and throw it out – one's self goes unscathed. But Shame condemns the person, the self. What you *did* was bad, so *you* are bad. Shame is a feeling that no one should ever have to suffer … however, what I said was alright, and I'll say it again!' David's thoughts went on in this silly manner for sometime while Nastya sat on the same bench, with a few feet of separation between them, and gazed at the same moon. Her thoughts went differently…

'I wonder why he's sitting so far away, right now. He had his soft hand on my cheek, and he told me that sweet thing, and now it's as if I'm a stranger seated beside him at a park.' … 'Nastya,' she continued, addressing herself, 'you too need to say how you feel. It is very dangerous to trust the wrong man; for at best… you'll lose yourself; and, at worst… you'll lose your life.' … 'But it is also dangerous – and *more* dangerous in my opinion – to distrust the right man. If you don't put faith in your intuition, and trust the man your heart tells you to trust, he will never be yours, and you risk something even more grim than losing your life. You risk never finding your soul.' … 'You know that that's true Nastya. You believe it entirely.'

And with that conclusion, Nastya turned to David, who was suffering from great anxiety due to the prolonged silence, and she spoke:

"You will think I sound stupid," she began, "but I think I really ran away to Paris to see the Seine and to meet you." And she paused and looked at him directly in the eyes. He looked away a moment and then his courage returned and he looked back at her, penetrating her eyes with his gaze that revealed so much joy and so much affection, that she then turned to blush. What she had said dissolved all of that miserable shame in his body and ignited a warm fire within him. Both David and Nastya then moved over on the bench to sit close beside each other. David wanted to show his gratitude to Nastya for saying what she had just said to him, however, his words failed him. So she continued to speak:

"I think I knew I would meet you," and then she smiled, "and I wanted to see the Seine, too. So much I wanted to! … but you are a man, and the Seine is just a river … no one has traveled so far, just for a river."

After hearing this, David was struck with such profound emotion that all he could do was take Nastya in his arms and embrace her with the full strength of his body. Nastya too embraced him with passion. Their bodies remained entwined, and neither wanted to end the embrace.

Finally David leaned back, and, with his hands on her shoulders, he gazed into her eyes, which reflected a thousand hues, bright as candle flames under the dark sky.

"You're not speaking," said Nastya.

"I want to look at your eyes, a moment … Never have I wanted to say so much yet been so unable to speak."

"You don't have to speak."

David spoke anyhow, without taking care to choose his words, "I have been ill for sometime now – living in a nightmare induced by chronic pain and the poisons the doctors have been giving me. It all began months and months ago in America, and led up to my being sent back here, to France, where the nightmare has continued – and has even intensified ten-fold. A nightmare is a gentle way to describe the pain I have been in. Yet, these few moments, I've known you … this is the first time that I have felt strong and healthy in a long time. My illness and confusion have vanished.

"But maybe you'll feel differently tomorrow." Nastya said, with a tinge of lament in her voice.

"Tomorrow I will be even stronger," David tried to articulate the ideas in his head that were yet to be examined, "The happy part of it all –

of experiencing a nightmare – is that in even the worst dream, you are a magician. Once you realize that the images you see and feelings you have – no matter how horrific they are – are not fixed, yet are malleable, and can be altered, you can change the whole dream – or at least wake from it." ... "I guess I speak of nothing." ... "But really, it's not nothing. You know, Nastya. In America, I had something. I had friends, and pleasures and ambitions, and then I was forced to come to France and I was stripped of all that I had. I wasn't even given the chance to say goodbye to those I knew back home. They just packed me up and shipped me eight-thousand kilometers away from everything I knew and loved. ...And now, Nastya, I am with you, and even if you leave me while the sky is still dark, I am with you now and I have everything. I have everything for the first time in my life and it came right after having absolutely nothing."

"I will not leave you while the sky is dark, David; I hope *you* will still be with *me* when the sky grows light again," Nastya paused, and bit her bottom lip, thinking about things. Then she continued, "I also had something in Russia: my father, my brother, a few friends, my mother and my home. But I didn't have everything. If I did, I never would have run away to France. I realize now my motivation was not really to become a dancer at the Opéra Garnier. That was more of a convenient pretext for coming. I could have continued my career just fine in Russia – near my home and my family. But something else drove me here." ... "You said, right when I met you that you had come to France by force ... I also came by force. I didn't really ever make a choice to come here. There wasn't a clear moment where I decided to take that train from Moscow. It was as if I, too, had to come. I was afraid to come, but I knew I would do it and I couldn't have stopped myself." Nastya paused for a moment, and then looking into David's eyes, she continued, "It was as if fate or God or something sent me here to experience this. ...To experience all of the sorrow and the confusion that I have known in this last week – and finally, to experience the happiness that I have right now." ... "Without this happiness," she takes David's hands in hers, "my coming to France would have just been some cruel trick by some fate or some God. But with it – by meeting you – the world seems to have meaning. This moment takes away all of my past regret." Nastya, at this point, was not afraid of speaking wantonly. She was no longer afraid of giving David too much with her words. She believed in what she was saying and she had full faith in how she felt and she was not ashamed...

"...I deeply love my father, and I know I hurt him by coming here," she went on, "but I think children are made to hurt their parents – only so that they may find their own life and their own happiness and find the one whom they can love ... so they can then make their own children, who will one day hurt them." ... "I know I hurt my father, but I know he understands. It is life, isn't it?

"...I also hurt my little brother," she continued, "he too is very sick. He has to stay in bed most of the time. I pray for him a lot and I do love him, but he is too young to understand how someone could leave him if they love him. When he is older, he will understand; and when he does the same thing, I mean, when he grows up and leaves our parents home to follow a dream or search for something, he will forgive me...

"...It is strange the way I packed up my suitcase and left Russia in the night – it was almost all unconscious. I just packed my suitcases and boarded a train and left everything I knew behind."

"And now you are free!" David smiled, "We both are. You talk of this Salaudski who wants to chain you up like a concubine; and I have this doctor who wants to keep me in fetters, but really, neither of us are chained up. We are both alive and we are both free. Our stories are amazing, really – quite unordinary – and things could have gone badly for either one of us. I mean very badly ... but they haven't. We are both alive and free and it is really beautiful." David pulled Nastya closer to him and continued speaking, "...What I love about this life is that at any moment – provided your legs work, and you are not locked up in a prison – but at any moment, you can just fly away ... just fly away! ...And if you don't find happiness, or love, or whatever you seek, just go somewhere else. It doesn't matter if you don't have the money to get there. If you have the ambition, you will find a way. The secret is to keep the ambition and the desire to live and embrace life. If you do that, eventually, happiness will come and love will come and all things will come. It could take a whole lifetime. But eventually, if you are a strong person, you will find what you've always dreamed of...

"...I think the tragedy of life," he went on, "is that we are much more free than we think we are. We human beings have infinite freedom; yet most people don't realize this until they are too tired to act. Still, tiredness can be cured, just as dreams can be created...

"...Back in America, I was tired and I was sick. But now my tiredness is gone and my dreams are born."

"David?"

"Yes, Nastya?"

"When you speak, I feel the last thing I want to do is go back to Moscow. I want to go away with you. To Spain or to Greece, maybe."

"And I want to take you, Nastya. I want more than anything to take you to those places ... Oh, I really want to." Then he sighed a rueful sigh, "...But I have no money, Nastya. It is not with me that you should go."

"But what you just said about having no money ... that makes it all untrue what you said before, about having infinite freedom, about being able to just *fly away*. 'Tiredness can be cured', you say. It doesn't matter if we don't have money. If we have the ambition, we can find a way."

"You are right, Nastya. What I said about us having infinite freedom was the truth. We *can* fly away and freedom and happiness will come with us ... what I said after that, about having no money, I said out of fear – just a flashing moment of fear. And fear can be strong. Fear can be an impetuous monster towering over one's head. But fear doesn't rule us. If it did, you would have never boarded the train to Paris. If it ruled us, I would go back to the doctor's right now and take my medicine, and be nice to this woman I loathe. I would mop the floors ten times over to earn a meager keep. But I am not going to do that."

"Yes, don't do that, my David, there are too many possibilities in this world to accept a fate like that.

"Can we walk a little, Nastenjka?"

"Yes, I like it when you call me that," Nastya laughed, crinkling her nose up. The two then stood and David held Nastya's hand and led her down *Quai d'Orsay* towards the *Pont Alexandre III*.

When they reached the bridge, they found it deserted of the midnight, errant Parisians who usually flock to it, along with the *Pont des Arts*. It was quiet and the anchored boats could be heard rocking underneath, sending little waves splashing against the stone walls beneath the bridge. David and Nastya walked back and forth down the *Pont Alexandre III*, holding each other's hands, ensconced in the new and happy romance each was experiencing.

Nastya admired the great bridge, built in the Russian style. At either end, stand granite pillars, seventeen meters high, with golden statues atop them. Numerous nymphs, and cherubs alike, adorn the old bridge, all participating in their own private, gilded orgies.

"I think this is the most beautiful bridge in Paris," David said, "I read a long time ago - before I ever saw the bridge – that it was the Tsar Nicholas II who set the first stone when this bridge was built. I love the stories of the Tsars."

"This bridge makes me melancholy. I love it, though. It reminds me of Russia." Nastya said, in a quiet, pensive voice, "I've only been gone a week, but I miss it."

"Many of these books about Russia imply that Russians are a peculiar variant of human," David stopped to laugh at how strange what he had just said sounded to him, "but they discuss the 'Russian soul' being so unique that it finds life in Europe or elsewhere too alien. 'It is too difficult for the Russian soul to be happy on foreign soil', I remember a Russian writer having said that."

"I believe it a little."

"Do you want to go back to Russia, Nastya? Since you are no longer going to try to be a dancer here?"

"Do you want to come to Russia, David? We could go to the Crimea. It would be good for my brother there. He needs the sun and the warm air."

"What is his name?"

"My brother? 'Dmitry' ... he's twelve. He is so cute. You should meet him. When he gets a little older, the girls are going to love him." ... "I just hope his illness goes away."

"What is his illness?"

"Consumption ... Tuberculosis ... unfortunately, it's in a very advanced stage. My mother has been getting very worried lately."

"Do you get along well with your mother?" David asked.

"Not too much. I love her though, of course. I love my father too, and I get along with him well. He and I have a perfect relationship. I miss him most of all."

"Do you want to go back to Moscow, Nastya? We can find a way, if you want."

"No. I am twenty-two years old and it's time for me to leave my parents. Can we sit here? On the edge of the bridge? I want to look out on water at those lights. Do you see all those different colored lights shimmering on the river's surface, right by those boats down there? ...

they are so beautiful." … "Anyway, maybe it's my culture," Nastya went on, "but I think it's natural for a woman to leave her father, and her father's home, to go give her life to the man she loves. Only I am different from most Russian girls. Even my best friends back in Moscow are getting married and having babies. Some are only nineteen! I think that's too young. I want have children someday; but first I want to follow my dreams, explore foreign countries, enjoy being young and free in this beautiful world. I need to do this. I can return to Russia later in life. I'll want to return someday, but, for now, I have to see the world, I have to experience the aspects of life that others find dangerous and threatening. I need to do this; I have no choice, and it scares me. It really scares me."

The couple sat beside each other, caressing each other's arms for warmth; their legs dangled over the edge of the Russian bridge and tiny fish leapt up to bite the soles of their shoes. Then Nastya began to cry. She did not cry much. She just sobbed lightly, and tears streamed down her cheeks.

"I'm sorry," she said, turning to David, wiping the tears from her cheeks, "I'm just thinking about Dmitry, my little brother. I get so worried about him sometimes. And I know he needs his sister. I know his health is probably even worse without me there. He really needs his sister. I feel so selfish. But his sister needs something else right now. She needs something besides Moscow. And she needs someone else, someone else besides her family. I just feel guilty for not being with him when he needs me. I wish he were old enough to understand," Nastya then laughed a little, choking on her tears. She then looked up into the night sky, "I wish *I* were old enough to understand. Maybe someday my brother will understand that *I* am young, too – just like he is young. I cannot be a parent. My parents remain with him because they are older and they have that wisdom and the ability to give up the things of youth, the dreams of youth, and youth's silly ambitions." She had stopped laughing, yet she kept looking up at the black sky. Her face then grew dark. There was a strange and inexplicable look of profound sadness that took hold of her face just then. David looked at her and felt a strong pain growing in himself, for he wasn't sure what was causing this grief in Nastya. He felt so happy to be with her, He was in heaven beside her; yet she … she looked up at the sky with a face that revealed to him her deep capacity for suffering.

"It is so beautiful," she suddenly smiled, still looking at the sky. When she smiled, her eyes laced with tears grew wide and the city lights around them caught these tears and made her eyes and eyelids sparkle as though they were set with millions of tiny diamonds.

David watched Nastya face lose it's grim expression and take on a hopeful and youthful smile, and this made him smile and be filled with joy.

"What's so beautiful?" he asked her, pulling her body closer to his.

"That solitary star in the sky!" Nastya replied, in a happy and innocent voice, "it's just one star, all alone in the sky. And see, there is its reflection in the river below. It is so very beautiful. I want to remember always this one lonely star in the sky...." David looked up at the star, hoping Nastya would continue talking about it – but she didn't. She just remained still. And slowly and steadily, the innocent look of joy faded from her face and her expression returned to that of profound sorrow – the expression she had had before, when she had been crying. She looked down again at the river below, and watched her legs dangle over the edge. Then, a new tear formed, a solitary tear, and it rolled from her eye, down her cheek, and dropped from her face into the dark waters of the Seine below.

"What is it, Nastenjka?"

"Sorry, I just started thinking again of my brother, and how I said that my parents can give up the dreams of youth, and youth's silly ambitions...." Then she paused and began to cry more. All the while, she looked down at her feet dangling over the river and more tears started to grow in her eyes and roll down her cheeks, falling from her face and landing in the dark water below.

"...Sometimes I am reminded of how much sadness there is in the world. There are so many things for people to be miserable about. Everywhere there are broken dreams, longings for things that will never come, hopes that soon turn to despairs. And joys that fall and turn to woe." Nastya spoke clearly and quickly through her tears, looking down all the while, "...And everyone has these broken dreams, and secret sufferings. Not just me, but my family too, my friends, and you too, I know. And It is hard enough that I have my own sufferings; but to know that those I love are suffering as well? That is enough to destroy me. This world can seem like the cruelest and most horrible place sometimes...."

As her words trailed off, David spoke: "But you needn't take the world's suffering on your shoulders; not even the suffering of your family, for that would only make their sadness harder to bear – knowing that you suffer for it too. You just need to be free from all of that. Just sneak off, Nastya; fly away! Everywhere in the world there is sadness but within every sorrow is an immaculate peace of mind, just around the bend."

"I was just thinking of my father – putting away the 'silly ambitions of youth'. He wanted more than anything to be a poet, but he gave it up to earn money for us. He's had to work for low-wages all of his adult life, and with those wages he's had two children and a wife to feed… So, he had no choice but to give up his greatest love." … "He's a good poet, too. No, he's a great poet! He has an amazing ability to write verse – like I've never seen before. He doesn't think I've read any of it. He keeps it locked in a drawer. But as soon as I was old enough to understand poetry – at about sixteen years old – I started reading his manuscripts while he was away at work. Oh, how I cried and smiled with joy and pride. I think all of my pride as a teenager came from my secret knowledge that my father is a great poet. He wasn't able to buy us a nice house or put a lot of food on the table, but I always held my head high when I was with my father – because, I knew what most others didn't know: what a beautiful man he is" … "and he conceals it and it's a shame. I've never mentioned poetry to him, except once. But, of course I didn't tell him that I knew of the existence of his poems, but we talked for many hours about poetry – all night, in fact. After all was said, he told me that once he had tried to become a poet. He said it with such lament in his voice. He didn't say anything else, but that once he had tried to become a poet. After that, he went off to bed, silently, with an air of melancholy. For almost a week after that, he walked around in a quiet depression. He went straight to bed every night after coming home from work. He wouldn't even eat dinner…." Nastya's words trailed off in a melancholic tone and she looked down again at the river, and studied two dark, silent boats trolling along the surface of the Seine.

David then pulled his soft bound journal out of his suit jacket pocket and held it in his lap for a moment, feeling the rough leather cover. "I write poetry too," he told Nastya, "It is also my dream to become a great poet."

Nastya's eyes beamed at this. She looked at David and smiled with great delight. David looked at her radiant eyes, framed by her tear-swollen eyelids, and her red cheeks streaked with tears; and he looked at her swollen lips, also wet with tears, that formed the kindest and most gentle smile, and he thought to himself that she was the most beautiful thing he had ever seen in his life. He smiled back at her, and she looked down at the journal in his lap and she asked him:

"Will you read me some of them?"

"No, not these. These were all written long ago. I have no connection to them anymore. I feel like, recently, I have become a completely different person. These poems," he tapped at the cover of his journal, "are dead."

Then he paused a moment, and then asked, "Do you have a pen? I will write you a poem."

"Oh, yes, you will write it right now?" She pulled from her purse a little silver-colored steel pen with black ink, and handed it to David.

"Yes, it won't take long. I have a lot of inspiration right now. You have given me an eternity of inspiration. It may not be a good poem, though, because I haven't written anything in a long time, but we'll see. Anyway, it will be for you – only for you."

"Oh, this is so nice, thank you." She kissed his cheek, very tenderly, for a few moments; and, as he settled on a blank page in his journal and took the cap from the pen, Nastya sat close beside him. She closed her eyes and rested her head on his shoulder. She wrapped her arms around his waist affectionately, and she remained still – so that he could write.

David thought deeply for a moment, running his fingers over Nastya's soft, bare arms, which held tightly onto his waist; and he looked up and around, to find the word to start the poem. He hoped the first line would be lying on the bridge. He looked at the bridge and its granite columns – pedestals for the statues of mythic heroes. He then looked down at the river - at those sad, unlit boats, trolling down the waveless dark waters of the Seine, passing by underneath the bridge. Then he looked up to the deep black sky, and he saw that solitary star that Nastya had found so beautiful. That star, all alone in the sky, a single shimmer of silver light, hovered over the city and over the river. How happy it had made Nastya, he recalled. How her face had transformed upon seeing that lonely star – all despair and melancholy giving way to hope and joy. David thought of all of these things; and feeling the girl pressed against him with her eyes closed, and feeling the wetness of her tears on his neck, he thought of how much he adored her, and he began to write a poem, which he titled: "Nastenjka".

When he finished, he closed the cap on the pen, and set it down. And he read over what he had written and he felt that it was good and this made him happy. It had been a long time since he had written anything that he liked. But now, with her, he felt capable of anything. It was, after all, his Nastenjka who had made his poem good, he thought. It had come from her. He had only transcribed it. And now, as she saw that he was finished, she lifted her head and listened while he read it to her:

"Nastenjka"

I swim in a river of the tears of Nastenjka.
You can see her alone, on a bridge she cries,
and the boats beneath, they pass on by,
down her river of tears, beneath the sky.

And our summer sky and gentle dawn,
and all that comes, does go along,
and all that goes, does go so far,
beneath this night,
beneath this star.

And lonely starlight lingering,
it does not light a single thing,
but looks around all through the night
for something dark it can give light.

That river that flows, beneath the skies,
my Nastenjka, she makes it with her eyes;
each tear that drops, it makes a wave,
each tear a wish, she'd hoped to save;

each wish, it drifted out of sight,
along that river, in the dark of night.

So Nastenjka she wept, with the tears that stained
her face, in the dark night that remained…
so dim and drear,
so dark and dear,
so came a new wave,
with each new tear.

And, just when the star gave up its dream
to give its light to some new thing,
he saw a hope on the river near –
a hope that was lost in Nastenjka's tear;
and his starlight caught it glimmering,
that tear it started shimmering;
then every wave was lit up bright,
and the river flowed with its new light,
like a string of diamonds in the night.

And such joy, this little star, it gave,
to see its light upon each wave
so brave he grew,
he felt so strong,
to see his river lit upon.

And the river flowed with serenity;
it flowed on to eternity.
That river, once lonely, dark and meek,
that began as a tear on Nastenjka's cheek,

now flowed and shined into the night
with all the world's and heaven's light.

And Nastenjka, seeing what she'd done,
looked to the sky, right at the one
who lit each hope she'd lost in fear,
who lit each wave made by her tear…

And the star looked back, and loved her so,
for making beauty, with her woe.

As soon as he finished reading his poem, he looked at Nastya, who had been quietly listening with rapt attention, while gazing at that solitary star – its 'lonely starlight lingering'. The poem, written about her, had touched her profoundly; and she looked into his eyes, and there was no mystery in her gaze. There was no confusion, nor misunderstanding, nor want of knowing, nor want of feeling; her radiant eyes expressed pure devotion to him. She adored him; and she gave herself up to him. And he vowed to himself to take care of her. He would do whatever he needed to do to give her 'all the world's and heaven's light'. He responded to her gaze with his own offer of pure devotion.

She then asked to hold the journal in her hands. He handed it to her, and twice she read her poem over again. She touched each letter and each line with the tip of her finger as she recited the verses aloud. Then, she closed the book, and brought her face close to his, whereupon, he took her in his arms and kissed her mouth … his lips, her lips; his mouth upon hers, in a perfect, warm embrace … he tasted the sweetness of her lips, he felt the softness of her face … she lingered on his gentleness, he lingered on her grace. And blessed it was, that their sorrowful journeys had finally led to this … the joy of their meeting, the strength of their union, and the glory of their kiss.

CHAPTER XVI

How the rain can hamper everything, when one is stranded in Paris, at night, with no place to go...

The rains had come again, and fell heavily, soaking the young couple kissing on the bridge where the *ping, ping, ping* of the downpour could be heard bouncing off the wrought iron lampposts, and off their bubbly, blown glass lamps, glowing with amber light, on the *Pont Alexandre III*.

The rain intruded incessantly on the lover's acts of passion. They might have made love right there on that old bridge, had the rain not been so heavy and cold.

Eventually, when thoroughly drenched, they were forced to unlatch from one another and go find cover. They ran down the deserted bridge, splashing through the black dirty puddles, holding hands in the darkness. Skipping down the quai, they both laughed merry and gay; but neither could be heard by the other, for the noise of the rain drowned out every sound.

After climbing up from the quai, they crossed the street and found cover underneath an overhang of a building near the *Grand Palais*. They stood, watching the rain, and they huddled together in their little dry spot. Then, with a clap of thunder the last of the showers came plummeting down. Then the downpour subsided, and the sky so gently drizzled.

"I have nowhere to take you, Nastya," David finally said, looking out from undercover at the rain a-constant falling, "I will walk you to this man's house if you want. I will hate it, believe me. I would hate more than anything to leave you there – with him ... but at least you will be warm and dry."

"I don't want to go to him. I don't want to go there ever again. Let me drown in the rain first!" ... "But you? ... what about you? Maybe you want to go back to this woman's house – the doctor's?"

"Let me drown in the river first! ...No, I will not go there. ... Come, we will walk a while longer." David took Nastya's hand and led her to find a nicer shelter. Nastya's black dress, once fine, felt like a wet rag wrapped tightly around her body, and David's suit too was saturated with the dirty rain. Though they had only met hours ago, they had met dressed in their finery, and now they cradled each other, dressed in their soiled rags.

Hand in hand, they walked on, passing many doorways, narrow passages, street corners, park benches, and other inappropriate places for new lovers to pass their first night together.

Finally they walked down an impasse, and at the end they found a tidy little romantic and deserted place where a stone arch provided shelter from the drizzling rain. The arch was cradled by ivy and looked a thousand years old; the stones were old and rough and half of the arch had crumbled to rubble.

They sighed with joy and serendipity upon finding this place to be. They had begun to feel weary from the long walk, but at last, they found their place. It was a small grassy knoll, beneath that crumbling arch, beside a golden gilded statue, aside an iron gate, that framed their little park. The park was a long slope of grass, filled with little trees and dotted with dandelions. All of the grass was wet – even the grass beneath the trees – but the grass upon the knoll was dry, for the crumbling arch that was built upon it, had shielded it from rain.

The park had a pastoral garden setting. Stone satyrs sat atop columns strung with ivy, playing their stone flutes; and marble nymphs lay in the grass, hypnotized by the satyrs' songs. It was late in the night, the satyrs and their nymphs had already had their orgy. And even Pan was growing tired. He had crawled off into a bush to sleep, and his rough hands and large fingers, and his massive hooves and horns, could be seen sticking out of the brier. The satyrs, however, did not take respite until the nymphs were ready. They sat atop their Doric columns, playing lullabies with their stone flutes. And the nymphs who lay upon the grass, all were lulled to sleep. Then the satyrs crawled down from their columns; and, rubbing their eyes in weariness, they lay down with the nymphs to join them in their dreams.

All of Paris was empty and tired. The buildings slept and the river did too. The *Sacré Coeur*, and the *Jardin des Plantes* were both exhausted, as were the *Panthéon* and *Père-Lachaise*, but that little pastoral park stayed awake for a long time, watching David and Nastya, ensconced in each other's embrace; and finally, when came the blae light of the crepuscule just before dawn, it sung them both to sleep.

Once the sober dawn had hunted and killed the drunken night…

Once the morning came, it came with its usual cruelty: that cruelty, which is taken out on anyone who passes the night prior in the fashion of a satyr, or the fashion of a nymph. Even innocent lovers, who pass a tender night of a quality, only slightly Dionysian, will find the next morning to be cruel.

It is the tragedy of Dionysus: Wear a black robe at night, and white you'll wear by morning; but wear a purple robe to the midnight feast, and when you wake you'll dress in black to mourn your soul deceased.

Often, the sobriety of morning sweeps completely away the love one had for oneself and for others only the night before. Not just the love, but the courage and the power and the dreams and desires. One wakes up a wretch sometimes – it's how things go.

But fortunately, for us – for you, the reader, and me – and for Nastya and David as well, the sobriety of morning did not diminish the adoration these two had for each other the night before. In fact, the next morning they adored each other more than ever. When David awoke beside Nastya, beneath that crumbling arch on the grassy knoll, he knew that she had become the most important thing in his life. And their being together had become the *only* important thing.

When Nastya had gone to sleep in David's arms in that little park, she felt that she would follow him anywhere – to Spain or Greece or Malta. Yet, when she woke up to the kiss of his sleep-swollen lips on her mouth, she decided that she would follow him even farther – to the Artic, to the edge of the Earth, to Venus, to Hell.

Though that morning brought neither of them regret for having met and shared what they had shared, there were definite stabs of pain, of a different sort, that were not there the night before. For, the night before, they were so blissful with each other that they didn't care about little things, like eating, keeping clean, keeping warm and dry.

If you had asked them the night before about these things, they would both have laughed them off as being stumbling blocks so innocuous that they really aren't even worth worrying about.

"If we have each other, we will be happy, and that will keep us warm. When we are hungry, we will eat. When we need to bathe, we will bathe together, with fine soaps from China and the warmest, cleanest water. Good things naturally come to those who are happy. If you are in love and happy, the world throws comfort at your feet...." ...That is what either of them would have said the night before on the subject of their poverty.

The next day, however, in the 'cruelty of morning', they were reminded – David especially – of the great threat their poverty posed for them.

'I found what I was looking for,' David thought, as he stroked Nastya's hair. She was still sleepy and was having a hard time keeping her eyes open, 'All I've ever hoped to have is right here resting on my shoulder ... yet, we cannot continue to sleep together in any old park in Paris. Soon she will be hungry, her dress will be tattered, and her shoes will be worn...."

"I'm unusually hungry, this morning." Nastya said, stretching and yawning, after she was finally awake.

'If I were not with a woman, I could live like this.' David continued thinking to himself, 'But with her it must go differently. Something must be done, and done right away....'

"We'll find you food, soon, okay?" David said tenderly, running his hands through Nastya's hair.

Meanwhile, Nastya's eyes wanted to close again; but she fought to keep them open, 'Oh, does it have to be morning already?' she wondered to herself, 'I feel as though I did not even sleep. I wonder what time it is. I wonder why nights as magical as last night have to end. I have this hollow feeling now. Maybe it's just from the hunger. But no, there's another hollow feeling ... as though he and I are destined to part. The last thing I ever want to do is to part with him. I cannot part with him. But what will come of us? Here, spending nights by the river, or in a park? With no money and no home, we will surely come to ruin....'

Then, as soon as Nastya was fully awake, she abruptly turned to David and said, "I want us to walk to Spain together … If we leave now, well cross the Pyrenees while it is still summer and we won't freeze. By winter we'll be in Andalusia, I'm sure. I've studied the maps and it doesn't seem like it would take us any longer than that. We'd certainly be through the mountains before fall – and once through the mountains, we'd be in Spain and it would be warm" … "In the South, in Andalusia, the sun will be hot; it will always be warm; we'll be able to sleep on the beach. We can pick fruit to eat, and sleep on the warm sand beneath a billion stars." … "And the people in the villages along the way will be so impressed that we are walking to Spain together – all the way from Paris – and they will find us to be a very cute couple, no doubt; so they will definitely give us food, and offer us beds in their homes as we go along." … "Those little villages in Southern France and Spain, they'll be so happy when news comes that that 'young man and his girlfriend who are bravely walking all the way from Paris to Andalusia' are about to pass through their village on our way south – they'll all begin cooking feasts and making up their guest beds before we even arrive in the village. I'm sure we'll be greeted by a huge crowd of happy villagers waving banners and shouting words of encouragement to keep our spirits high on our brave journey – I bet we'll have a reception like that in every village!"

"You have a great imagination, Nastya. I wish the world had been left up to you to design – we'd be a much happier species," said David with much sincerity, "but I think I'm going to find you some food and a train ticket back to Moscow."

"But I'm not going to go anywhere without you. If I go to Moscow, you will come too."

"Well," David replied, "it would be the hardest thing in the world for me to say goodbye to you. And I think it's unnecessary that we say goodbye. No one is pulling us apart. But one thing, for certain: you must live better than this. I mean, look at us! …one night outside and our clothes are already torn and dirty." … "Nastya," he continued, "I want us to be together, so we shall both go away from here. But if, for some reason, only one of us can go, it will be you who goes. You'll go to Moscow where you have people who love you."

"But you love me too, David. Right?"

David paused for a long time after that question just to make sure he was being honest with himself, "I do, Nastya. I really do. I love you and that's why I am going to take you far away from here, and provide you with a place to live and sleep and food to eat." ... "Just, if it doesn't work out for some reason, I will get you a ticket back to Moscow. This I promise you. You won't have to sleep another night outside."

"I trust you, David. I trust you and I believe you. But how are we going to get the money to leave here?"

"I have a little plan," he said.

All that follows David telling Nastya of his plan – a plan which didn't please her at all, until she had time to give it some thought...

"I don't think it's a good idea. It isn't ours to take."

"Nastya, I agree with you that a questionably immoral pursuit like this is best avoided whenever possible, but I argue that in *our* case, it is not an immoral pursuit." ... "I had the chance to take it before – right when I stumbled on it the first time. And I was all alone and could have easily gotten away with it. But I didn't take it. I didn't take it because I had moral objections to it. And I probably shouldn't have had any moral objections; because, for one, she is a rich, old woman whose life will go on just the same whether that money stays there or not. She has plenty more in the bank, I tell you. And, two, because she has made it her occupation since we met, to try to destroy me. She basically tried to enslave me, by getting me hooked on her arsenal of addictive poisons. She drugged me and wounded me." David then unbuttoned the first few buttons on his shirt and pointed to the puncture wounds that were still open and slightly infected, "I did not do this to myself! It was her. I remember it all now. Fragments of my memory have been coming back to me. The memory that was still completely lost only yesterday – the last time I saw her – is now coming back. She has treated me very badly. I believe she came close to even killing me. I spent a week with her and at the end, my health was worse than ever – a cause of her drugs and abuse. After one night with you, without any medication, I feel one-hundred percent healthy again. I have no pains anywhere in my body – except, of course, in these wounds that Odette inflicted on me..."

"...No, I didn't take the money then," he continued, "but if I knew then what she had already done to me, I could have taken it with a freer conscience. But I say a *freer* conscience and not a *free* conscience. Even then, with the knowledge of what she'd done, I wouldn't have thought it completely right. I still wouldn't have taken the money, because it would have still been an upset to my conscience – and a clean conscience is worth more to me that a bag full of money...

"...But the only reason it would have left a blemish on my conscience – even after that rationalization that it would be okay to take it, because she had already taken so many things from me, having successfully harmed me both mentally and physically – is because it would have been stealing just for myself. I didn't know you then and I was living just for myself. I could not argue that it would be right under any condition to steal if it is just for *my* benefit ... because then there is no higher good. The objective is only self-preservation, and I find self-preservation to be a ridiculous endeavor unless one preserves oneself for the purpose of giving service to a higher good. If the money is for me alone, I will not take it. But if it is for *us*, if it is for *you*, I will take it with fervor and pride and escape with the cleanest conscience in the world."

"David, I agree that if it is for *us*, it should be done. But if it is for *me* alone, I don't want it."

"That is fair, since I don't want it, either, if it is for *me* alone. ...So, it will be for *us* then!"

"For us!" Nastya replied happily. And the two kissed, and smiling, they headed off towards Rue du Dragon to scope-out the scene of the future crime.

CHAPTER XVII

"Now, there's a courtyard in the back," David began to explain to Nastya as they crossed the *Pont des Arts* on their way to Odette's place on Rue du Dragon, "...She lives on the ground-floor, and her windows face out to the courtyard. There are no bars on the windows, and I broke the latch on the shutters leading into her salon so that the window can be opened from the outside." ... "We will have to choose a time," he continued, talking excitedly with his confidence in his plan. Nastya also listened with excitement, "We'll pick a time and then you come to Odette's through the main entrance, and ring her buzzer. That will let you into the medical office. The money is in the other room – in her salon – locked in a drawer by the window with the broken latch...

"...So, you ring her buzzer at the appointed time and pretend that you are very sick and you need help right away. Don't let her take you into her salon. Make sure she keeps you in the medical office. Stall her...."

"What does that mean, 'stall her'?"

"*Keep her busy!* ...Because, while you are in the medical office, faking a medical emergency, I will have climbed in through the window and will be picking the lock on the drawer. Once I get the drawer open, I will take the money and the jewelry and put...."

"Not the jewelry," Nastya interrupted, "Just the money, you promised, remember?"

"...Right, just the money. I will take the money and put it in a large leather medicine bag that Odette keeps on the shelf by the desk. I will then climb back out the window, into the courtyard and run down the alleyway. I'll meet you at that cathedral I told you about – I'm going to walk with you there too, to point it out. It's called 'St. Sulpice', it's

252

hard to miss. As soon as you are finished playing the sick patient with Odette, you come to St. Sulpice – make sure no one is following you – and I will be waiting by the fountain in the square with a bag full of money – a ton of money!...

"Just one other thing," he added, "If, for some reason Odette discovers me in her house – if she is to walk in on me for some reason – first of all, you *don't* know me. You've never met me before, never seen me before, have no clue who the hell I am ... And second, if she walks in on me, I'm not going to try to jump out the window with the bag. If I do, she'll know exactly what I have done right away and within minutes she will have the police swarming around all the streets in the neighborhood. Therefore, if she walks in on me, I'm going to play stupid. I'll throw the bag full of money out of the window, so it lands in the courtyard, and then I will stay there and give her some story. If my story doesn't work, I'll restrain her from calling the police in anyway possible. Meanwhile, you leave. She won't be concerned with you anymore if she discovers that I've broken in to her place through the window. So then, you leave; and run around back, through the alleyway, to the courtyard, where you will find the leather medicine bag lying on the ground. ...Take that bag and run as fast as you can to St. Sulpice; and I will meet you there by the fountain...

"...If it goes that way, though, Nastya, I want you to only wait for me by the fountain for *ten minutes*. If it takes me any longer than that, I want you to leave with the money and go straight to the train station and get on a train for Moscow...."

"But, I won't. I'll wait for you by the fountain until you come – even if it takes ten hours!"

"Nastya, listen to me. If I am not at the fountain within *ten minutes*, you are to go to the station, *with the money*, and get on the next train to Moscow, is that clear? Will you do that?"

"Yes, I will do that."

David shows Nastya the splendid sight of the Cathedral St. Sulpice – where they intend to reunite with their new-found fortune...

"It's beautiful," remarked Nastya looking up at the great columns and enormous towers of the Cathedral St. Sulpice, which rise up in the air for hundreds of meters disappearing into the pastel blue sky.

"Yes, it is beautiful," David replied, "but we don't have much time if we're going to go to Salaudski's to get your clothes and your passport before we pull this off. We have to do this before the end of the day, before she stops seeing patients, otherwise she won't let you in to her office…

"This is the fountain I was talking about," David pointed to the stone fountain, guarded by stone lions, spouting water in the giant stone square of the cathedral. The two of them stood in the square and looked around. It was unusually deserted. The shops and the cafés surrounding the square were all closed. The square itself was completely deserted as well – only some flocks of pigeons gathered around the fountain.

"It's Sunday today," said Nastya, "that must be why it's so quiet." … "I hope the doctor will see me on a Sunday."

"Just remember to play that it's an emergency. Also, if you get a chance, and you are sure that she won't notice, cut the phone line in her office. I'm going to cut the phone in her salon, but she has a separate line in her office." … "Are you ready to go look at the courtyard?"

"Yes, is it far?"

"It's only about four blocks from here."

"Let's go."

A slightly discouraging discovery upon inspecting the courtyard of Dr. Moreaux…

"I love this little fountain," exclaimed Nastya, "those are beautiful plants, too. Look at the way the sun shines on the water – it's like a million tiny sapphires!"

"Yes, I also love that fountain. We need to be quiet a moment. There's her window," David said, pointing to the large shutters of paned glass between the fountain and the gate to the alleyway. They were closed and the curtains, too, were drawn in the inside. David approached the window silently. Nastya waited by the gate. After a few moments, David quietly crept back to the gate and said to Nastya...

"I'll have to think of a new plan. She obviously found out that I broke the latch on the window. There is a chain on the window now – with a padlock. I won't be able to open it."

Whereupon David is discovered lurking about in the courtyard...

Nastya was standing in the alleyway, on the other side of the courtyard gate. She could still see David in the courtyard, but she, herself, was out of view. David was passing behind the fountain to inspect Odette's other window: the window of her medical office; when he glanced over at the window to her salon, (the window with the curtains closed and the chain and padlock on the shutters), only to watch the curtains being thrown wide open.

David turned to face the salon window. Right at that moment the curtains were opened, and he then saw her figure standing behind the panes of glass. He saw her eyes beaming out at him like the cold blue flames of two candles. He stood only a few feet back from the window. Part of her body was obscured by the strong reflections of the sun on the panes of glass, but he could see most of her clearly. She looked at him with intense fury.

The old doctor was dressed only in a black bra and black underwear. Her stomach was bare, as were her legs. Her hair was messy – as if she'd been sleeping. 'It is still very early,' David thought to himself. Just then, he saw another figure come into view. It was the young, beautiful intern that works for Odette, and she was naked as she came to the window. Her blonde hair was also messy (perhaps from sleeping, as well) and she wore a cold expression on her face. She looked out at David with the same icy glare that Odette offered him. Her young, smooth skin, with its tawny complexion contrasted sharply with the withered and pale flesh of Odette, whom she stood beside. The young intern then pulled a white sheet up to cover her bare breasts and her naked body; and then fixed a glare at David even more icy and insolent than the last.

David stood frozen, struck dumb. Shocked to have been discovered lurking in Odette's courtyard. He just stood still, with his jaw dropped open, staring back at those four horrible eyes.

Perhaps it was only seconds later, though it seemed much longer to David, when Odette pulled the white curtains closed again. She did so, quickly, with a jerk of the hands and a final look of contempt. David, who was still rooted to the spot, looked over at Nastya who stood far off in the alleyway. Upon seeing her questioning face looking back at him, not understanding what had just happened, he realized he had better get her out of the alley.

She had not had a view of Odette's window from where she had been standing, so she didn't see the two women looking out at David. She just saw the expression on his face while he stood frozen, facing the window, and she became worried.

"Nastya, hurry away from here, and meet me down on the corner in a few minutes," David instructed her in a quick whisper after he reached the alleyway where she had been standing, "The corner of Rue du Dragon and Boulevard St. Germain. I'll be there in two minutes."

Nastya, without protesting or even asking David to explain, suddenly turned around and headed quickly down the alleyway, turning left on Rue du Dragon.

David then followed behind, walking slowly. When he reached the end of the alleyway, however, he turned right and walked towards the entrance of Odette's building.

Just when he was about to enter the code to buzz open the front door of the building, the door was opened from the inside – and Odette, now more or less fully-dressed, stood in the open doorway gaping at our young man.

"Why were you in the courtyard, just now, David? What are you doing here?" She spoke quickly, not concealing her suspicion and anger.

"Odette, I'm sorry," he swayed his head and spoke with feigned regret and submission, "I got stuck. I didn't want to bother you. I'm really sorry. I didn't have anywhere to go last night. The friend, whose place I was going to stay at, wouldn't let me stay there after all; and, since it was late, I didn't want to bother you; so, I looked around for a place to sleep and ended up in this park; but then the police came and hassled me, so I didn't know where to go – so I came here and slept in the courtyard out back. I was just waking up and getting ready to leave when you saw me a second ago."

"Well, you don't look like you got a very good night's sleep. Anyway, you were trespassing by being in my courtyard. You're still making your place to sleep my responsibility. There are a thousand other courtyards in this city. Why couldn't you sleep in any of those?"

"Odette, I'm sorry. I really am. I would have chosen another place to sleep but – you have to understand – I'm not used to being homeless, I've never had to sleep on the street before. I was already very tired when I was supposed to go sleep at this guy's place … but he wouldn't let me in. So, when I had finally just gotten to sleep in this park at four or five in the morning, the police came up and hassled me!" … "I was so tired, I just wanted to find the nearest place where I could sleep for a couple of hours … my legs were hurting from walking around all night … and your courtyard was the nearest place I knew of where I wouldn't be bothered. Odette, I'll never do it again.…"

"Alright, alright," said Odette, impatiently with a wave of her hands. Unfortunately, she wasn't wearing her Spanish bangles that sounded like horse hooves when she waved her hands impatiently like that – which she did so often… "And please stop saying you're sorry, it's annoying.…" Just then, Odette was interrupted by the sound of her intern's high-heeled shoes clicking on the marble floor in the vestibule, as she approached the doorway.

The young intern appeared and stood beside Odette in the open doorway. She scowled at David, with a look of disdainful repugnance. Her blonde hair, which had been messy when David saw her standing in Odette's window, was now neatly pulled back behind her head, and she was dressed in casual Sunday clothes. She wore no makeup yet her beauty was striking – even her angry scowls were beautiful. She was younger than David, about the same age as Nastya. David thought of Nastya, waiting for him down at the corner. This was the first time he'd been separated from her since the two had met. She had only been away from him for two minutes or so and he found it silly that he missed her so much. But he did.

The young intern flashed one more look of disgust at David and then turned to Odette, *"Je vais partir. On se voit la semaine prochaine, alors."* Saying goodbye to Odette, she leaned forward and kissed her twice – on each of the corners of her mouth. The young, pretty arm of the intern wrapped around Odette's old and slightly flabby waist.

"*Ouais,*" said Odette, "*lundi prochain, après mes vacances ... et merci, et gros bisous, ma chérie!*" Odette then slid her hand over the small of the intern's back and returned her kiss. Then the intern turned towards the street; and, giving David one more icy look of repugnance, she walked away – her high-heels going *clickety-click* on the pavement as she walked on towards Boulevard St. Germain.

"David," continued Odette, after she paused a few moments to watch the backside of her intern walking down the sidewalk, "I'm going to Strasbourg for a week – so you won't have me to rely on anyhow. You'll have to find some new parks and courtyards to sleep in on your own. And you'll have to find a new doctor to bother with your hypochondria." She smiled mockingly as she said this, "...Anyway, I have to leave here for the train station in no later than an hour and a half." ... "If you can help me pack and clean up, I'll pay you a hundred francs. At least then you won't be totally broke and miserable in Paris. You'll be able to eat for a couple of days."

"Yes, sure. Thank you, Odette," David was elated to receive this warm welcome into Odette's home. He wouldn't need to go through the window after all. "Thank you, thank you!"

"Alright, alright, would you please quit thanking me?" Odette said, annoyed again and waving her hands in front of David's face, "Just come back in ten-minutes. I have a phone call to make first and I want some privacy for it."

"Odette, do you think I could have the hundred francs now so I may go and buy something to eat first?"

Odette then smiled maliciously, gritting her teeth together, "I know that trick. I'll give you fifty now, and fifty after."

David didn't understand what she meant by 'I know that trick'. Certainly, David wasn't going to run off with Odette's hundred francs and never return. David had no intention of doing that.

She handed him a two twenty-franc bills and two five-franc coins, and instructed him to return in ten minutes.

"...But no more then ten minutes, because I have to leave here in an hour and a half, is that clear?"

"It's clear, I'll see you in ten!" David smiled as he turned away and happily ran down Rue du Dragon towards St. Germain where Nastya was supposed to be waiting for him.

David and Nastya reluctantly part ways, with promises, vows, kisses and the like…

"I thought you weren't coming. I got really worried," said Nastya who leaned against the wall of a building on the corner of St. Germain. She was pouting slightly, partially joking, yet seeing David again made her happy. It was obvious that she too had missed him. She squinted to see David's face, as the sun was shining brightly on hers. The sun always seems brighter the day after one stays up most of the night. The sun was clean and its light was white and warm. Nastya looked very pretty and much more innocent with the morning sunlight on her face. David had remembered how sensual and romantic Nastya's beauty was the night before, in the light of the moon, and the light of that solitary star. The night before, she had the real look of a sensual woman; and now her face seemed younger, more innocent, the face of a girl, beautiful though also pretty. Upon seeing Nastya standing on St. Germain, with the sun on her face, David's first thought was how much more beautiful she is than Odette's young intern.

"Of course, I came. I wouldn't leave you here," he said, kissing her warmly on the mouth, "I just had to talk to Odette. There's been a change of plans. She's leaving town in an hour and a half and I promised her I would help her pack. I actually have to be back there in ten minutes."

"She's leaving town! So we can do this after she's gone. It will be easier."

"No, it will probably be harder after she's left. I'm not sure how secure she'll leave her apartment, but, as we learned, there are already chains and padlocks on each of the two windows. Padlocks are easy enough to pick, however, they are on the inside – I won't be able to get at them after she's left. And I know how to pick little drawer and cabinet locks, no problem; but I never learned how to pick deadbolts on front doors…

"…I'll see, when I'm in there helping her pack, whether or not there is an entrance I can leave unlocked, but since she's going away for a while, she'll probably double-check all her doors and windows before leaving. And I seriously doubt I'll be the last to leave. It's too bad she doesn't like me or trust me very much, otherwise we'd have a place to sleep while she's away – and then we could easily take what we came for at any time."

"Even if she suggested that, I wouldn't want to stay there – not in *that* woman's home. I'd rather sleep with you in the park."

"Well, we won't have to sleep in the park, regardless," David attested, "Within a couple hours, we'll be rich."

"So, what do we do?" asked Nastya.

"Well, *I* need to stay here, and help her pack ... so I can't go to Salaudski's with you. I might even be able to get the money and the jewels right under her nose, while I'm packing her suitcases...."

"David," Nastya interrupted, smiling at the naughty boy, "you promised! *Not* her jewelry, just the money!"

"Right, I'm sorry, I forgot," David muttered between the kisses Nastya was planting on his face, "just the money!"

"So, go on!"

"Okay," continued David, giving Nastya the last of the instructions, "So, I may be able to get the money while I'm helping her pack – but I'm not sure. She may watch me the whole time. So, the plan stays pretty much the same. You go to Salaudski's and get your passport and clothing ... no, first you go and get yourself something to eat," David's voice sounded concerned, and he dug in his pocket to hand Nastya the fifty francs that Odette had just given him, "...Get some food and then go to Salaudski's and get your things. Do you think you can figure out the métro?"

"I think so. Anyway, I'll have to if I'm going to be back in an hour and a half. He lives clear on the other side of the city."

"But I'll need you to come back in *less* than an hour and a half. What time is it now?"

Nastya pulled from her purse the tarnished silver pocket-watch her father had given her, which she had taken on her voyage to France to remember him by. The time read: 10:38.

"So she'll probably leave right at noon, which means I'll need you back here at 11:30. You might not be able to make it that quickly. Just don't return any later than 11:45, okay?"

"Okay."

"It's just that she may watch me the whole time I'm packing, in which case, I'll need you to come and play the sick patient with an emergency in order to distract her." … "If I manage to get the money before you come, you'll know because why you are talking to her in her office, I'll drop the leather medicine bag next to the office door; then I'll come running in and grab Odette, and yell: 'Come quick, the shower pipes burst! The bathroom is flooded!' …or something to that effect. …And remember, when you see me, you *don't* know me, right?"

"Right, I don't know you, David."

"…Then, while I drag the doctor in the bathroom, you pick up the leather medicine bag – remember, it will be right next to the door joining her salon and her medical office – and you run out the front door and go as quickly as you can to St. Sulpice, where you will wait for me. I'll arrive within ten minutes. She'll obviously know that you left in a hurry, but she won't know that anything's been stolen." … "If we pull it off right, she won't realize she's been robbed until after she returns from her trip."

"It sounds like it will work well," said Nastya, "You know this money is for *us*, right? … for you and me. Do you think, though, I'll be able to send some to my father? And my brother too, so he can get better treatment and the more expensive medicine?"

"Of course, Nastya … but we'll have time to talk about that afterwards. Now, we have to hurry in everything we do. For the next hour and a half, every thing has to move very, very quickly."

"Yes, you're right. I'll go now to Salaudski's and I won't even stop on the way to get something to eat."

"Yes, Nastya, you *will* stop on the way to eat something. You *must* eat something. Just be quick. And make sure you have enough money left over for the métro. I think it's eight francs each way – but I could be wrong."

"Okay, my love, I'm going now – I'll miss you."

"But wait… that plan about you picking up the bag in the doorway … that's only if I've already managed to get the money by the time you arrive. Your cue, in that case, will be me running into Odette's office screaming that her pipes have burst. Unless I do that, we go on with plan 'A'…

"…Plan 'A', just to go over it again: You'll come back here by 11:30, or 11:45 at the very latest; since I think she'll be leaving here right at noon. That will only give us fifteen minutes. Push the code I gave you on the outside door, then go to the far door at the end of the hall. She lives on the ground floor, remember. There's a brass plaque that says 'Dr. Odette Moreaux' next to her door. Ring her bell until she answers, remember you are having an…"

"Emergency," Nastya finished David's sentence for him and then continued to speak, recapping their original plan, "…And I distract her in the medical office. I don't let her go into the salon *under any circumstances*. I'll fake an epileptic seizure…"

"Panic attack would be better," interrupted David.

"…I'll fake a panic attack and keep her busy as long as I can. I'll probably only get a few minutes with her if she's going to be in a hurry to catch a train. Oh, and I'll cut the phone line, if I can – the one in her office."

"On second thought, don't cut the line," said David.

"Okay, I'll skip the phone line. As soon as I leave, I'll go around back and find the leather medicine bag with the money in it lying on the ground below the window … were we still doing the window thing?"

"Yes, I'm still going to throw it out the window while Odette is in her office helping you. That's the most innocuous way to do it. The padlocks she has on those chains aren't hard to pick. I'll drop the bag through the salon window – the one closest to the gate in the alleyway."

"So, I'll go around back," Nastya reiterated, "and find the medicine bag in the courtyard. Then I'll run up to that Cathedral St. Sulpice and wait for you."

"Good memory. But remember, you'll only wait for me for ten minutes. Any more time passes than that and I want you to leave with the money and get on the first train to Moscow – and don't look back."

"I really hope it doesn't go like that."

"Me too, Nastya, me too." … "Now go and get some food and then get up to Salaudski's for your passport. Don't bring anything back that can't be replaced with money. We'll have plenty of money to buy you clothes and things … just get your passport and things of sentimental value. We'll have to travel light. Okay, my love?"

"Yes, my love. I'll hurry. Give me a kiss." The two then embraced and hung on each other's lips for several moments.

"I will miss you, my Nastenjka. I will miss you terribly." ... "I think there is a métro just down here on the right." He pointed down St. Germain towards Mabillon, "Yes, I'm sure I saw a métro stop down there."

"So, I probably won't see you at Odette's. Unless, of course, you come running in the room screaming. Probably, the next time I see you it will all be over. We'll have our fortune and we'll be together again. Oh, David, this will be a long hour and a half!"

"Yes, but I promise you Nastya, everything will work out well. We'll have each other and we'll have our fortune. We'll leave France immediately and set up a life somewhere together – somewhere quiet, in the sun, on the beach."

David's promise made Nastya smile and her thoughts flooded with hope and happiness. Both David and Nastya, upon parting, were so hopeful and happy for what was about to come, that they both giggled and laughed aloud with joy while kissing each other goodbye.

An account of David's brief employment as Odette's personal suitcase-packer and bidet-scrubber...

Running back up Rue du Dragon, David thought of how he'd been gone longer than ten minutes. He hoped this wouldn't cause any detrimental problems. He thought of Nastya, and asked the blue sky above to watch over her, and to make sure she eats and doesn't have any problems along the way that would prevent her from arriving safely back to Odette's office on time.

When he buzzed Odette's door, there was no answer. He buzzed it again. Still, no answer. He heard a muffled voice inside and waited. Finally, he heard a *click* and realized that she was probably just now getting off the phone. A moment later, she opened the door and ushered David into her salon.

"I have most of the packing done already. What I need most, right now, is to have my bidet scrubbed." She took him by the sleeve and ushered him into the bathroom. "Here is a bucket of water and *eau de javel*, and here is a sponge. Please make it spotless. I'll be out here packing in the salon."

David was left alone in the bathroom. There was nothing he could do in there except scrub that damned bidet that smelled like Odette and her girlfriend, that pretty intern – but mostly it smelled like Odette. He became a little sick imagining her washing her privates over the pink bidet that he was now scrubbing by hand, but there was nothing to do about it. Anyway, he was being paid a hundred francs for this, and he decided he should probably work to earn that money.

While he was alone in the bathroom, he reached his hand behind the toilet, searching for the plastic bag of medicine he had stashed there earlier. There was nothing behind the toilet except for pipes and mildew … the bag was gone.

"Damn it!" he muttered aloud, realizing what this meant… 'She knew about the window – as there are now chains and locks on both of them – and she also knows about the bag I stashed here! She knows that I'm trying to take her for something. I wonder if the money is still in that locked drawer. It is a good thing I didn't break that lock. But would she go and do a thing like move all that money to another location? If she put it in the bank, or packed it up to take on her trip, we're ruined!' … 'There's no way she would have packed all of that money to take on her trip. There was a lot of money in that drawer – I mean, *a lot of money!*'

After scrubbing Odette's bidet, David went out into the salon, where the doctor was seated at her desk, looking in a little hand mirror, and applying her makeup. When she noticed him entering she looked up from the mirror and asked, "Why did you just say 'Damn it!' like that?"

"Oh, because I stubbed my toe on your bidet."

"But you are wearing shoes."

"Flimsy shoes! … anyway, I scrubbed your bidet. It's more pink than ever!"

"Can you scrub the toilet, too? …And make sure to get behind the toilet, as well. It's really dirty back there."

'What is this woman trying to do?' David wondered, 'How much *does* she know? Why would she ask me to scrub *behind* the toilet? What game is she playing?'

"So can you do that, David? …No, on second thought, what I need more than that: Will you iron that stack of clothes on my bed and fold them up and put them in my valise? Be careful with the silks, though. Not too hot on the iron!"

"I'm not a very good ironer. How much time do you have?"

"The taxi will be here to pick me up at noon. It's 11:15 now."

"Alright, Odette." David walked over to the bed and picked up a crème-colored silk shirt from the stack of clothes and he stretched it over the ironing board. He then took the hot iron and tried to pull the creases out of the shirt. He had been at it for only a second when Odette threw down her makeup and ran over to the ironing board, grabbing the iron out of David's hands.

"You are such a simpleton!" she cried, losing her temper, "this is too hot for silks. Do you want to ruin my clothes?!"

"No, Odette, I don't want to ruin your clothes."

"But, why do you have the iron so hot, then?"

"I don't know how to iron!"

"Alright, stop. Sit down." David sat upon the bed; Odette moved the ironing board away from him and kept speaking, "I don't have time for this. Just fold the clothes and put them in my suitcase. Fold them very neat, though. Do you know how to fold clothes?"

"Yes, I know how to fold clothes."

"Okay, go ahead then." Odette, kept her eye on David as she walked across the salon and sat back down at her desk by the window. She didn't, however, resume putting on her makeup, she just sat there, in the desk chair, in front of the chained and padlocked window facing out to the courtyard where the beautiful little fountain sent cascades of sunlit water down upon the broad leaves of the tropical plants. She just sat there and watched David fold the clothes across the room.

'We'll have to go for plan "A",' David realized, 'It doesn't look like this old witch is going to take her eyes off me. She's literally sitting on her money over there at that desk. It's not going to be easy. I hope Nastya fakes a panic attack well. I hope she gets here on time.' While David was considering all of this, he absentmindedly folded the old woman's finery any which way and stuffed it into the valise. Looking at the valise, he remembered that he would be needing that leather medicine bag. His eyes drifted up to the shelving beside Odette's desk. He searched the shelves with his eyes until, to his relief, he noticed that the dark brown, leather medicine bag was sitting on the high shelf, right where it had been before.

"What are you looking for?" snapped Odette, as she watched David's eyes survey the room.

"A suitcase," he replied, "all your clothes aren't going to fit in this valise."

"There's an open suitcase behind you. The tan one. Take the little things out and put them in the valise, then there will be enough space in the suitcase for all of my clothes."

'I wonder if I'll have time to pick the padlock on that window' he thought to himself, while transferring Odette's clothes from her valise to her suitcase, 'I'll have to pick both the padlock *and* the lock on the desk drawer. That is, if she ever moves away from the desk. I hope the money is still in that drawer. I hope Nastya comes soon.

"Do you have the time?" David asked Odette.

"Why, is there someplace you have to be? Odette responded mockingly.

"I just want to make sure to have you packed on time."

"It's 11:30. We have time. I'm all ready to go. I'm just waiting for you.

'It's 11:30,' David thought, 'She said no later than 11:45. I hope she's on time. I really hope she didn't have any problems on her way. I hope that that Salaudski bastard didn't lock her up in a closet to punish her for not coming home last night."

At this time, David had no clue where Nastya was. Did she have problems with the métro? Had she been kidnapped by Salaudski? Had she decided that the two lovers' plan was foul and dishonest and she'd rather remain Salaudski's concubine than runaway with David and the doctor's dirty money?

...That last notion made David shudder with fear. He was falling in love with Nastya. Already, in the short time he had known her, she had become everything to him. Yet, he didn't have any address for her. He didn't know where Salaudski was living. He didn't have a telephone number for her. 'Maybe she'll decide that I'm no good. She said she agreed that stealing the old woman's money would be okay if it were for *us*. She also wants to help her father and brother with money. No, don't be silly David ... your connection with her is too strong. She's also falling in love with you...

'For me she's everything, I don't have family or friends, just her. But she has family and friends in Moscow, people she's known ages longer than she's known me. I don't expect to be her *everything*. ...But, still, I'm probably just being insecure. I know that I mean a lot to her. I know she is falling in love with me – not just falling, either, I think we are both already in love with one another. ...Still, I hope she comes here on time. Everything depends upon it. *Everything!*'

Such was the level of uncertainty in David's mind at the time, as he waited impatiently, while folding clothes, for his lover to arrive in a fit of panic, serious enough to take all of the doctor's attention away from David, her hired servant, for a few minutes.

David had no idea what Nastya was encountering on her way across town, nor had he any idea what was going on at Salaudski's. Fortunately, for you, the reader, I have all of this information and I can tell you exactly what happened on our heroine's journey – yet, so as not to write your eyes off, I'll leave out the parts that are inconsequential:

A brief and truthful account of Nastya's journey o'er the breadth of Paris, to the home of Salaudski, where a few things went awry...

Nastya had no trouble finding the métro at Mabillon. She stopped a moment when she reached the entrance. Two men, a short, good-looking Italian – about forty-two years old – and a tall, good-looking American – of about twenty-seven years – were approaching the same métro station that Nastya was entering. The American ran up and accosted Nastya in French...

"*Excusez-nous, Mademoiselle, mais....*"

But Nastya interrupted the American, "Do you speak English?" she asked.

"Yes," replied the American, "I can speak...."

"Good. Can you tell me how to get to the train station, *Gare de l'Est?* I'm in a hurry."

"Sure," replied the American, in a friendly manner, "take this métro one stop to *Odéon*, then change to the *line-four* and take that direction *Porte de Clignancourt*," said the American.

"I hope I'll remember that." Nastya sighed with a look of concern on her face.

"It's easy," said the Italian man in English, with a heavy Italian accent. "Listen," he continued, "We live just right here on Rue Montfaucon – the best street to live on in Paris – and I am great painter. Do you want to come up and have a drink with us and look at my paintings?"

"No, really, I'm sorry, I don't have time. There's someone I have to meet. I'm already late." Nastya then tried to hurry down the steps but the American accosted her again…

"Listen, you are Russian, aren't you?"

"Yes, how could you tell?"

"Your accent. Listen, I'm a writer. I'm writing a book about a Russian girl who comes to Paris and I need to research the life of a Russian girl at home and abroad – since I've never been a Russian girl myself, I could use a little help on the matter. Have you ever been in a book before?"

"No, but I've been in a poem. The most beautiful poem in the world was written about me … *about me!*" she points to herself and smiles coyly, fully aware of how arrogant she is sounding, "Listen, boys, I really have to go!"

And with that, Nastya turned away and ran down the steps into the métro station. The American and the Italian remained on the street at the entrance to the métro.

"She was a snob," the Italian said, "Let's go find another one, Roman."

"Sure thing, Guido, the day is just beginning. But I need to find a Russian one – as beautiful as that last one. I've got to get this book finished!" the American replied, looking around at all the young ladies passing down St. Germain in their pretty spring dresses.

On the métro, Nastya had no problems at all. She was alone in the car on *line-four* which is usually extremely crowded, and the métro cruised along at an efficient speed.

While sitting on the métro, she had a moment to think. She thought about Marick, that poor man who lives in a tent by the river. Although he had been mean to her – and to David as well – she felt bad for eating all of his food the night before. She wished there was enough time for her to go buy him some food with the money David had given her, but there wasn't.

'After this is over,' she decided, 'once we're rich – David and I – we'll go give Marick some money … enough for him to rent an apartment so he can find one of those French girls he wants so badly.'

Once she arrived at *Gare de l'Est*, she found the streets leading to Rue de Paradis quite easily. Along one of these streets, she saw a vendor selling crêpes. She ordered one with butter and sugar. It was too hot to eat right away but she managed to finish it before she came to Salaudski's street. She had been hungry that morning, when the two awoke under the arch in the park; she had even told David that she was hungry. But her appetite was ruined as soon as she set off for Salaudski's. Just the thought of seeing him again and of speaking to him – after the incident the night before on the terrace of the *Bistro d'Hiver* – made a wretched knot in her stomach and she felt like she was going to be sick. She just ordered the crêpe because she knew it was important for her body. She knew she'd need the energy that day; and besides, she promised David she would eat and it had meant so much to him.

It was when she reached Salaudski's street that the trouble began: Nastya turned the corner from Rue du Faubourg St. Denis and walked down Rue de Paradis. She knew she had to hurry but she dreaded the meeting immensely.

'All I have to do,' she thought, 'is tell him I found a place of my own, take my passport from the lining of my suitcase, take the few things I can't live without from my suitcase and put them in my purse, change out of these shoes into something I can walk in! … I'll change out of this silly dress too.' … 'Maybe I won't even talk to him. Maybe I'll just grab my suitcase and leave, and sort everything out once I get outside.' … 'Anyway, I have to hurry.'

When Nastya came to Salaudski's, the worst had happened. One of the reasons she had had that wretched knot in her stomach was because she was afraid that something would happen like what had happened.

There is a little strip of lawn in front of Salaudski's building. When Nastya neared his building she saw a lot of garbage strewn over that strip of lawn. When she got close, she could see that it wasn't garbage at all – it was her clothes! Right under the fifth-floor window of the room where slept, was her suitcase, lying open on Rue de Paradis – where any old gamine could come and steal her clothes. She began to cry, and raced for her suitcase. She wasn't crying for her clothes, however, she was crying because Salaudski had humiliated her. By throwing her suitcase out of the window, he reduced her already compromised position in society – or at least in Parisian society – to nil. He didn't steal from the poor, he just destroyed the poor's only belongings and then spread them out for her to see. Oh, what self-esteem she had had when receiving that letter from an 'aristocratic admirer abroad'; what pride she felt as she entered Paris for the first time with her head held high! ...Then, as soon as she meets Salaudski, he disarms her completely. He degrades her sexually. He attempts to enslave her, making her his lowly concubine. Nastya may have come from poverty, but her right as a human being to have pride and self-esteem had never before been violated. Nastya can live in poverty, but she cannot live without pride.

"And this man thinks that he can have me as a kept-woman because he'll buy me anything that costs less than a pair of shoes? He is out of his mind!" Nastya said aloud and angry as she dug through her open suitcase, looking to see if anything she valued was still inside. 'Basically....' she thought to herself as she examined one of her favorite possessions that had not survived the fall: it was a white ceramic plate with her footprints on it, made when she was a newborn baby. A few days after she was born, her parents took her to a place where they made these, and they dipped little Nastya's baby feet in blue ink – and then they stamped her feet on the plate and glazed over her footprints in a kiln of some-sort. That plate was twenty-two years old, it was her feet when she was a baby – the only surviving copies – one of her favorite possessions in the world, and it was now broken and shattered into little fragments of ceramic.

'Basically, he can't be happy just trying to destroy my innocence. He has to go even further and physically destroy a symbol of my innocence, and display it in the street, so as to force me to not be mistaken about what I actually lost. I can see it with my eyes: my innocence – broken and dead and lost forever on a filthy street in Paris.

Nastya was fully enraged and crying freely by this time. She had thrown a handful of fragments of her broken plate against Salaudski's building and she screamed a profanity in Russian up at the open window on the fifth-floor where the curtain blew in and out with the fickle changes in the wind.

Her anger reached its apex when she felt inside the lining where she had made a secret pocket for her passport and had sewn it shut. The lining was ripped – either by some street kid, or by Salaudski – and her passport was gone. How would she leave France without a passport?!

She was nowhere near calm; she was about as angry as one can be, but she still managed to change into the only pair of comfortable pants and shoes that had *not* been stolen from the open suitcase before her temper began to boil; whereupon, she ran towards the front door of Salaudski's building, determined to inflict as much pain on him as possible.

As soon as she entered the code on the door and it buzzed open, Nastya ran into the entryway and started up the stairs at incredible speed. Yet, she only made it up halfway of the first flight of stairs before the landlady hobbled out into the hall and began yelling at her to come back downstairs.

Nastya was crying and held her hands over her eyes.

The landlady spoke first. She was furious, and her angry voice resounded in the hall, "Your little *Salaud* has been making a mess of my building all morning! What do you want to do about it?! I can't have this type of circus happening here! What is going on?"

Nastya cleared the tears from her throat and answered calmly, "He's not *my little Salaud!* And, where is he? He threw my suitcase out of the window!"

"You think I don't know that? He threw all kinds of *merde* out the window. There's trash all on the street, and out in my halls, too! I call the police!" ...And with that, the little landlady turned and hobbled towards her apartment to phone up the cops. Nastya yelled at her back:

"Yes! Please call the police! Please call them," and the tears began to flow again, "please call them!" she begged, crying.

Hearing Nastya pleading with her through a veil of tears, the landlady stopped in her doorway and turned around to face the young girl, "I won't call them, my dear, but you tell him to stop this!"

Nastya then began to cry even harder and it became difficult for the landlady to understand her, as she was choking on her tears…

"No, please call them. He stole my passport!" Nastya then bowed her head to cry and the little landlady hobbled over to her and took the girl in her arms…

"It's okay, *ma petite*, Just wait a moment. Once you stop crying, we'll go to him together."

"Okay, thank you." Nastya replied with gratitude – and her crying began to die down.

"Just one moment, I have something that might cheer you up. Follow me."

Nastya followed the landlady into the vestibule of her apartment, nervously glancing around at the cluttered space decorated with gaudy ornamentation; she hoped that the something that "might cheer her up" wasn't a cake or something. The last thing Nastya wanted to do was eat. Then she suddenly realized, 'What am I doing?! I don't have time for this. Forget the passport, forget whatever this old woman has that's going to "cheer me up"; and, especially, forget that filthy, old pauper, Salaudski. Forget all of it, I don't have time for this … I have to go to the doctor's right now!'

Upon these words, Nastya turned around and bolted for the landlady's front door. She already had the door open and half her body through it, when the landlady waved her cane at her and said loudly…

"Well, don't run off like that! I have it right here. Here, take this, it's for you. It comes to me yesterday – in Saturday's mail." … "And, my dear, please close the door behind you or my cat will get out!"

Nastya took the envelope from the outstretched hand of the landlady. She examined it quietly, with an expression on her face that blended joy, misery, hope, and horror.

"It's from your family, I think. Again in Russian – just like the last letter." The landlady continued in her scratchy voice, "Who is it from?"

Nastya, silent and pensive, quietly turned the knob and opened the landlady's front door, exiting into the hall. Then, just as the last time she received a letter from her father – care of the landlady – she bowed her head and studied the writing on the envelope. This was postmarked the same day as the last letter he sent. Strange it should arrive much later. Her father's handwriting was much more of an illegible scrawl on this envelope. 'His hand must have been shaking when he wrote it,' she thought, 'no wonder it came later. The postman probably couldn't read the address.'

The landlady called out to Nastya as Nastya walked slowly but steadily towards the front door of the building, she wanted to leave Rue de Paradis as soon as possible, but the sealed envelope from Russia seemed to have hypnotized her and she could only walk slowly, completely entranced.

Like with the last letter, Nastya opened the envelope and begin reading as soon as she got outside of Salaudski's building. She stood on that little strip of grass where all of her belongings lay broken, torn and mangled, beneath the open window of her room on the fifth floor. She stood there silently, gently tearing the envelope, and pulling the letter out. She unfolded the stationary and read the news from her dearest father:

(Note: again I have translated the letter from Russian into English, for your sake. Please forgive me if you are a Russian scholar with a strong aversion to translated texts … one can't please ~~all of the people, all of the time~~ everyone.)

My Precious Nastenjka,

I sent another letter today too. I hope you already received that one. If you didn't, please wait for that letter before you read this one. Or, I guess it's of no consequence if you read this one first. Anyway, my Nastenjka, I wish you were here. Oh, I do. It is so hard to tell you this in a letter, it seems so wrong.

There has been a great tragedy and a great loss. The Lord took your brother yesterday. I want you to know that he was sleeping and went in peace. He is happier with the Lord, I know. His coughing got to be too bad. He suffered so much. The last few days, he was coughing blood every hour. The doctor came the night before last and was so worried about Dmitry's health that he stayed by his side all night. By morning, he had passed away. The doctor is a very kind man. I believe the Lord sent him to help us in your absence. He is still with us today, he has just cooked dinner for us – your mother and me. I hope your mother eats. He also helped us prepare for the funeral, which was early this morning.

Nastya, I buried your brother today; and in doing so, I learned the most bitter lesson one can learn. Your old father had thought that he'd taken the worst nails that life can hammer into someone. I thought no bigger axes existed than those that have struck my poor back. I realized today that the worst poison one can take, is to be forced to bury one's own child.

No child should die before its parents. It is unnatural. But the Lord will have mercy. The Lord will help us heal. I just don't think my old body – or your mother's old body – could take this happening again – to our only other child. Make sure you take care of yourself and please reconsider coming back home. I'll send you a ticket right away. I'll come meet you in Paris, if you need me to. Just please, my daughter, think about coming back. Your mother is so distraught that she can't even speak. She hasn't eaten since the doctor arrived. That was more than forty-eight hours ago. She just refuses to speak or eat or cry. She just sits there staring – I am very worried. I pray to see you soon, My Nastenjka, Dochenjka,

Your Devoted Father

PS: I have enclosed the last rubles of my paycheck in this envelope. It should be enough for you to board a train to Moscow – should you decide to come home.

Nastya read every word of that letter over and over. All of her emotions had mysteriously turned off while she read it. Her body knew she needed to read every word, so it saved her from despair just long enough to get to the last line. Then, once she had read all, the bright sky on Rue de Paradis turned to a dark and gloomy crepuscule. Her head began to spin with vertigo, a sense of ultimate doom pervaded every cell in her body; and then she fell, face first, onto the stone sidewalk below.

Her body collapsed and lay motionless near the wet gutter.

After she came to, she cried in a fit of tears, "My brother! …My little, baby brother! No! *Not him!*"

...It would be safe to say that no one in Paris ever suffered more than Nastya suffered at this moment.

Nastya's life has just fallen apart. Meanwhile, David is folding Odette's culottes....

"I love to wear black underwear, because it makes one feel so sexy. But I have to wear underwear that matches, and I hate wearing black bras because they can be seen through almost anything – well, the tops that *I* wear, anyhow...." While Odette played the little coquette, sitting at her desk, waiting for her nail polish to dry, giving David her dissertation on the sensuality of undergarments as governed by the laws of physics and physiology, David stood by her bed, in extreme agitation and worry. He folded her panties, just as she asked, and packed them into the tan suitcase. But he didn't listen to a word of what the old woman was rambling on about; and he wondered why she had hired him to do this, when she could have done it herself. After all, the only thing she did in the last hour was apply makeup to half of her face, and paint three of her fingernails. She looked ghoulish to David. The first time he met her, he thought she had the look of a benevolent, though slightly frail, older woman, whose body had only just started to wither with age. Now he looked upon her as a lecherous and ghoulish old hunchback who appeared to be stuffed with brittle bones, dried blood and pigeon feathers. And the worst of all was that David had to fold her underwear while she spoke in amorous detail about her own privates.

'Where is my Nastya?!' David thought to himself, imagining nothing but the worst.

"What time is it, Odette?"

"11:43. I'm going to have to go out and meet the cab soon. Are you almost done!? Boy, you are a simpleton, aren't you? ... look how you've folded these! They are not socks, they are panties!" Odette had come around to the bed to inspect her suitcase. "I don't even know why I should pay you for this. Didn't you have a mother growing up? Oh, that's right; you said she died ... well, no wonder! Look at this mess. You are not tying shoes, you are folding lingerie!..." Just then, Odette's reproaches towards David were interrupted when there was a loud knock at Odette's front door – the door leading into the medical office.

"Hurry and finish," she said, "I'll go see what they want."

When Odette turned her back and entered her salon, David quickly ran over by Odette's desk. From there, he could read the time on the grandfather clock.

"11:45! ...Oh, my Nastya, you did it! ... Oh, I love this girl." David clasped his hands together and gave thanks to whichever god was responsible for this. Then he fell silent, and crept over to the door leading to Odette's medical office, which she had left ajar.

He heard her unlatch the front door...

"Bonjour? Que-est ce que vous voulez, dit-moi?" She asked. The visitor then spoke to Odette, but David couldn't make out a word of it, the person's voice was too low-pitched and too muffled.

'It must be part of Nastya's ingenious act,' he thought, smiling as he crept back over to the desk to begin the mission.

"Vous êtes fous?! C'est la dimanche, alors! Vous êtes vraiment fous ... Allez!" was Odette's response to the muffled words of the visitor.

David looked again at the desktop, and noticed that his tools: the letter opener and the hairpin, were right where they should be, on top of the desk. As he grabbed the handle of the letter opener, however, he heard a loud crash in the other room. He dropped the letter opener on the desktop and ran over to the door to see what had happened in Odette's medical office.

Just then, Odette returned to the salon, with a satisfied grin on her face.

"What was that crashing noise, Odette?"

"Oh, that was just me slamming the door in the face of that crazy man – trying to sell subscriptions on a Sunday. On a Sunday, can you imagine? I told him how crazy he is!"

David thought about it, 'So, it was a crazy man and not Nastya?' ... 'But he came at exactly 11:45. Had Nastya sent him in her place? Selling subscriptions? What is going on here? I can't do this without Nastya. I don't want to do this without Nastya. Let me be poor and hungry, if I can't have Nastya. If I can't have Nastya, let me be dead!' ... 'But it's only 11:47 or 11:48, she's not that late. Yet she swore she'd return by 11:45 at the latest. But Paris is anything but efficient and she doesn't know the city, anyway. She'll come safely. I just hope it's in the next five minutes.'

"What are you doing, David"

"I'm finishing folding up your lingerie."

"You are tying it all in knots. Here, let me do it. I have to leave anyway."

"But you have over ten minutes."

"Boy, you are observing the time well, today. Your medication working out for you?" she jested, "Here, give me that. You go. I don't need anymore help. See! Suitcase is closed. Valise is closed. My shoes are on and my tickets are in my purse. I'm on my way out the door. If you're still bumming around Paris when I come back, drop by for a glass of tea … that's good you got off the medicine … see, I told you it was psychosomatic. Your as healthy as a snail! … Now go!"

" But, Odette… What about the other fifty-francs?

Odette pulled a fifty-franc bill out of her purse and held it up as if she was about ready to snatch it back away. "As if you deserve this, whew! … tying my panties in knots and drooling all over my bidet!" … "Whatever… a promise is a promise." And with that, she handed David the fifty-franc bill. David held on to it for a moment, rubbing his fingers against the banknote, deciding whether or not to keep it or throw it back in her face. Meanwhile, Odette began to speak with impatience…

"David, don't act like a simpleton. I asked you to go. Go see if the taxi's out front. I'm just going to lock up and I'll be out."

"Yes, I see you have some new locks on your house."

"Oh, you mean those," she pointed to the black iron chains and padlocks on the windows, "…I have to keep thieves out. I also have to keep thieves in, sometimes," she smiled at David mockingly, showing her small, yellow teeth. David thought she looked like a gopher whenever she made this particular mocking face that revealed her little, rounded yellow teeth. "…It seems," Odette continued, "that one of my patients decided to break the locks on my windows – whether to break in or to break out, I'm not sure. Anyway, I know who it was." Odette paused, looking at David with a mysterious glare, blending insolence and coyness. Her eyes burned with intensity as she glared at David. He, however, did not look away.

"It was that junky, Marick," Odette said matter-of-factly, "He was the one who broke the latches on the windows." David continued

277

staring at Odette with a blank expression. His insides were rotting away with the unbearable thought that Nastya may not ever come back.

"But I've cut him off, that Marick. He's not allowed to come near here anymore. I couldn't care less if he gets back on heroin now that his treatment has stopped. He shouldn't go around breaking people's things." Leaving it at that, Odette bobbed her head back and forth a few times, while grinning, and then stood back up, taking her suitcase and her valise in her hands. "…Do I hear the taxi out front?" Odette asked in the high-pitched, sing-song voice of a kindergarten teacher.

Just then, David walked right over to Odette and pressed the fifty-franc bill back in the palm of her hand. "I don't want this money, Odette. I just want my passport back."

"Well the passport is worth more than fifty-francs. I paid forty-three hundred francs for it. So when you pay me in full, I will return it to you."

"Odette, it is illegal to retain someone else's passport without their consent. I'm going to call the police." As he said this, the phone rang in the salon. Odette went to take the receiver.

"Too late, David, they're already calling us!" … "Hallo? … Oui?" … "Yes, I'm almost packed, I'll be outside in a few." … "I don't care if you keep the meter running, don't be insulting?" … "Really? Listen, young man, do you even speak French?" … *"très peu?"* … "Okay, keep the meter running, I'll be out when I'm out. Fine!"

Odette slammed down the phone against the top of her desk. "Go on outside, David. I'm going to lock-up."

"I told you, Odette, I'm calling the police if you don't give me back my passport."

"You will what?!" Odette cried, in a voice that quivered, "Why are you doing this to me the second I'm supposed to leave on vacation?" … "Why are you trying to hurt me, David?"

"Because, Odette, while you are in your first-class train car or in your five-star hotel beneath three-hundred thread-count bed sheets, eating your room-service off a tray of white gold, I will be hustling around Paris looking for rotten vegetables that have fallen to the gutters, so that *I* may eat. I will be looking hard for a place to lay my head that isn't wet from rain or wet from urine. I'll be dirty and ill and at the mercy of everyone. And the worst is I don't speak the language and I am without my passport. I won't have any proof that I am entitled to government aid. I won't be able to get a job, and my life will just get worse and worse, until my teeth rot and by scalp gets eaten by bugs and my intestines are devoured by tapeworms. And all I ask for is a chance … and it requires nothing of you, except that you let me have my passport back. …As soon as I land a job, I promise I will make payments towards my debt, I promise…!"

"Enough! … enough already! Must you be so dramatic? *Mon Dieu!* You are a character!" Odette's sobs have long since disappeared, and she resumes her tone of common anger, "I'll give you your damn passport, right now; but if you don't come back to pay me – if you don't check in at least once a week with me – I'll ruin you in this town. Am I perfectly clear? *I'll ruin you!* I know a lot of people in Paris. It's not such a big city. If you try to screw me over, I will absolutely ruin you, David." … "Now, wait here and don't move."

Odette looked over her shoulder several times as she made her way into her medical office to retrieve the passport from whichever hiding place it had been in. David heard a drawer slide open and a drawer slide closed. Then he realized, the plan wasn't going to work. It was already past noon and Nastya had not arrived. Then Odette exclaimed from her medical office, "Found it! It was right in the drawer – in plain sight. Surprised you never found it on your own." And her heeled footsteps could be heard *clicking* and *clacking* towards the salon. That's when David acted on *impulse*.

It wasn't as if he had had the time to actually make a decision right then. If all actions performed by human beings required that a decision be made first, before the action could be executed, David would not have reacted nearly quick enough.

If consciously making a decision was a prerequisite to taking any particular action, David would have had to first allow a question to enter his brain. He would have also been required to decide whether or not the question that had entered his brain was the appropriate question or not. We'll make things easier, though more outlandish, and assume that *it is* the correct question. David would, then have to decide whether or not this question should be confronted, or left alone. If he chose to confront the question, he would have had to decide whether or not an answer would be the best tool to confront it with – after all, answers are not the only known antidotes to questions. Questions have a vast array of unique predators.

Finally, after having decided that he should, after all, confront the question with an answer, he would have had to milk his brain for all the possible answers that are compatible with the given question. He would have to catalogue these answers and assign them values; and their values would be based primarily, yet not completely, on the most likely consequence that would result from using the answer in question against the initial question.

If some answers posed multiple consequences as probable, one would have to reason like a man at a roulette table – for chance and the laws of probability would play a significant role in deciding which answer posing multiple consequences should be considered. And all of this only brings the human brain to the 'considering phase'. The actual 'deciding phase' requires all of the steps above with the addition of other, more involved, steps, which the brain processes even slower and more prudently, for once you move the brain from the 'considering phase' to the 'deciding phase' you are placing it on the brink of action – where everything is happening in reality and the brain is actually risking peril and death. No brain ever died from 'considering' something. But 'deciding' and 'acting on your decisions' have resulted in billions of unnecessary mental and physical fatalities over the many centuries of modern man's errant excursions on the surface of this earth.

It can take nine million brain processes to momentarily 'consider' something. Another eighty-one billion brain processes (on average) are needed to turn a consideration into a decision. Once the decision is made, the amazing human brain drops at least twenty million safety nets to guard against the passage of a flawed decision into the action cue. The brain is aimed for self-preservation, and if one spoiled, rancid decision becomes a spoiled, rancid action, that action will physically bring the brain into harm's way. Yet, the brain is too clever for that – too clever for our own good!

And the problem is not that the brain is capable of performing these billions of processes, I just mentioned, instantaneously. The problem lies in the fact that the human brain is so powerful, and has grown up so much in recent years, that it is *now* capable of performing an almost infinite number of processes at one time.

If the modern brain was only capable of processing information the way I described it above, we would have no problem navigating safely through the world. But the fact is, The beautiful human brain is now capable of so much that every time a question arises, not only do numerous possible answers appear; but we also see the advent of counter-questions and pseudo answers, as well as decoy decisions, and holographic actions that are bred to protect the brain by not actually 'acting' in a physical realm, but by acting in a holographic realm, which fools the other, lesser brain processes into thinking that they have worked together to give birth to an action, when really they've done nothing.

We all know, the human brain is far more powerful than any machine built by man. The brain, unlike a machine, is *also* self nurturing and self-expanding. The human brain is rapidly mutating and we now have far more functions than we actually need – and these unnecessary functions have formed a mental bureaucracy that protects against their destruction. Basically, we have to live with them, for the modern brain has no veto power in and within itself. …It's amazing that we humans can move, or speak, or act at all, considering the amount of bureaucracy that goes into turning a 'consideration' into an 'action'. It's amazing that our bodies keep breathing.

Fortunately, the human brain – though far more complex than any machine – still falls prey to the same insidious worms that paralyze a machine's ability to execute processes. Like a machine, the brain, too halts its processes, now and again. Now, I'm not talking about the death of the brain, or the death of the body, when I speak of the halting of brain processes. I only speak of the death of logic.

And this! … to our great fortune, gives our immaculate brains an advantage over machines. Because when machines suffer the death of logic, they are truly lost and they are truly dead. But when a human being suffers the death of logic, we are blessed with the arrival of a new king: *impulse!*

[handwritten: shouldn't say that]

All of that long, nonsensical discourse I just made you the victim of was actually written for your benefit, *my good, faithful reader*. Let me recap the last few moments at Odette's:

The time was just after twelve noon… Odette had looked suspiciously over her shoulder many times as she made her way into her medical office to look for David's passport.

Moments after she disappeared into her medical office, David heard a drawer slide open and immediately slide closed again. Then, Odette yelled from her medical office, "I found it ... your passport was right in the top-left drawer, in plain sight ... I'm surprised you never found it on your own – the way you snoop through everything!" then she muttered, "I really shouldn't even give this back to you...."

While she was saying all of these things, she was heading back into the salon to give David his passport and kick him out of her building.

Had David relied on the bureaucracy of his mental processes – where, consideration, decision and action form the base – he would have never had time to act. Odette would have had given his passport back, kicked him out, and locked all the doors and windows to protect her home while she went on vacation, before he would have had even a chance to pick the best plan and go ahead with it – taking action. His brain, however, was too jumbled.

'What is right, what is wrong?' ... 'Where is Nastya? Is she coming? Why isn't she here yet?' ... 'Can I still pull this off? What are my chances of pulling it off? Is it worth trying, even if I win? Since Nastya is no longer with me, I will lose no matter what.' ... 'I meant it when I said that I would not steal just for myself. I have no higher good to serve if I steal for myself and myself alone.' ... 'But for Nastya, I would steal the gold out of a poor man's teeth without a second thought; I would dangle over the edge of the earth, if only I had one golden strand of her hair from which to dangle' ... 'I would....'

And David would have gone on praising Nastya like this for sometime, and all would be lost. But fortunately, his brain processes self-terminated for his own benefit. As a result, he was left with the one tool he really needed to go through with all of this; and this tool was: *impulse!*

Impulse struck David hard and fast while Odette came walking towards her salon with his passport in her hand. Pure impulse caused him to jump up from the bed at that moment, and run at the door, which Odette was trying to enter through. Before she could stop him by throwing her body in the doorway, David slammed it in her face and locked the deadbolt.

"What do you think you are doing, you bastard!?" Odette screamed from her medical office, while she tried to force open the door to the salon. It was no use, her locks were strong. David had to act quickly, impulsively, if he was going to pull this off. He could hear Odette's relentless screaming from the other room, yet he tuned it out and went about everything mechanically – like a skilled criminal.

He walked over to the shelving and retrieved the medicine bag off the high shelf. Then he took, from the surface of the desk, Odette's hairpin and letter opener. He then bent down, crouched between the window and the desk and slid the pin and letter opener into the brass lock on the drawer. Within seconds, the lock gave and the drawer slid open.

Odette had been screaming and pounding on the door in the other room this whole time; but right about the time he picked the lock, she became silent and not a sound was heard from the medical office. 'Has she gone to get the police?' he wondered, 'does she have the key for that door in there?' David remembered that she could lock the door from the side she was on as well. And she probably assumed he couldn't easily escape through the window barred by the chain and padlock. 'She has probably locked the bolt from her side and has gone to find the police. That's fine… I can pick that flimsy bolt, I did it only yesterday. I'll have to act quickly though if the police have been called.'

David pulled out the drawer and to his surprise, it seemed to be filled with even more money that the last time he had inspected it. There were numerous stacks of hundred-franc bills as thick as bibles. There were also dozens of bricks of two-hundred franc bills. The banknotes, alone, almost filled that large leather medicine bag. He had already swiped close to a million francs but he was going for all. He didn't want the credit cards or the travelers' cheques. He just wanted the money and the jewelry. And after all the colorful bricks of money tied-up with strings like little presents were in the medicine bag, he began to grab handfuls of the pearls and loose sapphires, the white opals and the fire opals. Not a diamond set in gold was spared. All the old woman's precious gold and gems went into that bag. There was even a bullion of gold at the bottom of the drawer – nothing was spared, nothing was left behind.

He had to stuff everything down in the bag with all his might in order to get the zipper to close.

In his fury and fervor, however, he did not hear the bolt unlock across the room. As he was trying to get the zipper to close on the bag overstuffed with his fortune, he did not see the figure of that person who had entered the salon and was running towards him. He didn't discover their presence until it was too late.

After he zipped the bag closed, he paused a minute to think of his next move – and that's when it came like bomb exploding in the eyes.

David was crouched down between the desk and the window when Odette ran up behind him and jumped on his back, stuffing a rag soaked with chemicals into his mouth and eyes. And the burn was immeasurable. He felt his eyes had been ignited with fire. He felt his retinas burning with corrosive chemicals, he saw nothing anymore. His breathing became difficult, his lungs began to burn. Every breath he took, it felt as though his lungs were being torn from his chest cavity. The old woman pressed the rag against his face while screaming and flailing about on his back where he was hunched over. She bit his shoulder and held those noxious chemicals to his face. Was it ammonia she was poisoning him with. Perhaps it was ether. He became very dizzy, and his brain had become unreactive, yet his body still managed to respond to the assault with a surge of adrenalin. Once Odette penetrated David's skin with her teeth, he threw his body upwards, causing the flailing old woman to fly backwards, hitting the wall. David had the fury of a fierce animal that has been ambushed. His eyesight was hindered and his sockets burned but he could still see. His inflamed throat was swelling painfully, but he could still breathe. His head was beginning to spin in dizzy confusion, but he didn't have vertigo yet, and he could still stand.

He had thrown that old doctor off of his back, which she had latched onto; and she now lay wounded on the floor with her head propped against the wall – and she squirmed.

David stood in place, looking down at the white rag soaked in chemicals, which Odette had shoved into his face. His lips began to burn, and he started seeing a mosaic of colored lights that interfered with his vision and judgment. He then looked at the door to the medical office. It was flung wide-open. He looked down at the medicine bag filled with money and jewelry. Then, in a swoop, clarity return to his mind, just long enough for him to realize that his plan had to go past step one.

He reached down and picked up the medicine bag by its two leather handles. He staggered forward, carrying the bag. Odette still squirmed on the ground like an insect stuck on its back, who is trying to flip over. The chemicals – that ammonia or benzene or ether or chloroform, or whatever it was – was hampering David's breathing and his judgment. Holding his throat, which smoldered with an intense heat, with one hand, and holding the medicine bag in the other, David staggered in a full circle around the room. Had he his wits about him. Had his judgment not been impaired, he would have, no doubt, escaped with the money through the open door of the medical office, through the hallway, out the front door and up the street. But his brain wasn't processing anything correctly so his body had to rely upon impulse.

Staggering past Odette, who was desperately trying to get her fingernails into his legs as he walked by, he came upon the desk once again. He looked down at the floor and saw the letter opener lying there. A ray of light came through the window, whose curtains were drawn, and it reflected off the blade of the letter opener, sending a shimmer of brass light into the retina of David's eyes. That letter opener looked like a dagger. David stood, eyeing it for many moments. The light shimmering off its blade had seemed to hypnotize him. Meanwhile he felt Odette's claws digging into the skin on his ankles. Then his hypnotic state subsided and his faculties returned to a slight degree. He thought of Nastya. Their plan wouldn't work if he didn't go past step one. This he knew well. A plan is only good if all the necessary steps are taken. This first part, step one, had gone beautifully, he thought, except for that chemical assault on his eyes and his brain, except for the damage done to his lungs and his throat. Other than that, and the little screaming beast that kept clawing at his ankles, step one had gone beautifully in his mind. But it was time to take step two.

David looked again at the letter opener – that brass dagger! Then he thought of Nastya and the window. 'It is too bad I didn't have time to pick the padlock, David thought. Then I could just open the window and hand Nastya the money.' It was as if he thought Nastya was waiting outside for him. It was as if he forgot that she hadn't come when she said she was going to. She had promised him: no later that 11:45. It was well after noon, and she still had not arrived. David wasn't realizing that he was on his own. Nastya was no longer in the picture. This robbery was a heist performed by David alone, against Odette alone. There was no party involved, it was just two people's – a man's and a woman's – fight to protect each one's self and destroy the other person. Nastya was nowhere near. Who knew if she would ever come. She had her own trauma to deal with. And perhaps the gruesome reality of her trauma, and how she actually felt it bite – *and how hard it bit!* – made her disinterested in pursuing a plan that could easily lead to more traumas – even greater traumas.

'Perhaps, Nastya sees me as her enemy. A monster bent on dragging her through a life of misery and unbearable tragedy,' this is all David could think about as he walked like a zombie, back and forth, past the window, while Odette scrambled to get to her feet.

Then he muttered something in the low, slow voice of someone whose body is being poisoned. "Nastya, please come to the window...." His eyes fluttered open and closed with the passing waves of vertigo that were beginning to mount. Then, another beloved wave of clarity and capacity passed through him and he took a step forward to the window, and – *blessed impulse!* – he threw his fist through the largest pane of glass, shattering it to pieces.

Punching out the window caused the skin on his hand and wrist to bleed profusely from the large gashes made by the shards of broken glass. He sucked at the blood pouring off his hand for a moment. It filled the recess of his mouth. The blood in his mouth seemed to ease the burning caused by the corrosive chemicals, and when he swallowed it, the blood soothed his throat.

Then, again void of his mental faculties, and again on impulse, David took the leather medicine bag filled with money, which he still held in his hand, and he stuffed it through the broken pane of glass on the window. The bag dropped through the window to the stone floor of the quiet courtyard out back and David peered through the pane of glass, seeing that immense fortune stuffed in an old leather bag, resting on the ground, out in the open, in the light of day.

Meanwhile, Odette had seen what had transpired. She had even managed to get to her feet at the moment David shoved the bag through the window. But she didn't attempt to attack him again. Her rag soaked in a chemical cocktail was lying on the ground near David's feet. He would squash her if she tried to reach for it. She didn't care about that rag. She had seen the bag. She had seen the bag and she had seen her drawer where she kept her valuables pulled out onto the floor. She had then realized what this was all about – why David had locked her in her office. When she saw him stuff the bag through the window, she realized what was in that bag, and she knew how crucial it was to get it back.

While David stood in demi-coherence, watching through the pane of glass, hoping that his Nastya would appear at any moment; and, smiling at him with that radiant smile of hers through the window, she would swipe the bag and run on to St. Sulpice.

While David stood watching the bag rest tranquilly on the stone ground in the courtyard, Odette, almost silently, ran towards her medical office. She ran slowly, limping from her injury, but she was determined to get away from David, and to get to that courtyard to reclaim her fortune.

As soon as she cleared the doorway to the medical office, she flung the door shut with all her might and turned the bolt, locking David inside. David, turned around when he heard the door slam and he looked at the closed door and laughed maniacally, exuding fumes of the toxic chemicals he'd inhaled.

Then, almost mechanically, he devised step three. It was obvious where Odette was going. It was obvious that she had seen him throw the bag outside and was going to retrieve it and run to the police. It was obvious that Nastya hadn't come, and was not about to come. He had not planned this heist as solo work. The thought that he would be alone on this mission never occurred to him. He wouldn't have done it if he thought it was going to be solo work. Yet, despite his mental confusion at the time, he managed to devise step three; and, as consequence of his severe mental confusion, that step involved actions of the most primitive nature: He would chase after that old woman and get the bag of money away from her. …First he would have to pick the lock.

Adrenaline is a powerful antidote to almost any poison. Once David realized how much was at stake with that bag being outside, and Odette chasing after it, and his being locked in her apartment, his adrenal gland provided a nice shot of animalistic energy and resilience to those horrid chemicals that were poisoning his glands.

The broken windowpane was too small to climb through. The lock on the door was easier to pick than the padlock on the window. He would have to follow her out the way she went. He bent down and quickly swiped the brass letter opener from the floor. He then charged at the door like a animal pouncing on prey and he shoved that letter opener into the door jam, turning it inwards, thereby freeing the bolt.

A moment later, he was through the medical office and out the front door running down the hall to exit the building. Once he got outside, the clear, white light of the sun hit his burning eyes and he doubled over for a moment. Then, lifting his head and squinting to discern his environment, he'd noticed something that he had forgotten might play a role in his plan that had suddenly ceased to be a plan and started to be an improvisation.

He noticed Odette's taxi parked right in front of her building. The driver was sitting calmly in the driver's seat looking at his watch. David didn't have time to pay this taxi any mind. He had to get to that courtyard and get the bag.

He raced around the corner, coughing from the chemicals and the strain the physical exertion was having on his damaged lungs.

When he reached the gate of the courtyard he flung it open and ran towards the window – yet he saw what he had feared he would see. The bag was gone. The courtyard was quiet. With the eyes of a hawk that were burnt and bleeding, he surveyed the courtyard looking for Odette – the woman who had stolen his fortune.

Only the sound of the stream of fountain water, reflecting the yellow shimmers of the sun, as it dribbled down over the broad tropical leaves into the fountain's basin could be heard. There were no other sounds. There were no voices, no footsteps, Odette was gone and the money was gone.

David didn't take the time to see if there was another way out of the courtyard in the back. Besides, he didn't think there was. He quickly turned around and ran back towards the gate, flinging it open and running out into the alleyway.

The alleyway was silent and Rue du Dragon, at the alley's end, also was silent. No cars passed down the street. No Sunday strollers walked by. It was deserted – as it often is on Sunday.

David didn't find an obvious step four. When he returned to Rue du Dragon, he saw that the taxi had left. He heard the sound of a car coming towards him – from behind – it sounded like it was going to run him over, its tires squealed. In sudden panic, David turned around and saw nothing. The car had only been part of his imagination.

Wrought with pain and hallucinations, David staggered back towards Odette's building. He didn't know where else to go. It was possible that Odette had grabbed the bag and was running through the streets of Paris in an effort to escape David and find help. What could David do? ...run like a madman through these winding cobbled streets looking for an old woman carrying a medicine bag? He'd never find her.

There were too many erratically winding streets in the neighborhood, and they all diverged into other erratically winding streets that went on for miles and miles.

'What is more likely,' he realized, 'is that she had grabbed the bag just before I entered the courtyard, and then exited through another gate on the other side of the courtyard, leading to another alleyway, which leads to Rue du Dragon, where she jumped in that taxi and rode off, with my fortune, in search of the police. That taxi was parked right here just a second ago. Then, a moment later, the bag was gone and the taxi was gone. That has to be it! But it can't be it! I *must* find that bag!'

David, having had no guidance in the planning of step four, had to rely on his own brain, which was, at that moment, less than adequately capable of strategic planning. He wasn't sure why he decided to go back into Odette's. The motive wasn't clear. She was obviously long gone and the police would, no doubt, be arriving there shortly. But, then again, what other choice did he have? Where else in the city of Paris did he have to go to, unless it was to Odette's?

He punched the door code and flung the front door open. He then ran quickly down the hall to Odette's door on the ground floor at the far end of the hall.

'What is she doing? Had she really been foolish enough to come back to her apartment?' David wondered. Her whimpering moans could be heard on the other side of the wall as David stood at the foot of her door, listening.

"Go away!" she moaned through heavy tears of panic and terror, "Go away!"

Was she really just on the other side of the door? It sounded as if she was sitting or kneeling just on the inside of her front door, trying to keep the door closed with the weight of her body.

The knob turned easily with a turn of David's hand and the door opened a few centimeters. 'This woman is really trying to block the door with the weight of her frail, little body. Doesn't she know how to lock her own front door? Has she lost the strength?' David thought with perplexity as he pushed lightly on the door.

As soon as he realized that the door actually was neither chained, locked, nor bolted, he gave it a firm and hard push – a push that made the door fly open – a push that made Odette's body fly backwards against the wall.

David entered Odette's office once again. The old woman was lying in a heap in the corner. When the door had been flung open, it threw her against the wall where she again hit her head, and then slid down to the floor where she now squirmed in her sweaty cotton dress, crying and begging the intruder to leave.

David closed the front door behind him, to keep the neighbors from getting suspicious. He sucked at the blood on his hand. It was still flowing freely from the gashes that were made when he punched out the pane of glass in the salon. The blood soothed his burning mouth and lips, and left a sanguine stain on his face.

"Where is the bag, Odette?!" he shouted at the injured woman sagging in the corner of her office. She didn't respond. She just moaned and squirmed and looked at David with eyes that he could not bear to look back at. *Those* eyes! How they burned with cold horror!

"Where is the bag?!" David shouted, "Quit moaning, Odette, and give me the bag!" He stooped down and grabbed the nape of her neck, squeezing it hard – his hand dripped blood on her skin and dress. She didn't scream, she just trembled and moaned like a dying woman, and looked at him with *those* eyes. Those eyes that meant to ask him *why?* *Why* had he done this? *Why* was he so desperate, and *why* all of a sudden? His body smoldered with a fierce fire that burned hotter than the chemicals in his eyes and his throat. Those chemicals, which had also made him dizzy and slightly delirious, were not the cause of this intense, monomaniacal drive – his body was running on adrenaline and gasoline.

Odette wouldn't answer. She just trembled and moaned, with a look of terror upon her face which was stained with the blood from David's hand.

He shook her again and pulled her forward, out of the corner; he suspected the bag might be tucked behind her. It wasn't. He released the nape of her neck whereupon she slumped back down to the ground. The money wasn't in her office. He stormed through her salon, entering into the bathroom – nothing but a clean, pink bidet. Madness drove his mind and there was no logic to where he looked. Back in the salon, he threw Odette's wooden odalisque against the wall and climbed the shelves looking for the leather bag. He tore the bed apart and ransacked her dresser. He tore her tan suitcase apart, which had been propped by the door with her valise in anticipation of her trip to Strasbourg. His blood left a trail around her apartment. Finally, he started to reason. Maybe the bag was still out back? Maybe he only hallucinated that the bag hadn't been there when he went out back to the courtyard. He distinctly remembered there only having been one entrance to the courtyard the first time he inspected it – when he had come with Nastya earlier in the day. If Odette had gone to her courtyard, he would have seen her coming back down through the alleyway. 'And why, if she took the bag, did she come back to her apartment? Why didn't she leave in the taxi?' he wondered, 'Yet, where did she go when she ran out of her apartment just a moment ago? Perhaps the money is still out back!...' But when he peered through the broken pane of glass out onto the stone floor of the courtyard, he saw the bare, stone ground below the window. The bag was really gone. It wasn't until he pulled his head back in and looked at the area around her desk that he noticed something peculiar. The desk drawer that he had flung out onto the parquet and ransacked, was now back in place in the desk. The drawer was shut and locked. His eyes lit up like red coals, still burning from the chemicals. All his attention fixed on that drawer. He tried the handle, but it would not budge. He would have to pick the lock again.

'So she *had* retrieved the bag, after all; and then she ran back inside to lock it up in the drawer,' David concluded, 'so where is that damned letter opener?!' He couldn't remember where he had last seen the letter opener. His mind was foggy from the chemicals he had been forced to inhale. It was as if each thought was pounding like a second heart beating in his brain, pushing at his skull, which was about to explode.

'The letter opener ... where did I use it last? Didn't I put it back on the desk when I was finished?' He threw the papers off the desk, looking for that, or any other object he could implement to free the lock. It was when he was bending over the desk chair, feeling the floor with his hands, that it happened. His head was bowed and faced the window in the salon, and his back, near the desk, pointed out into the room. Suddenly, he felt something on the ground he might be able to use to get that drawer open. He fixed all his attention on it.

Then it happened.

It felt like a bee sting at first. The chemicals and the cut and broken hand and all the adrenaline coursing through his veins made him nearly impervious to pain – therefore, it only felt like a bee sting.

In fact, what had happened was that while David had his back turned and was searching the floor for the letter opener, Odette who had managed to stop moaning and squirming on the floor in the other room, had entered the salon in order to ward off the intruder.

The many moments that David had spent ransacking the apartment and searching around for the bag, and later on the ground looking for the letter opener, had afforded Odette sufficient time to take one of her largest seven-gauge syringes and fill it with a vile chemical of some sort or another. And as David searched the floor, half blind, on his hands and knees, finally coming across a utensil that might be used to pick the lock, Odette overtook him and jabbed his back with the large needle. He dropped the utensil in surprise as she pushed the plunger in, expelling all of the chemicals from the syringe into the muscles in David's back.

The intramuscular shot hit him almost instantly. The chemicals surged his veins and pumped through his heart, causing a profound dizziness, an excruciating nausea, and terrifying, heart-pounding panic. He swatted his hands at the needle that was stuck in his back, but he could not reach it. Anyway, it was too late – all of the contents of the syringe had already entered his blood stream. He turned around and saw Odette standing a few feet away, by the desk. Her face appeared mangled to David who was, in his dizziness, barely able to focus on anything. She seemed to smile at him. She had a contorted look of fear, and horror, misery and pain; yet at the same time, she seemed to be smiling at him – mockingly – as if she were about to watch him die.

But he was not about to die. The shot had given him vertigo and nausea. It had made his muscles contract painfully, while his heart pounded at a terrifying rate; but his panicked body reacted to the attack by releasing more adrenaline and giving him a surge of energy, which gave him tunnel-vision and the strength of a wild cat.

Meanwhile, the pain increased and the area around the needle on his back burned like boiling oil had been spilled on his skin. He looked at Odette as her contorted face watched him steadily. She was weak from the struggle, breathing heavily, and she rested her weight upon the desk. David stopped swiping at the needle stuck in his back and he focused on the old woman who watched him from three feet away. His hatred for this woman intensified. She too, was delirious. Her horrific face smiled at him as he flailed his arms like an insect, trying to pull that syringe out. His hatred for her grew infinitely. He abhorred this woman who had just killed him with the venomous bite of a poison filled syringe. He was not dead, but apparently, she expected him to be, any moment. She alone knew what had been in that syringe; and she apparently took him to be fatally crippled and incapable of any kind of retaliation, for she stood only three feet away, smiling with horror and delight. His focus centered on this woman now. He no longer gave attention to the needle in his back, nor to the chemicals in his body that were eating away at his tissues – neither to the bag full of money that was God knows where. He looked at this woman with the bloodshot eyes of hatred, and behind those two burning red coals, his brain pounded with the desire for revenge.

She looked at him with her tight lips turned up, smiling and her eyes too burned, but with white fire. It was then that her contorted face mangled itself in an expression of fear, for she could see what he was about to do.

From the desk that stood between the two, David's eyes searched and fell upon an object. He looked at Odette again – her fearful face was about to scream. David reached out and wrapped his hand around the stem of the empty crystal cruet on her desk – which had once been filled with wine; and swinging his arm backwards, he brought it up and around, over his head, and down, clear in the center of her skull. With a crack like an eggshell breaking, or the breaking of ice on a pond, he felt the heavy bulbous base of the cruet with its multiple edges and facets, sink into her skull; whereupon she dropped to the ground, and lay still. Her matted hair became soaked with the blood from within her skull, where the cracks could be seen easily – from which the soft, swelling hematomas were pushing through. David's vision was impaired as the vertigo returned, stronger than ever. He became worried that he would faint right there, right on top of Odette's dead body. She was dead, there was no question about that; and there was no reason to lodge the crystal vessel in her head a second time. David tried to focus on something, to keep from fainting, to keep from dying himself. He looked at Odette's cracked skull on the ground. Blood, almost black in color, formed a puddle around her head. He could have sworn her brain was beating through her skull, in regular rhythms; he had never thought a brain would pulse like that after its skull is cracked open. He stood above her watching her, and then losing strength himself, he began to stumble. He dropped the cruet, which he had still been holding in his hand; and, stumbling, he stepped on the back of Odette's corpse, to catch his balance – to keep from falling. He could feel her nerves twitching violently beneath his foot. He could feel her coming back to life and pulling herself to her feet, to jab him again with another needle, this time filled with strychnine. But she wasn't pulling herself to her feet. She wasn't coming back to life. She lay dead on the floor of her apartment, as all the blood in her body formed a pool around her.

David had just killed the doctor. What hatred had caused him to do that – to kill her? The burning in his body momentarily subsided when he realized she was dead, sending a warm and pleasant sensation to his brain, to his thoughts, his goal had been achieved. He no longer thought about the money, the bag locked in the drawer of her desk. Perhaps that hadn't been his goal after all. Perhaps, all along, he had only wanted to kill the old woman. Perhaps, that was the result he had been hoping for. Or, maybe he wasn't thinking clearly. Maybe the sharp attack of delirium in his brain, caused by all the chemicals she had forced into his body, was confusing him. What was the goal he'd had in mind upon returning to Odette's, after he discovered that the bag had been taken from the courtyard? Was it to find the old doctor and crack open her skull? He couldn't remember. Maybe that was it. Regardless, that was over and now he was on to step four.

Before he could think about step four, viz., getting the money out of the locked drawer and getting the hell out of the dead woman's apartment, he had to get his vertigo to subside. It was threatening to take his consciousness – and perhaps his life – and send him crashing down to the floor atop the corpse beneath his feet. Then, he heard a sound. A distinct sound. The sound of sirens. Or maybe it was just one siren. A second surge of alertness and energy filled him upon hearing this: the most terrifying sound he could possibly hear. His head perked up and his eyes opened like an alarmed animal hearing gunshots in the jungle in the night. David staggered quickly to the door of the medical office, and advanced to the front door leading out – the door, which had remained closed during the killing.

He traversed the hall with quick movements, his energy was fierce from the adrenaline and fainting or falling was no longer a threat.

Quickly he pushed the button to release the front door leading out to Rue du Dragon. There was no doubt in his mind that the cops were outside. There was no doubt that they were surrounding the entrance to the building – with their rifles drawn.

CHAPTER XVIII

When David stepped out of Odette's building on Rue du Dragon, his hand was soaked in his own blood, his lips and mouth were gleaming with his own blood, and his shoes tracked the blood of Odette. When he stepped out of the building with the large, seven-gauge syringe still stuck in his back, he found the street to be deserted. No cars passed down the road. No strollers strolled, no taxis were parked out front, the shops were all closed – and no police sirens could be heard. Then he remembered, it was Sunday.

He turned down the sidewalk and staggered, injured and bleeding, his body was in tremors and the chemicals burned his insides more than ever; he couldn't tell if his heart was beating too fast, or not at all.

He headed off in tormented confusion. He walked away from St. Germain and came to the corner of Rue de Sevres. He wanted to stop and lean against the building, or perhaps fall to the street and let his body be finally devoured by those chemicals, which were corroding his insides. He rubbed his back against the stone wall of an apartment house on Rue de Sevres in order to extract the syringe from his muscle. The barrel of the syringe broke off and fell to the pavement below, the needle remained in his back. He swaggered forward through the deserted streets. The burning on his skin, in his lungs, and in his eyes continued. He sucked once again at the blood that still flowed heavily from his hand, letting it fill the recess of his mouth. He then swallowed it and it seemed to soothe him and revitalize him.

He had a hard time thinking clear thoughts, his brain was creating nightmarish visions that interplayed with all he took for reality and he didn't know which direction to follow. Had he really killed her? Oh, how her brittle skull broke through to the carriage of her brain so easily. How those three membranes protecting the brain instantly tore open allowing the contents of her head to seep out of her cracked eggshell skull, like a pot that was boiling over, with black blood. 'And did you see those eyes?' he thought, while crossing Rue de Rennes, sucking at the blood that dripped from the deep gouges in his hand. 'I can't believe *those* eyes! The way they looked at me, right before I did it – before I did *that thing!* For that brief moment she looked at me, with *those* eyes. I can't believe *those* eyes were hers!'

"What have I done, and what did I do it for? Where is Nastya?" he cried out in a voice of despair that rang through the empty streets, "Why didn't she come? It would have gone differently if Nastya had been there. Why hadn't she been there?"

And then the bells began to toll, and his thoughts were interrupted. He heard the bells afar and he counted twelve and he counted ten. 'How is it afternoon, and I count twenty-two tolls of the bells?' … 'Strange it's only afternoon, yet the sky is dark like twilight! It can be none other than the twilight that heralds the coming of death – *oh, wicked crepuscule!'*

After staggering across Rue de Rennes, he headed down the deserted Rue du Vieux Colombier and the cathedral of St. Sulpice loomed over his head with the silver light of twilight illuminating its grand towers, which disappeared into the glowing gray clouds of the crepuscular sky – *le ciel crépusculaire.*

Had there been any other spectators of the Cathedral St. Sulpice at this moment, it probably would have appeared to them to be a golden afternoon, with the soft light of May casting a warm yellow light on the cathedral and the giant square before it. And the fountain too probably would have appeared lit with sweet, yellow light; and its stream of water, ascending and descending into the stone basin below, would have shone to emit diamond-like shimmers of sunlight in all directions. But, for David, it was the crepuscule. His vision was darkening, and, though he could see the objects in front of him, they were dark and glowing silver and they changed shapes and deceived his perception like apparitions in the night. This crepuscular vision of St. Sulpice was how it was. It didn't matter if it appeared to others as a golden afternoon. There weren't any others around. It was Sunday and the square was deserted.

Standing in the vast square of the St. Sulpice, all that could be heard were the coos of the pigeons around the fountain and the flaps of their wings; the sound of the fountain water splashing in the basin could also be heard. David felt too weak to go any farther than that square. Each step he took sent tremors of pain up his body and he felt and tasted the blood, like gunmetal, coming up through his throat. Large, stringy vessels of blood came up to his mouth and he coughed, spitting them on the stone tiles on the ground of the square. He was too weak to walk much farther. In the distance he heard a police siren This time, it was clear. It was not a hallucination. On some not too distant street, a police car was approaching with its siren on. 'This is where it all must end.' David thought as he staggered over to the fountain to wash his face and hands in the basin of cool water.

'Nastya? Why didn't you come?' he thought to himself, as he looked around the deserted square, 'Did Salaudski make you a better offer?' ... he approached the fountain and submerged his head in the water. While underwater, he coughed, and blood came up. When he pulled his head from the fountain, he saw his blood adrift in the otherwise clear fountain water. He had lost more than he thought he had.

David stood wavering, almost ready to collapse, all the while trailing his hand in the fountain, to wash it clean from the blood. He heard the sirens approaching only too well, but what could he do? He was dying.

'Did Salaudski make you a better offer?' he repeated to himself, 'Oh, how could I even think something like that? That is not Nastya. That is not *my* Nastya! ... She didn't come because something has happened to her. She had an accident. She is just late. Perhaps Salaudski kidnapped her. Any of those – but purposely not come, she did not! That is not *my* Nastenjka! ... *not her!*'

'...Yet, whatever the reason, it doesn't matter; for I will die right here. I will either be caught by the police and then die, or I will die alone in this deserted square. Either way, it will be soon and it will be without Nastya. I just wished I could die lingering on the sight of her precious face, instead of dying with a view of this putrid fountain, filled with bloody water!'

As he washed again his hand in the putrid fountain water, which was becoming more and more red, he squinted his eyes and looked over yonder at the other side of the fountain. His twilit vision noticed a figure sitting on the base of the far end of the fountain, partially obscured by the statue of a stone lion. The figure had its back turned to David. 'Odette?' he thought, 'but it can't be!' ... 'it can't be *her!*' He backed away from the fountain in horror. He wanted to turn and run, but his legs had seized up and he was nearly paralyzed. Then the woman's head began to turn. He saw distinctly her cracked skull and her matted, blood-soaked hair, gleaming in the silver light of his dimming, twilit vision. She growled at him, her eyes of white fire, and her face stained with black blood – oh, how it growled!

Yet, hallucinations have the enigmatic tendency to eventually reform themselves into the actual objects that stand before the one who is hallucinating. And when David's horrific vision eventually reformed itself into a vision of reality, a great hope was born.

What he had seen there was not Odette, it had only been an apparition. There was no old woman sitting on the base of the fountain. That had been just a terrible delusion. Odette was dead, lying on the floor of her salon, beside her desk.

But it was not nothing, either, this figure. The figure he beheld was someone else, and the moment he realized who it was, his hope was born.

She had been crying this whole time, her head down in her lap as she sat on the fountain's edge. And when she saw David, she smiled a smile that he had never before seen. She then jumped up and ran over to him as quickly as she could with the look of pure love and happiness.

"Nastya!" he shouted, feeling divine hope and profound joy, "Nastya!"

"Yes!" she cried back, "Yes, it's me! It's your Nastya. It's your Nastya! ... David, what has happened?"

She embraced him hard, and she pressed her lips to his for a long time. He felt her body in his hands, her whole warm body pressed against his, and he felt like he was ascending to heaven.

"But you have blood on your lips!" she cried in alarm after kissing him. She too now had blood on her lips. It was not the blood from his hand, for he had washed that from his mouth in the fountain. This was new blood. Blood which came from his organs, which had traveled through his throat, filled his mouth, and stained his lips.

"It is not blood, my Nastya," he said, smiling in delirium, "they are stains of wine. And you have them on your lips, as well." He traced her blood-stained lips with his fingertip.

But you are hurt, my love. Look at your eyes! …they are so red; and your hand! …it is all cut up. And your skin is so pale; and, David, how you tremble! I'm worried David, why is there blood in your mouth?"

"I don't know Nastya. I don't know what happened. Where were you? You were supposed to be there. You were supposed to come to distract her, while I…."

"I know, David, I came late. I am sorry I came late. You look so hurt. You need to go to the hospital."

"No hospital, Nastya. If I die, it shall be here. I can't move anyway, I want to die here. I want my heart to stop as my lips rest upon your lips, as my eyes gaze into yours."

"You're not going to die, David," Nastya said with fear in her eyes and a nervous smile on her blood-stained lips.

Then she pulled back from David's embrace and helped him to sit on the edge of the fountain. He slung his head low and blood fell in steady drips from his open mouth. Nastya kissed his forehead and left him – left him sitting there. He watched her walk away and he felt his body starting to freeze. He felt his heart slow and his forehead beading with cold clammy sweat. His skin burned from the inside, but it was a cold, nauseating burn. Watching Nastya walk away through the twilit square, to where she disappeared behind the immense fountain made him seethe with sadness – sadness and desperation, and intense suffering.

"Now I must die without her!" he cried in despair. But that despair submitted to the even stronger physical sensation he was having. His throat was contracting and his organs burned in his gut. The terrible nausea reached an apex and he poised himself to vomit; and he knew if he vomited, it would be his blood and organs which would be expelled from his body.

Head bent over, and poised to vomit, he felt a warm hand pass over his cold scalp. With the touch of this hand on his head, with its soft, warm fingers running themselves through his hair, the nausea subsided, the burning subsided, and his pain nearly vanished.

He looked up at the girl who looked so happy and so beautiful – who looked so sad and so worried at the same time, and his hope returned. Nastya had come back.

She had only left him to retrieve something that was stashed beneath the basin of the fountain on the other side. And now she held it in her hand; whilst with her other hand, she stroked her lover's head.

David looked up at his girl, and then he glanced down at the object she held in her left hand. What she held was the medicine bag made of dark American leather, which David had thrown through the broken pane of glass in the window of Odette's salon down to the courtyard below. It was the bag he had filled with an incredible fortune of money and jewelry, and now Nastya had it.

He reached down and stroked the leather of the bag with his cut hand. "But how do you have this?" he looked up at Nastya, smiling at his beloved heroine.

"What do you mean, *how* do I have this?" she asked, "I did like you said. Since I came back too late to distract Odette, I instead went straight to the back when I heard the window shatter. Then I saw the bag lying in the courtyard beneath the window. I picked the bag up and ran here – to St. Sulpice – just as we'd planned. I ran here to meet you. To meet *you*, my love." ... "I know I disobeyed you. I waited here at St. Sulpice longer than ten minutes. But I wasn't going to leave without you. I don't want this money without you...."

"My Nastya...." He repeated her name three times, feebly, then mustered energy to stand to his feet. It was then he leaned forward and kissed her again, more passionately than before. His body felt like its tissues were deteriorating, and his brain produced increasingly nightmarish visions, his eyesight was failing him and more and more blood began to come up through his throat, filling his mouth and running down his chin.

"That was our plan, right?" Nastya asked between kisses.

"Yes, that was our plan, and you did it, Nastya! You are my heroine and my beloved."

"And this is our future?" She smiled with a great look of joy, as she pulled the heavy bag full of money up to her stomach and placed it in David's hands. He felt the heavy weight of the bag and he sat back down on the edge of the fountain and unzipped it. Looking inside, he saw all of the stacks of colorful money and the iridescent gems and pearls and strands of gold that he had filled it with. He zipped it back up and looked at Nastya, who had crouched down beside him, to also have a look at their spoils.

Nastya saw the jewelry and the gems but she didn't mention anything. By now, the details of the fortune were the last things on her mind. She was terribly worried about David's health. Oh, how he trembled all over, how red his eyes were, how his mouth was covered in blood that dripped down his face and soiled his suit. How pale his skin had become! It was almost blue. His breathing was getting shorter and shorter. Yet he managed to say: "You did it, my love. This is our future and it begins right now. Let's walk. Let's go, my love. All of Paris is behind us!"

The two began to leave the square, and walked down Rue Férou. Nastya held the bag of money and supported David with her arm. He had trouble walking but could manage to take small, slow steps. Nastya walked easily, as she had changed her clothes. She left her entire suitcase, and even her purse back at Salaudski's. All she carried was the money and her lover.

When the two reached the edge of the square, they stopped … or David stopped rather. His eyes were now closed and he, in his wavering consciousness, forgot to keep moving forward. Then another siren was heard, and then another - they were not too close, yet not too distant. Nastya turned to David who swayed back and forth, held up only by Nastya's arm and she saw that his eyes were closed. Through the thin membrane of his eyelids, she could see his eyeballs beginning to roll upwards.

"Wake up, David. Wake up, my love!" she cried, dropping the bag at her feet where it landed in the gutter.

"But I can't," he began raving, opening his eyes for merely a moment. They looked at her wildly, "…The birds are chasing us … the mice are biting our ankles … we have to run from here!" …Then his eyes closed again and he appeared lifeless.

"Wake up, David! Please don't fall asleep. We'll go to a hotel, or to the hospital. We can't take a train because I lost my passport. But we can go somewhere together. Just wake up, David! We'll go wherever you want to go."

301

Then, while his eyes remained closed, he spoke coherently for the last time...

"We can't go to the hospital, Nastya. I killed her. I killed the old woman. You have to leave me. Take the money and go hide. Just fly away! *Fly away!* Get a new passport as soon as you can and get on a train to Moscow. Take this money to your family. Take it for your father and your brother...." He tried to say more but his words trailed off. Nastya was stunned. 'He killed her?! And she has killed him?! And where was I at the time?!' ... 'Why couldn't I have stopped this? And, what am I to do now?' ... 'Oh, I don't care about that woman, or her money. I love *him*. I love this man, and now I'm going to lose him!'

Nastya pulled David's body close to hers. She tasted his blood on her lips, she felt his strong arms wrapped around her, desperately – as though he knew it was for the last time. Never again would he hold his Nastya – he knew this. He held her tight and she held him even tighter. Soon, his strength gave way and he lost his grip on her body. His legs began to falter and he slouched over Nastya's shoulder. He was too heavy for her to hold for too long. She never wanted this embrace to end but she knew she could not hold his weight much longer. She cried and pulled his body into hers as long as she could, until finally, his great weight slipped from her hands and he fell, face down, to the gutter below.

Hysterical, Nastya threw herself down in the gutter on Rue Férou and propped her lover's head up. His face was soiled with the grime from the gutter. She put her face under his and kissed his mouth as hard as she could. She tasted the blood on his lips and she drank the blood that dripped from his mouth – all the while, she cried in desperation. She wanted his blood to fill her body, so that he could go on living within her. She held her mouth against his, feeling the cold blood on her tongue. Then, in a flash, a great and horrible realization of what was happening filled her mind; and she broke into a violent fit of tears.

"His lips are cold, and there is no breath," she cried, choking on her tears, "...breathe David, please, open your eyes!"

For many moments, she lay on the lifeless body of her beloved, who lay face down in the gutter, and she cried in despair. Then, as though she could take no more, the despair left, the crying stopped, and her body became torpid and numb. She was overcome with silent delirium. It was her body's way of protecting her from the excruciating pain of what was real and now, and it hypnotized her and emptied her of all feeling; she didn't believe that he was dead. She stood up and looked down on him as though he were only sleeping. And then she decided he needed help. She didn't realize it was too late. In her delirium, she decided that the best thing to do would be to go and find an ambulance.

"I'll be right back, David, I'm going to find help. We'll get you to a hospital. Just wait here, my love." She stroked his back as she said this, and he neither moved nor responded, for the breath was completely gone from his body.

Nastya picked up the medicine bag. It was heavy under the weight of the gold bullion, the bills, and all of the jewels. She looked again at her lover, face down in the gutter. Then, she saw something sticking out of his back pocket. It was his journal; and she dropped the medicine bag in the gutter, and bent down to take it from his pocket. She left the medicine bag filled with money beside David's body, and started off down the street, holding his journal, in a daze of numbness, looking for an ambulance. Her brain was confused. She was suffering terribly from shock. She left Rue Férou and staggered down Rue Bonaparte, completely forgetting what she had set off to look for. Perhaps, she knew that an ambulance wouldn't help. Perhaps, she knew that his cells were dying, and his body was cooling and that he'd long since taken his last breath. Or, perhaps, she was just too torn from the misery of losing her brother and her lover in the span of one afternoon. Most likely, her mental faculties had escaped her to a degree that rendered her incapacitated, void of all thoughts and emotions – in short, her brain had shut down.

As soon as she had walked several blocks from Rue Férou and St. Sulpice, she could not remember where she was headed off to, or why. She walked slowly, trying to make sense out of the nonsensical thoughts that swarmed in her mind. Then her thoughts left her completely, and she ambled slowly down Rue Bonaparte, flipping through the pages of David's journal, trying to find the poem he had written for her: the poem called "Nastenjka".

When she found the page, she read it aloud. She read it aloud and walked on directionless. She did not cry, she did not tremble. She only read that poem aloud, with her glazed eyes and blood-stained lips, stopping on these lines which she read over and over:

...And the river flowed with serenity;
it flowed on to eternity.
that river, once lonely, dark, and meek
that began as a tear on Nastenjka's cheek,
now flowed and shined into the night
with all the world's and heaven's light.

And Nastenjka, seeing what she'd done,
looked to the sky, right at the one,
who lit each hope she'd lost in fear
who lit each wave made by her tear.
and the star looked back, and loved her so,
for making beauty with her woe.

EPILOGUE

Nastya continued walking in a daze for several hours, reading over and over the poem David had written for her; and she was already very far from St. Sulpice when a policeman accosted her on Rue du Petit Musc - on the other side of town, near the Bastille.

The policeman saw the young, pretty girl walking down the center of the street with blood on her clothes and on her lips and he stopped her and began to question her.

Nastya could not answer his questions, as they were in French; though even if the policeman had been able to speak English, she wouldn't have responded. She made no effort to speak and her glassy eyes revealed someone who had been deeply traumatized beyond repair.

After two more policemen arrived, Nastya had come to her senses enough to acknowledge their presence; though, the whole time she was questioned by the three police officers, she just stared off into the distance while the rest of her body trembled in a sort of mild, and barely visible seizure.

Later, the second policemen said while recalling the incident: "As we interrogated [Nastya], she looked us in the eyes, though she seemed to be looking *through* us and not *at* us" … "It was like there was nobody home." Eventually, she displayed having some sort of memory, as, just before nightfall, she started to lead the police officers across the river to the square at St. Sulpice. Although no one knew what was going on in Nastya's head at the moment, it would be fair to assume that she led them to St. Sulpice to get help for David – who was probably, in her mind, still alive.

By the time Nastya and the three policemen reached Rue Férou – which took quite a while as Nastya refused to speak and she kept getting lost on the way – David's body had already been removed and the blood had been cleaned from the cobblestones of the street and the gutter.

Nastya smiled when she saw that David was no longer lying in the gutter. She probably believed that he had come to feel better and had left to go find her. One can assume that she was also glad that the bag full of money was no longer there, for she wouldn't have wanted him to forget that.

The police were well-informed of the incident that had occurred hours before – both at Odette's place and near St. Sulpice; and, as Nastya's face and clothes were bloodied, and, as she had led them to the very place where the young man had died only hours earlier, they had little doubt that she had had some involvement in the crime.

Nastya was detained for ten days in Paris. The first five days were spent at the sixth precinct, in a holding cell. Then, after she refused to eat on each of those five consecutive days, she was transferred to the psychiatric ward of the hospital: *Hôtel Dieu*.

At *Hôtel Dieu*, she was force-fed through intravenous methods, and her strength improved but her delirium did not subside. The doctors also gave her regular injections of benzodiazepines and anti-psychotics (which only made her mental state even more disconnected and confused).

In all of the ten days of her detention, she did not speak, except for once when she mentioned to a doctor in English that she had to go take "the first train back to Moscow".

The doctor, hearing these words, and noticing her distinct Russian accent, arranged for her to be transferred to a hospital in Moscow until she was fit to give testimony to the French police.

On the thirteenth of May, Nastya was sent on an airplane to Moscow. She never returned to France.

The Monsieur de Chevalier (who, we must add, never had a drop of aristocratic blood in his body; and whose real was "Jean-Marc Colin"), waited "faithfully" for Nastya to return for about two weeks. Then, in the middle of May, he forgot about the beautiful Russian ballerina, when he met a Ukrainian girl of just eighteen, named Vera, who was working illegally as a seamstress at one of the many sweatshops on Paris' Rue St.

Denis. Vera was desperately trying to attain French citizenship so she could work legally, and on the first of June, she consented to marry Jean-Marc "Salaudski" Colin. And, although Vera was embittered towards this "vile, old drunk" who was three times her age, she proceeded to marry him after he promised her that once they were married, she would no longer have to work.

The two were married in July and they immediately took a short honeymoon to the seashore at Concarneau; but when they returned, Vera's new husband forced his wife to continue working as a seamstress, as his injury pension was not large enough for a husband *and* a wife.

Two weeks after being hospitalized in Moscow, Nastya – still suffering from hysteria, and acute delirium – escaped in the middle of the night and found her way to her mother's and father's apartment on Sokolniki Street.

The anti-psychotics and hypnotics, which were given to Nastya at the hospital, only increased the severity of her already confused mental state; and, on the night she ran away to find her parents' home – running through the streets of Moscow, glassy-eyed and dressed in a hospital gown – she was worse then ever. As soon as she entered her apartment, she was surprised to see that her brother wasn't in his bed, sleeping. She couldn't understand why his bed and his clothes were no longer in the apartment.

She called to her brother, "Dmitry?" and looked for him in the cupboards. She called for her father too, "Papa?" …But, her father wasn't in it. Her mother was the only one home. Nastya refused to speak to her mother but her mother had plenty to say. She explained to Nastya that her father had taken leave from work and went by train to Paris, to track down his daughter. He had been gone almost a month when Nastya arrived at the family's home in Moscow, and he was, as her mother put it, "determined to stay until Nastya, his only living child, turned up!".

Nastya, made no attempts to communicate with her mother – neither by speaking, nor through facial expressions. Still with the jerky movements and the confused glassy eyes, that radiated no spirit and no soul, Nastya took to her bed behind the gauze curtain where she remained motionless for seven days.

After a week of taking care of her daughter, Nastya's mother was fed up. Her daughter refused all food and drink, and she wouldn't respond to anything her mother did or said. As Nastya's father still had not returned from Paris, there was no one to stop Nastya's mother from committing her to an insane asylum.

In the asylum Nastya was given heavier drugs than before, and was left mostly alone. During her entire stay there she only had one visitor: the Director Lavretsky of the Bolshoy Theatre.

Monsieur Lavretsky became very dispirited upon seeing Nastya in her comatose condition, in the dreary environment of the asylum. He had entered her room with a cheerful grin on his face, happy to see his favorite ballerina again; yet, she didn't seem to recognize the director; and he left less than five minutes after he arrived, discouraged and depressed. He would make no further attempts to see her again.

Nastya remained incarcerated in the asylum until the following December, when the building caught fire and burnt to the ground, taking her life.

Odette was cremated and her ashes were sent in an urn to her husband in Strasbourg; where he made a place for them in his attic.

David's autopsy report stated that his death was a result of toxic blood levels of phenobarbital, acetic acid, and acetylene dichloride. His body was buried in one of those vast, unnamed, mass burial sites, which no one ever hears anything about; yet, which are so common in and around the great city of Paris.

THE END